Readers' comme

'This is great! Your best yet. I really enjoyed it!'
Hazel

'Lovely images of the area surrounding Shaftesbury. Didn't guess the culprit, although had plenty of my own ideas!'
Jeannette

'Good portrayal of life in a country town and the people and animals who live there, and the fact that crime even goes on in these lovely idyllic places.'
Fiona

'I loved it, easy to read with all the twists and turns. When's the next one?'
Lydia

Also by Kathy Morgan

WOODFORD MYSTERY SERIES
The Limner's Art
The Bronze Lady
Death By Etui
The Mystery of the Silver Salver
Deadly Philately

OTHER WORKS
Silver Betrayal
Snowflake, the Cat Who Was Afraid of Heights

Kathy Morgan lives in Dorset, where she has an antiques business with her partner. They have a variety of animals, and Kathy enjoys exploring the countryside around Shaftesbury with her horses and dogs.

Kathy has a regular equestrian feature, 'Horse Tales', on Shaftesbury's local radio station Alfred 107.3fm, and occasionally manages to persuade antiques dealers to chat with her for another feature called 'Antiques Natters'.

Copyright September 2023 Stormybracken Publishing
Kathy Morgan
Printed by KDP

1st edition September 2023

The author Kathy Morgan asserts their moral right under the Copyright, Designs and Patents Act, 1988, to be identified as the author of this work.

A CIP catalogue record for this title is available from the British Library.

Field Murder

Yvonne Parker Series

By

Kathy Morgan

THANK YOU!

I love the enthusiasm from friends and family when I tell them I am writing another book, and the generosity of time and skills they are willing to give me! Social media is my friend when I am writing, and thank you everyone who engages with endless posts about chickens, cats, dogs, horses and 'Book Questions'.

Thank you Fiona, Lydia, Nova, Hazel, Jeannette and Annette for your time and encouragement. I am extremely grateful.

Martin The Editor has seemingly endless patience, and humour, both of which I appreciate and make the writing process far easier than it could be.

Thank YOU for picking up this book and starting to read it – I hope you make to the end, and enjoy the pages along the way.

And Bob, thank you for accepting my answer 'I'm Writing!' to almost any question when I am in my office xxx Love you!

Thank you Hannah Freeland Photography ABIPP for a lovely morning at the horses' field, resulting in lots of super images of us! I have used one of Bramble and me on the back cover. Thank you.

Chapter 1

Yvonne Parker and her horse Toby were enjoying an early morning ride through the fields of their local farm, both appreciating the warmth of the June sun after several days of rain and winds. The bees were buzzing in the clover, and the birds were noisily warning each other away from their young. The fresh green grass of the sheep field was soaked with dew, and Toby's huge hooves were leaving clear outlines of his bare feet in a wandering trail behind them. Yvonne never took these moments for granted and was allowing her gaze to meander along the distant landscape while a broad smile formed on her face. From west to east she could see St James' church, the back of the Abbey Primary school, the top of the Trinity Tower, and the curve of the cottages on Gold Hill. She enjoyed the gentle rhythm of her horse's four-beat walk, and her body moved steadily with him. Who needs yoga and meditation when you have this? She thought smugly.

The peaceful moment was abruptly halted when Toby snorted and faltered, causing her to look around at what was alarming him.

'Uh oh' groaned Yvonne, as she and the horse stopped in their tracks at the sight of the body lying on its back in the field. 'That's not a good start to the day is it Toby?'

She peered about to see if there was anyone else nearby, but at half-past five in the morning on a beautiful sunny summer's day in Dorset, she was the only person taking advantage of the cool and quiet lanes and tracks of Hannam, a village on the outskirts of Shaftesbury. She patted her thigh to check her phone was in the pocket of her black and orange riding tights, stroked the solid brown neck of her horse, and asked him to walk on again.

Horse and rider continued towards the sheep, who was feebly waving her legs in the air in an attempt to right herself. When they were roughly ten feet from her, Yvonne took her feet out of the stirrups, swung her left leg over the saddle behind her, and carefully lowered herself to the ground. Toby was a huge horse, and she'd learned not to leap off him after jarring every joint in her body the first time she dismounted. At almost fifty years old she was experienced enough to take care of her body whenever possible. She hooked Toby's rope reins through the Velcro which attached the orange saddle pad to the shiny black leather saddle, and left him to graze while she went to investigate. She and Toby were used to finding sheep who had lain down only to find their unshorn fleeces had become sodden with the overnight rain, and the weight of their coats prevented them from pulling themselves upright again. As Yvonne approached the sheep it began to wriggle more frantically.

'Hey, I'll do that!'

Yvonne spun round at the sound of the male voice behind her. She glanced at Toby and sent a silent rebuke. 'Some guard horse you are.' Toby carried on munching the grass. She wished she'd brought her dog with her. Zebedee would have warned her there was someone close by, and her Staffy X appearance was a great deterrent for would-be attackers.

'Oh I'm sorry!' the man said and stopped moving, holding his hands up to show he was harmless. He had clearly been running through the field towards them and was wearing a loose black sleeveless top and black shorts, with lime green running shoes. 'I didn't mean to frighten you. Here, she looks heavy, not that I don't think you're capable,' he quickly added.

Yvonne watched as he grasped a couple of handfuls of fleece and hauled the sheep to her legs in one smooth movement. She guessed he was over six foot, with the lean muscular build and tanned skin of a regular runner. His short dark hair was slick with sweat, and his dark eyes were fringed with long dark eyelashes. Why do men often have the best eyelashes, she wondered?

After a moment of hesitation as the sheep suddenly found herself upright, she quickly recovered and ran away to join the rest of her flock without a backwards glance.

'You're welcome!' called Yvonne to the fast-retreating dirty white backside.

The man laughed 'They're never grateful.' He wiped his hands on the wet grass in a vain attempt to wash away the smell of sheep. 'I won't shake your hand for obvious reasons, but I'm George.'

'Hello George, my name's Yvonne. I was hoping we had lost that ghastly tradition of shaking hands after the pandemic,' she laughed. 'Thank you for saving her. You're right, I am perfectly capable, and Toby and I have saved a couple already this year, but if someone else can do it instead then I'm happy,' she grinned and with relief she saw that he was smiling back.

'Do you often ride through here?' he asked.

Immediately her innate warning bell rang, and their isolation from anyone within shouting distance made her answer carefully 'Occasionally we do. I always let the farmer know the sheep are OK, or if like today one of them has been stuck I let her know that too. In fact, I'd better do that now.'

She pulled out her phone and messaged the farmer to let her know what had happened, and that she was with a man called George. She knew that Tabitha Leighton would already be somewhere on the farm, and didn't worry about waking her or her girlfriend. Within seconds Tabitha had replied with a thumbs up emoji and a kissy face, which was their normal communication when one had done a favour for the other, followed by 'George who???' and a winking emoji.

Yvonne glanced at the man, to see he was watching her. Satisfied that he knew she was in contact with someone as they spoke, she asked him 'What about you? I haven't seen you running here before.'

'This is the first time I've followed this route. It's a good one.' He looked back over the fields. 'Yes, I'll do this again. Do you need a leg-up?'

Yvonne started to back away, and she saw his face change to embarrassment. 'Oh I'm sorry, I've done it again,' he said. 'My mum used to have horses, so it's what I'm used to. But of course you don't want some random stranger doing that.'

Yvonne couldn't think of anything to say; the situation was just so awkward. She had no doubt that he could easily fling her up into Toby's saddle, but to do so he would have to bend down and grasp her leg, and have a full face view of her bottom as she jumped upwards. Then she was saved by a glint on the ground. Peering closely, she walked towards it, and saw that in the flattened grass where the sheep had been lying was a small pile of jewellery.

'What on earth is all of this doing here?' she wondered aloud.

'There's some more,' said George, as he stooped to pick up a couple of rings which had been squashed into some sheep poo. He did his best to clean them in the long grass, before handing them to Yvonne. 'I have never seen rings like these before. Is that hair?'

Yvonne glanced at them, before nodding. 'Yes. Although it seems macabre now, one, two or three hundred years ago jewellery was made incorporating strands of hair or teeth. These are probably mourning rings, look, you can see the inscription.'

George peered closely at the rings. 'Is that a *K* and a *V*? And the other one looks as though it is a *C* and a *K*. Eugh, I don't like the idea of wearing anything like that.'

Yvonne shrugged, and said 'These days people have bracelets made from the hair of a horse's tail. It's no different. I don't think we should leave this lying here, and the police won't come out for anything less than a stabbing or shooting. I'll pop it into the police station when they open at nine o'clock.'

Fishing out a dog poo bag from the pocket of her hi-vis waistcoat, she began to scoop the pieces into it.

'We'd better check we have found it all,' said Yvonne, and for a few minutes they searched the grass around the area where the sheep had lain. Yvonne found another necklace, and George found an earring. Yvonne found the other one, and she linked them together through the butterfly clips on the back.

'Neat,' George nodded. 'You'd better let your farmer friend know about this too. The police will need to be involved to find out who has lost it all. It has probably been stolen locally and dumped here, so the thieves can retrieve it later.'

'An odd place to hide it,' said Yvonne. 'In the middle of a field, on a path.'

George shrugged. 'Maybe they dropped it while running from the police. Of course, we've both covered it all with our fingerprints, and trampled over the crime scene. Morse, Lewis and Barnaby would be quite cross with us.'

Yvonne laughed. ''Round here the police wouldn't even come out to view the scene.'

'True,' said George. 'But you still need to contact them. Here, this is my number in case they need to speak to me too.' He pulled his phone out of the thigh pocket of the tight running shorts underneath the outer looser pair and pressed a couple of buttons.

Yvonne's phone pinged, and she saw his number appear. She added him to her contacts list. 'George who?' she asked.

'George Gumbleton. If you're sure you're OK to get back on your horse without me, I'd better get moving, or I'll seize up if I stand around for much longer at my age.'

Yvonne wondered what that was. Mid- to late forties like her? Early fifties? 'Yes, thank you, I'll be fine. You carry on with your run. And thank you for saving that sheep.'

'Anytime,' he smiled, and began to jog along the worn path next to Toby's hoofprints which could still be seen in the dew on the grass.

'Right then Toby, let's see if I can get on without too much drama this time,' Yvonne said as she put a hand on his reins and began to walk in the direction of the ditch which ran along the north side of the field. The last time they had done this, Toby had jumped when a deer emerged from the bushes, just as Yvonne put her foot in the stirrup, and she ended up flat on her back. She hadn't been hurt, and had lain there, giggling, for much longer than necessary.

Obediently Toby followed her. He was ten years old, and Yvonne had bought him when he was four. During their six years together they had forged a strong bond, and Yvonne regularly told him he was the best decision she had ever made. He was over seventeen hands tall, and if she was honest he was bigger than she was comfortable with. Yvonne Parker was forty-nine years old, with shortish dark hair she could style either straight or curly depending on her mood. She was five foot six (she still worked in feet and inches) and usually a size twelve, depending on the clothing manufacturer. She had womanly curves, rather than the boyish figure so many designers preferred, and was often frustrated that waists, sleeves, and hemlines didn't compliment the amount of material needed for her bust and bum. Fortunately riding tights and the V-neck technical sports t-shirt with short sleeves suited her shape perfectly. Even the hi-vis waistcoat was made for the female shape. She had an antiques shop in a little road off the main High Street in Shaftesbury, where she rented space to twelve other dealers, as well as having her own area where she sold a range of decorative homeware and jewellery. Her dog, Zebedee, was usually found curled up in her bed behind the counter or sitting looking hopeful whenever the biscuit tin was produced.

Officially Yvonne was retired, having made a fortune when she sold her antiques business almost twenty years ago. These days she preferred to spend a few hours most days inside her cosy little shop, rather than driving up and down England's motorways and organising massive antiques fairs and managing huge antiques centres in prime locations. On mornings like these her early start was prompted by the rising of the sun, rather than three alarms set five minutes apart lest she fall asleep after the first or even the second one, and her health was all the better for it. She loved pulling on her riding clothes, making a cup of coffee in a travel mug, and driving five minutes down the road with Zebedee to the livery yard where Toby lived. He recognised her car as she drove past the field he shared with seven other horses, and would be waiting at the gate for her to loop a rope over his neck. Zebedee would mooch around the yard with the rest of the pack of stable dogs who either lived there, or belonged to other livery owners, each separating themselves from the others to supervise their humans as necessary. Together the three of them would walk to Toby's stable where Yvonne had already placed a bucket of food, and while he ate his sugar beet and minerals, she drank her coffee and ate a granola bar. Within twenty minutes of arriving at the yard, Toby would be tacked up, Yvonne would be sitting in his saddle, and the pair of them would be heading out into the countryside. Often Zebedee came with them, trotting along behind as though she was herding them, but today Yvonne had planned to ride along a stretch of relatively busy road and so Zebedee stayed behind, keeping watch through the open boot of the car for them to appear at the end of the drive.

Did she miss the early morning routine of shower, hair, make-up, smart clothes, several miles of driving before the first open service station, crappy coffee, greasy sausage rolls, more miles of driving before ending up either at a showground where the officious managers would treat her as though she was an unwelcome and demanding relative rather than the person responsible for helping to pay their wages, or a huge building where the managers were either suspicious of her because they were stealing from her, or hopelessly ineffective and allowing the customers to steal?

No, she did not.

Together, horse and rider reached their destination at the edge of the field, where Toby walked into the big dry ditch, and Yvonne smoothly swung herself into the saddle from the bank. No deer interfered with the manoeuvre, but just as Yvonne was settling her other foot into the stirrup, Toby tensed, and began to step backwards, snorting and eyeing something in the ditch. Rather than look to see what he was worried about, once they were level with the flatter part of the bank where he had walked into the ditch, Yvonne asked him to step out, and away from whatever it was that was scaring him. Probably a bird in the brambles, or a sheep or something, she thought. Checking her watch, Yvonne was surprised that only twenty minutes had passed since they first spotted the distressed sheep. They still had time to finish the ride she had planned.

As they walked away from the ditch and headed for the part of the field where it was safe to have a canter, she was aware that Toby hadn't settled into the easy walk they were used to. He kept looking back, and flicking one ear in that direction, and although his gait was energetic, there was a tightness she did not like. Perhaps there had been a snake in the ditch, or an animal in distress. Sighing, Yvonne turned around, and because he was not keen to walk back that way she jumped off again, fixed his reins so he couldn't tread on them, and left him to graze while she returned to the ditch. If there was a sheep stuck in those brambles, she was calling Tabitha to get it out. No way was she ruining these riding tights, or her hands.

She looked back and saw that Toby was not grazing as usual, but was standing watching her, his ears on alert. She hesitated. Was he going to run away? Tabitha was happy for her to ride through the fields because Yvonne and Toby didn't churn the ground up, or leave gates open, but if Toby started to run amok who knows what damage he could do to the ground, the fences, the pregnant ewes, or anyone else using the pathway.

Deciding that he wasn't going to move anywhere, and that she needed to see what was going on, Yvonne continued towards the ditch. A voice called out 'Are you alright?'

19

Yvonne turned back, to see George Gumbleton walking towards Toby but looking at her. Toby flexed his neck around and lowered his nose to George's outstretched hand, before snapping his head back to its previous watchful position. Yvonne wasn't sure what to do. Had the man been the cause of Toby's unease, and was now going to take him, or worse, injure him?

'Are you alright?' repeated George, as he laid a hand on Toby's huge shoulder. Making sure her phone was close to hand, Yvonne replied 'We're fine thank you. I'm just going to check there isn't a sheep stuck in this overgrowth.'

Feeling his eyes on her back as she approached the brambles, she tried to hear any noises which would indicate an animal in distress, but the only sound above her pounding heart was that of bees and birds. Peering over the bank, ready to run if there was a snake or jump over it if she sensed that George had come up behind her, she looked up and down the ditch, but could see nothing. She glanced back and was reassured that man and horse were still standing in the same spot, so she stepped closer and peered into the brambles which filled the end of the ditch where the stream appeared from underground, but could not see a struggling white shape, or flapping wings of a pheasant. There was something in there. She stepped into the ditch to take a closer look.

The world went white, and then black, and then red. Oh, so much red. And the smell! How had she not sensed it earlier? The body was half in the brambles from the other end, and the half that Yvonne could see was the head, neck and chest of a woman. A dead woman. A very bloody, dead woman.

Chapter 2

While Yvonne was throwing up the coffee and granola bar she had enjoyed less than an hour before, George Gumbleton rang the police. Yvonne could hear him using the What3Words app to give their exact location, as she broke off some beech leaves from the hedge to wipe her mouth and face.

'There are no telegraph or electricity wires across this field, and it is open and flat.'

'Yes there are sheep, and a horse.'

'Two. Two people. Well, two that are alive.'

'I'm not sure, because I came over the stile.' He looked at Yvonne. 'They're asking about gates into the field. Can you talk to them?'

As he handed her his phone, he rummaged in his shorts and produced a small refillable bottle of water. She took it gratefully and used it to swill out her mouth before taking a drink, not caring that the water was warm. 'Thank you,' she said as she made to pass it back to him, but he shook his head and indicated she could keep it. 'Hello? Yes, there are two gates accessible from the road for vehicles, and yes I'm sure you can drive any car or van on this ground.'

George and Yvonne looked at each other in surprise when they heard the sound of sirens so soon after the initial contact with the emergency services, and Yvonne answered the call handler's question, 'Yes, we can hear them now. No, the gates are not locked. I'll contact the farmer, thank you.'

'I'd better give Tabitha a ring, and let her know what's happening,' she said, as she handed George his phone.

The next hour and a half was a mixture of frantic activity as vehicles drove towards them across the field from two directions and a helicopter landed close by, and hanging around waiting as one officer after another, with ever increasing rank, came over and spoke to them. Yvonne wasn't sure how Toby would react to the sight of the helicopter and its rotary blades coming down to land, so she had a hold of his reins, but although he stopped eating – something he had started to do while she was busy throwing up in the ditch – and the down draft made them all turn away as it landed, she was surprised that he was more concerned about the noise from every officers' radio than the helicopter. It wasn't long before he resumed munching.

Yvonne recognised two local policemen, Tom Archibald and Tim Smith, because her antiques shop was opposite the police station on Angel Lane in Shaftesbury, and both men were among several local regulars who were offered coffee and cake whenever they popped in. Shaftesbury wasn't a high crime area, but it didn't hurt to let the public know that The Law was never far away, particularly when some items of stock cost a few thousand pounds.

Tabitha was one of the first to arrive, driving her green Land Rover to where the sheep had congregated as far away from all the fuss as possible. She jumped out, opened the gate into the next field, sent her two dogs away so that one was positioned behind the flock, and the other to the side, and between the three of them they sent the sheep through the gate. The whole manoeuvre took less than a couple of minutes.

'I'm impressed,' commented George. 'I've never seen anyone herding sheep in real life. That's Tabitha Leighton, isn't it?'

Yvonne thought he was coping with their discovery better than she was. She nodded, as she watched her friend shut the gate, send the dogs into the open back of the Land Rover, and then climb into the driver's seat. 'Yes, Tabitha is the farmer here. This is her field, and those are her sheep.'

She could see that Tabitha was on the phone, and guessed she was phoning Alison Jones, her girlfriend. The pair took it in turns to take Alison's children to school, enabling Alison to open her hairdressing and beauty salon before eight o'clock in the morning a couple of days a week, and today was Tabitha's turn. The salon would be opening late today. Tabitha finished her phone call, and drove towards them.

'What have you two found?' Tabitha asked as she pulled up.

'The body of a woman' replied Yvonne.

'A woman? The police told me there was a body, but no more. Who is it? What's happened to her?'

Yvonne shook her head 'I don't know who it is, but whatever has happened to her was brutal.'

Tabitha looked at her, wondering what to ask. Yvonne was shocked, and Tabitha guessed the experience was grim. 'Has she had a stroke or a heart attack, or has someone attacked her?'

George could see that Yvonne was struggling to speak. 'There is a lot of blood, so I would guess someone has attacked her. We don't know anything else, just that there is the body of a dead woman over there.'

Tabitha looked him up and down, assessing this man who was standing calmly with her friend, who was upset.

Sensing she was wondering if he was involved, George quickly explained 'I was running through your field from over there, when I saw Yvonne standing near her horse. I thought perhaps she had fallen off him, but it turns out she had dismounted to help one of your sheep. Neither of us knew anything about the human body until Yvonne took Toby over there so she could reach the stirrup to remount.'

Tabitha looked at Yvonne 'Are you alright?'

'I will be' Yvonne said. 'It's all a bit upsetting. I agree with George that she must have been attacked. It's a horrible mess over there. I am glad you were here George, I wouldn't have liked to discover it on my own.'

'I wish I hadn't seen it, but I know what you mean' said George. 'I'm glad I wasn't here on my own too.'

'There's three of us now' said Tabitha briskly. 'I have just the thing you two need to help with the shock.'

Yvonne's attention was drawn to the team who were trying to erect a forensic white tent over the brambles which secured the gruesome body. It took eight people over forty minutes to find the correct size to fit over the awkward spot. By this time she, George and Tabitha were sitting on the back of the Land Rover with the dogs, while Toby grazed nearby. Yvonne had taken off her riding hat, and run her fingers through her hair so it wasn't completely plastered to her head. Tabitha was wearing her customary baseball cap over her dark hair which was plaited in one rope down her back. She was roughly the same height as Yvonne, and more straight up and down and stockier. As Tabitha produced a flask of hot water, and dished out a small coffee and two teas, complete with milk, no sugar, for the three of them, the toned muscles in her arms and bare legs were evident. Yvonne felt a pang of jealousy when she noticed George appraising her friend.

Where had that come from? It was a long time since she had felt any emotion other than irritation or tolerance towards a man, and she had certainly never felt envious of her friends' figures. Tabitha was used to handling sheep, bales of hay and straw, and goodness knows what else farming entailed, whereas Yvonne hauled a few boxes of antiques now and then, and lifted Toby's saddle on and off his back. Her arms weren't flabby, but they could be more toned. She resolved to do something about them, but then Tabitha also unearthed an open packet of chocolate Penguins and all thoughts of health and fitness flew away. It felt wrong to be enjoying herself in the circumstances, but Yvonne found herself laughing at the silly jokes in the wrappers of the chocolate biscuits, and giggling at Tabitha's running commentary on the lack of progress of the forensic tent team.

'I think I need to accept my run is over,' said George as he climbed out of the Land Rover and proceeded to do some stretches. 'If I don't do these I'll seize up for the next two days, and won't be able to get out of a chair or walk upstairs without groaning. Being in the presence of death sharpens your mind about what is important, doesn't it. Whoever that person is underneath the forensic tent won't be doing anything ever again.'

The three of them stared at the people who were working around the body. Yvonne wondered if this was the first time some of them had encountered a murder victim.

'I wonder if their family know what has happened? Perhaps their killer was someone they knew. It is horrible to think about it' said Tabitha.

'I'm sure I read that over fifty percent of murders are carried out by a family member' said George.

'Yes, I think I have heard that too. I wonder if that is what has happened here. I hope the people responsible are caught soon. Once they've finished with you,' Tabitha tipped her head in the direction of the largest group of police, 'I'll run you back into town if you like. It's The Abbess Aethelgifu, isn't it?'

'Thank you, that would be kind of you.' He glanced at his watch, before frowning and pressing buttons. 'Damn, I forgot to turn it off. I was recording my run,' he explained when he caught sight of Tabitha's confused expression.

Yvonne processed the information. The Abbess Aethelgifu, or TAA as the people of Shaftesbury preferred to call it, was a restaurant on the High Street. It had opened three years earlier, in the space left by a much-loved family business which had suddenly closed after over sixty years trading. Rumours that the family had sold out to a city trader were confirmed when the window displays of duvets, curtains, balls of wool, fire guards, mops and buckets had been replaced with blackout blinds, and a tremendous amount of interior renovation had taken place. The businesses either side refused to engage in the general fury by the townspeople that some out-of-towner had dared to flash their millions, leading to the assumption that they too had been paid off. Everyone declared they would neither work there nor buy whatever was going to be for sale.

The local people who were doing the renovations, and supplying the materials, kept quiet, many not telling their partners where they were working, such was the venom directed at the new venture.

Eventually the word got out that it was to be a beauty salon, causing a new flush of rumours that it was paid for by drugs money, and was going to be a brothel.

After a few days the rumour mill decided it was going to be a night club, where again prostitution and drugs were involved.

Finally the positive official press began, with leaflets, posters, advertisements in the local press and on the radio, and the local workers and suppliers began to emerge from hiding. Shaftesbury was to be the latest addition to the cities and towns across England to have a Jimmy Mack. Jim Mack was a popular TV chef, who had capitalised on sourcing and producing delicious food from an expert team of people who project managed an increasing number of cafés, restaurants and hotels around the country, each with its own unique flavour for the surrounding area. In the space of one day the Shastonians were completely behind this new venture in their town, although the name of The Abbess Aethelgifu gave them some pause for thought, until they realised that she was the daughter of their own King Alfred, and the first Abbess of Shaftesbury Abbey. The monogram TAA appeared between the blackout blinds and the glass windows, the signwriter produced a beautiful sign across the front of the building, and the local food producers began to tout their trade. To be given the Jim Mack seal of approval was considered to be better than a Royal Warrant.

Yvonne now remembered that George Gumbleton was the name of the manager of The Abbess Aethelgifu, because he had been prominent in the publicity for the new restaurant for its first six months. If there were prizes to be donated for a local primary school fete then he was there with vouchers for meals; if there was a charity cycle race, he was leading a team of staff; if there was a venue needed for the Shaftesbury Fringe then he was volunteering a room at The Abbess Aethelgifu. He had then disappeared from the limelight, although the restaurant and its staff had continued to maintain and expand their involvement in the local community. She realised that she had been staring at him while he was completing his post-run stretch of hamstrings and quads, and blushed even though she hadn't seen him because she was too busy thinking about past events.

'I don't mean to be disrespectful to the poor soul you two have found, but I hope we're not going to be stuck here for much longer,' said Tabitha as she checked her watch. 'I have my final fitting for my wedding dress at eleven o'clock, and have to make myself clean and presentable before then.'

'When's the big day?' asked George.

'In two weeks' time, at Kenyon Hall.'

'Nice!' commented George.

'Oh, it is,' agreed Tabitha. 'It is very nice. I can't believe I'm getting married in such a beautiful place. Me and Alison are so excited; we're determined to enjoy every minute of it, and not let it pass in a blur. Charles Diamond, you know, the wedding coordinator there, is such a charming man. Nothing is too much trouble, and he has given us lots of advice about everything from wedding invitations to flowers to photographers.'

'Is Alison your fiancée?' asked George.

'Yes she is. We have been together for five years, and decided a couple of years ago to get married. We have saved hard for this day, and have had a wonderful time choosing all the different elements of it. It's a lot of fun. Neither of us will let the other be a bridezilla, and we have similar taste in everything so we haven't had a serious disagreement about anything.'

'Except for the cake' teased Yvonne.

'Ha ha, yes, except for the cake,' laughed Tabitha, but before she could explain the cake saga to George one of the policemen walked over with the two local coppers, Tom Archibald and Tim Smith.

'I don't think we can do any more with you here. Thank you very much for waiting, but I would like to talk to you all again. These two have your contact details,' he said, with Tom and Tim nodding their confirmation, 'and I'll be in touch later today.'

Tim, the taller and younger of the two, said 'If you have any questions, or think of anything else which might be useful, you can always message one of us.'

'Yes, don't hesitate to talk to us if you want to,' agreed Tom, fixing his blue eyes on Yvonne.

Their senior officer continued 'Please do not talk about what you have found today with anyone. We suspect the body is that of a local elderly lady who has been missing since Monday, and as it's now Thursday you will appreciate that her family are very worried. If they hear any rumours at this stage it will be devastating, whether the body is hers or not, so please, please keep all of this to yourselves.'

Yvonne couldn't resist a glance at Tabitha because she knew that Tabitha would have already told Alison everything she knew when she phoned her about not being able to take the children to school. Tabitha avoided her eye.

'Yes, of course,' said George. 'If there is anything else you need from me, I'm going to be in Shaftesbury for a few more days. However, I am due to fly out to Ireland for a meeting next Wednesday. Do I need to check with someone about that?'

'We should have finished with you by then, but let me know the details, and I'll check for you,' said Tim, and Yvonne noted that he and George obviously knew each other socially from the way they talked.

'Your horse has been very calm,' said Tom. 'We could do with him if we decide to open a Shaftesbury Police Horse unit.'

'Yes, he's lovely,' agreed Tim as he patted Toby's neck. 'I used to ride when I was a boy. My mum took me and my sister to the riding school every Saturday afternoon. We loved it, except when the weather was bad. I can't remember why I stopped.'

'I used to work at my aunt and uncle's stables, and it was either pouring with rain or so hot the flies were everywhere,' laughed Tom. 'I haven't ridden since I joined the army thirty years ago, but seeing your horse has reminded me how much I used to love it. I could do with starting again on a calm chap like this one.'

Yvonne felt ridiculously pleased with the compliments Toby received, even though she knew it was his belly that was dictating his behaviour. 'He's pretty good most of the time. I can't imagine a life without horses. If we're free to go, then I'll climb on from the back of your truck, if that's OK,' she said to Tabitha, who nodded, and Yvonne called Toby over as she clambered onto the Land Rover. Obediently he walked over to her, sidled into position so she could swing herself into the saddle, and stood patiently as she sorted out stirrups and reins.

'Very good,' nodded George, impressed. 'I have never seen a horse do that before. Usually they need someone holding their reins and stirrup to keep them still. You've trained him well.'

Yvonne chose to accept the compliment, and not start lecturing everyone within earshot about listening to a horse who doesn't want to be ridden.

'I'll have that lift now, if it's still alright, Tabitha?' said George.

'Of course, let's go,' said Tabitha, as she secured her dogs in the back of the Land Rover, and with one more check over the hedge at her sheep in their new field, she and George drove out onto the lane outside.

It was too late in the day to continue with her planned ride, and so she turned Toby for home, and they walked most of the way because the lanes were too narrow and busy with walkers and cars to pick up a decent pace. It was only as Toby broke into a trot on the approach to the drive up to the livery yard that Yvonne remembered the stash of jewellery in the dog poo bag in the pocket of her hi-vis waistcoat. 'Oh well,' she said to Toby. 'I'd better pop into the police station before I go home.'

Chapter 3

Yvonne felt highly visible as she drove into the small parking area behind her home, even though as an antiques dealer she was used to carrying stock and cash worth a lot more money than the jewellery she was carrying in the dog poo bag. For some reason, being in horse riding clothes made her feel vulnerable, whereas in her antiques dealer clothes of long floaty skirts she felt invincible. Zebedee's presence was mildly reassuring whenever she was with her, but the dog couldn't prevent someone from watching her.

Yvonne's home was also her place of work. After a few years' sabbatical she had decided to return to the antiques business, and surprisingly quickly found the ideal building from which to trade. Her previous experience had been a multi-million-pound family business, incorporating seven antiques fairs and forty-two antiques centres. Suffering from burn-out as a result of personal tragedy, she had sold the business, and could live off the proceeds without ever working again. She spent over ten years trying to find peace. Self-help gurus whose only purpose was to take her money, businesses for which she had no passion, looking for help in diets or fitness schemes, isolating herself, throwing herself into good works, joining every social group in the area, nothing seemed to work. It wasn't that she didn't enjoy many of the experiences; she loved most of them, but couldn't fill the void. The tragedy had destroyed her trust in those around her at the time, and she no longer had family or friends she could turn to. Fortunately she was the type of person who could easily make friends, and now there was a trail of people around the country she could call up at a moment's notice and plan to meet at a theatre or pub. But there was nobody to make her a hot drink when she came home from a walk in the freezing cold rain, nor anyone she could buy a Christmas present for and see them open it on Christmas Day year after year.

One day she was sitting on a bench by a Derbyshire canal, enjoying watching the flashes of blue as a kingfisher darted along the bank, when a couple of horse riders came by. Yvonne had ridden as a child, but not since then. The sound of the horses blowing through their nostrils, and their smell as they walked by, awoke a memory of a happier time, and she resolved to find a riding stables and start lessons. The kit had changed a lot since her childhood, but not much else had, although she didn't remember aching after those horse rides. The morning after her first lesson she couldn't lower herself onto the toilet seat without her leg muscles crying out, and as for attempting to go down the stairs, they had to be taken one at a time, very carefully. She increased her lessons to three times a week, so that the aching merged into one pain, and studied the horsemanship course offered by the riding school. There was an antiques shop near the café Yvonne and her fellow riders used to frequent after a lesson, and one day she absent-mindedly walked through the door. Instantly the musty old smell flooded her senses and brought about a feeling of excitement that nothing else had evoked. There was a flea market at the local showground that weekend, and with her heart racing she went along. Within minutes she forgot about feeling anxious, and enjoyed being anonymous as she browsed the stalls, taking in the sights and the sounds of the traders.

Ten months after those two horses and their riders came past her bench, Yvonne moved into the Angel Lane premises in Shaftesbury. A former flower shop, the building was ideal, with a small road frontage enabling security to be tight, leading to a large space inside. The antiques shop filled four rooms on the ground floor, and the double garage at the back which led to a small yard. The yard was closed off from a public carpark by electronic wooden gates and provided easy access for deliveries and collections of antiques of all sizes. The cool, dark area which had been the storage space for plants was renovated into a light warm kitchen/ living room thanks to the installation of underfloor heating and lots of wall and ceiling lights. The upstairs flat had also been used for storage, and it was here that Yvonne indulged herself by creating a private stylish and comfortable home.

The antiques shop took three months to fill with a dozen dealers, Zebedee moved in after being abandoned by a man who moved to another continent, and Toby caught her eye when she was perusing a horse rescue website. Yvonne had found peace for eight years; she was happy and content with her life. Although meeting George had awoken a new need in her.

Yvonne could tell by the cars in the yard that several of the dealers were already in the shop, and knew that the person on the rota for working that day would be preparing to open the doors to the public. A time check on the local radio station told Yvonne it was half-past eight, and as she knew the police station wouldn't open its doors until nine o'clock, she decided to have a shower and change of clothes before handing in the jewellery.

Rather than going through the back door and the small shop kitchen to her own large kitchen/ sitting-room, Yvonne jogged up the outside wooden staircase to the private entrance of her home, beaten to the top by her dog. Once inside her bedroom, with Zebedee sprawled on her blue padded dog bed for a change, Yvonne tucked the dog poo bag inside her underwear drawer, stripped off her riding clothes and put them in the laundry bin, and walked through to her bathroom. She loved her bathroom. It had a white floor, and white walls with turquoise and silver detail, a large bath with jacuzzi jets, and a separate huge walk-in shower with several different settings. She only used one of the settings, but every now and then she experimented with a new one, before reverting back to her original favourite. There was also a television, radio and telephone on the walls, but today she made sure the switch for all three was set to OFF, and luxuriated in the shower for several minutes as the shocks of the morning were lathered and rinsed away with the shampoo and body wash.

She quickly towel-dried her hair, deciding it was going to be a messy curly day today, dried and moisturised her skin, carefully smoothed her favourite Skin Shade by Tropic onto her face, and moved into her dressing room. Yvonne chose jeans shorts and a navy-blue vest top, slipped her feet into white moccasins, brushed mascara over her eyelashes and applied a rose-coloured lip gloss. She checked her appearance in the floor-to-ceiling mirrors at either end of the room and nodded her approval. Slim with curves, weird tan lines thanks to horse riding and dog walking around the beautiful local countryside, more wrinkles than she would like to see on her neck and face but satisfied that she looked good compared to her grandmother who had been an old woman at fifty, shuffling from one room to another in polyester dresses, tights, and slippers.

Yvonne retrieved the jewellery from its hiding place, laid it out on her duvet, and carefully photographed every piece. Once she had finished, she wrapped it back up in the dog poo bag and put it into her navy-blue shoulder bag where she also put her phone and purse. Picking up her keys, she said goodbye to Zebedee who had now moved to her customary position in the middle of Yvonne's king-size four poster bed, and locked the door on her way out. She decided to walk through the public carpark around to Angel Lane, rather than through the shop and risk getting into conversation with anyone. Mission accomplished, within two minutes she was inside the police station. Handing over the jewellery proved more complicated than she expected, and it took more than forty minutes of repeating her story to several different officers – Yvonne had no idea Shaftesbury police station was staffed by so many people – before she saw a blond head through the frosted glass and Tim Smith appeared. He read her statement, took the jewellery into his custody, and with a voice dripping with suspicion, said he would also need to talk to George Gumbleton about their find. Yvonne didn't blame him for his reaction but was also a bit put out that someone almost half her age was talking to her in this way. She understood that it did look odd neither she nor George had mentioned the jewellery to anyone when they were being questioned at the field, but the shock of finding the human remains had made her forget about it. She wondered why George hadn't said anything.

'Why on earth didn't you tell us about this when we spoke to you?' Tim repeated, as he looked down at her from his six-foot two height compared to her five-foot six obviously cross with her, his blue eyes cold.

36

'I'm so sorry,' said Yvonne, feeling guilty even though she knew she was innocent. 'It completely went out of my mind when I saw that … that body.'

Something in her voice or her face must have convinced Tim that she was telling the truth, because his eyes softened, and he said 'Alright, I do understand what a shock that was for you. I can put you in touch with someone you can talk about it with, if you like? It would be a good idea to do so. It is not every day you have a traumatic experience like the one you had a few hours ago.'

'Oh no, thank you. I'll be fine.' Yvonne decided not to tell him it wasn't the first time she had seen a mutilated dead body. 'I can talk about it with George, because he was there too.'

'Yes, George,' said Tim, the grimness returning to his voice. 'I'll be needing a word with him too. Keep in touch, please, and let us know as soon as you think of anything else.'

Feeling foolish, and a little resentful at the way he had spoken to her, as she left the building Yvonne immediately texted George to warn him that Tim was on the warpath about them not giving the jewellery to the police at the scene. 'I completely forgot about it until I got back to the stables' she typed.

She was thrilled when he replied almost immediately with 'Thanks for letting me know. I forgot too! Hope you're OK. Drink later?'

Not wishing to appear too keen, Yvonne waited until she was through the front door of her shop, all of twenty seconds later, before replying 'That would be nice. The Shaston at six o'clock this evening?'

Within two seconds George replied with a thumbs-up emoji.

37

The smile on her face meant that no one in the shop had any idea about Yvonne's horrific experience that morning, and she was easily able to engage in conversations with customers and dealers about antiques for the next hour. A text from Tabitha enticed her to a local café with a stunning view over the Blackmore Vale for brunch. Both were surprised to find they had large appetites, despite the shocks of the morning and the number of biscuits they had eaten in the back of Tabitha's land rover. In quiet voices they talked about their morning between mouthfuls of sausage, bacon and egg. From their seats they could not see the murder site, but flashing blue lights were sporadically driving around the lanes below them, which was possibly the first time Yvonne or Tabitha had seen anything like it in all the years they had lived in the area.

Yvonne returned to her shop, made everyone who wanted one a cup of tea or coffee, valued some items brought in by one customer, sold an expensive sewing etui to another, and relaxed into the humdrum routine of a day in an antiques shop. There had been a time when she had thought she would never want to be near another antique again, and on occasion the sight of certain objects could invoke an involuntary shudder, but normally the shape, smell and history of an item made her feel pleasantly excited.

By midday the tension in the shop had risen, caused by a woman who came in and started to talk about the sirens and noise of the police helicopter which had woken her up. Yvonne was amazed this hadn't been the main topic of conversation until now, but none of the antiques dealers lived in Shaftesbury, and the handful of customers they had seen had also driven from outlying villages. Immediately the only topic of conversation in the shop was about the belief that the local missing woman had been found. Yvonne tried to concentrate on some admin work in her office at the end of her kitchen/ living room, and moved between her office and the shop for the rest of the day. The snippets of conversation whenever she re-entered the shop informed her that the woman had been found dead, or alive, or almost dead, or in a confused state, or died in the ambulance. She managed to keep her own role in the morning's proceedings quiet, and no one who came into the shop knew that she had been the one to discover the body.

She caught herself checking the time every few minutes from three o'clock onwards, and wondered whether to change into a skirt or dress. As six o'clock approached she decided to keep it casual, and other than changing her top for a flowery shirt, adding some powder foundation and touching up the mascara and lip gloss, she left the dealers to lock up the shop whenever they felt like it, and walked up the High Street to The Shaston, the hotel and restaurant where she was meeting George. As soon as she walked in through the big glass doors and saw him sitting in the courtyard beyond, she knew she had made the correct decision, because he was also casually dressed, and looking handsome in navy blue chino shorts and a pale blue t-shirt.

'George, hello, what can I get you?' she gestured towards the almost empty glass in front of him.

She could see him trying to decide if he should insist on buying her a drink, or worrying if that would cause offence, when they were both saved by a waitress asking if she could take their order. George gestured to Yvonne to choose first.

'Thank you, I'll have a raspberry mojito.'

'I'll have another of these,' George gestured to the bottle of locally brewed beer on the table. When the waitress had gone, he said 'How have you been today?'

'I've been fine,' Yvonne assured him. 'I don't know if the shock hasn't set in yet, or if I got rid of it all in the field.' She was embarrassed about throwing up, but George set her mind at rest.

'I was very close to joining you,' he grinned.

'How have you been?' she asked.

'I didn't get as close as you did to the body, but it has affected me a little,' he admitted. 'I have never seen a dead body before, let alone a murdered one.'

Yvonne nodded, and took a sip of her drink.

George continued 'I am intrigued about the jewellery. Tim asked me to come into the station after you'd been there this morning, and I told him as much as I knew, which was very little. He kept asking me to list the items we found, but I'm afraid it's all a bit of a blur. I was just trying to clean the sheep poo off everything I picked up! All I could specifically remember were those two mourning rings, the pair of earrings you matched up, and a necklace.'

'There were a lot more rings, and necklaces with pendants. I would say these are high quality antiques, and must be from a much larger collection. No doubt the police will have something on their database and be able to match it up with the legitimate owners. There is nothing we can do about it, whether we remember the pieces or not. The police have them all now, so our memories of them doesn't matter. It's that body I can't get out of my thoughts. I wonder who she was? That poor family if it was the local elderly lady who has been missing for the last few days.' Yvonne took another sip of her drink. 'Mmmh this is delicious. Do you have plans for the rest of the evening, or shall we have something to eat here?'

'Good idea. I haven't made any plans, and I would love to eat here.'

'Hello! Mind if we join you?' Tabitha appeared behind George, pulling ooh-la-la faces at Yvonne. 'This is Alison, my fiancée. Alison this is George, Yvonne's friend with whom she found the body this morning' she said, as she pulled up a couple of chairs from another table, and not waiting for either George or Yvonne to agree, sat down.

Yvonne noticed that George was now granted friend status, even though they had only met that morning, and the circumstances had been macabre. Tabitha looked completely different to the farmer with her hair tucked into a baseball cap and wearing cargo shorts, vest top, and sturdy walking boots of that morning, and this evening her womanly physique was on display in a short black sheath dress with a random large gold leaf pattern, the colours of which matched her long dark loosely curled hair now streaked with gold extensions and stunning eye-makeup. Yvonne guessed that Alison or Maisie, Alison's business partner in the beauty salon, had been practising Tabitha's wedding-day hairstyle and make-up, and the couple had come straight from the salon. Several people were admiring Tabitha's transformation, including a man who appeared to have moved his chair so he could get a better look at her.

The waitress reappeared, more drinks were ordered, and Tabitha continued 'The body still hasn't been removed from my field. It's a nuisance because I don't want the sheep to stay in the one next door for too long. I'm planning on cutting a second lot of hay from there, but if the greedy buggers are in there for much longer I won't be able to.'

'Tabitha!' remonstrated Alison, who this evening was looking her usual elegant self with her long blond hair immaculately straightened, minimal make-up, in contrast to her fiancée, and wearing a long sleeveless sheath dress in a similar pale blue to George's t-shirt.

'I know, I know,' grumbled Tabitha. 'I am being insensitive. But I do have a living to earn, and farming is hard enough without people inconsiderately murdering other people on my land. Why couldn't they have done it in the bottom field where the sheep will be living this winter? The police could stay in there all summer for all I care.'

'Oh, ignore her,' Alison apologised to George. 'She's just upset because we've had a bit of a setback with our wedding plans.'

'What's happened?' asked Yvonne.

'Well, you know Charles, the wedding coordinator, promised us that delicious seafood menu? We had an email from him this afternoon saying would we be happy with chicken as an alternative.'

'Chicken!' complained Tabitha. 'We can have chicken every day of the week!'

'As well as sheep we have a couple of hundred chickens on the farm,' Alison explained to George.

'We won't for much longer if this avian flu keeps coming around every year,' muttered Tabitha.

'Of course,' said George. 'You are having to keep them undercover during the winter?'

'Yes we are, and I don't like it. We've always had free-range birds, and it's been a joy to see them scratching around in the fields, but housing them in the barn is messy and takes a lot of work. More importantly it is not the life I want to see them living.'

'Anyway, back to our problem' said Alison. 'We both love seafood, and for us it was to be a real treat to have oysters and crevettes, and a monkfish curry as our wedding feast. Obviously we did have a chicken alternative on the menu, and a courgette and chickpea choice too, for those who don't like seafood or spices. Chicken is not a celebratory meal for us; it's everyday kitchen supper food.'

'Why can't he supply the seafood menu anymore?' asked Yvonne.

'He hasn't said he can't supply it, but it is not sounding good is it! We can't get hold of him on the telephone,' complained Tabitha.

'That's unusual,' observed Yvonne, who was Matron of Honour for Tabitha and had been involved in the wedding organisation since Tabitha and Alison proposed to each other. No one had been able to ascertain who proposed first, but it didn't matter because they were both obviously in love and in agreement about the future they wanted together. 'Charles always either answers immediately or returns our calls within the hour.'

'Not today he isn't,' said Alison, darkly. 'He has a definite case of avoiditis as far as using the telephone is concerned.'

'Charles Diamond of Kenyon Hall?' queried George. 'Where you're having your wedding?'

'Supposedly,' muttered Tabitha. 'Less than two weeks to go, and he's changing one of the reasons we chose that place. We're spending a fortune on all of this on the basis it will be the best of the best, and at this rate the 'best' will be chicken! We eat chicken at least three days a week, and we know what sort of a life those chickens have lived. I'm not paying for or eating chickens who have been kept in anything other than free range and organic conditions.'

'We rarely eat meat anywhere else,' explained Alison. 'Both of us need to know the animals have had a good life before they end up on our plates.'

'At least he didn't offer us lamb,' sighed Tabitha. 'We eat that three times a week too, and I never eat lamb from anywhere else, however well they have been kept. I am so cross with him; I am tempted to cancel the whole thing.'

'Me too,' agreed Alison, 'although it will break my heart if we don't go ahead with our wedding.'

Yvonne could see that both Alison and Tabitha were close to tears, and fortunately the waitress arrived with their drinks order, distracting them from the stress of wedding preparations as the glasses were passed around to the people who ordered them.

Alison checked her watch. 'Scott has to leave by half-past seven for cricket practice, but we have plenty of time to enjoy this.' She raised her glass to everyone, and seeing George's quizzical expression she explained 'Scott is my ex-husband, and my children's father. It is all terribly civilised, and he pops round to look after them so we can go out now and then. Thank goodness he could take them to school this morning.'

Tabitha yawned. 'He is really good about taking care of his children, and it's not like either of us want to stay out late tonight. I have to be back on the farm by five o'clock tomorrow morning. I have been so caught up with wedding preparations this afternoon I haven't had to time to find out what is going on over there. Have either of you heard any more developments?'

Yvonne and George both shook their heads, a silent exchange confirming they wouldn't mention the jewellery.

'Your hair and make-up does look amazing,' commented Yvonne.

Tabitha looked a little embarrassed. 'Both Alison and Maisie practically held me down to do this' she gestured to her face. 'I think it's far too much, but they both said it would look good if we decide to change for our evening party. I don't think we will though?'

'No, I think we'll stay in our wedding finery. You look gorgeous,' said Alison as she leant over and kissed Tabitha on the cheek. 'Don't worry, I would never let you walk down the aisle looking over-made-up. You are just not used to it, and if you still don't like it on the night then we won't do it like that.'

'I do like it!' Tabitha was quick to reassure Alison, and self-consciously smoothed her hair with her hand, 'and I love my hair. I think I should keep it like this.'

Yvonne nodded 'Those highlights are stunning. They wouldn't look out of place on the farm either.'

'My hair is always under a hat when I'm there, so it wouldn't matter if they did look a bit too glamorous for shearing sheep or dealing with foot rot.'

'You shear your own sheep?' George said with amazement.

'Of course!' laughed Tabitha. 'How else do you think I get this level of tone on my arms.' She flexed both biceps revealing an impressive set of muscles.

'I worked in Australia for a couple of years for a shearer, and it is bloody hard work. How many do you have to shear every year?'

'That's useful to know in case I need any help,' grinned Tabitha. 'I usually run a flock of about five hundred, but not all of them need to be sheared, and I take my time and shear them over a few weeks. That one you and Yvonne rescued this morning is in the last tranche; she'll be done tomorrow.'

45

'I'm impressed. I couldn't do it now! This was thirty years ago when I was a young man, and I found it tough then' laughed George, holding his hands up in defence.

'Oh well, if you start training now I reckon I could make use of you by the time you're needed next year.'

Alison's phone dinged to signal she had received a message. 'Scott wants to know if we would like some of the supper he has made for himself and the children? He has made a pasta bake.'

'I love Scott's pasta bake' said Tabitha. 'Let's go back now!'

They swallowed the last of their cocktails and said their goodbyes.

Tabitha gave Yvonne a wink as she left.

Chapter 4

Yvonne and George declined the waitress's invitation to move to the dining room for their dinner and decided to stay where they were in the courtyard after Tabitha and Alison left. They chose starters and mains from the menu, and both moved onto tap water rather than continue with alcoholic drinks.

'Two glasses are about my limit,' confided Yvonne.

'So's mine,' said George with a grin, 'and I've had three!'

Throughout the evening there was no opportunity for awkward silences to creep in, because their meal was continually interrupted by friends and acquaintances stopping by their table to say hello.

'I think we're about even,' said George, 'although you are perhaps a little ahead of me. If this was a competition I would start to text friends to come here on purpose.'

Yvonne laughed 'Next time let's eat out of town.' Realising she was being presumptuous she blushed, and took a drink of water.

Smoothly George said 'Yes, if you're free on Sunday I'd like to try a pub over in Marnhull; I've heard good things about their Sunday lunch and want to try for myself.'

'So long as we can leave Shaftesbury after one o'clock, I would love that. We're having a Yard Ride on Sunday morning, and by the time I've got home, washed and changed it will be about that time.'

'Sounds perfect. I'll book a table, and pick you up at one?'

They were interrupted by someone wanting to say hello to George, and after they had gone he said 'It sounds as though things are not going smoothly at Kenyon Hall for their wedding.'

Yvonne shook her head 'It does doesn't it. When we all went to have a look at it last year we were so impressed with everything. It is Alison's second wedding, and Tabitha's first, and they wanted it to be really special to celebrate their relationship, without costing the earth or being formal and stuffy. Charles Diamond made it all sound exactly what they were looking for, with the formal intimate wedding ceremony in their beautiful secret garden and the folly with decent space for a dozen people, so it could be inside or outside depending on the weather, and then open up the orangery on the other side of the secret garden, which is stunning and will be where we are joined by the rest of the guests for the wedding dinner and dancing. Kenyon Hall's house band are brilliant, and will be playing during the ceremony, during the dinner and then ramp it up for the evening.'

'I think they have about fifty members, don't they?'

'Yes, I think so, which means that all types of music can be played, and different songs, but they won't all be playing at Alison and Tabitha's wedding. The setting is fantastic, and they can accommodate all the guests on a beautiful day or a typical English summer rainy day. They also have His and Hers dressing rooms and bathrooms for last minute hair and make-up, although they will be Hers and Hers obviously for Alison and Tabitha, and both brides are going to change for the evening party. They are also going to have a couple of nights there for a honeymoon, rather than go away anywhere. Scott will

48

have the children while they are on their honeymoon, and they will be bridesmaids along with some other nieces and nephews of both Alison and Tabitha. Me and Maisie Day, Alison's partner in the beauty salon, are both Matron of Honour. The brides will lead us all up the Rose Walk in the secret garden, assuming it's not raining too much, to the place where they will make their wedding vows. The legal wedding is going to take place in Shaftesbury Town Hall with a few of us present, but Tabitha and Alison are planning to make their personal vows to each other in front of everyone. The amount of organisation they have done is amazing, and none of that has changed, so I hope they can resolve this catering issue.'

'I remember our wedding day. The stress of choosing, booking and paying for everything was enormous. It was so expensive! We both had a fantastic day, as did our guests, but I wouldn't like to go through all of that again,' said George.

Yvonne was momentarily silenced while she absorbed the news that George was married, before rallying. 'I don't think it has been stressful, until now,' she said. 'It has been a lot of fun, with the four of us looking through ideas on the internet or in magazines, and Alison and Maisie have had plenty of suggestions from their clients at the beauty salon. Kenyon Hall was the obvious choice, and they didn't look at anywhere else, but I think it is a bit worrying if there are major issues with sourcing the food at this late stage.'

'It does sound like it,' agreed George.

'The menu agreed with Charles has already been paid for by Alison and Tabitha. Even if they receive any refunds for the lesser quality, the shine must have been lost from their day with this change to their plans. It's very strange because we have never heard a bad word about the place before, and it's not like covid or Brexit can be blamed anymore, since they have had numerous big celebrations there whenever lockdown rules have allowed.'

'I agree; I have never heard anything negative about Kenyon Hall, or Charles Diamond, except the occasional niggle from people you would expect to have a moan about something. But even they have generally been enthusiastic, and I don't think I have ever heard anything bad about the food or drink they serve up there.'

'Oh yes,' agreed Yvonne, 'there are always those people who will nit-pick about something, but this is way beyond a niggle isn't it. It is also odd that Charles hasn't given them any explanations, or even spoken to them. Usually we speak with him in-person, or on the telephone, and he emails confirmation of our conversations. It is a good system, because it means we don't get bogged down in a long email thread, and if something has been misunderstood in conversation it is picked up very quickly. I hope he is alright, and nothing has happened to him.'

George shrugged 'I suppose if he has picked up a cold or covid or something he may have trouble speaking which could explain why he isn't answering his phone, but you would have thought he would have explained that in the email.'

'True. Is there something going on in the food and drink world that those of us outside know nothing about?'

George shrugged 'Not that I know, and I would hope I would know about it. I am surprised that Charles knows with a fortnight to go that they will be unable to supply any of the seafood, because there is still plenty of time for it to be caught and processed. But I suppose we use local suppliers, or at least from somewhere within a day or two of delivery, always fresh unless we have agreed to buy frozen, and although we plan our menus in advance we won't know until the day before the delivery whether we can put some dishes on the menu. But crevettes, oysters and monkfish are always available if pre-ordered. It is supplies of fresh fish like sardines or sea bass, or crabs and lobsters, which can be affected by the weather preventing the fishing boats from going out to sea. If Charles buys his seafood frozen, from an international or global supplier, then any issues possibly wouldn't have come to my attention yet.'

It was the first time they had touched on the subject of his job, and Yvonne was curious to learn more.

'Is TAA the only restaurant you manage, or are you the area or regional manager for all of them around here?'

'I manage several of the Jimmy Mack restaurants, but I live here in Shaftesbury. Although I do travel and so it's probably fairer to describe my flat as my base rather than my home.'

Yvonne risked probing further 'Do you have family?'

George allowed himself a small smile 'Yes, I have family. I have two grown-up sons and two grown-up daughters, an ex-wife with whom I am definitely not on good terms with like Alison and Scott appear to be, as well as brothers, sisters, and parents and cousins. But none live locally. And I am single. What about you?'

Yvonne absorbed the information he was divorced. She rarely talked about her family because during the eighties and nineties the name Parker was synonymous with the English antiques business, and everyone knew who she was and who she was related too. Once that was all sold and finished with, she had retreated into a quiet life and had little contact with family or the other people she had worked with, and now it was all so long ago that only the antiques dealers or collectors who had been in the business in those days would have any reason to question her about her heritage. She delivered the speech she usually gave when asked about her personal life. 'I'm single, no children, no family to speak of, no exes lurking in the background. I live above the shop in an apartment I designed for myself, Shaftesbury is my home, and I rarely leave here except for two or three times a year when I take Toby with me for horsemanship camps.' Before he could ask any more, she said 'I think I am too full for pudding, but if you're having anything I could squeeze in some sorbet.'

George recognised she was cutting off that line of conversation, and following her lead he studied the menu. They decided on a blood orange sorbet for Yvonne, and cheese and biscuits for George.

'Oh no, I can't,' Yvonne said when he offered to share the enormous cheese board when it arrived. 'I love cheese, but it gives me nightmares if I eat it after lunch.'

'Luckily I don't have that problem,' he said as he tucked into a mouthful of blue cheese. 'With your professional hat on, what did you think of the jewellery we found? I have no idea about jewellery, as my ex-wife will testify, but I am sure you will have been paying attention.'

After her shower Yvonne had taken time to study the pieces they found in the field and she had taken photographs. She was impressed with the quality and age of the gold and the precious stones, but she decided not to reveal anything about it to George in case it jeopardised the police case or even her life. By her estimation the collection was worth in excess of three million pounds, and as there were several complete pieces comprising of matching necklace, bracelet, ring and earrings, and many single earrings, or necklaces and ring, she suspected that the ones they had found were only a part of a much larger haul. She would have expected matching tiaras to many of the pieces, but they hadn't seen anything like that. If the jewellery was linked to the body they had found, she doubted she was a much-loved grannie from Shaftesbury.

Cautiously she replied 'It looked as though there were some lovely items which would sell well in my shop, but like you I was too busy trying to scoop it all up to take much notice. I think I'll give that particular field a wide berth for a few weeks, because I can't think of any innocent reason why it should have ended up in there.'

'It must have been a burglary gone wrong. I wonder if she disturbed the intruders, and then chased them down the lanes into the field. Brave old bird if she did, but I shouldn't worry about going in that field,' said George. 'With the amount of police activity in there at the moment, no criminal is going to think that even a cigarette butt or chewing gum wrapper will still be in there after they go.'

'Do people still buy chewing gum?' mused Yvonne. 'It was forbidden in our house when I was young.'

'Mine too!' laughed George. 'Yes, people do chew gum. As soon as I see a member of staff with it I know they are either a smoker or a drinker, or both.'

The conversation progressed to sweets from their childhood, and together they shared happy memories of penny sweets including Black Jacks and Fruit Salads, and more expensive ten penny sweets like chocolate logs and liquorice sherbets.

At the end of the evening both declined the waitress's offer of tea or coffee, and Yvonne accepted George's request to pay the bill on condition she paid for their Sunday lunch, a financially unfair exchange for him in her view considering the amount of alcohol they had to drink that evening, but it was very nice to be treated once in a while.

Slowly they walked down the High Street together, taking a detour to the top of Gold Hill where Yvonne was glad she had kept her sensible shoes on as they walked over the cobbles.

'We are lucky to live here,' said George as he gazed over the iconic view.

'Yes, we are,' said Yvonne as she looked over the Blackmore Vale which was gently lit by moonlight, and with streetlights twinkling in the distance.

Together they headed towards Yvonne's home, past George's restaurant, and at the electronic gates which separated her parking area from the council's carpark, George gave her a delicious kiss on the cheek. Feeling herself blushing again, Yvonne pressed the remote control for the gates and walked through as they were opening, turning to give him a wave before opening the back door to the shop and going inside. Zebedee greeted her with her usual enthusiasm, and as Yvonne was buzzing too much to go straight upstairs to bed, she made herself a cup of peppermint and liquorice tea and flopped down on one of the sofas with the dog to watch some telly and allow her mind to quieten. She could feel George's lips on her cheek for over half an hour, and even after that she could conjure up the memory.

But Yvonne was old enough to know that first impressions were not always to be relied upon, and there were a few niggles about George Gumbleton that upset her dreamy state. The most prominent was the way a man at the restaurant had positioned himself in a chair some distance away from them. At the time Yvonne had thought he was looking at Tabitha, who was a bit over-dressed for an evening in The Shaston, but now she thought he was observing George and all who came over to speak to him for the entire evening. When they left The Shaston he had followed them, and although he didn't walk down the cobbles to the top of Gold Hill when they did, he was loitering at the start of Park Walk off to the left when they walked back up to the High Street. She hadn't seen him again, and she was sure he wasn't watching them with the intention of seeing when they parted because she had scanned the carpark as she always did before opening her gates, but she guessed that he knew where they were going and didn't feel the need to stalk them to her home.

When either of the policemen Tim or Tom next came into the shop she would quiz them about George Gumbleton, and she would be on the lookout for his shadow on Sunday.

Chapter 5

Fridays were rest days for Toby, and Yvonne's day on the rota to supervise the shop.

Yvonne had developed an area at the rear of the shop, where the original double garage used to be when the building was a house and which had then been used as a dark cool room for storing the flower shop's deliveries. In its latest incarnation the space was occupied by the stock of a man who specialised in automobilia. It wasn't unusual for a small vintage car or large motorbike to be in there, although most of the stock was rusty old signs, lamps and several cabinets filled with Mercedes badges, Jaguar brooches, and Alfa Romeo merchandise. The dealer, Rob Kemp, was a few inches taller than Yvonne, with untamed curly black hair and direct blue eyes, and arrived shortly after nine o'clock.

'Morning Yvonne,' he said, as he walked in carrying a jewellery box. 'Can you cast your eyes over this for me please? Tell me what you think?'

Yvonne, who had decided to go for loose curls and a light fringe today, was wearing a V-neck skater dress in yellow which showed off her curves and tanned arms and legs, opened the small red velvet jewellery box and glanced at the cufflinks inside. Rob was a true fan and collector of automobilia, and loved to show off his latest finds, even though no other dealers in the shop were particularly interested. 'They look like a very nice pair of cufflinks with the initial B,' she said as she handed the box to him.

He pushed the box back across the counter 'Take another look.'

Yvonne did as she was asked, this time taking each cufflink out and using her loupe to peer closely at the marks on the metal. 'Oh,' she said, frowning slightly as she placed them carefully back in the box and closed the lid, leaving her fingertips resting lightly on the top. 'That's a B for Bentley, isn't it? And that family crest is interesting.'

He nodded, a broad smile on his face 'You think the same as I do?'

Instead of directly answering him, she said 'Where did you get them?'

'They were tucked under the seat of an old Jaguar E-type I'm working on at home. I've had the car for years; I bought it at auction in Sherborne after one of their large house clearances, but I can't remember where the house is or who the previous owner was. I'll have to have a look for the registration documents. The car was in a terrible state then, held together by bird poo and cobwebs. I cleaned it up as soon as I brought it home, but haven't done much more until last week when I cleared my diary and got stuck in.'

Rob enthusiastically began to tell Yvonne about the renovations so far, and his plans for the car. Yvonne was half-listening, while also trying to process the fact that she had seen a similar pair of cufflinks covered in sheep poo the day before. The cufflinks yesterday had not particularly caught her attention, but now that Rob had made her look more closely at these in the red box she could see that they bore the mark of a rich land-owning family, whose ancestry could be traced back several hundred years.

They were interrupted when the two police officers Tom Archibald and Tim Smith came in through the front door. Rob casually pocketed the box, and asked if they and Yvonne would like a tea or a coffee? 'I've brought in a box of home-made ginger biscuits,' he grinned as everyone chorused 'Yes please!'

Rob's homemade cakes and biscuits were legendary, and on days when he oversaw the shop, Yvonne allowed him to use her kitchen to bake more, because the kitchen she provided for the staff was a basic kettle, sink, fridge and microwave affair. It was a mystery to everyone how Rob and his wife managed not to be the size of the Michelin man statue he had at the back of the automobilia room, next to the roll-up shutter.

'Any news?' Yvonne asked the two police officers. 'I assume that's why you have come in?'

Tim glanced to the back of the shop where Rob had disappeared to make their drinks. 'Actually, we've come in to see if you can shed some light on where the jewellery you found might have come from.'

Yvonne shook her head 'What do you mean?'

'You must have noticed the marks on most of the pieces,' said Tom. 'We were wondering if you had heard anything about items with those marks being stolen, or turning up in auction or private sales?'

Yvonne shook her head. 'Not that I can think of. I did notice those marks, and I was going to do a little research because they are interesting to me. I'll let you know if I hear anything, of course. I thought you were coming in to tell me you have identified that poor woman I found.'

They could hear the kettle boiling and the biscuit tin opening. Tim leaned in and said quickly and quietly, 'We will have some news for you soon.'

Rob appeared through the doorway with a tray of teapot, cafetiere, glass milk bottle, mugs, spoons, plates and biscuits, closely followed by Zebedee. Yvonne wanted Tim to tell her more, because he obviously knew something, and found that she didn't have the stomach for food, but the policemen didn't appear to be having the same problem, and within minutes their used mugs were back on the tray, and the biscuit plate held only crumbs. Tom was a keen enthusiast for Austin-Healey Sprites, and he and Rob chatted about Tom's latest acquisition and how he was going to renovate it, while Tim and Yvonne quietly sipped their coffee and listened. A few members of the public came in, and after an initial smile and nod of welcome, Yvonne left them to wander through the rooms in their own time. She could see them on the CCTV screen on the wall, and when one couple looked as though they were interested in viewing something in a cabinet, she made her excuses and walked through to the area where a large amount of collectible porcelain was held. By the time she returned, with the couple and the three items they wanted to purchase, the police officers had left, Zebedee had taken herself back upstairs to the flat, and Rob had cleared away the tray of food and drinks.

For a few minutes she had the place to herself, while Rob busied himself in the garage, and another two dealers were tidying their stands in another room.

By mid-morning the day had returned to a level of normality, with two or three other dealers in and out at any one time, refreshing the stock and rearranging their stands, and the shop was busy with three coach loads of tourists who were visiting Shaftesbury for the day. Fortunately they didn't all try to come into the building at the same time, but staggered their visits over several hours, whether by arrangement or accident Yvonne didn't know, although she suspected the drivers had something to do with the timings. She always made sure the coach drivers were included in the coffee and biscuits routine and allowed to use the shop's toilet. It cost her nothing and filled her shop with people who were looking for a souvenir of their visit to the ancient hilltop town of Shaftesbury. Business cards for Angel Lane Antiques were readily available on the counter, and resulted in a few thousand pounds of online business throughout the year.

The rhythm of the morning was again disrupted when the door was flung open, and Tabitha and Alison walked in.

'You will never guess what's happened now,' cried Tabitha. 'Charles Diamond has completely changed the menu, and it bears no resemblance to our original choices.'

'What is he offering you now?' asked Yvonne.

'Oh, he's not offering, he's telling,' said Alison. 'If it wasn't for the beautiful setting and the fact he won't give us our money back, I'd rather cancel the whole thing and invite everyone to a picnic on Castle Hill. He's told us we're having a buffet, and it's all cold. Cold rice, cold couscous, cold pasta. It sounds as though he is going to raid the delicatessen counter of one of the local supermarkets!'

'Has their kitchen broken down, or their chef left?' asked Yvonne.

'Who knows? He is refusing to explain, and keeps making it sound as though we should be grateful and trying to fluff it up so it sounds grand, instead of something you can eat any day of the week,' cried Tabitha.

'Surely it's a breach of contract? By changing the menu, and not providing the food and drink from the sources you have agreed, he is not fulfilling his part of the bargain.'

Tabitha was too upset to reply, and Alison said 'the agreement has all these get-out clauses in Kenyon Hall's favour, so we don't have a hope in hell of seeing any of our money again. This whole business has tainted it for me.'

'Oh, don't say that,' said Tabitha, who looked so miserable Yvonne came around the counter and gave her a hug.

'I am so sorry this is happening. It all sounded so perfect when we saw Charles last year! Something catastrophic must have happened because you confirmed the menus with him two weeks ago! Has he given you any explanation at all?'

'Nope,' said Alison. 'He won't answer our phone calls, and all we have got is an email stating the changes they are making.'

'Have you tried speaking to someone else at Kenyon Hall? Would you like me to try?'

'I did speak to a receptionist, but all she could do was transfer me to Charles' phone, which of course he did not answer.' Tabitha pulled away from Yvonne and took a deep breath. 'I think we should go up there and find the little weasel. Make him tell us to our faces what is going on.'

'Good idea,' nodded Alison. 'My next two clients have cancelled thanks to covid, and I know that Maisie was going to be doing the books today. I'll give her a ring and see if she's free.'

'I'll see if someone can cover me,' said Yvonne, and went to the back of the shop to find Rob. As she expected, he was standing in the shop's carpark with a customer and their classic old open-top sports car. The two men were peering under the bonnet. 'Rob, I hate to ask, but is there any chance you can cover the shop for me for a couple of hours please?'

'Yes, no problem,' said Rob. Turning to the customer, he said 'you've done a fine job there. That was a tricky thing to fix.'

He followed Yvonne through the open shutter, and waving the man good-bye, pulled it down behind him.

'Sorry to drag you away,' said Yvonne.

'Oh no problem, you did me a favour. Once he gets started talking about that car, he doesn't stop!'

Fortunately Yvonne was walking away from him as he said this, so he didn't see the small smile on her face at the irony of Rob complaining about someone else's non-stop obsession with cars.

Yvonne, Alison and Tabitha left the shop together, and walked up Angel Lane and around the corner to Bell Street, where Alison's business and her car were located.

'Good news,' Alison said. 'Maisie says she hasn't started on the bookwork and is only too keen to avoid it and come with us.'

Maisie, another tall, slim blond like Alison, but nearer Yvonne's age, was waiting next to Alison's stylish silver-blue Mercedes, and the four women settled themselves inside. From her vantage point in the back seat, Yvonne enjoyed the view of the Blackmore Vale as Alison drove them fifteen minutes to Kenyon Hall, an estate whose history went back centuries and had certainly profited from the slave trade. Despite its inhumane past, the drive up to the building was stunning, with mature oak and beech trees lining the road, the lake over to the left which looked cool and inviting in the hot sunshine, and the peaceful sight of horses and sheep grazing the pasture together.

'We should have a plan of what we are going to say,' suggested Maisie.

'Yes, we should,' agreed Alison. 'I want Charles to tell us why he is changing our menu so drastically.'

'But even if he tells us why, it doesn't change the fact that it is not going to be anything like the once-in-a-lifetime experience we have been looking forward to,' Tabitha said quietly. Yvonne thought she was looking pale and tired, nothing like the energetic figure she was used to seeing striding around the farm.

Tentatively Maisie said 'Before we see him, Alison and Tabitha do you think you ought to have a think about whether you still want the wedding to be held here? It seems to me that the stress of all these last-minute changes is tainting the venue, and that could have an impact on your memories.'

'Maisie is right. Let's pull over in that gateway up ahead and make a For and Against list. If the aspects of the venue you love outweigh this cock-up with the food and drink, then now is the time to adjust how we are all thinking about what is happening. However, if the issue with the food and drink is too momentous to overcome then we do need to find an alternative venue very quickly indeed.'

'That is impossible,' Tabitha dismissed Yvonne's suggestion immediately.

Alison turned off the road and switched off the engine. 'Nothing is impossible, Tabs. We have already said that a picnic on Castle Hill would be amazing, and the way I feel we are being treated by Charles is turning me off the idea of celebrating anything here.'

Maisie was delving in her beautiful purple velvet shoulder bag with beaded detail of a peacock. Yvonne shivered and looked away. No antiques dealer will have anything to do with peacocks, because they all know they are bad luck.

'Here we are,' said Maisie, as she pulled out a purple notebook with silver detail of a unicorn on the front, and a matching pen which neatly slotted inside. Yvonne nodded

63

her approval of this design. Maisie was keeping meticulous notes of the wedding plans in the notebook, all timed and dated, and she scanned through it to remind herself of Alison and Tabitha's original wishes when the four of them first sat down to plan the highlight of their social calendar in Yvonne's sitting room, with a Thai takeaway and a couple of bottles of wine.

'Let's start with things which haven't changed,' said Yvonne. 'Our wedding outfits are all divine.'

Everyone nodded in agreement, and a short discussion about how gorgeous they were going to look, with Alison and Maisie sharing their plans for everyone's hair and make-up, and the timeline for manicures and pedicures, taking into consideration Tabitha and Yvonne's habit of using their fingernails for scraping mud off animals.

'Our jewellery is ready,' said Alison. They had chosen a local jeweller to make their engagement rings, wedding rings, and a bespoke set of earrings, necklaces and bracelets for each bride and matron of honour which reflected their individual interests.

'I cannot wait to wear mine!' said Maisie. 'Oh, I'm so excited!'

'Me too,' grinned Yvonne. 'Almost makes me want to get married again! Almost.'

Maisie laughed. She was the only one of the four who was still with her original partner. They were childhood sweethearts, started 'going out' when they were fourteen-years old, married at nineteen, three children, and twenty-five years later they were still happy together.

'The guest list is awesome,' said Alison, the enthusiasm from Maisie and Yvonne rubbing off on her.

'Yes, it is!' shouted Maisie, and everyone laughed, even Tabitha joined in.

'The legal part will take place regardless of the party venue,' said Tabitha.

'That's right' agreed Maisie. 'The four of us at Shaftesbury Town Hall for eleven o'clock in the morning. One advantage of moving the celebration party to a venue nearby is that more people could attend the wedding ceremony.'

'I'm not sure I want more people there,' said Tabitha. 'I'm going to be nervous enough, without being watched by tons of pairs of eyes.'

'I agree. I like the thought of just the four of us being there for the legal part of it' said Alison. 'We don't need anyone else for that, but I would like the opportunity to celebrate with as many people as would like to join us afterwards.'

'Well we don't have to decide anything now' said Maisie 'But it is worth noting that having more people around, maybe immediately after the ceremony for photographs on Gold Hill or Park Walk if the weather allows, could be something to put in the plus column.'

'True. I hadn't really thought about having any photographs taken in Shaftesbury, I was seeing that as the legal bit we had to do, and then coming here to this beautiful setting for photos and videos,' said Alison.

'Yes it is beautiful here,' said Tabitha, as she watched a couple of chestnut horses grooming each other.

'It is a beautiful setting,' agreed Yvonne, 'but Maisie is right; Shaftesbury does have beautiful views, and it would be lovely to have photos taken in your home town. Of course it is a bonus to have amazing scenery and stunning architecture like this, but it doesn't change the joy of the day if those things aren't there. It is the people who make the wedding day, and you two are going to look gorgeous wherever the pictures are taken.'

'And if the people are eating bad food and drinking rubbish wine they won't be happy,' Tabitha said quietly 'which is all we will remember when we look at the photographs.'

'Come on,' Alison restarted the engine, 'let's go and find out what the man has to say, and if we can get any satisfaction from him.'

Maisie and Yvonne looked at each other and began to giggle. Alison was the first to catch-on, and she too started to laugh. Tabitha had been lost in her reverie and looked at the others trying to work out what was so funny, until eventually she too realised what Alison had said, and by the time the car pulled up outside Kenyon Hall all four women had tears of laughter running down their faces.

Chapter 6

Their meeting with Charles Diamond was short, and unsatisfactory. At first the reception staff tried to tell them that he was unavailable, no they didn't know when he was free and please could the brides-to-be go home and telephone tomorrow, to book an appointment. Alison and Tabitha refused to accept this, stressing that their wedding day was in a fortnight's time, and there were urgent issues they needed to discuss. Next, the staff told them that he was not on site, but Maisie had done her homework and knew there was a wedding in progress, and he would be in attendance. Yvonne felt sorry for the staff, because she could see that they were not happy at the situation they were in and guessed that Alison and Tabitha were not the first people to turn up without an appointment and demand to see Charles.

A manager appeared and invited the women into one of the restaurants and ordered tea and cakes for them while he promised he would try to find Charles. The restaurant was called The Stables, and as the name suggested it looked as though it had been converted from the original building used to house resident and visiting equines. Yvonne could imagine the noise and smells as the ostlers washed down the carriage horses, forked out the muck, and swept the passageways. The brickwork had signs of restoration, as did some of the wooden beams, and the wooden dividers between individual seating areas and the floor were modern, which was a good thing since the original stalls would have rotted and worn to the point of being dangerous and unusable. The Stables was almost empty, with only one other cubicle occupied. The elderly couple were seated on the wooden benches with large cushions in cream and blue flowery design, at a long table covered in a matching tablecloth, and with a vase of sunflowers for decoration. They were having afternoon tea, and Yvonne didn't like the look of the thin white bread of the sandwiches, and small portions of cake which looked as though someone had bought packets of three different mass-produced patisserie and cut them into quarters.

No one had eaten lunch, but when their food and drink arrived they were disappointed and found their appetites had disappeared, because instead of fresh milk in a pretty jug, the milk for the tea was individual long-life portions in plastic cartons, and the cakes were clearly from a cheap supermarket. The women were shocked, because Kenyon Hall was famous for its spectacular afternoon teas and delicious lunches, and the last time they had come here a matter of weeks before they had enjoyed a feast of homemade lemon drizzle, chocolate brownies, and a white chocolate and raspberry heaven on a plate.

'I can't eat this,' said Tabitha as she pushed her plate away, and looking at Yvonne she explained 'and it's got nothing to do with that poor woman you found in the field, although that experience has affected my sleep and my eating habits. This cake tastes cheap and nasty, and I wouldn't eat it whatever has happened recently. If this is the standard of food they are expecting to serve at our wedding we're not having it here.'

'I can't drink this,' said Alison, who hadn't even poured herself a cup of tea but was looking at the milk cartons with distaste. 'I'll force it down if I have to in some bed and breakfast or motel, but a so-called country house hotel like Kenyon Hall should not be serving this muck.

'Let's go and find him and get some answers, then we can make a decision one way or the other.' Tabitha stood up, and the other three followed her in the direction of the orangery.

'We don't want to screw-up anyone's special day,' urged Alison.

'Of course not,' agreed Tabitha, 'but we do need to speak to him now.'

The sound of raised voices drew the women towards the secret garden, and as they approached they could just about see the top of Charles Diamond's head. He was surrounded by three men, all dressed in morning suits, and all three had glasses and plates in their hands.

'This is not what we have paid for,' one man, in his sixties and with the figure of someone who enjoyed his food, was shoving his plate in front of Charles's face.

Charles was holding his hands up in surrender and looked as though he was about to burst into tears.

'And this is not the French champagne we paid for!' a second man held his glass up for all to see. 'It's the kind of fizz my wife buys when she and the girls are having a session with crisps and curry. How dare you fob us off with this crap.'

Yvonne noticed four men nearby watching the scene. The way they held themselves indicated they had been in the armed forces, the outline of taut midriffs and bulging pectorals visible under their black polo shirts bearing the Kenyon Hall logo on the front, and when Charles caught the eye of one of them they moved forwards, revealing the word SECURITY on the back. A fifth man appeared to the side, dressed in a dark suit, and stepped forwards, drawing the attention of the three angry guests.

69

'Please, come this way and let me see if I can resolve the situation,' he said as he walked through a doorway and out of sight of the four women. The security guards formed a human barrier separating the men from Charles, and shepherded them after the man in the dark suit.

'It's not just us, then,' said Alison to Charles, who looked around in horror. Charles was a lean man in his sixties, who always looked dapper in a silver-grey suit, white shirt, and pink tie, his white hair smoothed back from his tanned face. That tan stayed the same whatever the time of year.

He had clearly thought he was on his own, and the relief which had smoothed his face when the reinforcements saved him from the tense situation disappeared, and he now looked like a much older man, the skin on his face grey and lined underneath the fake tan.

Charles Diamond had none of the confidence and swagger of the man they had met on their previous trips to Kenyon Hall. He spread his hands in front of him, and in a small voice he said 'I am sorry. I am so sorry.'

Maisie spoke 'We are here to inform you that because of your inability to fulfil your side of our agreement, the wedding of Alison Jones and Tabitha Leighton is cancelled, and we expect a full refund in the next three working days. You will receive a letter from our solicitor to that effect, and we will take you through the legal system if you do not immediately comply. Come on ladies,' Maisie gestured to Alison and Tabitha to follow her, and Yvonne took up the rear.

All four walked out to the carpark, and into the safety of Alison's car. Everyone sat in silence while they processed what had just happened.

Eventually, Tabitha said 'What will we do now?' and burst into tears.

In a surprisingly determined voice, and while fishing in her handbag for tissues, which she handed to her fiancée, Alison said 'We go back to Yvonne's house, Maisie will go and buy some sandwiches from the bakery, and some proper cakes, we will make a big pot of tea, and plan an amazing wedding ceremony where no one will feel the need to turn their noses up at the food or spit the drink on the floor.'

Alison spun the car around, sending gravel flying towards the huge stone steps leading up to the open double doors of the hall where Tabitha and Alison had thought they would be posing for wedding photographs in just two weeks' time, and floored the accelerator as she sped down the driveway.

'That's if we all make it there alive,' said Maisie.

'Sorry, sorry,' said Alison, and immediately took her foot off the accelerator until they had slowed to a more sensible speed. 'Although I do feel better now.'

'Me too,' said Tabitha. 'I didn't realise cancelling would feel so good. Thank you, Maisie, for making that decision for us.'

'My pleasure,' said Maisie, whose colour had returned now that she didn't think they were going to die in Alison's Mercedes.

Chapter 7

As Alison drove into the carpark at the back of Yvonne's antiques shop, Yvonne was sure she caught a glimpse of the man who had been spying on George Gumbleton disappearing up the walkway towards the library.

'What's up?' asked Maisie, as Yvonne twisted in her seat and tried to peer around the wall which was blocking her view.

'Oh, nothing,' shrugged Yvonne. 'I thought I saw someone, but it wasn't him.'

'I don't know about that,' grinned Alison, looking at Yvonne in the driving mirror. 'Is he who you were looking for?'

Again Yvonne turned around so she could see through the rear window, just as George Gumbleton walked around the corner and waved as he caught her looking at him. Involuntarily a smile moved her lips, and she returned his greeting with a raised hand. Embarrassed she realised that everyone in the car was watching her, and she said crossly 'What? I can wave at someone can't I?'

'You've gone a lovely shade of pink,' teased Tabitha.

By the way her cheeks were burning, Yvonne suspected her face was puce rather than a delicate English rosé.

'Yvonne and George had a date last night,' Tabitha said to Maisie in a confiding tone.

'It wasn't a date!' protested Yvonne. 'We were discussing the body we found together. Anyway, what's wrong with me going on a date?'

'Nothing,' said Tabitha, 'it's just that in all the time I have known you, you have never dated anyone, either male or female.'

'Well, I still haven't,' retorted Yvonne. 'Come on Maisie, I'll help you shop for our lunch. Here are the keys to my home Tabitha. Let yourselves in and put the kettle on.'

By the time Maisie and Yvonne returned fifteen minutes later with a box full of small rolls containing chicken, beef, or egg mayonnaise, some peaches, and four slices of mandarin and chocolate cake, Tabitha and Alison had laid the table and made a pot of tea. Maisie had popped home while they were waiting for their lunch order to be made up and collected the huge wedding folder in a matching unicorn design to her notebook, in which she kept every sample of menus, materials, price lists, addresses of every supplier whether they were chosen or rejected, and Yvonne retrieved her wedding book from her office. Tabitha and Alison already had theirs, because they had been expecting to go through it with Charles Diamond. Between them they had the order of the day at Kenyon Hall, and the menus. Starting with a venue, the four friends brainstormed possibilities, none of which matched up to the splendour of Kenyon Hall, nor its perfect facilities, but all of which had their own unique atmosphere which could make the wedding day special. By the time the rolls and one pot of tea had been finished they had a list of three possible places, and so they started on the menu.

'We need to decide what is essential to the day,' said Maisie. 'There are so many things on this list which Charles promised us and are unique to Kenyon Hall, but we probably don't need if we are having the celebration somewhere else.'

'I'd like to add those beef rolls,' said Alison, pointing to the empty space on the plate where the rolls had been.

Tabitha laughed 'We could always do a lamb roast and have it with flat bread and mint and yoghurt dressing.'

'Oh yes, my favourite!' agreed Alison.

'Well, if you are serious,' said Maisie as she studied her list, 'that only leaves this place as a viable option.' She pointed to one of the local vineyards.

Yvonne nodded 'Shall we make a ghost plan of your wedding day using the vineyard? Until we know if it is available we can't make firm decisions, but at least this way if anything pops up which makes it totally unsuitable we don't need to take it further. I'll make us another pot of tea.'

'I'll give them a ring and see if it is a possibility' said Maisie, and stepped away from the table to make the phone call.

Alison and Tabitha ran through the lists together and agreed that so long as they had their wedding outfits, weather-proof space for their guests, the rings, and decent food and drink, then everything else would be a bonus.

Maisie came back 'The vineyard is available, and we can go up there now and talk to them!'

Everyone moved as one to Alison's car, and within ten minutes they had arrived at the vineyard.

'Now this would be perfect,' said Tabitha. 'I can see my farm from here!'

Everyone looked in the direction of the farm, their eyes drawn to the police tent and vehicles in the field.

'Have they told you when you can move your sheep back?' asked Maisie.

'Not yet, but I'm working on it being at least a fortnight, if not longer. They have closed the footpath through there, and the order says for at least six months, but I imagine that is a generous timescale.'

'Let's hope so, for your sake,' said Maisie.

The four friends were regular visitors to the vineyard, which had a restaurant serving tasty breakfasts, lunches, afternoon teas, and evening meals, as well as fantastic English sparkling wines. They walked in through the big open wooden doorway and turned left to the restaurant which had one wall of windows allowing the diners a panoramic view of the vineyard.

'This would be perfect for our guests,' murmured Tabitha to Alison, who nodded.

The owners recognised the four women, and came over to greet them, before ushering them to a large round table next to the window wall. The restaurant was half-full, with a mixture of families and couples eating a late lunch or afternoon tea, everyone looked happy with the food, and there wasn't a plastic milk carton in sight.

The owners were keen to find out news about the murder in Tabitha's field, because visitors to their vineyard could see the police activity from a distance and it was the main topic of conversation amongst their local diners. Although it appeared to be good for business while it was current news, they didn't want their beautiful view to become notorious as a place to see the murder site, and Tabitha agreed. She didn't want her farm's name to become synonymous with the murder either.

The owners and Tabitha and Alison discussed the brides' wishes and the vineyard's ability to meet them. The vineyard would have to be compensated for closing their restaurant for the whole day, their food and drink was pricey, and it soon became clear that without the refund from Kenyon Hall the cost was out of their reach. Entertainment would be extra because that had been included in the fee Charles Diamond was charging, additional toilets would need to be hired because the vineyard only had two, the carpark was too small for the invited guests' vehicles meaning that additional parking would need to be rented from the next-door farm. With two weeks to go, the chances of finding someone who could supply posh bogs or standard portaloos was slim, let alone decent entertainment for the evening. No one had much hope that any kind of refund would be forthcoming from Kenyon Hall within the next fortnight, let alone the demanded three days, and everyone needed to be paid up front, or at the least given a healthy deposit.

Alison and Tabitha thanked the owners for their time, and their kindness when it became clear the wedding could not take place at their business. The couple gave Alison and Tabitha several names and contact details of people who may be able to help if they could find another venue.

'This is why the vineyard is one of our favourite places,' whispered Yvonne to Maisie as they followed the dejected brides-to-be back to the car. 'That family are so generous, you could see they were willing to bend over backwards to accommodate us, but at the end of the day they need to make a profit.'

It was a subdued carload of women who drove back to Yvonne's place. The determination which had filled them after their encounter with Charles Diamond at Kenyon Hall had dissipated, and the difficulty of their situation was overwhelming. As they dragged themselves out of Alison's car, Yvonne said 'Come on, let's go for a drink in the Shaston. I can't face any more tea, or coffee, and it's perfectly acceptable to have a cocktail after five o'clock in the afternoon on a sunny day.'

Alison said 'I'll have to ask Scott if he can have the children. Give me a minute and I'll ring him.'

'I'll let Andy know what I'm doing,' said Maisie, and sent her husband a text.

Yvonne popped inside to check everything was OK with the shop, and that Rob was happy to close up for her. He was deep in conversation with another man, and gave her a nod when she stuck her head around the corner and waved her keys at him. He put his hand in his pocket and pulled out his keys which he waved back at her without faltering in his conversation. Satisfied, Yvonne joined the others, and together they trooped up the High Street. As they passed The Abbess Aethelgifu, Yvonne glanced through the tinted windows. It was a while since she had been in there for a meal, but she remembered that the last time had been for her birthday when her fellow antiques dealers at the shop had treated her to a celebratory dinner. She smiled at the memory. They were a nice bunch of people, and she felt lucky they had chosen to be a part of her business.

Once settled at a table in the courtyard, with drinks in front of them, Tabitha said 'We could clear out one of the barns of all my machinery, beg and borrow tables and chairs, hire portaloos, and then we have a weather-proof space, and the fields are fine for parking. Where we get the portaloos from, I have no idea, what we do about the catering, I don't know. We need a wedding cake from somewhere, and these things need to be ordered months in advance. The option of using the Town Hall is starting to look like a decent one, but we need to let the officials know if we need it for a couple of hours. We need to find entertainment for the evening.' She slumped in her chair, looking close to tears.

'It is overwhelming' said Alison, and gave Tabitha a hug. Looking around at The Shaston's outdoor and indoor spaces, and the lavatory doors she said 'It is a shame this place isn't available and would probably be out of our budget anyway.'

Maisie sighed 'It's the weekend tomorrow, so it will probably only be us silly buggers who are working. It's going to be difficult to get hold of anyone to ask about facilities and prices now until Monday.'

'Right, we need a plan of action,' said Yvonne. 'There are too many ifs and buts. Your marriage is the most important thing, and that is booked at the town hall. Your dresses, your hair and make-up, your rings, your fantastic Matrons of Honour are all organised and ready to go.'

'Hear hear!' said Maisie. 'At least we won't have to go and choose wedding shoes again.'

Everyone laughed 'I don't think that saleswoman will ever forget offering you one gold sandal for your right foot' giggled Alison.

'What did she think I was going to wear on my prosthetic leg?' asked Maisie. 'It's not as though I walked in on a blade or something. I was wearing a pair of shoes, right shoe on my right foot and left shoe on my left foot! That never happens when I wear the skin-coloured sleeve on the outside. It's my fault, I didn't think.'

'Oh god, her face when you pointed it out, Yvonne' by now tears were pouring down Alison's face.

'It took her a while to realise what she was saying, but once she did she couldn't stop apologising. I bet she still wakes up in the middle of the night in a hot flush at the memory' said Yvonne. 'It is lucky you are so well-balanced about it, Maisie.'

Maisie shrugged. 'I have been living with the loss of my left leg for over twenty years. I am used to comments like that. Remember when I was in your shop and the television crew arrived to film an episode for their Antiques Road

Trip series, and they went off at a tangent because one of the dealers had three artificial legs from the fifties on their stand?'

'That was your fifteen minutes of fame!' said Yvonne. 'If only you had repeat fees for that episode. I am always seeing it pop up in the afternoons. Anyway, the point is your wedding can go ahead, we just need to sort out the party.'

Maisie said 'Yvonne is right; the important part of the day is in place, so let's raise our glasses and make a toast to our beautiful brides-to-be. Cheers to Tabitha and Alison.'

No one had touched their drinks, and so four full cocktail glasses were raised, clinked together, and sipped, followed by murmurs of appreciation.

'Let's divide up the main outstanding tasks, and see if we can find some more things we can tick off this list,' said Yvonne. 'I'm going to bear in mind your idea about the barn and the field Tabitha, and I'm sure there are enough antiques dealers who have tables and chairs stored away in various warehouses around the area. I can think of seven tables and countless chairs in my antiques shop now, not the rare and pricey kind, which I could persuade the dealers to let us borrow. We could turn it into a 'try before you buy' event, because you know what it's like when you go somewhere and see the perfect table for your kitchen, or chair for your office. But I would also like to have a go at finding an alternative venue. I can't think of anywhere we haven't already discussed, but I will ask my colleagues and any customers who come into the shop tomorrow if they have any ideas. I could also ask for suggestions for entertainment, if that will help someone who would like to take on that task.'

'I can do that,' said Maisie. 'I am sure my kids will have some ideas, and I will do the same as you, and will ask all of the customers who come into the salon tomorrow for suggestions for venues and will pass them onto you.'

'Thank you Maisie, I'll do the same and between us we shouldn't miss anyone,' said Alison, who looked a lot brighter now that the ideas were starting to flow again, along with the cocktails. 'I also have an idea for the catering, and for the cake. A lady who regularly comes in for a colour and trim has her own business, and although I expect she is fully booked she is bound to know someone who can help.'

'Well, that leaves me with the portaloos,' laughed Tabitha. 'I will ask the chap who chairs the organising committee for our local show if he has any suggestions.'

'Same place, same time on Sunday evening?' asked Yvonne.

'Same place, same time!' chorused the other three, as the cocktail glasses were clinked again, and the remains of the drinks were downed.

Chapter 8

Saturday was a busy day in the antiques shop, and although Yvonne started the day full of hope for ideas of venues and entertainment for the wedding from her fellow dealers and customers, by lunchtime she still only had the names of the same three venues, all of which were already booked, and numerous suggestions for the entertainment along the lines of 'oooh that chap we saw at Muston's, you know, the one with the guitar' and 'the band we saw at thingy's birthday party, you know, the ones who sang Mustang Sally'. Children's magicians, face painters, and sing-along entertainers also featured.

Just before midday the door opened, and Yvonne's heart jumped. George Gumbleton, dressed in black shorts and a red polo shirt which set off his dark hair and brown eyes, was smiling at her as he closed the door behind him. 'I'm popping out for a sandwich and wondered if you have time to come too?' he asked. 'Or I could bring one back here for you and we could eat them while you carry on working.'

'I'm not officially here today, so bunking off for a sandwich is perfectly legal' she grinned, glad that she had taken the time to style her hair rather than towel-dry it and hope for the best, which usually resulted in a fluffy halo around her face.

Aware that all eyes in the shop were on them as they exited onto Angel Lane, Yvonne could feel her cheeks burning.

'Phew, it's hot out here!' she exclaimed, fanning herself with her hand as they walked down the road. 'Where were you thinking of going for that sandwich?'

George looked up and down the High Street, which was busy with people and vehicles. 'Come on, let's try the deli and see if they have a free table out the back.'

Luck was on their side, and they slid onto the pretty wooden chairs either side of the small table in the window overlooking the vale.

Yvonne sighed as she gazed over the countryside 'We are so lucky to live here. My horse is just the other side of those oak trees!' She pointed in the distance to a clump of trees on a small green hill.

'Ah yes,' nodded George seriously. 'I can see him.'

They laughed at the absurdity, and the waitress appeared at their table to take their order. Neither had looked at the menu, but a quick scan and Yvonne chose the cheese ploughman's, knowing how delicious the cheeses were in the cabinet in the shop. George copied her, and they both ordered ginger beer.

'We're like two of the Famous Five' laughed Yvonne. 'Perhaps we should find another couple of people and a dog and solve the murder in Tabitha's field. That poor old woman's family must be beside themselves by now, with everyone talking about it.'

'Oh, haven't you heard?' said George. 'Her name is Mrs Gooch, and she has been found safe and well. Apparently she went on a last-minute holiday with a friend of hers, and they came home first thing this morning, completely oblivious to all the stress they had put Mrs Gooch's family through.'

'Thank goodness for that!' Yvonne paused as the waitress put their drinks on the table. 'Where had she been?'

'They were staying in Swanage, at a caravan park. Her friend was meant to be going with her daughter and her family, but one of the grandsons tested positive for covid on Saturday morning, so she invited Mrs Gooch to go with her instead. It turns out she isn't as frail and batty as her family were making out, and the pair of them have been enjoying hiking along the coast and through the countryside to pubs and cafés for lunch during the day, and playing bingo and watching the cabaret entertainment in the caravan park in the evening! Her interview on the local radio is hilarious; she is cross about all the fuss and waste of police resources, and furious at the description her family put out about her.'

Yvonne laughed 'Oh my goodness, I was not expecting that. How brilliant! Although it is nice that she has people who would miss her if she disappeared for a day or two, don't you think? Didn't she tell anyone where she was going?'

'She didn't tell her family because she speaks to her daughter every Friday evening on the telephone, and of course she didn't know she was going until the Saturday morning, and she rarely speaks to her son, but it was he who raised the alarm. He was working in Shaftesbury on Monday and decided to treat his mum to lunch, but when he turned up at her house there was no answer, so he let himself in with his key and was concerned to find milk and chicken in the fridge which needed to be thrown out. He went back on Tuesday, and it was obvious she hadn't been home since he was last there.'

'He must have been worried about her. I can understand why he contacted the police.'

'The funny thing is, Mrs Gooch had told her neighbour, who also has a spare key, to come in and help himself to the milk and chicken, and also to the fruit and vegetables in the larder, but he was involved in an art exhibition at Shaftesbury Arts Centre this week and forgot all about it, and of course was never at home when the police came round to ask if he'd seen her. If the neighbour had collected the food, or if he had been home when the police called, then the concerns about her safety would not have been raised.'

'But surely the neighbour had seen or heard the news? I did, and I didn't know her.'

'No, he doesn't have a television, and isn't on social media. He does listen to the local radio, where there were a lot of appeals for information about her, but because of the exhibition he hasn't been listening to that all week either. Mrs Gooch didn't switch her mobile phone on because she only has it for emergencies, so although she was carrying it with her every day on their hikes she didn't hear any of the voicemail messages left by her son and daughter. She's insisting her son and daughter take her out for a meal tomorrow night to make up for the embarrassment of arriving home to find the police had sealed the front and back doors and left a card telling her to contact them as soon as she arrived home. She thought a crime had been committed at her house while she was away. I think the last straw was when she saw the photograph they had chosen to use.'

'Go on,' said Yvonne, leaning forward, a smile of anticipation on her face.

'In their defence, the son and daughter said it was the only one they could find where you could see her face, because usually their photos of her are taken from behind as she walks up some hill or other, or with her face turned away as she watches one of her grandchildren in a paddling pool or on a swing. The one they chose was from last Christmas where she had a paper cracker hat on her head a bit skew-whiff, and a mug of tea in her hand. It does look as though she is in an old folk's home, rather than sitting down in her favourite armchair having just cooked and cleared away a full Christmas dinner for fourteen people.'

'How old is she?'

'Sixty-four years old. I expect to still be running at that age.'

'I might have started running by that age,' grinned Yvonne.

Their plates of food arrived, and just as Yvonne expected, the cheese was delicious. She and George made easy small talk, shared the bill, and parted company outside the shop with a wave and a confirmation of their lunch date the next day.

Yvonne walked back to the cool interior of her shop, and stood just inside the door quietly observing the energy of the people within. She walked through and unlocked the door to her kitchen, wondering how soon she would be missed if she was murdered. She was greeted by a rush of Staffordshire Bull Terrier x Collie, her dog Zebedee, and an offer of a cup of tea by the antiques dealer who was manning the shop that day, and realised that without noticing her life had become full of people and animals with whom she interreacted on an almost hourly basis. There had been a time when weeks had gone by without a conversation with another human being, and with no animals in her life she didn't even have them for companionship. Before she had a chance to analyse when all of that had changed, and why, Alison and Tabitha were pressing the button outside the gates in the carpark.

'Let us in!' called Tabitha.

'OK!' laughed Yvonne at the sight of them looking pleadingly at the camera.

Once inside, Tabitha began telling Yvonne all about the generous offer the local bakery had made. 'They heard about our plans falling through, and have offered to make us a three-tiered wedding cake in time for our wedding day!'

'That's amazing!' exclaimed Yvonne. 'I didn't even think of asking them; I didn't know they made bespoke orders.'

'They don't' said Alison 'but because we've been supplying them with eggs for all these years, they wanted to help us out. I can't believe it! What a weight off our minds.'

'That really is so kind of them,' agreed Tabitha. 'So, Miss Yvonne, what's going on in your life? A little birdie told us you and a certain Mr Gumbleton have been seen enjoying a romantic tete-a-tete at the deli this lunchtime?'

'Yes, do tell. What did you talk about?' urged Alison.

'Honestly, this town! I can't remember what we talked about. Probably not a lot other than the so-called missing grannie has turned up,' laughed Yvonne. 'Did you hear her on Alfred radio?'

'Yes!' laughed Alison. 'Wasn't she brilliant? Even though I don't know who she is, I am pleased it wasn't her because she sounds like such a character. Although she is grumpy about all the fuss.'

Yvonne said 'She was fortunate that people were missing her enough to look for her, because whoever that poor soul is in the field doesn't appear to have been missed by anyone. No other suggestions have been made as to her identity. Everyone was convinced it was the missing grannie.'

'So, who was that dead woman in my field?' asked Tabitha.

There was a knock on the door from the shop, and when Yvonne opened it the two policemen were standing on the other side.

Tim looked in, and seeing Tabitha and Alison sitting on the sofa, said 'ah good, three of the four of you we wanted to speak to are here. Can we come in?'

Yvonne opened the door wider so they could walk through, and feeling uncomfortably guilty, she sat down next to Tabitha and Alison, leaving the two policemen to sit on the other sofa opposite them.

'What's up?' asked Tabitha. 'Have you managed to find out who is lying in my field?'

Tom nodded, his blue eyes contrasting sharply with his black hair. Yvonne wondered what position he had held in the military. He was always smiley and friendly when they met, his size seemingly made him less intimidating than his taller partner, but she'd seen him tackle a local drug dealer single-handed while off-duty, after the man had stabbed one of his associates and was threatening another outside one of the pubs on the High Street. The man was terrifyingly out of control, screaming and shouting obscenities, the veins in his neck and head standing out in an alarming manner, and the blood of his former business partner covering his t-shirt and bare arm and the hand still holding the knife. A crowd of onlookers had gathered, police and ambulance were called, but no one knew how long it would take them to arrive, and no one wanted to risk also getting stabbed by trying to help the bleeding man on the pavement, or trying to wrestle the knife from his attacker. Tom had moved like lightening out of the crowd behind the man, and in a second had him on the floor with his hands handcuffed behind his back, the knife kicked away and out of the man's reach. Once the man was secured, Tom carefully picked it up and put it in an evidence bag he produced from a pocket in his jacket. He then had a word with the man who had been lucky to avoid the knife, before joining another man and a woman in giving first aid to the stab victim, and when the police arrived he had a word with one of the officers, handed over the knife, and walked away, unnoticed by everyone except Yvonne. She had never forgotten how quietly he dealt with the drama, how cool he was under pressure, the physical and mental strength he employed to rapidly get the scene under control, and how he had handed over responsibility to the officials when they were able to take charge.

Tom sat quietly next to his colleague on the sofa, and it was Tim who spoke first 'It's not official yet, but we believe the dead body is that of Jane Poundsmith.'

From his tone he sounded as though he expected them to know who he was talking about. The three women looked at each other with raised eyebrows.

'Who?' asked Yvonne.

Tom answered her 'The body hasn't been formally identified, but Jane Poundsmith has been under surveillance for years by various police forces, and by Revenue and Customs. No one has seen her for at least two weeks, and the body does resemble her in size and age. Her face was too disfigured for family to view, her hands had been removed so no chance of fingerprints, and there are no British dental records because we believe she always went to Romania for dental work. DNA is our best hope, but the sample we have on record as being hers is a bit suspect, something to do with the officials involved in processing it have since been removed from the service, so it is possible we will never get a positive identification.'

'Does that mean she was dismembered in my field' asked Tabitha.

'Yes. She was tortured and killed there. That is why there was so much blood.' Tom said.

'That must have taken some time. And whoever did it must have come equipped. I can butcher a lamb in about half an hour, and I know what to do. Someone who is inexperienced would struggle to remove her hands.'

'Nice topic' observed Alison, who had gone a ghastly pale colour.

'I'm just saying' said Tabitha. 'It won't have been as simple as dumping a dead body there. It must have been planned, which means whoever did it probably had local knowledge about my field. It is truly awful to think about it. That poor woman.'

Yvonne was struggling with the visual imagery, but tried to stay focussed. 'We didn't see any tyre tracks, so presumably she was alive and walked to the spot?'

'Or was carried' said Tabitha.

'I can't bear to think all that was going on here' said Alison. 'It is so awful.'

'But did she have a connection to Shaftesbury?' asked Yvonne.

'We weren't aware of one' said Tim. 'That is why we are so keen to learn more about the jewellery. It is unlikely that her murder and the jewellery being found nearby are not connected.'

'What jewellery?' asked Alison.

'There was a substantial amount of jewellery found near the body' explained Tim. 'More than you would expect to find on one person.'

'Is there any news as to where it was stolen from?' asked Yvonne.

'We don't know it has been stolen' said Tom. 'For all we know it was hers.'

'I have jewellery but I don't walk around the fields of Shaftesbury with it during the night' said Alison, who was starting to gain a little colour into her cheeks.

'And why didn't the people who murdered her take it with them?' asked Tabitha

'They must have been disturbed' said Yvonne.

'Very' remarked Alison.

'What time did you finish checking the sheep that night?' Tom asked Tabitha.

'I didn't. I walked through the field in the morning, probably at about seven o'clock, but I didn't go back there again until Yvonne called me the following morning. They are not due to lamb for a while yet, and have all the food and water they need, so I don't usually check them more than once a day.'

'Is that your regular routine? To check them at seven o'clock in the morning?'

'It is at the moment' said Tabitha. 'Once they get close to lambing I'll be there early morning and late evening until all the lambs are born and healthy. After that I will keep checking on them at least twice a day, but probably won't be regular times.'

'It would be a good idea to vary your routine' said Tom, looking steadily at Tabitha.

She looked back at him, understanding dawning on her face. 'That's a bit tricky, because the times when they lamb are usually before dawn and after dusk, and that is also when predators like foxes are around. I always have my dogs with me, and they would alert me to anyone nearby. It is not as though I am going to be walking around with pockets full of jewellery, is it? All I have in my pockets are sheep nuts, dog treats, a couple of penknives and baler twine.'

90

Tom and Tim shared a look. 'Is there anyone who could come with you?' asked Tim.

'No' Tabitha said in a defiant tone. 'All the other sheep farmers will be busy, and Alison has the children and her own business to run. I could probably get someone to come with me now and then, but not all the time. What are they meant to do, follow me around all day every day?'

'Of course, sorry, I appreciate it isn't practical' Tim said, and with a nod from Tom continued 'We'll make a point of driving past the fields when we can, and look out for you. Give us a wave if you are able to please? Just so we know everything is alright.'

'Fair enough, thank you' said Tabitha.

'I can make a point of walking Zebedee or riding Toby in the area more regularly' said Yvonne.

'I think it would be good for the kids to have a few early mornings, and I know they would love to have barbeques and picnics in the fields in the evenings' said Alison. 'I am sure between us all we can make sure that anyone watching would be unsure who else is going to pop up and where from. That's the idea isn't it?'

'Yes, that would be good. We don't want to alarm you, but if the body is that of Jane Poundsmith then the game has changed, and the people involved are more dangerous than we were assuming' said Tim.

'Is there anything you want to ask us?' Tom addressed Yvonne, but then included Tabitha and Alison.

The three women looked at each other. 'I don't have anything to ask now, but it is overwhelming' said Alison. Tabitha and Yvonne nodded their agreement.

'Have you had any more thoughts on the jewellery?' Tom asked Yvonne.

'No, I haven't, I am sorry I have been busy with the wedding planning,'

'Ah yes, the wedding of the year' said Tom, with a smile. 'How are the plans coming along?'

'Other than we don't have a venue, or toilets, or food, it's going great!' laughed Tabitha.

'But we do have a cake' said Alison.

'That's great, we all need cake' teased Tom.

'Yes, thank goodness the bakery has come to our rescue.'

'Which one?' asked Tim.

'The one on the High Street.'

Again, Tom and Tim looked at each other, before Tim said 'Um, I hate to tell you, but they have been closed down. I can't give you details, but you will need to find somewhere else for your cake.'

Chapter 9

Still reeling from the shock that the wedding cake supplier had been snatched away from them, Yvonne decided to do something different. She went into the antiques shop and offered to mind the counter for an hour, so the dealer who was in charge that day could deliver some chairs a customer had bought that morning. Yvonne had never heard of Jane Poundsmith, so tried to google her, then look her up on Facebook and Twitter, and even had a search on Instagram, but no results were found. Rob came through from his room and asked her what she was doing.

'The police have just told us they think the body is that of a woman called Jane Poundsmith who they seem to think is a familiar name to everyone, so I was looking her up.'

A couple were interested in some items in one of the locked cabinets, so Rob busied himself with unlocking the doors and discussing the items inside.

Out of interest Yvonne googled herself, and was horrified to find that photographs of her thirty-something face were all over the results page. Hurriedly she shut down the site and placed her phone under the counter as though that would make it all go away.

A couple of regular customers came in, and then a family with young children. A dealer asked Yvonne to help him move a table, another dealer asked her opinion on some silver she had bought, and the telephone rang three times, all with queries about the antique shop's opening hours. The dealers began a discussion about a recent auction, and which items they were surprised at the high prices they fetched, and which sold for so little it spelled doom for the antiques market in general, and then continued to predict a miserable future for their businesses.

'At least the subject of the murdered woman seems to have been forgotten,' Rob whispered, as he finished wrapping up the couple's purchases.

Yvonne pulled a face and said in a low voice. 'That's a bit sad though, don't you think? I don't even know who Jane Poundsmith was?'

'I am sure I have heard of her,' said Rob, 'but I can't think where.'

On cue, the door opened, and Tom and Tim walked in, causing the two dealers to decide they needed to get back to work and stop dwelling on a miserable fate which had yet to befall them.

'Twice in one day! I am glad you two have come in because I do have a question for you. Can you tell us who Jane Poundsmith was?' asked Yvonne. 'Neither of us have heard of her, and I can't find anything about her online.'

'We can have a go,' said Tim Smith, looking hopefully towards the back of the shop, in the direction of the kitchenette.

'Did you hear the kettle boil?' asked Rob, picking up the unsubtle hint. 'You're in luck; I have brought some raspberry and white chocolate muffins in with me today.'

'Perhaps you could do the catering?' suggested Yvonne, only half-joking. 'Can you do wedding cakes?'

'Never tried,' called Rob over his shoulder, as he disappeared into the kitchen.

'Of course, you need to find someone else to make Tabitha and Alison's wedding cake. That's just fruitcake covered in icing isn't it?' said Tom.

'We had one fruitcake, which was the top tier, one chocolate cake, for the bottom tier, and a gluten-free lemon drizzle for the middle tier' said Tim, with a smile on his face as he remembered the taste of all three. 'You're meant to keep the top tier as a Christening cake, but as we're never going to have our kids Christened, we ate most of it on the night.'

'Who made it?' asked Yvonne, hopefully.

'My mum,' he replied. 'She used to make all our birthday cakes, and Christmas cakes. Her Easter cakes were the best.'

'Used to?' Yvonne's heart had sunk at those words.

'My parents moved back to Yorkshire ten years ago, so we don't see much of them anymore. She always bakes when we see her, and she is the best I know.'

'I don't suppose she's coming down here in the next two weeks, is she?'

'No, sorry.'

All thoughts of Jane Poundsmith, Kenyon Hall, and other people's cakes disappeared as Rob walked in carrying the tray of teas, coffees, and the all-important cake tin, accompanied by Zebedee.

'I know we have only just asked you this, but have you had any more thoughts about the jewellery you found?' Tim asked Yvonne.

'I'm sorry Tim, I haven't had any time. As I said we are all too busy trying to sort out the wedding venue and everything else, but I will do some research. Have you heard any more?'

'Nothing,' said Tim, in a way that told Yvonne he had. She understood he couldn't tell her everything that happened in the investigation, but there was something about the jewellery that was stuck in some inaccessible part of her brain, and if only he could reveal something it might unstick itself.

'How about Jane Poundsmith? What can you tell us about her. Assuming the body will be identified?' asked Yvonne.

Tom thanked Rob as he picked up a mug and a muffin from the tray. 'These look delicious, thank you. Jane Poundsmith has been a Person of Interest for many years, but we have never been able to find enough strong evidence to charge her with anything. All we have is rumours, so we can't talk about those, I am sorry.'

'Can you at least tell us the area of crime she has been of interest in?'

Tim answered 'The range is so wide that basically you name it, her name has been linked to it.'

'Although not in this area,' commented Tom. 'She is known to our colleagues in Kent, London, and Liverpool, but she hasn't been connected to anything here in the Southwest. In answer to your other question, then no the body has not been identified yet, but we're not looking at anyone else. Tabitha should be able to have her field back on Monday.'

'So soon? She will be pleased!' said Yvonne.

'There wasn't much evidence, other than the body and the jewellery you found. Of course there is no CCTV or other security cameras in the area, and no reports of mystery vehicles, screams, or blood-covered people. The field and lanes leading to it are too rural for any hope of eyewitnesses. The investigation team is struggling, so anything you can tell us about the jewellery could be vitally important,' said Tim, looking at Yvonne.

They were interrupted by the door opening, and a young couple who Rob recognised walked in. As he struck up a

96

conversation with them, and the three moved towards his room at the back of the shop, Yvonne tidied up the tray in preparation of carrying it out to the kitchenette. Before she could pick it up, Tom laid a hand on her arm.

'Please Yvonne, let either of us know anything you can think of about that jewellery. Anything at all. You have my number?'

Yvonne nodded 'Yes I do, and of course I will. But I also wanted to ask you about George Gumbleton. I met him for the first time on Thursday, and I was wondering if there is anything I should be aware of?'

Tim winked 'Is this romance I can sense in the air?'

'Don't be silly,' Yvonne could feel herself blushing, and the sensation of George's lips on her cheek came flooding back. 'It is far too soon to be talking in those terms. But I would like to know sooner rather than later if there is anything dodgy about him.'

The policemen looked at each other and shook their heads. 'If there is then I haven't heard anything, but you know him better than I do,' said Tom to his partner.

'I certainly haven't heard of anything,' agreed Tim. 'He has an ex-wife and grown-up children, and I haven't heard of any girlfriends, gambling debts or parking fines. When he is in town we often team up for the pub quiz at The Mitre with a couple of his staff, and they seem to get on well with him.'

'He does a lot for charity' said Tom, in his best Smashie and Nicey impression.

'Thanks a lot you two,' laughed Yvonne. 'I think you have been a great help.'

'Any time you want someone to vet potential boyfriends, then just ask us,' teased Tom.

Yvonne felt she couldn't mention the man who appeared to be stalking George, or was he stalking her? It all seemed so tenuous, and paranoid.

With the tea party over, and the clearing up completed, Yvonne went into her office to focus on the photographs she had taken of the jewellery, and do some research on the internet, while Zebedee lay at her feet under the desk. The family crest on many of the pieces was of the Speake family, who had been major landowners in Lancashire for centuries, and their hereditary titles were passed down to the present day. They owned several estates around England, and their family home in Dorset was Kenyon Hall, built by the family in the fifteenth century. It had remained in the family since then, was never sold, and members of the family still lived there. In the first and the second world wars it was used by the military, and returned to the family afterwards, although from what Yvonne could understand the family had always remained in residence. In the nineteen seventies two of the brothers turned it into the leisure facility it was today, and were still involved in the running of it in their eighties. It was difficult to work out who was in charge, but from what Yvonne could deduce, it seemed that one of the brothers had two sons and a daughter, and the other brother had one daughter, and all four were managing the estate. Other members of the family lived on a smaller estate in neighbouring Somerset named Kenyon House, and the Speake name was common in the area. As with all landowners from centuries gone by, the Speake family had connections with the slave trade and corrupt politicians, but Yvonne knew the present-day Speakes as good employers, fair traders with their farming and equestrian businesses. Feeling that she had exhausted the internet for the time-being, Yvonne picked up her mobile, and rang a couple of contacts in the antiques world to see if they had heard anything about stolen jewellery.

It was twelve years since she last spoke to the first person, and he was pleased to hear from Yvonne. They spent a good thirty minutes chatting about old acquaintances and past times in the antiques trade, but he had nothing to share about either Jane Poundsmith or the Speake family, or about any stolen jewellery. They ended the call promising to meet up, and Yvonne hoped they would. Many years ago she had chosen to remove herself from her old life in the antiques business. With some people it had been a sharp cut, and with others, like the man she had been speaking to, it was a gradual moving apart with no effort on her part or his to maintain the contact because they no longer moved in the same circles. She had enjoyed their chat and realised how small her world had become since moving to Shaftesbury. It was a healing place for her, and the main part of her decision to move had been precisely because it was a town which provided everything she needed, from social groups to decent eateries, arts and entertainment, excellent hairdressers, and beauticians. Her antiques shop was one of many within a ten-mile radius, and if she wanted to drive for an hour in any direction she could reach many more antiques auctions and shops. She enjoyed the relative anonymity of Dorset, Wiltshire and Somerset, because her family's business had been centred around London, Sussex, the Cotswolds and the Midlands, but talking with a former colleague brought up some of the old adrenaline she used to thrive on.

The second person was less enthusiastic to receive a phone call from Yvonne Parker, and Yvonne couldn't blame him. It was thanks to Yvonne's evidence in court

99

that his father had gone to prison for ten years. Although his father had been released many years earlier, and as far as Yvonne could make out was as rich as before, if not more so, the son was not going to forgive Yvonne for her actions in committing him to a prison sentence. Grateful that he didn't hang up when he heard her name, nevertheless it took Yvonne a few minutes of gentle persuasion before she heard the thaw flow down the phone line, and the man began to share his knowledge about the Speake jewellery. Once upon a time they had worked closely together, and the familiar rapport was still there, if a bit rusty. He told Yvonne that the Speake family jewellery was renowned in the specialist jewellery trade because it rarely came on the market. There were a small number of family members who kept it securely passed down from one generation to another, and when the occasional piece did surface it made a big stir in the antiques world, but it was often a member of the family who would purchase it back. This contact of Yvonne's turned out to be someone the family would use to buy their heirlooms, because otherwise the price would rocket if it became known the family wanted it. Yvonne thanked her lucky stars that gut instinct had prompted her to phone him, and that he had been forthcoming about his association with the family. She took this as a sign he at least understood her motives for acting in the way that she did in the courtroom. As their conversation developed he was keen to learn which items she had found, and she listed most of them for him. That same gut instinct told her to hold some details back, although why she did not know. Like Yvonne, he had not heard of any items being stolen, or if he had he wasn't telling her. Yvonne believed him. It was difficult to keep something like that quiet in the trade, and he didn't have anything to gain from keeping it from her. However, when she brought up the name of Jane Poundsmith he abruptly, but politely, ended the call by saying he had a meeting with someone who had just arrived at his door. Yvonne sat at her desk for a long time afterwards looking at the notes she had made during the conversation. It felt good to have finally had a constructive conversation with him, the first since his father was convicted, and she appreciated the time he had given to share his knowledge. It was interesting that he wasn't prepared to extend that generosity to the subject of Jane Poundsmith, and Yvonne wondered why.

She checked her watch and saw that it was almost six o'clock in the evening. The time had flown by. She popped through to the shop and had a brief chat with the dealers who were closing up. Everyone had had a good day, and the takings were healthy, and so they were heading into town for a quick drink. Yvonne declined their invitation and rushed upstairs to change into her riding clothes. Within an hour she and Toby were strolling along the country lanes with a couple of fellow livery owners, Sally and Charlotte, enjoying a beautiful summer evening. The sun was still relatively high in the sky, even at that time, and the three women took advantage by heading over the busy main road to Ashmore Forest, where they had a couple of canters, before heading back home at quite a fast pace so they didn't get caught out by the setting sun.

'We should do a night ride,' suggested Sally.

'A what?' asked Yvonne.

'A ride in the dark,' explained Charlotte. 'Everyone wears a head torch on their helmets, and there are various places we can attach lights to ourselves and our horses. We could plan a route so we are off-road as much as possible, although with enough of us riding together we'd be more visible than some of the vehicles that drive around here.'

'That sounds amazing! Count me and Toby in.'

'OK, let's have a look at the calendar and see when the moon will be bright,' said Sally.

'We'll need to ask our friendly landowners for permission to cross their land,' warned Charlotte, 'and weather-permitting we'll go for it.'

The three continued chatting as they rode into the yard, and by the time Yvonne left they had recruited another horse owner to join in.

Not for the first time, Yvonne thanked whatever god was out there that she had her interest in horses to take her mind off the horrors of life. She drove home with a smile on her face, which was wiped off when she spotted that same man lurking by the library as she turned into her carpark.

'Yvonne! I'm glad I caught you.' George jogged across from the direction of the Italian restaurant, having changed out of the clothes he was wearing at lunchtime, and still looking good in stone-coloured shorts and a black polo shirt. 'Have you got time for a chat now?'

Yvonne glanced down at herself. She was relatively clean after her adventures on horseback, and she wouldn't have thought twice about popping to the pub with Tabitha without changing first, but she wasn't sure that passed for polite company. 'Can it wait until tomorrow? We're still meeting for lunch aren't we?'

'Yes, yes of course, but I've been thinking about the problems Tabitha is having with her wedding venue, and I have an idea.'

Yvonne checked her watch. All she really wanted to do was have a quick shower and cook up some pasta, washed down with a glass of wine. As if reading her thoughts, George said 'Have you eaten yet?'

She shook her head. 'No.'

'Neither have I. How about I pick up something for both of us and come back in roughly half an hour? Say no if you'd rather wait until tomorrow, but it's no trouble for me if it's alright with you.'

Yvonne smiled gratefully at the thought of someone producing food for her; she was hungry now she thought about it. 'That would be really kind, thank you.'

'What do you like: Chinese, Indian, Italian, chips?'

She nodded towards the Italian 'I love any of those, but their pizzas are delicious. Anything from their menu would be lovely, thank you.'

'Great, I'll go and get that sorted,' he looked happy that she had agreed to eat with him. Yvonne thought she could get used to this.

'I'll open a bottle of wine,' she said as she climbed out of her car and opened Zebedee's dog cage in the boot to let her out too. 'What colour?'

'Whatever you're drinking,' he said, and walked back across the public carpark towards the Italian.

Yvonne checked the path up towards the library but could not see the spy. She and Zebedee ran up the external staircase to her flat, where she turned at the top and looked back towards the library. Sure enough, the spy, or someone, hurriedly pulled back around the corner out of sight.

Usually if a friend was coming to see her, Yvonne would leave the back door to the shop unlocked so they could let themselves in, but this evening she left it and the electric gates shut. She wasn't sure if George was at the level of friendship where he could let himself into her home, but regardless she didn't feel safe leaving any door unlocked while that man was lurking.

103

Chapter 10

Fresh from the shower, Yvonne walked down the spiral staircase to the living room, popped a couple of plates into the oven to warm up, and studied her well-stocked wine rack. The days of drinking Bacardi and coke or Southern Comfort and lemonade were long gone, and she had never really had a taste for vodka or gin, although Pimms was always welcome. She almost selected a bottle of French red wine to go with the pizza, but decided she preferred chilled rosé instead and pulled a bottle from the fridge. Zebedee was sitting by the dog food cupboard, her eyes never leaving Yvonne until Yvonne glanced at her, and Zebedee eloquently gave a sideways glance at the cupboard before fixing her eyes on Yvonne again.

Laughing, Yvonne picked up Zebedee's food bowl from the draining board and pulled out a tray of food from Zebedee's cupboard. 'Here you are,' she said as she put it on the small mat, holding one hand out with its palm facing the dog so that she would stay sitting until released. After a few seconds Yvonne said 'Eat up!' and Zebedee wolfed down the food before Yvonne could finish laying the table.

The sound of the buzzer on the electric gates sent Yvonne to check the small monitor at the back of the kitchen, where she could see George holding a couple of pizza boxes and a brown bag. Wondering what else he had bought, she pressed the button to unlock the gates, and walked through to let him into the building.

'Come in!' she said, and on seeing the size of the bag he was carrying 'how much food have you brought for us?'

He grinned. 'I hope you're hungry. It all smelled so good in there, I bought pizzas which we can pop in the oven to keep warm, and some starter things too.'

Together they unpacked the food onto the table, Yvonne swapped the warmed plates in the oven for the pizzas, and they spent the next few minutes helping themselves to the mix of small dishes George had selected, including garlic mushrooms, calamari, olives and cold meats.

'I don't think I have room for a whole pizza now,' complained Yvonne.

'Nor me,' said George, sadly. 'Sorry, my eyes were bigger than my belly. Shall we just have one between us, and leave the other for tomorrow?'

He took one pizza out of the oven and together they tucked in to their second course. Yvonne noticed the comment about saving one for tomorrow, and the assumption they would be eating together in the evening after their Sunday lunch but chose not to respond. It was a long time since she had made day-to-day plans with someone else, and she wasn't sure how she felt about it. For the time being it seemed right.

'So, what's this idea you have for Tabitha and Alison's wedding?' asked Yvonne, as she refilled their empty wine glasses.

'I can't offer the use of our restaurant because it is almost fully booked, but we do have an outside catering company we are just starting up, and although their wedding is about two months earlier than we would like, I have had a chat with the team and they would love to use Tabitha and Alison's wedding as an opportunity to try out their plans.'

'Use them as guinea pigs, you mean?'

'I suppose so, yes, although less than two weeks' notice will not be their usual way of working.'

'Of course not, sorry.' Yvonne realised she had sounded a bit critical. 'What did you have in mind for the menu, and don't forget we still haven't sorted out a venue.'

'Ah, well I might be able to help with that too. The back of the restaurant faces the old coaching stables from the days when everything was delivered by horse-drawn wagons, and between them is a large courtyard. We have planning permission to make that whole area part of the restaurant, and building work has already been done to renovate the walls and roof of the former stables. The roof is now weatherproof, and the walls won't fall in on us, but the floor is uneven, and as you would expect is made from cobbles rather than smooth concrete. There is electricity and water, but no appliances or furniture.'

'Tabitha was thinking about using one of her farm buildings, so your courtyard and derelict coaching stables already sounds better than that. What about carparking?'

'Ah, now that I cannot help with, I'm sorry,' said George. 'There isn't room for more than ten vehicles out the back there.'

Yvonne was surprised. 'As much as ten? Where on earth do they come into the space?' she was trying to picture access from the High Street and could not think of anywhere.

'There is access from Bell Street, next to the café, and that is where our deliveries come for the restaurant,' explained George.

'I have never even thought about your deliveries, although now I am I cannot remember ever seeing anything delivered to the front of the restaurant.'

'No, all deliveries come through the large wooden gates off Bell Street, so we don't cause any congestion on the High Street. Would you like to have a look?'

'Now? Yes please!' Yvonne jumped up and began to tidy away the empty food containers and plates. 'I can't believe how much we have eaten.'

'Nor me. You were right though; the Italian was a good choice. I'll wash up.'

Yvonne looked at Zebedee, who was waiting expectantly for any leftover food. 'Sorry Zeb, there's nothing for you sweetheart.' What she wanted to say out loud was 'Blimey, he's chosen and bought delicious food, and is washing up! Let's keep him!'

They had only used a couple of glasses, some cutlery and a couple of plates, so by the time Yvonne had slipped her bare feet into a pair of comfortable loafers, checked her pockets for dog poo bags and treats, and clipped Zebedee's lead to her collar, the washing up was drying on the draining board. The three of them left through the back door together as if they did it all the time. Yvonne set the alarm and locked the door, and then let them out through the electronic gates, glancing across the carpark as she did. No sign of any movement.

'Let's go in through the Bell Street entrance, rather than through the restaurant,' said George. 'I'd like to share my vision of how the happy couple could see their wedding reception venue after their marriage ceremony.'

'I'd like to see that too. I am also curious to know where this entrance is. I must have walked along that road thousands of times, and can't picture anywhere a delivery lorry, let alone a large van, could drive in.'

The sun was going down, and the light was failing, but Yvonne never worried about being on her own in Shaftesbury, and as usual there were a few people walking to their cars in the well-lit carpark. The narrow path leading out towards the road was a bit spooky with high hedges and nooks and crannies around the library building where a potential attacker could hide, but Yvonne had always reasoned someone would have to wait a long time for a lone person to walk through without any other random strangers in the vicinity in the next few minutes. Also, she trusted that Zebedee would alert her to anyone lurking nearby, and sure enough as they walked towards Bell Street Zebedee turned her head and stopped to look at a couple walking up behind them.

'Hi Yvonne,' said Tim Smith. 'Hello George.'

There was no mistaking the inuendo in Tim's greeting, and Yvonne was glad of the dusk as she felt her cheeks burn.

'We've enjoyed a lovely meal at your restaurant,' Tim's wife said to George.

'That's good to hear,' smiled George. 'Were you celebrating anything?'

'Yes, our twelfth wedding anniversary. My mum has the kids for the night, so we're making the most of it,' grinned Tim. 'We're heading home for a full night's sleep without any interruptions.'

'That's right,' laughed his wife. 'A child-free night should mean nooky, but we're seizing the opportunity for a night without having to get up for glasses of water, toilet trips, or arguments about who has which toy when no one should be playing with any toys because they should all be asleep.'

Together they turned right up Victoria Street to their home, while Yvonne and George continued along the road until George said 'Here we are.'

Yvonne looked up at the huge black gates between two shops, and said 'I swear these were not here last time I walked past!'

George laughed and pressed the key code to unlock the gates. As they opened Yvonne gasped at the sight of the tall greenstone walls on either side, lit with electric flame-effect torches and leading into a courtyard with the black framed floor-to-ceiling windows of the back of the restaurant in front of them through which they could see groups of people eating, drinking and laughing. There was a fountain against the wall to their right, and as they walked into the courtyard and the gates closed behind them, the noises of the street outside were silenced and replaced by the gentle sound of the water flowing from the fountain.

'This is huge!' exclaimed Yvonne. 'I had no idea this space existed right in the middle of Shaftesbury.'

George shrugged. 'No reason why you should. It is fully enclosed if you want to let Zebedee off the lead.'

'But I've eaten in there lots of times, so how come I haven't seen this?' Yvonne unclipped her dog, and looked at the diners seated on chairs she had sat on several times since the restaurant opened.

George smiled 'Can you remember what you could see while you were sitting in there?'

'Of course I can. It's that stunning mural of Shaftesbury in years gone by. Horses, carriages, cars, buses, nuns, families, people in rags and people in rich clothing, dogs, cattle, geese.' She peered at the windows, trying to see the pictures in her mind transposed onto the glass. Suddenly aware she was rudely staring at a couple eating their meal she drew back.

George laughed 'Don't worry; they can't see you. You are right, from the other side of the window you can see everything you described. These windows are switchable two-way glass, so we can make this courtyard private for events, without making the restaurant dark. We can make this side frosted so that people attending an event in here can't see the people eating in there, and the other side is permanently decorated with the scene of Shaftesbury through the ages. If we wish to use the restaurant and the courtyard together then these windows fold back. Unfortunately we wouldn't be able to do that for Tabitha's wedding, as we already have several bookings in the restaurant, but if you turn around and look at the former stables opposite you can see that there is plenty of inside room we could use.'

Together they crossed the courtyard, as Zebedee checked and sniffed her way along the walls surrounding them. George opened one of the doors which fronted the building, and Yvonne peered inside before withdrawing.

'I can't see a thing, sorry.'

'Here,' George switched on the torch on his phone, and together they went inside. He slowly illuminated the interior from left to right, and waited for Yvonne to comment.

'Mmmh, it doesn't compare to the Orangery at Kenyon Hall.'

George kept quiet, seeing that Yvonne was still processing what she was seeing. By now she had taken out her own phone and switched on the torch light, and she began to pace around the interior.

'There aren't any toilets?' she queried.

'None that are plumbed in yet, but the restaurant's toilets are just inside that door,' he pointed to the far right corner of the courtyard behind them, 'and we have a connecting door beyond this door,' he pointed, 'to the café on Bell Street. They close at three o'clock on a Saturday afternoon, meaning we can use those toilets in there. The toilets for this building are also through this door, and it may be possible to persuade the workmen to plumb them in time for the wedding, but I wouldn't like to make that promise at this stage.'

George opened the door, and by the light of their phone torches, and closely followed by Zebedee who had now completed her inspection of the courtyard, they walked into an area which was as big again as the space they had just viewed.

'Wow. What is this for?'

George began to pace and point 'Here is where the toilets will be, with a large hallway between them and this area here which will be the kitchen. The fridges will go here, freezers over there, the ovens here, and the sinks and dishwashers here. This section of the wall has a serving hatch, so we can have pizza evenings and Italian nights where the guests can see the kitchen working, or for an event like a wedding it will be closed so that everything appears to be magicked out of nowhere.'

Yvonne could see his vision, and his passion for the project, but she had a concern. 'That is all very exciting, but it will take a while to install and set-up won't it? How could we cater for Alison and Tabitha's wedding in a fortnight's time?'

'Aha!' said George with a triumphant smile on his face. 'That's where our outside catering company comes in. Our plan is to have a business where all of the food is planned for the facilities available, and prepared off-site away from the event, using the restaurant's and the café's kitchens when they are not in use. For example, if someone wanted a birthday party in a field, the food and drink would need to be suitable for transporting straight to the tables, with minimal cooking or chilling. We have a former horse lorry which has been equipped with freezers, cookers, fridges, and water, enabling us to at least do something if there is no access to running water or electricity.'

'Do you own the café too?'

'Yes, we do. We bought it at the same time we bought the building where the restaurant is now.'

'I had no idea it had changed hands!'

'The original owners still run it, but they were struggling with making it pay for itself, and so when we offered to buy the building and the business, which was making a loss, and pay them a regular wage to keep managing it, I am pleased to say they were keen to shake our hands.'

'But if they were making a loss, why would you want to keep them on?' asked Yvonne.

'Because it wasn't anything they were doing wrong,' explained George. 'You must have been in there for breakfast or afternoon tea? Their service and food are excellent. The problem was their margins were too small to pay for the costs of the building, and staff too. Now we combine the food and drink orders for the café and the restaurant, there is no waste because both can use each other's stock, and because we are buying large amounts the costs are affordable for both businesses.'

'I had no idea about any of this, and I live and work in this town. I feel as though I have been walking around with my eyes closed,' laughed Yvonne.

The three of them walked back out into the courtyard and stood quietly for a few moments.

Eventually Yvonne broke the silence 'What would it cost for Alison and Tabitha to hire this space for their wedding?'

'The cost of the food and drink' replied George. 'None of the facilities are finished, so we would not charge rental; the team have not catered an event yet, so we would not charge for them or the expenses involved in the preparation of food and drink, nor utensils, plates, glasses, washing-up, nothing. Only the cost of the food and drink.'

Yvonne shook her head. 'This is amazingly generous of you. Are you sure?'

'Of course. As I said, this is our outside catering team's opportunity to put their theory into practice, and although I am confident they will provide a first-class service, there will be teething problems, and so long as Alison and Tabitha can cope with that, and it won't ruin their special day, then they would be doing us a favour by allowing us to use their wedding as a first try-out. What do you think? Will they go for it?'

'They would be mad not to.'

Chapter 11

Yvonne woke up to a beautiful sunny morning, and stretched luxuriously in her bed, her foot meeting Zebedee's solid body. Checking her phone she saw it was just before six o'clock in the morning, and with a yawn she rolled onto her side and sat up with her feet on the soft cream-coloured woollen rug next to the bed. She knew Tabitha would already be out in the fields checking the sheep, and she texted 'Ring me when you have five minutes.'

Immediately the phone rang, with Tabitha's name lighting up the screen. 'Morning! What's up?' Tabitha asked.

'I think that George may have found a solution to your venue and catering problem,' said Yvonne, as she stroked Zebedee's head. 'I won't be back in Shaftesbury until later this afternoon, but could you and Alison meet us here at about four o'clock?'

'Yes, we can do that. Where is the venue?' asked Tabitha.

George and Yvonne had talked about their plans as he walked her back to her flat, and they decided the best approach was to surprise the two brides-to-be. 'Can you see if Maisie is free too?' asked Yvonne, ignoring Tabitha's question.

'I know she is because she and Alison are going to be playing hairdressers with each other's wedding hairdos. When are they starting on yours?'

114

'On Wednesday. I doubt they will make it look anywhere as good as yours does; your hair looks gorgeous. I am enjoying all this beauty pampering!'

'Me too, although I am surprised how much I am enjoying it,' said Tabitha. 'Don't be mistaken; I could not look and stay like that every day, but it is good to know I can look a little bit glamorous!'

'Ha, you looked very glamorous on Friday night! No need to dress up for this afternoon, unless you want to, and I'll see the three of you here at the shop by four o'clock,' said Yvonne.

After the call had ended, Yvonne checked the time. She and her fellow livery owners were not due to leave for their ride until eight o'clock, giving Yvonne plenty of time to enjoy a cup of coffee and slice of toast, staying in her pyjamas, and doing some research on the jewellery for another couple of hours.

She was finding the research frustrating. Normally this was the part of her antiques business she loved. There was little information about the family in the numerous books on her bookshelf, and the internet kept throwing up a limited version of their history too. The information gleaned from her second phone call the day before helped a little, but the internet was behaving like a closed book and yielding nothing new. After another fruitless hour she abandoned the research, showered and dressed, and together with Zebedee drove to the yard. A few of the other livery owners were already there, and Zebedee leapt out of the car, eager to join a couple of Jack Russells and a collie whom she had been playing with the evening before while Yvonne and Toby were out on their ride.

The horses lived out in herds of between two and eight, depending on their needs and personalities, and all were barefoot. Toby was in the largest herd of eight, in a six-

115

acre grass field during the summer, with two large shelters facing each other, and one at the end with only three walls and a hexagonal shaped roof. During the day the horses were confined to a one-acre paddock, with access to hay supplied in three round cattle feeders which had been adapted so that no horse could get their leg or head stuck between the bars however hard they tried. At night the gate was opened, and they were released onto the remaining five acres, until whoever arrived first in the morning gave them breakfast in their day paddock. The three shelters were positioned in a horseshoe shape facing north-east, so that all eight horses could be sheltered from the sun or the driving rain if they chose to be, and at this time of year the horses would gather in the shade to swish the flies away from each other with their tails. Yvonne and her fellow livery owners had a rota for morning and evening yard duties, and she could see the herd had already been fed their breakfasts. When he saw her, Toby left his field mates to saunter over to the gate.

'Good morning!' she called, and she and Zebedee walked through the gate to greet him. Formalities over, which included a little cuddle and a horse treat from her pocket, Yvonne smoothly put the bright orange rope halter over his head, and with the matching twelve-foot lead rope over her arm she walked up the track to the yard with her horse and her dog.

By eight o'clock the dogs were all together in the kitchen of the farmhouse, watching the family as they ate their breakfast. It was too hot to leave them in their cars, and the farm owners were always happy to dog-sit, so Yvonne left Zebedee with her doggy friends, while Yvonne and Toby rode out of the yard with their horse and rider friends. Twelve of the twenty-two livery owners were riding together to the small café at the local airfield, across the tracks and fields, and the noise of the bare hooves on the roads brought a smile to Yvonne's face. Some of the horses and riders were a little nervous of riding in such a large group, and so when the opportunities arose on the quiet lanes or through one particular field, the riders played leapfrog to settle the nerves and excitement. While everyone else stayed in walk, the horse and rider at the back would trot slowly past the line to the front and take up the lead. This was a great exercise for horses who didn't like to be passed by other horses, horses who didn't like to be in front, and horses who didn't want to be left behind.

The final track through the woods was a long climb up to the airfield, and usually when Yvonne rode this route she and Toby would canter up it, but because of the heat of the day and the number of riders, everyone agreed they would stay in walk. She and Lindy, on a beautiful palomino, rode side-by-side chatting about their horses and the weather, and what they were planning to eat at the café.

'I am looking forward to having a bacon and egg bap, with a mug of tea' said Lindy. 'I haven't eaten anything yet, and I'm starving.'

Mindful she had eaten a small breakfast and was going to be eating a huge Sunday lunch, Yvonne said 'I think I'll just have a toasted teacake.'

'My grandmother used to love toasted teacakes!' said Lindy. 'They always remind me of her when I see them. She lived in a small cottage with a large garden, and she and Grandad were pretty much self-sufficient with their fruit and vegetables, a couple of dairy cows, chickens and a couple of pigs. She was always cooking and baking, and we used to love staying with them as children.'

'Where did she live?' asked Yvonne.

'They lived on the family estate in Somerset.'

117

Yvonne's ears pricked up. 'Which one?' she tried to sound casually interested, but her heart was racing.

'It's called Kenyon House. That's my dad's family. My dad still lives there, and my mum. They used to live in one of the estate cottages, and that was where I grew up, but now he's inherited the estate from his uncle, he and mum have moved into the house itself. Well, they have moved into one wing of it. It is huge, and they are both in their seventies now.'

Yvonne's mouth had gone dry, and because she wasn't paying attention she narrowly missed getting poked in the eye by an overhanging branch. This caused great hilarity for the riders behind her, and the opportunity to ask Lindy any questions was further lost by their arrival at the road leading to the airfield. The group walked along a short stretch of the road, and turned into the carpark. They were met by another four livery owners who had walked on foot with their horses and ponies for a couple of miles along the lanes of Hannam to the airfield. The owners of the airfield had constructed a solid post and rail fence around a paddock area, with tie-up rings for the horses and hay nets. Nobody wanted loose horses on the grass runway. Numerous partners of riders, together with a couple of other livery owners without their horses, had driven up with hay nets and the paddock was ready for the sixteen horses and ponies. Everyone had ridden with halters and lead ropes under their bridles, and most people took off the bridles but left the saddles on their horses' backs.

Once the horses were happily munching, the riders could buy their drinks from the wooden coffee shack on the edge of the carpark, order their breakfasts from the waiting staff who were hovering with pens and notepads, sit down on the picnic benches arranged between the horse paddock and the grassy airstrip, and watch the small airplanes land

and take off. The horses were used to the environment, and on the occasion a new horse came to the yard this was one of the first things they did together, so that the new horse and rider could be with others who were confident with all the noise and activity. Everyone there were veteran airfield breakfasters, and there was no drama for either horses or riders as one after another a series of small planes took off and flew into the sunny blue distance.

In less than an hour all breakfasts had been consumed, toilet visits completed, and bridles put back on horses' heads. The paddock was poo-picked using a couple of handy manure scoops and scrapes which permanently lived in the paddock, and the manure was thrown into the hedge which separated the carpark from the road. There was a water trough outside the paddock, conveniently situated along one wall of the coffee shack with the guttering and drainpipe leading into it to catch the frequent rainfall. Sometimes it needed topping up with buckets filled from an outside tap on the other side of the airfield's office building, but fortunately today it was more than three-quarters full, and any horses who needed a drink could help themselves on their way to the mounting block. The old stone mounting block was all that remained of the original Georgian building on the site until the nineteen forties, when the land was commandeered during World War Two as a military airfield and the building was destroyed by an unfortunate and fatal landing.

Once all the riders were mounted, the whole group posed for a photo taken by the man who was working in the coffee shack, with the hilltop town of Shaftesbury in the background. Then the riding group waved off the walkers and ponies who were going to make their way back along footpaths across fields where there were no stiles, and those who had driven to the airfield waved off the riders as

119

they turned right onto the road, crossed the busy C road at the end, and onto the permissive bridleways crossing private and National Trust land. The views were spectacular on such a clear day, and lots of photos and selfies were taken as the horses and riders walked along in groups of three or four.

Yvonne managed to ride up next to Lindy and her palomino horse, and tried to resume their conversation, but Lindy's phone rang, and with a silent apology she answered it. Not wanting to listen in to her private conversation, Yvonne joined Sally and Charlotte on their matching chestnut mares, who were deep in conversation about the recent murder.

'It has made me nervous about riding out on my own,' confessed Sally. 'I never used to even think about it before, so long as I had my mobile phone on me, and hi-vis reflective clothing, as far as I was concerned that was all I needed.'

'You do write up on the board in the tack room where you're going and the times you left and are expecting to get back though, don't you?' said Charlotte. 'I know you do because I see it.'

'Oh yes, but that's more as a precaution in case I fall off!' laughed Sally. 'It isn't going to stop anyone from attacking me, is it. It just means my body might be found earlier rather than later.'

'Yes, that is a horrible thought isn't it. That poor woman's body was lying there for days before you found her, Yvonne' said Charlotte, before seeing the look on Yvonne's face. 'Sorry, I don't want to bring up any ghastly memories.'

'Don't worry about it,' said Yvonne. 'I don't think that image is ever going to leave me. I would like to know who she was, and how she ended up in such tragic circumstances. It would be reassuring to know if she was mixed up in some kind of crime, and this wasn't just a random killing which could have happened to anyone.'

'Yes, I know what you mean,' said Sally. 'I think that's why I have stopped riding out on my own. The thought that there could be some mad man lurking around our countryside, just waiting to jump out and attack, is really upsetting me.'

Charlotte shook her head. 'I do understand, Sally, but it is very unlikely to be the case. There is going to be a sinister reason behind her killing, and a lone madman is not going to be the reason. We all ride with cameras on our hats, we are all on horseback, and none of us regularly ride the same route at the same time or day, and so the chances of someone lying in wait with murder in their heart is so minimal as to be inconsequential.'

'Logically, I know you are right' Sally shrugged. 'My self-defence training is top notch, so I know I could defend myself in an attack, and this one' she gestured to her chestnut-coloured Arab horse 'can outrun any man, but I am still too scared to ride out alone.'

'Don't push it,' advised Charlotte, 'there is no point having sleepless nights and tense rides out with your horse for the time being. Perhaps once we know what has happened we can all return to normal. There is always someone willing to go for a hack, isn't there.'

'Oh yes, that is what is so lovely about our yard; everyone gets out and about whether on foot or in the saddle. I love days like today where almost everyone from the yard joined in. And look at this view!'

The group had come to a halt while a gate was opened. It was half off its hinges, and not possible to open or close from horseback, and so one of the more agile riders, Daniel, had volunteered to jump off his big grey Percheron horse and open the gate for everyone else. One by one they filed through, and waited for him to securely close the gate, before effortlessly mounting from the ground.

'I wish I could do that' the admiration in Yvonne's voice was clear.

'I can on a good day,' confessed Sally.

'Me too,' said Charlotte. 'But it's not good for the horses' backs, that's why I don't do it every day,' she grinned.

'Me too,' agreed Sally, laughing. 'Obviously I would mount from the ground every day if it was actually good for my horse.'

'Of course you would!' laughed Yvonne. 'I must confess I have never managed to get on Toby from the ground. I have to put him in a ditch, or I climb on a gate.'

'I doubt you can get your foot in the stirrup from the ground can you?' observed Sally.

'Not without letting them down to the last hole, and then the leathers are too long for me to get my other leg over the saddle!' said Yvonne.

'What's all the laughing about?' asked Lindy as she joined them.

'We were talking about mounting from the ground, and how obviously we can do it as easily as Daniel does but only choose not to because of our horses' backs,' explained Sally.

'Yeah right' said Lindy. 'Although I can get up from the ground, but it is a struggle, and not pretty,'

'Same here!' said Charlotte. 'How are the party preparations going?'

'Very well thank you. I hope you will all be able to come?'

'What's this?' asked Yvonne.

'I'm having a fiftieth birthday celebration next month, but typical me I have left it all until the last minute. I must post an invitation to everyone on the board in the tack-room when we get back. It's nothing formal; just jeans and t-shirts or whatever you'd like to wear for a party, and a few drinks and nibbles, but it would be nice to see everyone for a relaxed evening without our horses, as much as we love them.'

'Where will it be?' asked Yvonne.

'At my parents' home, at Kenyon House so there will be plenty of room for parking,' grinned Lindy. 'I think there are going to be around three hundred people there.'

Chapter 12

The welcoming committee were waiting at the yard when the group rode back up the long beech-lined drive, and it wasn't long before Yvonne had untacked Toby. After she gave him a quick shower under the hose, managing to get a fair amount of water over herself too, together with Zebedee they walked back down the hardcore track to the paddock. Toby had a thorough roll in the bare earth inside the gateway, ensuring he rubbed his wet head and ears into the ground so that when he stood up and shook there were lumps of mud hanging on to his body. He looked nothing like the smartly turned-out horse in all the photographs taken of them during the ride, and he happily took himself off to join the rest of his herd.

Yvonne gave his tack a wipe over to remove the worst of the sweat, and left the saddle, bridle and girth in the tack room to give it a thorough clean when she came back the next day. She and Zebedee drove home, and Yvonne only had time for a fifteen-minute turnaround from Happy Hacker to Sunday Luncher. A quick shower and hair wash, towel-dry and smother her body in moisturiser, brush on some make-up, pull on underwear and a long turquoise summer dress, feet into flat gold sandals, fingers run through hair, fix earrings to ears, a matching floaty long turquoise scarf around her neck, white shoulder bag, and job done. She gave herself a once-over in the mirror, agreed with Zebedee who was supervising from Yvonne's bed that she looked amazing, and left her flat.

By the time George pulled up in his midnight blue Jaguar XK8 convertible, Yvonne looked as though she had been leaning on the wooden balcony rail at the top of the stairs outside her flat for hours. She waved, and skipped down the stairs, enjoying the feel of the dress as it moved with her body.

As she emerged through the electronic gates, George said 'I'm sorry, have you been waiting long?'

'No, not long!' said Yvonne, deciding not to admit she had only been standing there for about ten seconds before he drove into the carpark.

'Would you like me to put the roof back up?'

'No, this is lovely, thank you. It will dry my hair, and I can always put my scarf over my head if it's getting too blowy.'

The drive to the village of Marnhull was through windy country roads and took less than a quarter of an hour. During that time Yvonne and George chatted non-stop about the scenery, the weather, Yvonne told George about the yard ride up to the airfield, and George told Yvonne about his ten-kilometre run with some of the members from his new running group, the Hindon Runners.

'It was a great run, with a super bunch of people,' he said 'but what I can't understand is how it was nearly all uphill? Surely we must have been running downhill an equal amount as it was a circular route.'

The pub was busy, and they had to wait a short time for their table, but neither minded the delay and chose to sit outside in the sunshine to enjoy a pre-lunch drink.

'I don't usually drink alcohol during the day' explained Yvonne as she ordered blood orange San Pellegrino 'but as you're driving I might have a cheeky glass of wine with my food.'

'I have witnessed too many boozy so-called business lunches to think that lunch-time drinking is a good idea,' said George as he ordered a pint of Coca-Cola. 'If nothing else, it makes me fall asleep. But if you were driving I would probably do the same.'

The waiter took their food order, and as they both claimed to be starving after their individual activities that morning, they ordered bread and olives to keep them going until their Sunday lunch arrived.

'Have you heard anything else about the body we found?' asked George as he pushed the china ramekin containing olive oil and balsamic vinegar towards Yvonne so she could dip her freshly baked bread into it.

Yvonne took her time before answering. She was wondering whether to share the news that she had discovered one of the livery owners was part of the Speake family, and that she had been invited to a party at the estate. Part of her was desperate to talk about it with George, but there was a little something she couldn't define and made her withhold the information.

'Mmmh that's good,' she said, pointing to the dipping sauce. 'No, I haven't heard anything. Have you?'

'I have been trying to find out more about this Jane Poundsmith, and it is possible there is a link to the problems Charles Diamond is having with supplies up at Kenyon Hall.'

'Really? From what Tim was telling us she doesn't sound at all like the kind of person I would have expected someone like Charles to have dealings with.'

'I agree. As I said, I have only heard very good things about Kenyon Hall, and Charles in particular, but that is from guests. We don't share the same suppliers, and so I haven't heard any of the usual gossip you get from delivery drivers and ordering departments, but one of our chefs has recently joined us from another top-notch venue who were having similar supply issues to the ones Charles appears to be having for Tabitha and Alison's wedding.'

'Do tell' said Yvonne, leaning in closer across the table so they could not be overheard.

'According to her, they went from having superb quality produce to having to scrabble around from local supermarkets. One minute they were receiving vanloads of seafood, meat, fruit and vegetables to the kitchen door, and the next she was being sent off to Asda and Morrisons with a shopping list and a handful of notes. Obviously the supermarkets could neither supply the quality or the quantities their kitchen required, and after three days of being unable to produce the menus the clients had ordered and paid for, she quit.'

'But surely if the guests had paid up-front like Tabitha and Alison have, there would have been the money to buy and produce amazing quality menus? Obviously you want to eat what you have paid for, but let's be honest, when you are attending a birthday party or wedding celebration so long as the food is hot or cold as it should be, and tastes reasonably good, you're happy? Any good cook can create a celebratory meal from what is available from the supermarkets?'

'Don't forget that catering for a party of two hundred and fifty people requires more ingredients than could be bought from the shelves in one day, let alone three days' worth, particularly if there is more than one party on a particular day.'

'Of course, it's not like you can buy two hundred pork chops, and the ingredients for fifty nut cutlets. I was thinking of one of my dinner parties where I probably have a maximum of eight people round the table!'

'Sounds like fun,' grinned George, and Yvonne found herself smiling back. 'But that's the other problem. From what our new chef was telling me, there was no money. Although the guests had paid the full invoiced amount, the money was nowhere to be found, and the cash she was being given was coming from other parts of the business such as the gymnasium and the spa. The Finance Director has disappeared, and the accounts staff are unable to track down where the clients' money has gone.'

They had to sit back in their chairs while the waiting staff cleared away the empty plates and dishes from their bread and olives, and placed the plates of roast lamb for Yvonne and roast chicken for George in front of them. Dishes of roast potatoes and vegetables, and a small gravy boat were also put on the table.

'That's not going to be enough gravy for both of us,' observed Yvonne.

'Can we have another gravy boat please?' asked George, and within a minute another one appeared.

'I like this place' said Yvonne.

'Good choice' agreed George.

For a few minutes they ate without talking, until Yvonne asked 'When did all this happen? To the chef at the other place?'

'At the beginning of last week' said George. 'Or at least that's when the supplies seemed to suddenly stop. According to her, things have been a bit sticky at times for the past six months, but they have always been able to conjure up something, until Monday which is when the Finance Director failed to turn up for work.'

'So how does Jane Poundsmith fit in to all this?'

George laid down his knife and fork and leaned in. Yvonne did the same. 'Apparently at about eleven o'clock last Monday morning the Finance Director's wife came looking for him. It was a friendly place to work, and family and friends were welcome to drop in for a few minutes, so long as they didn't interrupt the flow of the work. It is the same policy I adopt in my restaurants. I expect my staff to work hard, and often long hours, and I feel it is unreasonable to stop them from talking to people for a few minutes here and there.'

Yvonne thought of her antiques shop, and the regular cups of tea and coffee she provided to the dealers and their friends and families. Sometimes the tea parties went on a bit, but no customer was ever ignored, and everyone who walked through the door received a warm welcome from everyone already taking up position with a mug in their hand. Her business had been profitable from the first month, and had never failed to clear its expenses, including her wages. She thought back to the days when she had no time for friends, was always working, too tired to go out in the evening if she was at home. When it all came crashing down around her she had no one who wasn't connected to the family business she could escape too. Now she had a relaxed and productive work environment, her equestrian friends, and local friends who had nothing to do with antiques or horses.

She realised she had been looking down at the table, and George was waiting for her to acknowledge what he had just said. She simply nodded her agreement, and George continued 'The difference this time was that the wife was clearly in a bad temper and was on the warpath. She went searching for him, but he was nowhere to be found, and no one had seen him that morning. Apparently he had gone away the previous Friday on a stag weekend and hadn't come home. He was due back on the Sunday night. The rest of the stag party said he hadn't turned up at the airport for the trip to Budapest but had sent a text saying he was sorry, he couldn't get away from work, and he hoped they all had a good time. He wasn't at work on the Friday and hadn't been at home since the Friday morning when he told his wife he was getting a lift with one of the other stags to the airport.'

'She must have been worried out of her mind!' exclaimed Yvonne. 'Why was she so angry?'

'Because when he didn't come home on the Sunday night she had contacted one of the other stags who told her he hadn't been with them all weekend because of work, so she messaged one of his assistants who told her he hadn't been at work on the Friday, and there had been no drama that day worthy of his attention. She searched his home office and found a mobile phone hidden in a bag in a filing cabinet. She unlocked the phone using the passcode he used for everything.'

Yvonne raised her eyebrows 'A Finance Director who didn't have a variety of passcodes?'

George shrugged 'And on that phone she found a series of messages to and from someone called J.'

'He was having an affair?'

'Don't know. It doesn't sound as though they were romantic messages, but they were dates and numbers, possibly times or amounts of money. The wife had gone through their friends' list and contacted everyone who's first or last name began with a J without any joy, no pun intended, and ended up at his workplace to check for herself that he wasn't there.'

'So, you think J could stand for Jane Poundsmith?'

'Could do' said George, and picked up his knife and fork to carry on eating.

Yvonne followed his lead, and it wasn't long before their plates were empty. Leaning back in her chair, Yvonne asked 'I take it he hasn't turned up anywhere?'

'I assume not. Our chef left there on the Wednesday and started work for us this morning, so he could have turned up since then, but she is in contact with the colleagues who are still working there so I think someone would have told her if he had walked in through the door. From the sound of it most of the kitchen staff have left, and there is no shortage of alternative hospitality places for them so they won't be hanging around for long if things are not resolved soon. It is a bit of a coincidence.'

'It is a bit' Yvonne agreed. 'How old was the Finance Director?'

'I didn't ask. Why?'

'I'm just wondering. If he has done a runner with this Jane Poundsmith, he is probably near her age wouldn't you say? Late fifties? It just doesn't sound like the sort of age to go on a stag weekend to Budapest.'

'You are making a lot of assumptions there' laughed George. 'But you do have a point. It isn't likely that anyone in their twenties, or even thirties, would be the Finance Director for a prestigious venue like the one our chef has come from, and I can't imagine anyone in their forties or fifties wanting to go on a stag weekend in Bournemouth, let alone Budapest. Any of my friends who get married now have had their stag nights or weekends when they were in their twenties, and these days we possibly would go on an experience like track racing or off-road driving, but spending lots of money to go abroad and get drunk isn't fun anymore. I'll have to quiz her about him when we get back.'

'Speaking of which, it's three o'clock already. The time has flown by!' said Yvonne. 'Shall we go back to mine for a cup of tea, before the girls turn up?'

Chapter 13

Yvonne opened the gates so George could park his car directly outside the shop, and let him in through the back door. Rob popped his head out of the kitchen to see who was coming in.

'Hi. The kettle is on if you two would like a cuppa.'

'No thank you, Rob,' said Yvonne. 'We're due to be meeting some friends any minute now so we'll go on through to my kitchen. Is everything alright here today?'

'Yes, of course, running smoothly as usual!' he grinned, before disappearing from view as the kettle came to the boil.

'I have never been in here before' said George, as he peered through to the shop.

'Go and have a look around, while I put the kettle on' said Yvonne. 'I'll be with you in a minute.'

The sound of a thump and running paws down the stairs forewarned of Zebedee's greeting, and she threw herself at Yvonne as if she'd been on her own for several days.

Yvonne filled the kettle and switched it on, before running up the spiral stairs for a visit to her bathroom. When she came back down there was no sign of George, so she went in search of him with Zebedee at her heels. The shop was empty of customers, and Rob and another dealer were the only people in there, so Zebedee decided to guard them and sat looking hopefully at the plate of biscuits on the counter. Yvonne found George hunkered down in front of a cabinet, looking at a set of medals awarded to a soldier in World War I.

'My great grandfather had these' he said, pointing at them. 'My mum has them in a cabinet like this one in their living room. I always think of him when I go in there. How can anyone sell them?'

'Maybe he didn't have any relatives to leave them to, or the family line has died out after his family inherited them' explained Yvonne.

'That is so sad. When you think about what those men went through, and now they are forgotten. Oh well, at least it looks as though someone is making a good living out of them' he gestured to the gaps on the shelving. 'Someone has had a busy weekend judging by the sparse contents of this cabinet, and that one.'

Yvonne frowned as she studied the remaining stock. 'This cabinet is rented to a lovely lady, Marion Close, who is on holiday. I think she has gone somewhere lovely and hot like Majorca, so she'll be pleased to see how much has sold when she gets back. But the other one should be maintained. The dealer is almost the complete opposite of Marion, Juliette Monk, and is a complete baggage.'

George laughed 'What do you mean?'

'Oh, you know those women who can't say anything without criticising? She'll walk through the shop and pass comment on the prices other dealers have marked their stock, or laugh at the descriptions and try to show off her own knowledge about the pieces. To be fair she does know her stuff, and is usually right, but it's just the way she does it, you know what I mean?'

George nodded. 'I am surprised you allow her to stay. It seems to me you have a relatively harmonious group of dealers here.'

Yvonne shrugged. 'She hasn't done anything so bad that I can terminate her contract. Yet.'

Juliette's stand was looking neglected. There were plenty of spaces where items had been removed, and nothing had been put in to replace them, and no one had shuffled the remaining items so the gaps disappeared. There were only two stands in that room, Marion's and Juliette's, and looking at Marion's stand, which included a bookcase in the corner, a couple of tables, one chair and a fire guard, Yvonne thought it also looked a bit neglected which was to be expected, but wasn't a good look for customers.

On Juliette's stand there was a layer of dust on the tables, and two clean circles where she remembered a pair of plates had sat for a while. She wondered when Juliette had last been in to clean and restock her stand. It was a condition of being in the antiques shop that the dealers took a turn working on the tills and telephone once a week, and kept their stands clean and well-stocked. Yvonne tried to remember when she had last seen Juliette, and other than when she had brought in a particularly fine Vienna cold-painted bronze of a bear at least three weeks' ago, she couldn't think of a more recent occasion.

The rota for working in the shop was informal and fluid, and people signed their name onto the big calendar located on the desk to claim their days, and as there were usually at least two if not three or four people signed up, if one person was off sick or needed to change their day because a particularly lucrative buying call had come in, it didn't make much difference to the running of the shop. Yvonne went and checked the calendar and saw Juliette's name written both for the day before and the Tuesday earlier in the week.

Her phone pinged a message from Maisie to signal the trio were waiting outside the gates in the carpark, so

Yvonne called to George that everyone had arrived, and went to let them in.

'What is going on?' asked Alison. 'Your message sounded intriguing.'

'Have you really found us a venue and solved the catering problems?' asked Tabitha.

Yvonne saw the excitement on their faces, and suddenly felt worried. What if the romance of the evening before had made the courtyard look more appealing than it really was? What if it was too late to complete the amount of work required to cater for a big wedding? She did not want to give them false hope; these two had enough disappointments and tragic events to deal with.

Holding her hands up in defence she said 'Hold on. We are just going to have a look at somewhere close by. It is not ready yet, and there is a large amount of unfinished work to do, but just possibly George may have a solution to the venue and catering problems' explained Yvonne. 'Do you want to come in and talk about it first, or shall we go straight there?' she asked, as George appeared behind her.

'I think we should go straight there. Zebedee too' he said.

'Come on then ladies, follow us' said Yvonne, before yelling for her dog to join them.

'I don't think Zebedee's coming!' yelled back Rob. 'Don't worry, I'll pop her in your kitchen if you're not back by the time I go.'

Yvonne wasn't keen on anyone going into her home without her, but decided it would probably be easier to have a discussion about the venue without the dog exploring everything and distracting them.

'Thank you, Rob, you're very kind. But don't give her any of those biscuits!'

'I won't' he called. 'I remember what happened the last time she had anything with coconut in it.'

'That was disgusting, poor Zebedee. We won't be long' she added, thinking that would discourage any ambitions he might have to go snooping in case he got caught.

'Where are we going?' asked Maisie. 'Do I need to go and fetch my car? We can't all fit in George's flash motor.'

'Very nice' said Alison, admiring the Jaguar. 'I have always wanted one of these.'

'My idea of hell,' muttered Tabitha. 'If you can't tow a trailer, drive across a muddy field, or put a sheep in the back of it, then what's the point?'

Laughing, Yvonne opened the gates and lead them out into the carpark. 'Come on, this way.'

'We're obviously not going to TAA' said Tabitha. 'Not if we're walking up towards Bell Street.'

'Would you have wanted to have your reception there?' asked George.

Tabitha shrugged. 'I must admit it wouldn't have been my first choice, even if we could afford it, sorry. One of the reasons we loved Kenyon Hall was because it had both inside and outside space, whereas your restaurant is entirely indoors. The vineyard would have been great for that too, and my barn ticks those boxes.'

George said nothing, but shared a conspiratorial look with Yvonne, which Tabitha saw. 'Where are you taking us?' she demanded.

'Keep walking this way!' said Yvonne, as the group made their way out of the carpark and turned left onto Bell Street.

'At least it's not the library,' said Alison. 'Are we going to Muston's?'

'Obviously not' said Maisie, as they continued past Mustons Lane.

'Morrisons!' said Tabitha triumphantly.

'Nope' said Yvonne.

'The Arts Centre?' asked Alison.

'Here' Yvonne gestured to the large black gates, and George opened them so that everyone could see through the entrance to the edge of the courtyard.

'Where on earth did these come from?' asked Maisie. 'I have never seen these before.'

'Nor me' exclaimed Tabitha. 'How long have they been here?'

George shrugged 'They have been here as long as I've been here, and this gateway dates back hundreds of years.'

'I can't believe that' muttered Tabitha, before asking Alison 'Are you coming?'

Alison was standing on the pavement looking down through the gateway with a smile on her face. 'Yvonne, this is perfect!'

'Come on, come and see the rest of it' said Yvonne, as she led them down between the buildings on either side until they arrived in the large courtyard.

George closed the gates behind them, and walked down to join them, standing back and letting the women take in the scene.

'You've been busy' said Yvonne.

'Not me' he admitted. 'I was running this morning, and out to lunch with you after that.'

Maisie, Tabitha and Alison all said 'Ooooooh!'

'Never mind all that,' Yvonne flapped her hands. 'Look at all this!'

Lights were strung up around the walls and ran overhead on a series of archways and trellis. Wooden barrels filled with plants were positioned on either side of the doorways.

The fountain was bubbling away noisily, and lights had been strategically placed so that the water appeared to twinkle as it cascaded. Metal chairs with silver-coloured cushions, and matching tables with silver-coloured tablecloths and silver and white table decorations were arranged around the arches and under the trellis. Lined up against the far wall which ran between the end of the restaurant and the back of the café were three rose-coloured sofas with silver throws and cushions, and three low tables with silver-coloured tablecloths and vases containing peonies were in front of them. The doors to the kitchen area opened, and a woman dressed in black and carrying a champagne bucket walked through, followed by another woman carrying a tray with five champagne flutes, and then a man carrying three plates of food.

'Please, make yourselves comfortable' said the woman, as she gestured for them to follow her to the sofas. 'Would everyone like a glass of champagne?'

The wedding party did not need to be asked twice, and Tabitha and Alison sat on the middle sofa, Yvonne and Maisie made themselves comfortable on the sofa nearest to the restaurant, and George perched on the edge of the sofa nearest the kitchen, where he was joined by the woman after she had poured their champagne.

'This is the person who has been doing all the work' George introduced her. 'Her name is Lesley Martin, and she is the person heading up TAA's outside catering company. All this decoration can be loaded into a lorry and transported to any location. If you do want to hold the wedding in your barn, Tabitha, we can move all this furniture, lights and plants over there.'

Tabitha nodded. 'That would be amazing.'

For the next hour a series of tasting dishes and drinks were brought out to the four women, who sampled

139

everything with enthusiasm, and discussed with Lesley what they would and would not like on the wedding menu. There was very little they rejected, but one non-alcoholic cocktail reminded all four of vomit, and two of the desserts were tricky to eat as they tended to shoot off across the courtyard when anyone pushed a fork or spoon into them.

'I should have brought Zebedee' joked Yvonne, as one of the staff cleared away the mess with tissue, soap and water.

'What do you think of the décor?' George asked, indicating the courtyard in front of them.

'I think it is gorgeous' said Alison, 'We didn't have a choice about the colour scheme at Kenyon Hall, because everything is already in place and everything was cream. It was up to us to have the colours we wanted in the flower arrangements and our bridal clothes. I think we went a bit overboard with the colours in the flowers, just to compensate for the blandness of the furnishings. With this silver and white detail, and the colours of the sofas and peonies, we would not need even a third of the flowers we ordered.'

Tabitha nodded 'You're right. The lights, the stone floor and walls, this amazing wall of windows hiding the restaurant, and the stone walls and wooden doors of the kitchen are all beautiful and do not need to be swamped by a mass of cut flowers which are going to die within hours if not days.'

'What about your wedding outfits? Is this going to suit them?' asked George.

'We're not giving anything away! But yes, this will all be the perfect backdrop.' Alison looked at Tabitha, who nodded her agreement.

'I think you may have saved the day, George Gumbleton' said Tabitha. 'Now all we have to do is discuss the cost.

Although it would be wonderful to hold our wedding on our land, I think this is a better place. What do you think Alison?'

'I agree with you. As romantic as it would be to have it on the farm, it would also mean a lot of work clearing out that barn, and we would still have to find and hire toilets. I do have one question though. What do we do if it rains?' asked Alison.

'I am glad you asked me that' grinned George, and jumped up from the sofa. In three strides he was at the wall to the new kitchen and pressed a large green button. A whirring sound heralded the appearance of a canopy which had been housed inside what Yvonne had taken to be a protruding lintel above the door. The lights which trailed over the archways and trellis appeared to pull the canopy across the courtyard, and in less than a minute the whole area was enclosed by a brightly lit roof. Two of the waiting staff appeared, each carrying a chandelier, and using a pole with a hook on the end they effortlessly hoisted the chandeliers into position. Lesley walked in with a tray of candles in glasses filled with silver-coloured beads, and placed one onto each of the tables located around the courtyard. Within five minutes the courtyard had been transformed from a secluded and tranquil space to a room with pizzazz.

'Wow! Obviously I don't want it to rain on our wedding day, but I'm not going to mind if it does!' said Alison.

'I sincerely hope it doesn't rain,' said George 'and we will probably do this for the evening when the temperature drops. Do you like it? Would you like to hold your wedding here?'

'Yes please!' chorused Tabitha and Alison.

'I hope we can afford it' said Tabitha.

'I had a thought about that' said George. 'You can pay for the cost of the ingredients on the menu, no charge for the preparation or serving, and no charge for hiring our courtyard. You would be the first people we are catering an event for, and there are bound to be hiccups and mistakes, although obviously I hope there are none. Therefore we would not charge you for being our guinea pigs.'

'That is very generous of you' said Alison.

'Or, and this is the option I am hoping you will choose, but of course it is up to you.'

'Go on' said Alison.

'You allow us to use your wedding as our advertisement. We take photos and videos of everything, we ask you and your guests for quotations about the experience, and we use them repeatedly over the next year in print, on the radio and on social media. We will not charge you a penny.'

'I'm up for that!' said Tabitha.

'Me too! We could get some free publicity for our business' Alison said to Maisie.

'Absolutely. We could do a tie-in with your salon for future events if you wish.'

'But' cautioned Yvonne 'how will you afford to do this? Surely you need to make this pay?'

George nodded 'We blow our entire advertising budget on this one event. The alternative is to have staged and posed pictures, which is an option, but less authentic.'

Lesley appeared with a small silver-coloured box for each of them, decorated with rose-coloured beads in the shape of two hearts entwined on the top and tied with a matching ribbon. 'We would also still have to put in a lot of work to achieve those pictures. I would prefer to be making and serving the food and drink for a real wedding party, and

142

see them enjoying themselves, than produce a menu just so that models can pose and discard. These are four different party favours for your guests. Have a look and taste of each one, and let me know if you like them, and if so how many of each you would like. No, don't do it here' she interrupted as Alison was about to open hers. 'Please, take them home, and have a look at them on your kitchen table or living-room sofa, because that is where your guests will be opening their boxes.'

'Good idea!' said Maisie. 'I vote we all go back to Yvonne's kitchen and share the goodies.'

Reluctantly, Tabitha and Alison eased themselves off their sofa. 'Would you mind if I took some photos?' Alison asked.

'No, please do take photos' said Lesley. 'We can't give you a brochure or point you towards a website, and you need to know what your wedding venue is going to look like.'

Once Alison was satisfied she had a record of everything, George led the way back towards the gates, and they emerged onto Bell Street.

'It is like another world' observed Tabitha, as the usual late Sunday afternoon bustle of tourists and local dog walkers weaved their way around each other along the pavements and into the road. 'While we were sitting in there I completely forgot we were literally sitting in the middle of town.'

Maisie was looking back at the gates 'I really cannot remember ever seeing them before.'

As Yvonne turned to look at them she caught a flash of movement out of the corner of her eye, and sure enough the man who appeared to be stalking her was disappearing around the corner of the bank. She could see his reflection in the windows of The Shaston.

'What is it?' asked George, peering in the direction Yvonne was staring.

'Nothing. I thought I recognised someone, that's all.'

Appearing to accept her answer, he said 'I'll leave you four to discuss my proposals in peace. I really hope you choose to have your wedding here, but whatever you decide I hope you have a beautiful day.'

'Thank you George, we'll give you a ring tomorrow morning if that's alright?' said Alison.

'Of course, I will look forward to hearing from you.'

The four friends walked back to Yvonne's home, chatting about the food, drink and colour scheme, holding their little silver box. Once inside her kitchen, Yvonne made tea for everyone, and they sat around her kitchen table and opened their boxes. Each was beautifully packed with a mixture of gifts. Between the four of them were small heart-shaped photo frames, sweets and chocolates wrapped in silver-coloured paper, a tiny bottle of locally made rosewater, a small bottle of silver nail varnish, a tiny silver sheep charm, and a silver-coloured tealight from the artisan candle shop in the High Street.

Alison turned her box upside down and noticed there was a list of ingredients. 'Mine has gluten-free sweets.'

Maisie did the same 'Mine has sugar-free sweets. Mmmh you would never know; they taste delicious.'

Chapter 14

After everyone had left, and Yvonne had tidied up, she noticed there was a WhatsApp message on her phone. Sally had posted on the livery yard group chat that she would like to do the night ride the following evening, and was anyone else interested? Both Charlotte and Lindy had already responded affirmatively, and Yvonne added her name to the list. They agreed to be ready to ride out from the yard at half-past eight on Monday evening, with the aim of being back on the yard by half-past ten.

Yvonne went into the little room off the kitchen, which was officially her downstairs toilet but had been turned into a home tack room, complete with a saddle horse on which sat Toby's dressage saddle, and five bridle hooks attached to a plank of wood secured across the end wall where various bridles and halters hung. The general-purpose saddle, bridle and basic grooming kit she used every day were in the secure tack room at the yard, but in the downstairs loo she had a box containing a lot more brushes, hoof picks, and sweat scrapers. Considering she had only had her own horse for eight years she had accumulated a lot of stuff. Of course, the equipment at the yard was in Toby's orange and black colours, whereas in the box were blue hoof picks, a pink sweat scraper, and green rubber curry combs. On the shelf next to the spare grooming kit was another box containing high visibility bits and pieces. Usually Toby wore fluorescent leg bands in orange, with a reflective strip, when they went out hacking, but Yvonne knew he needed more than that if they were to be riding the lanes in the dark. She pulled out the LED taillight, orange of course, and a couple of lights she would attach to her stirrups. It was a while since she'd used the head torch, so that was added to the pile, and she carried them all through to the living room where she plugged them in to charge ready for the next day.

It was still early in the evening, so after Zebedee had eaten her dinner the pair of them went out for a stroll. Yvonne had only intended it to be a twenty-minute walk around the roads, but it was such a lovely evening they ended up walking down Tout Hill to Enmore Green, through to Breech Common, and back up through St James' to Park Walk, where they and several other people enjoyed watching the stunning sunset over Duncliffe Woods in the distance.

'Aren't we lucky to live here,' said a male voice next to her, and turning she saw that Tom Archibald was standing with his dog also taking in the view.

'Hi Tom, yes we are.'

Zebedee and Tom's dog, Stan, of indeterminate hairy breed, ignored each other while their owners stood in companiable silence for a minute or two.

'I really should be going home. I'm on duty at six o'clock tomorrow morning, but I'm not ready for bed yet. Fancy a quick drink at the Shaston?'

Yvonne was a little taken aback, as although he was a regular coffee and cake member of the antiques shop, he rarely came in without Tim. Thinking about it, she wasn't sure she had ever seen him without Tim Smith. Her face must have shown some confusion because he quickly followed up with 'I'm not asking you on a date or anything! Sorry. I just fancied a drink and didn't want to drink on my own.'

'Oh, of course, I didn't think anything like that!' lied Yvonne, feeling her face blushing and giving her away. 'A nightcap would be very welcome. Come on dogs,' and she led the way out of Park Walk and up the road to the Shaston.

It was now too cool to sit out in the courtyard, so they ordered their drinks at the bar – Tom insisted on paying – and sat together on the only available seat, which would not have been Yvonne's first choice, a deep faux leather sofa, with the dogs at their feet.

'Lie down,' murmured Yvonne to Zebedee, who had form for being a bit protective of Yvonne if other dogs came near. She didn't want her fighting with anyone, especially not the local policeman's dog. Zebedee did as she was told, with an audible grumble.

'There, you see Stan? That is how a well-behaved dog behaves,' said Tom. 'I've got no chance with him. He was my mum's dog, and I inherited him when she moved abroad in February. We're still getting to know each other, but he has made it clear that training commands are a waste of breath.'

Yvonne laughed. 'He's alright sitting there. How old is he?'

'Mum says the rescue centre guessed he and his siblings were only a few days old when they were dumped, with their mother, outside their gates. That was a couple of years' ago, in March.'

'Oh no, how sad! How many were there?'

'It is sad, but at least they were all together, and pets cost a lot of money so I would rather they were dumped like that then left to suffer. He's fine, he knows no different, and the other people who adopted his mum and brothers and sisters have all kept in touch. They have a puppy party once a year where all five of them plus their mum go on a walk. This year it was along the beach at Bournemouth, ending with a cream tea for the humans. Because mum had left, I went with Stan, and it was great fun. We walked with them on leads for about half an hour, and then we reached a quiet area with no other people or dogs around and let them off. Oh my goodness, it was hairy noisy mayhem. They all charged around, including their mother, kicking up sand whenever they came near us, shooting off into the sea. None of them had a fear of the cold or the waves, and we ended up huddling together as a human shield around the older members of the group as the dogs kept running back to us and shaking sea water over everyone. Someone had booked us in to the café in advance, and they reserved one end for us, in front of a wood burner, so we all dried off and warmed up.'

'That sounds amazing.'

'It was. Next year we're planning to walk through Longleat Forest and end up at a café or pub. I didn't want him when mum originally suggested it, but he is a lovely dog, and is giving me a focus outside of work.'

'How does he cope when you are at work?' asked Yvonne. 'I'm lucky because Zebedee can come to most places with me, and of course I mainly work at home, or someone is around in the shop who can keep an eye on her when I'm out, but that's not possible for you with your job.'

'No, Stan is not police dog material, even if I was a trained dog handler. Although now I have him, I am thinking about doing that. There is a woman in Hannam who does doggy day care, so Stan goes there every day.'

'What, even when your shift starts at six o'clock?'

'Yes,' Tom nodded ruefully. 'I have to drop him off for about quarter to six in the morning and collect him any time between five and seven in the evening.'

'That must cost you a fortune!' exclaimed Yvonne.

'It costs mum a fortune,' grinned Tom. 'She pays for all of his bills, and I get all the fun, don't I mate?' he said as he rubbed Stan's head. All judgemental thoughts flew out of Yvonne's head as she saw the devotion in Stan's eyes as he looked up at Tom.

'You two have obviously bonded well' she observed.

'He's a lovely dog. Oh it's closing time, and I think we're being chucked out. Thanks for keeping us company,' said Tom as he sprang easily to his feet.

Yvonne managed to push herself out of the depths of the sofa in a far more ungainly manner and accepted his offer of a hand on her arm to help her stand up. Laughing, she said 'Sorry, I have seized up! We had a super horse ride up to the airfield this morning, and my body has decided to mould itself to the sofa.'

Together they walked out of the Shaston, and along Bell Street, chatting all the way. 'Didn't you say you used to work at your aunt and uncle's stables?' asked Yvonne.

'I did, yes, my mum's sister and her husband had a riding school in the Meon Valley in Hampshire. The horses and ponies all lived out in the fields around the yard, and I used to cycle over from our house in Droxford to their yard in Soberton. In the summer some of the horses and ponies stayed in a field near our house, and I would ride one and lead the other three along the lanes in the morning, and ride back with them all in the evening.' He sighed 'Those were the days.'

'But you don't have anything to do with horses now?'

'No, I haven't even thought about them for years, until I met your big lad the other day. I wouldn't have time now;

particularly as I have Stan to look after,' he said as he looked fondly down to the hairy dog. 'How do you find the time?'

Yvonne shrugged. 'The yard where I keep Toby is like a doggy day care centre, I suppose. The owners have a fully enclosed garden where dogs can stay while we're out riding our horses, and there are some off-road routes where we can ride with the dogs. Although they do have to be sociable and relatively well-behaved,' she grinned as she looked at Stan, who ignored her. 'He is obviously well-socialised.'

'Yes, he is. He is usually fine with other dogs. But I would worry about having him loose around horses.'

'Probably best to keep it like that. You don't want to find out the hard way and end up with a huge vet's bill for either him or a horse, or both. Even if your mum is paying' she teased.

'True! I don't think mum would appreciate it.' They had arrived at the gates to Yvonne's home. 'We'd better head off home. Early start in the morning. Thank you both for the company,' and with a cheery wave Tom continued to walk on down to the High Street, with Stan trotting along beside him, big fluffy black and white tail waving goodbye.

Yvonne and Zebedee waited until the gates were fully closed, and then raced each other up the wooden steps. Zebedee won, obviously, and waited at the top with her Staffy grin showing she knew she would always win that particular race. As she unlocked the door, Yvonne quickly glanced over her shoulder, but nobody darted into the shadows and she could not see anyone around.

Once inside she slipped off her sandals and went straight into the bathroom and turned on the bath taps. Her whole body ached, and she knew it was her own fault for not stretching before and after the hack in the morning. She could remember the days when she could just hop on a horse and not even notice it the next day, but since she'd reached her forties, and the menopause had crept up on her, she had to take more care of herself. She poured a few drops of Pure Lakes muscle and joint bath soak into the water, and walked into the dressing room to undress and pop her clothes in the laundry basket. She suddenly remembered all the lights which were recharging in the sitting room, and so she ran down the spiral stairs and unplugged everything, leaving them all in a neat line on the kitchen table. Zebedee had followed her down and was drinking from her water bowl, making the loud slurping noise all dogs do, and so it was a few seconds before Yvonne heard the buzzer on the monitor for the electronic gates. She walked over to the monitor, and even though she knew the person standing outside couldn't see her while she could see them, she felt vulnerable without any clothes on. The person was standing with their head turned away, as though they were looking at something behind them.

'Hello?' said Yvonne, feeling her heart race. It was after half-past ten at night, and none of her friends would call on her unannounced so late. In fact, none of her friends would call on her unannounced as they always texted or messaged beforehand, because everyone led such busy lives.

The person looked at the camera, and she saw with relief it was Tim Smith. 'Hi Yvonne. Don't worry, I was just passing and saw your lights on, and wanted to give you an update on the case. Are you decent?'

Yvonne paused for a moment. What on earth could be so important that a policeman would need to come to her home so late on a Sunday evening? She decided honesty was the best policy 'No, I'm not, sorry, and the bath is running. Can it wait until tomorrow?'

'Oh I'm sorry, yes, yes of course it can. So long as you're OK, I'll pop into the shop tomorrow morning?'

'Thank you, that would be better,' said Yvonne. 'I'll see you in the morning.'

'Bye!' he said with a wave at the camera, and she watched him as he headed up the carpark towards Bell Street.

'Well, that was weird,' she said to Zebedee, and felt comforted as her dog followed at her heels as she switched all the lights off and walked back up the spiral stairs.

She turned the tap off in the bath and went and stood looking out of the windows to the north and west which overlooked the carpark, careful to stand to the side so no one could see her even though it would be difficult from that angle below. There was one couple walking to their car, setting the lights flashing as they approached and unlocked it. Then three young men walked through the carpark from one end to the other, and another two couples walked to their cars. More people began to walk down the path from Bell Street, and Yvonne guessed that something at the Art Centre had just finished. Still feeling unsettled, Yvonne pulled on a t-shirt and shorts, and went back downstairs. She unlocked the connecting door to the shop and checked that the alarms and door locks were set properly by unsetting and resetting them all. Then she checked the back door and the double garage doors, and then relocked the connecting door, all the time being followed by Zebedee. She knew that the dog would alert her if anyone was close by, and she felt reassured. As an afterthought she turned on one of the wall lights in the sitting room. If Tim had thought she was still up because he saw the lights on, then other people must think the same. Because her home was so tucked away she didn't really think about what it looked like from the outside, and how that might lead passers-by to conclude whether she was at home. She resolved to have a look tomorrow evening when she came back from the ride, and that maybe in future she should always have a light on somewhere in her home. Perhaps in the shop too? Lots of business owners did that. Because the windows and door at the front of the shop had iron grills on them, and the back was defended by the gates, she hadn't given any more though to her own security when she was at home.

As she walked back into her bedroom she noticed a message on her phone from Tom.

'Just to let you know we've had an update in the case. Will see you in the morning to keep you informed.'

Feeling hugely relieved and also really stupid for over-reacting about Tim's visit, Yvonne gave Zebedee a big cuddle, even though she had positioned herself in the middle of Yvonne's bed, and went back to finish running her bath. She decided that nice soothing music was required, and selected Camille Saint-Saens' Danse Macabre, one of her favourites. She hadn't watched any Jonathan Creek for a while and sank into the bath wondering if any of the programmes were available on a streaming channel. It wasn't long before she was conducting the music and singing along. Thank goodness I don't have any neighbours, she thought, as the orchestra came together in a crescendo before dying back down to a single violin.

By the time she was ready to get out, she had stretched her aching muscles and luxuriated in the warm bathwater and was feeling much calmer. Wrapped in a towel she went back into the dressing room to pick out an outfit for the morning. The window at the end was high and faced east, overlooking the police station which would have been closed since six o'clock that evening. Yvonne had never drawn the blind because she was one storey up and was never in that room while the police station was open, but the relaxing bath and music and the message from Tom had obviously not completely put her mind at rest, because she drew the blind.

Chapter 15

The next day was a busy one in the antiques shop. Mondays tended to be quiet in Shaftesbury in general, and therefore the dealers who rented space in her shop made the most of the available parking spaces nearby to restock their stands. Rob always brought in a delicious treat from his kitchen, and today one of the other dealers, William Drake, a large grey-haired man in his sixties who specialised in militaria, also brought in a couple of homemade quiches.

'This one is tomato and cheese,' said William 'and this one is salmon and asparagus. Both organic, and the salmon one is dairy free. Tell me what you think.'

He had already sliced them into slim wedges and arranged each quiche on its own plate. Although it was only ten o'clock in the morning, Yvonne wanted to try the dairy-free salmon one.

'Mmmh, this is tasty,' she said, through a mouthful of her lunch.

William beamed 'You'd never know it was dairy-free, would you?'

Yvonne shook her head 'No, absolutely not. Did you grow the asparagus yourself?'

'Of course!' William said proudly.

Their conversation drew other dealers to the table where William had set up the food. Rob made a pot of tea and a pot of coffee, and for almost an hour the shop was empty of customers but full of antiques dealers eating, drinking, and talking loudly. Cooking, gardening, and shopping were the main topics of conversation, and it wasn't long before all of William's quiches and most of Rob's chocolate brownies were devoured. Only Yvonne, who was sitting behind the counter for the most part observing and listening to the people enjoying each other's company, noticed the door open and Tim walk in. He looked a little shocked by the party scene in front of him, and she indicated for him to join her in a quieter part of the shop. Squeezing around the edge of the counter, the pair of them walked through to the next room where they sat on a couple of Windsor chairs at a Pembroke table.

'What's the occasion?' Tim asked, nodding his head to where the laughter was coming from.

'There isn't one,' said Yvonne. 'We seem to be having a spontaneous social gathering. You've missed out on the savouries, but there might still be some of Rob's brownies left.'

'No, no, I can't eat any of those today' smiled Tim. 'Have you had any more thoughts about the jewellery you found?'

'Yes, I have.' Yvonne decided to share some of her findings. 'I believe it is part of a collection from the Speake family, which to my knowledge is still owned by them and for it to be in Tabitha's field, it must have been stolen.'

Tim nodded. This was not news to him, but he didn't interrupt.

'Specifically, from what I can remember of the items we found,' Yvonne wasn't going to let on she had taken photographs of everything and had spent hours studying them 'it looks like a collection belonging to Lady Margaret Millicent Speake.'

'What makes you think that?' asked Tim.

'Although there isn't much in the way of public documentation, I do have a contact who is familiar with the family's jewellery, and there was a particular mourning ring they believe belonged to Lady Margaret's great great great grandmother, to commemorate the death of her baby son at seven weeks' old.'

'That is interesting. The jewellery is still at the station; would you like to come over and have another look at it?'

'Yes please!' said Yvonne, because although she had the photographs, there was no substitute for handling and looking at the real thing. Assuming he meant for her to see the jewellery immediately, Yvonne stood up.

'Alright, how about tomorrow afternoon? Three o'clock?'

'Oh, yes, that would be good,' said Yvonne, hoping she had successfully covered up her mistake.

'Is business good?' asked Tim.

'Yes, ticking over nicely.'

'Do you mind if I have a wander through the shop?'

'No of course not.'

Yvonne left Tim to browse and began to sort out the stock book. Although every dealer had their own designated space within the shop, they also marked their stock with labels on which were written a short description of anything from two to ten words, price, and the dealer's unique code which was usually their initials. Yvonne's was YMP, Rob's was RLK and so on. Customers rarely bought from one dealer's stand, and so when they came to the counter to pay, the prices and codes were entered onto the computer, and labels were removed and put into an old ice cream box, and the customer paid the total amount rather than sums of money to each dealer. Yvonne had a ledger into which she would write everyone's sales, and at the end of every day she would double check the computer's lists with those in the ledger. It was time-consuming and probably not necessary, but it ensured any transposing of letters was picked up, and if the computer became corrupted in some way there was always a paper copy. It also meant the dealers could easily check their sales for the day or week in the book without using the computer when it was needed for serving customers.

Tim reappeared, brushing his sleeve where dust had transferred. 'There are some fascinating things in here. Are the owners responsible for cleaning their own stock? It looks as though someone is lacking in the dusting department.'

Yvonne glanced in the direction he was looking, beyond the tea party, and frowned. She couldn't see the area he was talking about because it was in another room, but she guessed he was referring to Marion's stand, although the one next to hers was also a mess. Juliette had clearly still not been in and tidied her stand, let alone replenished the stock. Perhaps her neglect could be the reason Yvonne could give for giving her notice to leave, as well as for missing her shifts running the shop. Another burst of laughter came from the room next door.

'It is their responsibility, yes. Are you talking about the one in the corner of the end room?'

'That one and the one along the wall on the other side.'

'One of them is on holiday, and is due back any day now, but the other dealer is usually conscientious about keeping her stand up together. I noticed her stand was looking a bit neglected yesterday and she's missed a few days working in here. Thank you, you have reminded me I was going to try and get in contact with her and check she is alright.'

'Good, that's good. I am sorry, I hope it didn't sound as though I was criticising anyone.' said Tim, as he walked towards the door. 'I'll see you tomorrow afternoon.'

'No problem, and yes, tomorrow' Yvonne nodded.

The bell sounding on the door as Tim opened it caused the dealers to realise how long they had been standing around gossiping, and within minutes the plates and cups were washed up, and the gathering had dispersed. Left with only William, Rob and a couple who dealt in vintage and antique linen, Yvonne casually asked 'Has anyone seen Juliette recently?'

The couple both murmured to each other and shook their heads. The wife said 'Now you mention it, no, I can't remember the last time I saw her. Her stand is in a bit of a mess, so it must be weeks rather than days.'

'She didn't turn up last week when we were on the rota together, but I didn't mind. She can be hard work,' said the husband.

Rob shook his head too 'I can't think when I last saw her either. She's usually around at some of the auctions I go to, but I think the last one must have been a month ago. I don't think I've seen her since then. She seemed perfectly fine at that one.'

'I think I'll give her a ring, and just check she's OK' said Yvonne. 'I thought I'd ask in case anyone knows if she's gone on holiday.'

'Not that I know of' said Rob 'but then we're not particularly friendly so she wouldn't tell me anyway. Marion is on holiday, isn't she?'

'Yes, I know about Marion. She's due back any day now I think' said Yvonne, before winking suggestively and saying 'Does that mean you are friendly with Marion? Does your wife know?'

'Marion's holiday is marked on the calendar!' laughed Rob. 'She's a lovely lady, but no, not my type at all. My wife has nothing to be concerned about.'

'Or hopeful' teased William.

The group dispersed, still sharing jokes and laughing, and Yvonne wondered if they would have been so relaxed if Juliette had been there.

She walked through to her home office and looked up Juliette's phone number, but she had second thoughts and sent her an email instead. She decided it might be good to have a paper trail, in case Juliette was planning on leaving without paying her final month's rent. While she was checking the bank statement, Yvonne saw that Marion's monthly direct debit had failed to enter the account on the first of the month, and Yvonne resolved to hold onto Marion's share of the shop's pay out at the end of the month, although she was sure it was just a mix-up possibly caused by a problem while she was trying to pay for goods in another country. This was standard practice with a dodgy dealer who was skipping without paying their rent, but Marion had come with great references from everyone, was one of the dealers who had been with her from the beginning, and had been an asset to the business by always having interesting stock on her stand, and even though she wasn't attracting buyers through Instagram or other online outlets, she regularly brought people into the shop by her positive reputation in the trade.

Juliette was a different character. Prolific online, positive social media content, and fastidious about promoting her stock with photographs and video reels. When Yvonne checked she could see that Juliette hadn't posted anything on social media for a fortnight. Yvonne hoped something hadn't happened to her, but she didn't like the way things were looking. It wasn't part of her agreement with the dealers to have a next of kin listed, and Yvonne didn't know anyone else to ask. She decided to wait a couple of days for a response to her email, and then she would phone her.

Zebedee was laying her head on Yvonne's knee and gazing up at her with a pleading look in her eyes, and so Yvonne took the subtle hint, and the pair of them left Rob and the antique linen dealing couple in charge and walked over to Castle Hill for an hour.

Once back home, it was only three o'clock in the afternoon, even though Yvonne felt as though it should be much later in the day, and as Rob and the couple were happy to close the shop up when the time came, she and Zebedee withdrew to Yvonne's bedroom and curled up on the bed together with a paperback by Kate Morton. Inevitably Yvonne (and Zebedee) fell asleep after a few chapters because the room was warm and the bed was comfortable, and when they awoke it was six o'clock. Feeling foolish for sleeping so long, and muzzy headed from sleeping in the afternoon, Yvonne went down the spiral stairs for a drink of water and to make herself a light supper and feed Zebedee. She took a quick peek into the shop to check everything was locked as it should be, and the alarms were on. She realised how unnerved she had been the previous day by Tim's unexpected visit to the back gate, and yet this morning he had been perfectly normal and had made no mention of it. She wondered if that was why she had slept so deeply in the afternoon; her sleep the night before had been fitful.

Soon it was time to change into her riding clothes and gather up all the lights and high visibility equipment, and head out for the night ride. Yvonne was very excited, and had butterflies in her stomach, something she hadn't felt before riding for years. She decided it was best for

161

Zebedee to stay at home; it was a bit much expecting the livery yard owners to dog-sit her dog at night as well as during the daylight hacks, and Zebedee was happy to return to the middle of Yvonne's bed for more sleep.

Yvonne loaded up her car with the equipment, and a few snacks in case they wanted to hang around at the yard after their hack and drove to Hannam without seeing anybody suspicious. Sally was already there, and Lindy and Charlotte pulled into the carpark as Yvonne was getting out of her car. No one else was around, and the four women collected their horses from the fields, tacked up, discussed their lights and reflective clothing, and spent five minutes or so studying the route Sally had organised.

'We have this landowner's permission to ride through these fields' she said, pointing on the map 'which will make a big difference and mean we can miss out the whole of this road. The gates are all open because he has taken the first cut of hay off the fields at the weekend, and he is happy for us to ride across them, rather than stick to the field margins.'

'That's brilliant, thank you' said Lindy. 'So, we don't need to ride on the roads until we cross the A350 into Ashmore Woods?'

'Correct' nodded Sally 'and at this time of the evening we will clearly be able to hear and see any oncoming vehicles, and the road will be a lot quieter than when we cross there during the day. Once we are in the woods we can go down here, along here, all the way along here, and back up here to cross over at the same point, and ride back through the fields. Is that OK? I know we're basically going and coming back along the same route.'

'It's perfect!' said Yvonne. 'It will be dark in the woods but being able to ride across these fields in the moonlight coming home will be like a dream come true. A dream I didn't know I had until just now.'

Everyone laughed, and after Sally had written up a condensed version of their route on the white board in the room they called the 'snug', the four of them set off across the fields of the livery yard, to the adjoining farmland where they had to negotiate their first gate. Because this was not a usual permissive riding route, it was a traditional metal farm gate rather than a horse-friendly gate, and so Lindy volunteered to jump off her palomino mare and open the gate for everyone.

'Come on then, Lindy' said Charlotte. 'You were telling us yesterday you can mount from the ground!'

'Of course I can!' she said, as her mare lined up next to the securely closed gate. 'But it is just as important to practise mounting from a gate.'

Everyone laughed, and thanked Lindy for her efforts. Yvonne admired how deftly Lindy climbed onto the gate and swung herself into her horse's saddle.

'You made that look easy. Having long legs helps' commented Sally.

'Thank you' said Lindy, checking her long black and grey curly hair was still caught up in its hairband below her riding hat. 'I find as I get older I need to work harder at being able to do moves like that.'

'Do you do anything in particular?' asked Sally.

'Every morning as soon as I get out of bed I spend a few minutes stretching, and a couple of times a week I go to a class with a Strong Nation trainer.'

'What on earth is that?' asked Sally.

'It's a high energy class with strength training and a bit of self-defence' explained Lindy.

'All sounds a bit like too much hard work' said Charlotte. 'Mind you, if it means you can do gates like that one as

163

easily as you did, I think it's something I may need to start doing.'

Lindy laughed 'You're young, I am sure you can do gates like that.'

'No' admitted Charlotte. 'I'll do the next one, and you'll all be able to hear that everything creaks and squeaks when I try to climb onto a gate. And I'm not talking about the gate!'

The women laughed, and began to discuss their various fitness routines, or lack of them, with Lindy and Yvonne at a similar age and sharing their experiences of perimenopause, and Sally and Charlotte both in their early twenties and realising neither of them were as fit as the two women who were at least twice their age.

The four riders and their horses walked across the field together, admiring their shadows on the ground and looking back occasionally to see the beautiful sunset behind them. Charlotte managed to take a selfie with all four riders, parts of their horses, and the sunset in the background.

'Shall we trot through this next field?' asked Yvonne. Everyone agreed, with Lindy setting the pace as hers was the smallest horse. Every time they rode out in company Yvonne thanked Toby for being so good. It hadn't always been the case, and she couldn't have imagined riding alongside three others across an open field a few years ago, but after some intense practice with a handful of willing fellow livery owners, he had been a joy to ride out in company ever since. Charlotte's horse was a little excited at first, but it took them almost six minutes to reach the next field, and by then she had settled into a steady rhythm.

The sun was out of sight, but the sky behind them over Duncliffe Woods was spectacular, and they turned their horses around to face the view as the colours changed from fiery reds and orange to paler pinks within minutes.

'Come on, let's canter up this first field, and bring everyone back to a walk for the final field heading up to the road' suggested Sally.

As Sally and Charlotte's horses were used to going out together, everyone agreed that they should lead the canter, then Toby and Lindy's horse, Astrid, could set off together. If anyone's horse bolted everyone else would come back to a trot or walk as appropriate, if they could, but all four horses behaved as though they did this every day of the week, and by the end of the field they were riding in formation in canter up the hill together. It was no problem to bring everyone back to walk, in fact all the horses were offering it, and so the four of them walked up to the main road on a loose rein.

They hadn't needed to have any of their lights switched on, and even now they could see in the growing dusk without them, but everyone turned on their head torches and, because Charlotte's horse was still a little on her toes, it was Sally who dismounted to open and close the gate. Before doing so she walked around the back of each horse and carefully switched on their taillights. She handed the reins of her mare, Polly, to Charlotte and took a photograph of everyone from behind. Then she took back her horse, who had not moved an inch, opened the gate, and because the other three were high up sitting on their horses' backs they had a good view to check when the road was clear, just in case some dangerous silent electric vehicle drove by, and everyone crossed safely over to the other side where there was an easy horse gate to open. This time Yvonne did the honours, grateful for the tall handle designed for equestrians and which she could reach from 17.2hh (approximately one- hundred- and- seventy- eight centimetres tall) Toby, and she and Toby held it open while the other three walked through. A well-placed tree stump gave Sally the step up she needed to remount Polly, and still with their lights on the four horses and riders walked down the woodland track, with Yvonne and Toby leading the way.

Yvonne was familiar with the woods, but had never been there in the dark, not even on foot with Zebedee. She was surprised how peaceful it was, with just the sound of the horses' hooves padding on the earth and swish and creak of the saddles as the riders' bodies moved in rhythm with the horses'. The owls were noisy, calling and answering around them, and there were occasional rustles in the undergrowth either side of them. Suddenly two pairs of eyes were shining in the light of her headtorch and she gave a start, but they stayed motionless and Toby did not react. Feeling foolish when she realised they belonged to deer, Yvonne tried to shake off the tension which had shot back into her body. She jumped again when there was a shout behind her.

'Oh my god, I thought they were human!' laughed Lindy, who had also spotted the two deer.

They came to a T-junction as their track joined a main path, and although they could have ridden two abreast as it was at least three times as wide as the one they had walked down, everyone was content to follow one behind the other, with Charlotte and Sparkle bringing up the rear.

'We usually trot along here' Yvonne called back to the others. 'What do you think?'

'Yes, let's go for it' called back Sally. 'This section is clear of tree roots, so Toby should be able to see where he is going.'

With everyone else's agreement, Yvonne led the ride in trot for a few minutes, until they reached the part where the track began to slowly go uphill, fenced off to one side where there was an open field to their right, meaning there was more opportunity for the full moon to light their way. Someone suggested they canter, as they usually would in daylight, and as Yvonne thought everyone was in agreement she asked Toby forwards into a canter, mindful that his huge stride could cover the ground easily and perhaps cause the smaller horses behind to travel faster than was safe in the dark. She tried glancing back to check if everyone was alright, but was met with a glare of head and chest torches which blinded her. Guessing what she was doing, someone, maybe Lindy, yelled 'Keep going! This is great!' and a chorus of 'Keep going!' persuaded her all was well.

The track turned into a steep incline, so Yvonne let Toby move up a gear for the short distance until it levelled out again, where she asked him back into his steady canter. She realised there was a bit of a commotion off to the right, and looking towards the noise she could see a badger caught in the light of her head torch bounding along a tram line in the crop parallel to her and Toby. Seconds later it had disappeared, and as she continued to look across the field she could see five deer silhouetted, watching them.

She gradually brought the group back to a walk by using their usual signal of holding up one arm, and as they approached the next turn-off, she asked 'Does anyone else want to lead?'

'Can I have a go please?' asked Charlotte.

Yvonne, Sally and Lindy made sure their horses were over to the left so that Charlotte and Sparkle could trot past to the front. Sparkle had lost her eagerness to charge off, and Charlotte was having to ride her into the lead. Once there, Sparkle became quite spooky, and Charlotte decided that being in the front perhaps wasn't the best place for them to be.

'We'll try this another day, if that's alright with you' she said, as she asked Yvonne and Toby to re-take the lead, and Sparkle gratefully tucked in behind Toby's orange-lit bottom.

They turned onto the narrower woodland track, and walked in silence, each enjoying the experience with their horse. At the main road it was Charlotte who dismounted to be on gate duty, and after checking all was clear she and Sparkle led the group across to the metal double farm gate on the other side of the road, opened it wide for everyone, closed it, and used the gate to re-mount.

'I think that is the first time she has ever stood calmly next to a gate for me to mount from before!'

The full moon lit the fields in front of them, and everyone turned their lights off, leaving the horses' taillights on. The four of them walked back the way they had come, chatting as they did so, and admiring the landscape. The lights of distant hamlets, villages and towns were visible, but did not detract from their experience of riding in the moonlight. More deer could be seen, and owls could be heard, the occasional fox calling to her young, and sheep bleating to theirs. On the road behind them a car or lorry would go past, to remind them they were not far away from other people, but in the silence in between the traffic it was easy to believe they were the only ones awake.

'If you look over there, you can see the curve of Gold Hill picked out in the lights of the houses and the streetlights' said Lindy as she pointed to their right.

'Can you imagine if we rode up there one night' said Charlotte.

'I think we should! We could ride up there, down the High Street, down Great Lane, turn right to St James, past the bottom of Gold Hill and stop at the Two Brewers for supper, before riding back down the lanes' said Sally.

'I'm not sure I want to ride along those roads in the dark' said Yvonne.

'How about we organise a yard ride, at Halloween or Christmas or something, and we could have people walking with us. Not like yesterday's breakfast ride where we split into two groups, and the walkers took one route and we took another, but we all walk along together?' suggested Charlotte.

They had reached the last gate, so everyone dismounted, loosened their horses' girths a hole on each side, and walked the rest of the way back to the yard.

'I must admit, I am feeling two long rides in two days' said Yvonne, as she felt the tiredness in her legs.

'Me too' said Sally. 'Worth it though.'

'I think Sparkle is worn out!' said Charlotte, as she looked at her chestnut mare walking quietly alongside her, 'both mentally and physically. This has been a brilliant ride, thank you so much everyone.'

The yard's outside lights were on as they walked in, and the owner came out to greet them. 'Hello everyone, did you have a good time?'

They realised she had been worried about them, and they reassured her all was well. 'Maybe I'll come with you next time! There is some chilli left over from supper in the pot on the hob in the snug, if you're feeling peckish,' she said. 'Help yourselves.'

'Thank you!' they said, and as they watched her disappear through her garden gate, Lindy said 'and that is why I love it here.'

Within minutes the horses were untacked, their sweaty bits including where the girth, saddle and bridle had been given a wipe over with a wet sponge, feet checked for stones, and all turned back out with their mates.

'She's enjoying that' observed Charlotte, as Sparkle sank to her knees and proceeded to roll in the dry earth. As if on cue, the other three in their fields did the same.

Yvonne fetched the bag of bread, butter and cold chicken from her car, and joined the other three in the snug, where Sally was doling out the chilli into mismatched bowls. Charlotte had also brought food, and the four of them sat around the old wooden table eating chilli con carne with fresh bread, chicken sandwiches, and finishing up with cups of tea and small blueberry muffins.

'Did you make these' Lindy asked Charlotte.

'I did. I will admit to you all that these are left over from today, and as I can't sell them tomorrow I thought you wouldn't mind.'

Yvonne's ears pricked up 'Are you a baker?'

'Yes. Me and my mum have the bakery on Coppice Street.'

'I didn't know there was a bakery on Coppice Street,' said Yvonne, feeling foolish, since Coppice Street was the next road from Angel Lane. 'These are delicious.'

'We only opened last week, but we haven't advertised it or anything because we are still finding our feet. We started a home delivery company during the first Covid Lockdown, you know cream teas and mini sandwiches, pies and so on. Although the demand has dropped off now that people can go out to eat together, we have enough regular customers to keep going, and as the business was taking over my mum's house we decided to move into the building next to the hairdressers. It has been a nightmare trying to keep supplying our customers while getting the new building ready, but my dad and husband have been brilliant, and we had our grand opening last week.'

170

'I am so sorry! I missed seeing any of this going on' said Lindy.

'Don't worry! We haven't really told anyone, and there were only the four of us at our opening. It was eight o'clock at night, dad had finished painting the last windowsill, and my husband had wired in the big oven, so we opened a bottle of fizz and bought in fish and chips from up the road. That was our grand opening' she laughed.

Yvonne said 'Would you be able to make a wedding cake for less than two weeks' time?'

'Two weeks!' exclaimed Charlotte. 'There must be a story behind that. Wait a minute, I didn't know you were getting married?'

'No, no, not me!' laughed Yvonne. 'Friends of mine have been having a difficult time with their wedding plans. We're not really sure what has happened but suffice to say they had everything booked at Kenyon Hall, and now it has fallen through.'

'I had heard there were a few problems at Kenyon Hall' said Charlotte. 'Give them my number and I'll have a chat to see what they would like. I am sure we can work something out, but I need to hear what they would like before I agree to do anything.'

'Kenyon Hall is my uncles' and cousins' business' said Lindy. 'What's this about there being some problems?'

Yvonne was careful about what she said, not wanting to spread rumours or unjustly damage a family business. 'You know Tabitha Leighton and Alison Jones were getting married there?'

'Yes, I'm invited to their wedding. What has happened?'

'It's a long story' said Yvonne, 'but there are supply problems up there. Tabitha and Alison have had to move their wedding somewhere else.'

171

'Tell us more?' Sally urged. 'I was invited too.'

'And me!' said Charlotte. 'What's going on?'

While everyone finished eating, Yvonne told them some of what she knew, mindful that Lindy's family were involved with the issues at Kenyon Hall, and the jewellery. She would like to know what was going on too!

Chapter 16

It was midnight by the time Yvonne drove back into Shaftesbury, and rather than going straight home, she parked on Salisbury Street outside the butchers, and walked around the corner up to Charlotte's new bakery. The signwriter hadn't started work yet, and other than a notice on the door with opening times and contact details, there was nothing to indicate that a new business, let alone a bakery, was there. Feeling slightly better that she hadn't noticed, and relieved that the wedding cake situation had been satisfactorily resolved, she walked back down the hill and up Angel Lane. She had purposefully left some lights on inside the shop and her home and was pleased to see that from the outside it looked as though the building was occupied, but no one could see through the windows.

'Yvonne? Are you alright?' a voice out of the darkness made her jump. The streetlights had gone off for the night, and she hadn't noticed Tom and his dog Stan walking up the road.

'Bloody hell Tom!' she shouted in a whisper. 'You scared the fucking life out of me!'

Tom looked a bit shocked at her outburst, but she didn't apologise. What the hell was he doing here at this time of night?

'Sorry, sorry' he whispered. 'I've just come off duty, and I can never go straight to sleep, so me and Stan have a

173

little walk around the roads for half an hour or so. It's lovely out here at night, with no one else about.'

'Well, I'm about' said Yvonne, crossly.

'What are you doing out here?'

Yvonne's mind went blank. How could she explain what she was doing?

After a few awkward seconds inspiration struck, and she said 'Did you know we had a new bakery in town? I have heard it is somewhere round here, but I can't see it.'

'Yes, it's around the corner' said Tom. 'Come on, we'll show you.'

Together, the three of them walked the few steps back the way Yvonne had just come.

'There it is,' Tom pointed to the non-descript building. 'They haven't put any signs up yet, because they are still settling in, but I have tasted the donuts and they are delicious.'

'That's not stereotypical for a member of the police service at all' teased Yvonne.

'Ha ha, no, not all. I was impressed, because they were made with proper raspberry jam; none of this apple sauce or caramel nonsense. Isn't that your car?' he said, spotting Yvonne's car on the road.

'Yes, yes it is. I parked it there while I looked around.' Yvonne was feeling unreasonably guilty, and was sure she was blushing, but hoped it was too dark for Tom to see. 'Thanks for that, it's always good to be able to support a new business. I'd better be heading home now and let my dog out for a wee before bed. Bye Tom, bye Stan.'

Yvonne drove her car the short distance to her gates, waited until they were closed before she got out, and ran up the wooden staircase to let Zebedee out. She sat down in the area on the balcony she called the Tree House, on a swing seat and looked across the carpark and at the roofs of the nearby buildings, while her dog pottered around in the small garden below. There was no traffic noise, and she wondered if it was the first time that she couldn't hear any cars or lorries whilst sitting there, and no other background noises. Yvonne didn't think she ever sat down in complete silence. In her home there was always the buzz of the fridge, or the sounds of people and traffic on the road outside, or the noise of dealers and customers in the shop next door. When she was with Toby on one of their early morning rides she often revelled in the quietness of their surroundings, but while out on a hack there was always the sound of the horse's hooves as he walked along roads or tracks, inevitable traffic noise, birds, sheep, cows, airplanes from the nearby airfield or military aircraft flying to or from the many bases in the area.

The tap tap tap of Zebedee's claws on the wooden stairs broke her reverie, and she eased herself into a standing position. Ohhh she ached!

'Come on puppy, let's go inside.'

Soon the bath was running, and she poured herself a glass of water to drink. The exhilaration of the ride, and all that food and chat afterwards, had given her a thirst. She set the jacuzzi jets and luxuriated in the pummelling on all the sore spots on her body, contorting herself into some strange positions to get the best access to the water massage. Eventually she turned off the jacuzzi, put on an audio book, and sank back into the water, resolving to listen to one chapter.

Three chapters later she forced herself to get out of the rapidly cooling water, dried herself, cleaned her teeth, pulled on a cute t-shirt and shorts pyjama set in pale pink with white hearts, and curled up in her bed with her snoring dog beside her.

Too soon she was woken by a text, from Tim. It was one minute past seven o'clock in the morning. 'More news on jewellery. Message me when you're up.'

Again, Yvonne felt that shiver of unease. How did he know she was still in bed? On a normal day she would be out with Zebedee or Toby by now. And surely the police didn't privately message people? This was hardly an emergency, and she was meant to be coming to the police station that afternoon to talk about the jewellery.

Yvonne carefully got out of bed, searching for and finding aches and pains as she did so. She smiled as she remembered the fun she had acquiring them. She and Toby deserved a day off today, but she would go over later and give him a good brush, to make sure no rubs or sores were developing after two long rides two days in a row. She needed to move around, and so she messaged George.

'Are you free for breakfast? Feel the need to dine out.'

By the time she had washed and dressed – denim shorts and loose flowery blouse, hair tied back in a scarf today – there was a reply 'Starving. Just got back from a run. Meet at café at 8?'

Yvonne groaned at the thought of running. She did not see the attraction. 'See you there.'

She then replied to Tim 'I'm up. Kettle's on. Come to gates.' That would give them half an hour, and a way out if he was up to no good, because George would be texting, and would come looking for her if she didn't turn up. He wouldn't be able to get in through the gates, but at least he'd make a commotion outside, and attract other people's attention. She didn't seriously think Tim was going to murder her in her kitchen, but she wasn't comfortable with the attention she was getting.

By the time she and Zebedee had run down the spiral stairs, Tim was already pressing the buzzer at the gates. A

176

quick glance at the monitor to confirm it was him, and Yvonne pressed the button to open them. She unlocked the back door to let Zebedee out and Tim in and left the door open so Zebedee could come in when she was ready, and also in case George needed to scale the gates, which would automatically close behind Tim. She had a feeling this last reason was unlikely, but Tom's unexpected appearance last night, and now Tim's out-of-the-ordinary message this morning, were making her uneasy.

Yvonne wasn't feeling particularly sociable, so she just asked 'Tea or coffee?'

'Coffee please. Thank you, Yvonne. Sorry to bother you so early.'

'No problem,' she lied.

While the coffee was brewing, she fed Zebedee, and made a cup of tea for herself. Tim made himself useful by putting a couple of mugs on the table, and fetching the milk from the fridge, before sitting at the table with the jug of coffee. Yvonne wasn't sure she liked this over-familiarity, after all for several years he had never been any further than the counter in the antiques shop, and although a regular tea and cake consumer when he did come in, always with Tom, he had been served his drink by herself or Rob or one of the other dealers, and had never washed up the mugs or helped to clear away. What had been pleasing from George was intrusive from Tim. But it did mean she didn't have to make small talk with him.

When she could no longer delay, she sat down at the table with her tea, and waited.

'Mmmh, good coffee, thank you. Have you heard anything more about the jewellery?'

'No, I thought you were here to tell me something new?'

'Yes, I am. I was just checking. I'm sorry but we'll have to cancel your visit this afternoon. I'll admit, I don't know what is going on, but the jewellery was removed from our station by some officials during the night. Obviously no one was on duty there, because it closes at six o'clock in the evening, and hasn't opened yet, but the cleaners went in at half-past six this morning and found the official notice stating what had happened on the internal door. They contacted my superintendent, who contacted me.'

'What officials?' asked Yvonne, now intrigued rather than suspicious.

'Some serious crime bods, I'm sorry I don't know exactly who.'

'Can they do that? Surely they must speak to someone at the station. They can't just break in and take anything they want?'

'Unfortunately for us they can. Or at least they have the keys and alarm codes, so no breaking in was necessary. The pictures or descriptions must have been flagged somewhere and triggered this action. We are no longer investigating the jewellery.'

'What! What's happening then?'

Tim shrugged his shoulders 'I'm sorry, I do not know. All I know is that we have been taken off the investigation and have been told to get back to our normal local policing duties.'

'That's mad. What about me and George? Are these new people likely to want to talk to us?'

'Again, I don't know. Possibly they will, but it will depend on what they already know. I am sorry not to be more helpful, but this is how they treat us. Like mushrooms' he grinned.

Yvonne wasn't in the mood. 'I'm seeing George in a minute, so I'll let him know. Do you know if the body has been identified yet?'

'It still hasn't been officially confirmed, but we are working on the assumption it is that of Jane Poundsmith, and as she wasn't local to this area we are no longer involved in that investigation.'

'But surely the two things are linked, and they were both found here? You must be curious?'

'Oh, I am more than curious' Tim briefly let his frustration show, before returning to the professional policeman she was used to dealing with. 'Anyway, there is no more I can do, and the people who have taken over the investigation will be privy to far more information than I am. I just wanted to tell you myself, because you were the person who discovered the crime scene in the field and have been very helpful. Are you OK? That body was not a pleasant thing to see.'

Yvonne appreciated his concern and fiddled with her empty mug as she wondered whether to tell him. She decided it was time, but stayed looking at the mug in her hands. 'I am fine, honestly. It is not the first dead body I have seen as the result of a brutal attack, although at least I was expecting to find the first one.'

She looked up in time to see him nod, and in that instant she knew he was fully aware of her past.

Smoothly, Tim said 'Shock can play funny tricks with us, so if you ever want to talk about it, it doesn't matter what time of the day or night, just text me. If I can't talk, you know because I've drunk too much or am diving for treasure off Old Harry's Rocks, then I will get back to you as soon as I can. I promise.'

179

He held her gaze for several seconds, before standing up and reaching over for her mug, and washing everything up in the sink.

'Go and enjoy your breakfast' he said with a smile and left the room.

Yvonne sat at her kitchen table for several minutes, running over old memories and wondering how a young local policeman like Tim Smith would know about the gruesome discovery she had made almost twenty years before.

She had been born into a family of antiques dealers. Her mother's father and grandfather had run a pawn broker's business, with shops all over England. Her father's father had worked for them, and then branched out into house clearances and junk shops. When her parents married it was as though the whole of the second-hand market in London, Sussex and Surrey was combined. They met at an auction house in London, where her dad was a porter, and her mum was working for a year gaining experience after completing a degree in antiques and fine arts. Both came from large families, and Yvonne had grown up with numerous uncles and aunts, cousins and second cousins, as well as her own five siblings. These days she occasionally saw one brother and his family because his wife had been her friend before falling in love with her brother, and they had remained good friends, and although one sister had moved to Norway so they didn't see each other, they kept in touch online. But ever since she had found her cousin, the son of her mother's brother, lying in the antiques shop he and his wife ran, with his head caved in, she had withdrawn from all other members of the family. Her cousin was not the first in her family to die in brutal circumstances, but his was the first death to be caused at the hands of another member of the family.

The fallout had been enormous. The families fractured, the businesses broke up, thousands of people were financially affected as the supply of antiques, vintage goods, and junk came to an abrupt halt. The shops, auctions and fairs on which people's livelihoods relied disappeared. Trust was destroyed.

Yvonne had moved away, changed her name in all but official documents, and laid low for years. Although fresh in her mind, particularly on days like today, the events had died away from the public's awareness. Many of the people involved had died, whether through so-called natural causes, at their own hands or at the hands of others. Some were still in prison. Others had been released and come out to find their social landscape had changed which suited some, but left others desperately trying to recreate the good old days of violence and intimidation.

A text on her phone reminded her she was meant to be somewhere. Quickly she typed 'So sorry, got held up. On way now. 2 minutes. Mine's a tea and sausage bap.'

'Cheeky' she grinned at Zebedee 'but I don't think he'll mind. Come on pup, we'd better get a move on!'

It took less than a minute for them to reach the café, and as they walked through to the tearoom at the back Yvonne hesitated for a moment. George was sitting at a table for two in the window, in the beautiful summer sun shining in through the open window. He really was very good looking! Before he could sense her staring, she urged Zebedee forward, who didn't need telling twice.

'Hello Zebedee!' he made a fuss of the dog, before standing up and giving her a gentle kiss on her cheek. A broad smile spread across her face, and she busied herself with sitting down and arranging Zebedee at her feet under the table so she couldn't reach other customers and beg from them.

181

'I've placed our order' he said, as the large, flowered teapot with matching cups and a miniature milk bottle-shaped jug arrived. The jug had the name of the local dairy on it, and George had also ordered both a glass of blood orange juice. 'I'll have yours if you don't like it.'

'No, I love this juice. It's my favourite,' she said, taking a sip. 'Sorry I was late but wait until I tell you who I have been speaking to.'

Mindful there were other people in the room, Yvonne and George leant in closer so they could talk in low voices.

'I have just had a visit from Tim Smith, and he told me the local police are no longer investigating either the murder or the stolen jewellery.'

'That doesn't surprise me,' shrugged George. 'It is a serious crime, both of them are, not just the murder. Our local police force does not have the capacity or experience to deal with it.'

'But surely the local police should still be involved? After all the woman was murdered in Tabitha's field, and the jewellery was left there too? Only someone with a local connection could know about that field?'

'Not necessarily. It has a public footpath running through it, and gates at either end big enough for vehicles to drive through. Anyone involved in hare coursing probably knows about it.'

'Do you think so?' Yvonne was horrified.

'Of course. It is the last of Tabitha's fields and leads through to the arable field belonging to the next farm along. And every year those crops get damaged by vandals.'

Yvonne shook her head 'I had never connected that with hare coursing. I always thought it was idiots making crop circles.' She shivered. 'I like to think we are in a cosy relatively crime-free area here, but I am having to reassess.'

'We are in a relatively crime-free area,' George tried to reassure her, 'and although the murder did take place in the field I can't imagine any of the people involved are local, can you? That makes a difference, you know.'

'I hadn't thought of it like that' said Yvonne, feeling better. George really was a lovely man.

Their breakfasts arrived and while they ate, George told her about the plans for Tabitha and Alison's wedding.

'They came back last night to double-check a few things, and I must have given them the right answers because they have booked their wedding with us. I am pleased for Lesley and her crew, because Tabitha and Alison are local businesswomen, with families here, and so not only do they understand the challenges of working in this area, but if all goes well, as I am sure it will, they will be great promotors for the catering team.'

'That reminds me, I must text them and tell them I have sorted the wedding cake problem.' Yvonne stopped eating long enough to search in her handbag for her phone and type a WhatsApp message to the wedding group. A flurry of celebration, cake and thumbs up emojis appeared before she resumed eating.

'Who did you find to make it?' asked George.

'One of the girls I was riding with last night has opened a bakery opposite the post office, and she said she'll do it. It is who you know in this life that matters' she grinned and winked at him.

'What bakery?'

'That's what I said! She and her mum have been running a small business from home since the first lockdown, but the business has kept going, unlike so many others once everyone started to get back to "normal" life, and they decided they couldn't allow it to take over the house anymore. She happened to mention it to her hairdresser, who told her the business premises next door was available, and it all went from there.'

'That is useful to know. I'll tell Lesley in case they can work together in future. Out of interest, does Tim often drop in when the shop is closed?'

'No, he has never done it before, he must have really wanted to let me know what was going on' said Yvonne, and was just about to tell George about her unexpected encounter with Tom the previous evening before realising that George wasn't thinking about the investigation, because there was a hint of jealousy in his voice. Putting that to the back of her mind to mull over when she was alone, she said 'it's funny, but both Tom and Tim keep popping up unexpectedly at the moment. I don't think I have ever seen so much of the pair of them, even when you add up all their coffee breaks in the shop! I probably won't see either of them for weeks now the investigation has been taken away from them.'

'Mmmh' said George, as he lay down his knife and fork and making an obvious change of subject. 'That was delicious. What are you doing for the rest of the day?'

'I have some shop work to do, I think I had better catch up with the girls about how the wedding plans are now coming together, and I need to spend some time cleaning tack and grooming Toby, and taking Zebedee for a good long walk. What about you?'

'Ditto with the restaurant work, although everything seems to be running smoothly and going to plan we all know what happens when you get complacent. I have a good team working with me now, and it is great to see they are as passionate about our business as I am. They are working very hard, so I am planning a Thank You for them after Tabitha and Alison's wedding.'

'Oooh what are you going to do?'

'I thought maybe we could hire a minibus and driver and go to somewhere like Marwell or Longleat for the day.'

'That sounds like fun! I have never been to either of them.' Yvonne wondered what an antiques dealers' outing would look like. Probably a trip to antiques fairs at Ardingly or Newark.

George walked Yvonne home, and again he gave her a gentle kiss on the cheek when they said goodbye. Although they hadn't made plans for their next meeting, Yvonne was sure it wouldn't be too long.

Chapter 17

Yvonne spent a couple of hours in her office catching up on admin for the antiques shop, and when she emerged the place was quiet. She and Zebedee wandered through the rooms until she found the dealer who was in charge that day, William Drake, studying one of the stands selling antique linen.

'Morning William, this isn't your usual interest' she teased.

'Ha, no, but my wife is after a pretty tablecloth for an occasional table we have in our sitting room, and I wondered if one of these would be suitable.'

Together they pulled one out, studied and refolded several prospective purchases, before William chose an Irish linen tablecloth, decorated with lace and embroidery. He took a photo of it and messaged his wife, who replied 'Perfect'.

'That was easy!' he said, as he and Yvonne made their way back to the counter so he could pay. 'Before mobile phones I would not have been allowed to make a purchase on my own, but would have had to spend many days over several weeks trailing around shopping centres in the area trying to find the exact one.'

Yvonne laughed at his expression. 'I should think your wife feels the same.'

'What is happening with Marion? I haven't seen her for weeks, and her stand is looking neglected too. Is she on a cruise again?'

'I don't know where she has gone, but she was due back by now. She usually does let me know if she's not going to be here for a while, but not this time. To be honest I am getting a little worried about her. I will contact her and check she is alright.'

'That is a good idea' he said. 'I don't know of any friends or family. Is she married?'

'I don't know. Although she is always lovely when she comes in, I don't think she has any particular friends amongst our dealers, and I don't remember her mentioning any children or a partner. I think I will give her stand a bit of a clean and tidy up now, because you are right, it is looking a mess.'

'I'll give you a hand' said William, as he headed off to the cupboard next to the kitchen where the vacuum cleaner and bucket of polish and dusters were kept. Most dealers brought their own cleaning equipment in with them, because everyone had a preferred pot of cleaner or wax polish, but Yvonne liked to keep a supply handy so there were no excuses for an untidy display which could reflect badly on the rest of the shop. Between them they cleaned and tidied Marion's stand, including taking everything off the bookcase in one corner and giving the ornaments, plates and books a wipe to remove the dust which had accumulated. William also set to work in the display cabinet, which did not need dusting because of its locked doors, but there were relatively large expanses of bare shelves and he rearranged the contents so it looked attractive again, and he gave Juliette's stand the once over with the duster too. William then took on the task of vacuuming the rest of the shop's carpet while Yvonne gave the general counter area a good clean. It was the practice of everyone to tidy the worktops, and clean with an anti-bacterial spray the computer screen and keyboard, telephone, and surfaces as part of their closing up routine, ensuring the communal work area always looked appealing. Yvonne pulled everything out including the screen, loose pieces of paper, the shop's A4 diary, and numerous pens and washed the counter, before drying it all with a clean tea towel, and wiping all the pens and scissors and other random stationary which had appeared in the 'Life is better when you're an antiques dealer' mug. She discovered three staplers, although no boxes of staples, and wondered when she had last stapled anything, and an opened bag of mint humbugs which had stuck together.

The door opened with its welcoming bell, and three women came in. Yvonne recognised them as locals, and after a brief exchange of greetings she left them to browse. She could still hear the vacuum running, and guessed William would stop when they reached the room he was working in. Sure enough, while she was checking the surfaces were completely dry and replacing almost everything back in its place, she heard the noise stop, and then the sound of William reeling in the cable.

'I almost reached this room,' he said as he walked past carrying the vacuum cleaner. 'I'll finish it before I go tonight, but I'll leave Rob's space alone. I am sure he wouldn't appreciate it if I tried to vacuum in there.'

Yvonne laughed. 'I don't think running a vacuum cleaner around in amongst the automobilia would make much difference to the general appearance of the garage. Thank you, William. Between us we have done a good job in here today.'

'I have made a ham and tomato quiche for lunch. In fact, I made two, but there doesn't seem to be anyone else here today, so I'll leave the second one with you if you like. It will last for a few days in your fridge.'

That's very kind of you, thank you William. I'll make us a salad to go with it.'

The rest of the day continued in a similar relaxed and productive way, with a rush of customers after three o'clock who all bought something and allowed William to excel in his customer service persona, and then no one else came through the doors until they decided to close at five o'clock.

Yvonne's phone had been busy with positive messages between the four women about Tabitha and Alison's wedding, and the two brides-to-be had already met Charlotte and her mum, and everyone was happy with the plans for the wedding cake.

Yvonne changed into a faded red polo shirt, cargo shorts with plenty of useful pockets for horse treats and hoof pick, socks and paddock boots, and together with Zebedee drove the short distance to the yard to see Toby. It was a gorgeous warm and sunny evening, and several people were around. Yvonne collected her grooming kit from the tack room and walked with her dog down the track to Toby's herd. He stayed where he was when she arrived, and so she brushed his coat and mane and tail where he stood, occasionally fending off interested noses from his field mates. Zebedee drank deeply from one of the water troughs, and then settled down to sunbathe alongside one of the wooden shelters. By the time she had finished grooming him Toby didn't look much different to when she started, but she still felt satisfied with her efforts. One of the other livery owners was walking down with her horse to return him to the paddock after a schooling session in the menage, and they chatted for a bit as they watched him have a roll in the dry sandy soil, and then the

189

herd of eight horses decided silently to walk out into the field together and away from them.

Once home Yvonne took a quick shower to wash away the grime from the antiques shop and her horse, had a light supper of quiche and salad, not minding at all that it was the same meal she had eaten for lunch, and then headed for bed before the sun had gone down completely.

She slept soundly but was wide awake just before five o'clock. After a few minutes of discussion with herself because her bed was comfy, she decided to get up and take Zebedee for a long walk. They went through town to Tout Hill, along to Breach Lane, and spent a happy half an hour wandering along the paths on Breach Common, enjoying the countryside and peacefulness, ignoring the traffic noise on the nearby A30. By the time they crossed over to St James' the rest of the world had woken up, and speeding drivers on their way to work broke the calm of the morning. They walked along the road past houses where the occupants were still asleep, a few other early morning dog walkers, and several individual runners, until they reached the bottom of Gold Hill. Yvonne marched briskly up the cobbles and turned back at the top to enjoy the view which was particularly spectacular in the early morning sunrise. It also gave her a chance to catch her breath. They continued up the steps past the church and came out on the High Street.

'Good morning Yvonne!' a voice called out.

Yvonne looked around, but although there were now several people walking either with or without dogs, she could not identify the person who had called to her.

'I'm up here!'

The sound was coming from a building opposite, and looking up Yvonne saw George holding a mug in his hands, and leaning out of a window three storeys up. He waved, and she waved back.

'Do you want one?' he asked, holding up the mug.

'Yes please!' she called.

'Hang on, and I'll let you in.'

Yvonne looked around for a small staff door on either side of the restaurant but couldn't see any, and waited for George to open one. The sound of several locks could be heard, and George opened the main doors to the restaurant. 'Come on in' he said. He was wearing navy blue chino shorts and a light blue t-shirt and looked gorgeous with his smiling brown eyes and dark brown hair still damp from the shower. Yvonne was suddenly aware that she was sweating in the surprising heat of the early morning after her march up Gold Hill. She hoped her white t-shirt didn't reveal the perspiration but had a feeling it probably did. They walked through the first part of the restaurant and George opened the door into the kitchen, which almost filled the middle of the long room, and divided it into two parts accessible to each other via a corridor with a floor-to-ceiling mural of local scenes on one side and an enormous fish tank on the other. Yvonne had never seen this part of the restaurant before and was struck by how clean and sparkling the empty work surfaces were. Between the fridges and freezers and the sinks was another door, and George held it open for her to go through. A plain staircase ran up to the next floor, but George said 'keep going up!'

Yvonne and Zebedee continued up the next flight of stairs, lit by a glass atrium another flight up.

'She'll be fine off the lead' said George. 'She can't get into the restaurant.'

Yvonne unclipped her lead, and Zebedee was off exploring. They were standing in an enormous room, with a large kitchen area to the left, obviously spanning a similar area to the restaurant's kitchen but with floor-to-ceiling slate-grey cupboards, a black range-style cooker, a double sink along the wall, and an island topped with a black marble-effect surface with golden flecks in the middle. Beyond the kitchen area was a large glass oval dining table with eight chairs around it, and floor-to-ceiling windows with a similar covering to the street scene downstairs in the restaurant, but instead of showing Shaftesbury through history, this one depicted a calm seascape with rocks and cliffs on either side and the horizon in the distance with the sun either rising or setting, its rays laying a golden path towards it.

'There you go' said George, having opened one of the cupboards and producing a dog bowl. He filled it with water, and placed it in front of Zebedee, who drank as though she had been left without water for days.

'She was thirsty' observed George.

'We have been out for a while' explained Yvonne, glancing at her watch and seeing it was now half-past six.

'What would you like? Tea, coffee, juice?'

'A coffee would be lovely, thank you' said Yvonne, who had been able to smell the delicious blend he was drinking since she had walked up the stairs. She noticed a travel bag on the floor. 'Are you going somewhere?'

'Yes, I'm off to Ireland for a couple of days, to meet up with Jim Mack. Have a seat' George gestured to her right, and she saw there was another table, this time a small square wooden table in front of the window George must have seen her from.

She walked over and looked out of the bay window. 'Wow, you can see everything from here! Look at that, the town hall looks totally different from this angle. There are the tops of the houses all the way down to Tabitha's fields, and you can see Toby's livery yard!'

'Can you?' he asked, coming to stand next to her. 'Where's that?'

'You see the farm buildings over to the right of the waterworks?'

'Yes, I see them'

'Those are the house and the stable yard. Spanning away from them in a fan-shape are the four sections of the fields where the horses live. You see? The one on the left runs alongside the driveway and is for horses and ponies who cannot tolerate grass at any time of the year. It is all hardcore, sand and woodchip tracks, with a section at the end which was grass, but is now either mud or bare earth. The next three are all grass, except for where those shelters are, can you see? They are fenced in so that the horses can be kept off the grass during the day and live on the same type of surfaces as the end section, but then in the evening the gates are opened so that they can access several acres of grass at night.'

'I thought horses ate grass? What's the point of that?'

'Horses are not designed to eat the types of grass land we have in this area' explained Yvonne. 'If you think about it the countryside we can see from here is all farmland, and most of it is or has been dairy farmland. The types of nutrition dairy cows need are very different to those of horses who are foragers and browsers. You think about the grazing available to an Exmoor pony compared to a horse living in a field around Shaftesbury. An Exmoor pony has many miles to move, for one thing, with a variety of surfaces under their hooves. They have gorse, moorland, heathland, bogs, heather, trees and hedges to nibble on, and ancient lanes and hedges to shelter in and behind. Compare that to putting a horse or pony on an acre of ryegrass, with a post and rail fence probably with a strand or two of electric tape running along it. No diversity of nutrition. No access to bark or anything other than grass. No natural shelter, and in many cases no man-made shelter either. No variety of surfaces. By creating the living areas in the way they have, the owners of Toby's livery yard have created a healthy environment for our horses to live in.'

George said 'I had no idea keeping horses was so complicated. My mum used to keep her horses in a field at the back of our house during the day, bring them in at night, and that was it. Other than the hours of poo-picking we all had to do. Mmmh, smell that? I popped some rolls in the oven to warm-up.'

In no time Yvonne was sitting at a table in the sunshine, overlooking the Blackmore Vale, drinking coffee and eating warm cinnamon rolls, with a man she liked very much indeed.

Glancing around the room, she wondered where he slept, and what his bedroom looked like. So far everything she could see was to her approval, even if it wasn't exactly to her taste. Seeing her looking around he said 'If you need the bathroom it's upstairs, next to my bedroom.'

Oh, the humiliation! She didn't know which was worse: George assuming she needed a wee, or George reading her thoughts about his bed.

'Thank you, but I'm fine. No, I was just thinking this is a large space. I don't think I have ever looked up above the ground floor of these buildings.'

'It is far too big for one person, but I have got used to having my own space.'

'I know what you mean; I can't imagine living with someone again. I love having my bathroom to myself, and my bed to myself. Except for having to share my bed with Zebedee, but at least when she hogs the duvet or starts snoring I can kick her off the bed.'

They laughed, and Yvonne felt as though they had engaged in an important conversation about their future, without any awkwardness.

'Come on, I'll show you the upstairs if you like. If you think the view is good from here, wait until you see the view from upstairs.'

Together they cleared the table, and George popped their cups and plates in the dishwasher hidden under the island. Then he led the way up the stairs to the next floor. This space was approximately a third of those of the rooms downstairs and was decorated in a clean blue and white. The bedroom and bathroom were one room, which was a little disconcerting in Yvonne's view, but then she didn't have to live with it. The room was light thanks to the atrium above and the narrow long window on the back wall over the bath.

'Come and look at this' said George and opened one of the two small casement windows at the front.

Yvonne came and stood next to him. The windows were chest-height, but she was able to see the view for miles below them. 'Wow, this is what you wake up to every morning! I have a carpark and roof tops' she laughed.

'We do live in a beautiful area' he said.

They stood at the window for several minutes, discussing various places they could see, and some they couldn't. When they eventually turned away Yvonne let out a yelp 'Zebedee, no!'

Zebedee was stretched out, apparently sleeping peacefully in the middle of George's bed, the wide blue and white horizontal stripes of the duvet were of varying widths and at the point she was lying they were thick and blue surrounding her white body. Her dog opened one eye, and then closed it again.

'Off off off' said Yvonne, climbing onto the bed to push her to the floor. 'I am so sorry' said Yvonne, as she desperately tried to straighten the duvet, and check for white dog hairs on the cover.

George stood and laughed 'Don't worry! It's not a problem. At least she is comfortable here. It means you can come over for dinner one evening with her or come and have another early morning breakfast.'

Yvonne was practically lying across his bed and couldn't look at him; the whole thing was too embarrassing. It was a long time since she was in any kind of intimate relationship with a man, and she didn't know if he was hinting at something, or just being friendly. Part of her wanted to be in the bed with him; part of her wanted to run away as fast as she could. What had been an easy relaxed time together had suddenly become fraught with social traps. She could feel her cheeks burning.

'Come on you' she said to Zebedee, before turning to George. 'Thank you so much for breakfast, and again, I am really sorry about your bed.'

Chapter 18

The next Saturday evening was Tabitha and Alison's hen party. Scott had Alison's children for the weekend, and as neither Tabitha nor Alison wanted to go out of Shaftesbury, nor have the type of party where male strippers and tiaras were in evidence, they chose to have a couple of drinks in The Shaston with anyone who wanted to join them, and then go back to Yvonne's house for the remainder of the evening. Maisie had made a lamb curry which she brought around to Yvonne's before the party started, and the two of them walked up to The Shaston together, passing TAA as they went. Yvonne managed not to look in, but Maisie did, and said 'Oh there's George!'

Of course Yvonne had to look, and wave too, or it would have been odd. There he was, sitting at a table in the window with two young women and two young men. He waved, holding her gaze as he did so. She smiled, he smiled back, and all the embarrassment she had been feeling since they last saw each other evaporated. She wondered if those young people were his children.

Maisie and Yvonne were the first to arrive at The Shaston and were already sitting down with their drinks when Tabitha and Alison came in, followed by the other hairdressers and beauticians from Alison's salon, the farmhands from Tabitha's farm, and over the next hour assorted friends and neighbours. At one point it seemed that everyone in The Shaston was celebrating Tabitha and

197

Alison's hen party, and that was when George appeared. Yvonne spotted him as soon as he walked through the door, and he was miming 'did she want a drink' before she could pretend she hadn't seen him. She shook her head and raised her half-full glass so he could see she had one. She didn't know why she was behaving so awkwardly and was beginning to get annoyed with herself. She lost sight of him for a while, and when she next saw him he was in a corner with Tabitha and Alison, their three heads together indicating they were planning something.

'Hello Yvonne, how are you?' Tim Smith was now standing next to her.

'Oh hi Tim. I'm fine thank you. Are you here to wish the happy couple a fun hen night, or just popped in for a drink?'

'I'm here with my wife and some friends. We're waiting for our table. It is certainly popular in here tonight.'

'It should get calmer in a moment because I think we're about to leave' said Yvonne as Maisie beckoned to her from the door. She could see Tabitha and Alison were already walking outside, and a quick glance failed to reveal where George was. She wanted to ask him how his trip had been. Ireland was one of the few countries she had not visited, and she was thinking it would be a good place to have a short holiday in the Autumn. To Tim she said 'That's it, we're off. Have a good evening!'

'Thank you, and you too.'

Yvonne weaved her way through the crowd and joined her friends outside. The four of them walked along Bell Street, past the black gates closing off the courtyard.

'I still find it incredible that an amazing space is behind those gates' said Maisie. 'Even though I now know it exists, you would never know from here would you?'

'It makes you wonder what else is behind the various doorways and gates we pass every day' agreed Alison. 'Look at this door. It appears to be the front door to the terraced house, but how do we know how big the house is? Is it divided into flats? Is it offices? A government agency?'

'Blimey, what have you been drinking!' laughed Tabitha. 'Don't start going all conspiracy theorist on us!'

'Wait until we get onto the subject of the tunnels!' grinned Alison.

'What tunnels?' asked Yvonne.

'Have you really never heard about the tunnels that run underneath our town?' asked Alison.

'No!'

'Oh yes, a lot of these buildings have basements and cellars with openings into tunnels. Attempts have been made to explore them, but nothing has ever come of it. I think there are too many engineering challenges due to roof falls and blockages.'

'What were they built for?'

'I don't think anyone knows. Rumours range from they were escape routes for the nuns in the Abbey, to transport routes for provisions from one end of town to the other.'

'My building has a cellar but I haven't really explored it.'

'Let's do that now!' exclaimed Tabitha.

They had arrived at Yvonne's gates which she opened, and they went in through the shop's back door. Yvonne led the way through the shop around to the end room, where she put her shoulder to one side of a freestanding bookcase which stood at an angle in the corner and moved it further away from the wall. In doing so she revealed a small door behind it.

'Follow me' she grinned and unlocked the door.

Giggling, the women followed her around the back of the bookcase and through the open door.

'Where are we going?' asked Alison.

'Down to the cellar. I did come down here when I first bought the building' Yvonne explained 'but I have had no need to come back since then. Here's the light switch.'

The four friends followed each other down the uneven stone steps and into a room with a low curved ceiling.

'Wow, this would make a perfect wine cellar' said Maisie.

'Wine never lasts long enough in my house to store it in a cellar' laughed Yvonne.

'This would make a perfect locked room' said Tabitha as she looked around the space. 'You know, one of those adventures people pay good money to do.'

'Well let's not get locked in here' said Alison, as she ran back up the steps and pulled a small chair from the room above to hold open the door.

'Thank you, that was a good idea' said Yvonne. 'Here is the door I was thinking of. It must lead to underneath the carpark. The estate agent opened it for me when I was viewing the property, but I don't remember it having a lock on it. I wonder where the key is?'

'Is that the original door do you think?' asked Alison. 'It doesn't fit very well, does it. Look at these gaps all the way round. You can see where an extra bit has been added on down the side so that there is something for the lock to slide into.'

'Here, let me have a look and see if I can find the key' Tabitha took the bunch of keys from Yvonne and methodically held the keys up one by one.

Yvonne said 'Front door, also front door, my kitchen, my upstairs door, back door, garage door, and the door into the cellar. That's it. There are no more keys.'

The four of them studied the locked door in front of them.

'That is a modern lock' observed Maisie. 'It is newer than the one on the door at the top of the steps.'

'It isn't brand new though is it?' said Yvonne. 'It's been there a while. Perhaps the estate agent forgot to add the key to that bunch with the rest of them. I doubt they still have it after all this time.'

'You know, I can get that door open' offered Tabitha. 'It's easy to do. It will damage the lock though.'

Yvonne studied the door. Whether buoyed up by alcohol or encouraged by Tabitha's enthusiasm to show off her door-breaking skills, she nodded. 'Go for it. I'll have a new door made, and one that fits this time.'

Tabitha grinned. 'Watch this.'

She handed her jacket and shoulder bag to Alison, slipped out of her pretty gold sandals which had two-inch heels, and proceeded to man-handle the door off its hinges. Because the door was too small for the doorway she had room to manoeuvre, and although she was planning to lift it out of the hinges on the right, as she started the process they could hear the splitting sound as the section of wood which Alison had pointed out was a recent addition came away from the wall. Tabitha changed tack and pulled the door open.

The four women peered into the darkness. Almost simultaneously three phones were produced, and the torch app switched on.

'What on earth is all this?' exclaimed Yvonne, as their torch lights shone on dozens of boxes stacked on top of each other along the left-hand side of the tunnel. 'Hold this' she instructed Tabitha as she handed over her phone and ducked through the doorway.

The tunnel was cold, made of green stone, and although high enough for five-foot six-inch-tall Yvonne to stand upright, she instinctively stooped. While the other three held their phones to illuminate the nearest boxes, Yvonne reached into the top one and tentatively lifted the lid. Inside was full of jewellery boxes. Yvonne picked one out and opened it.

'Wow!' breathed Maisie, as the diamond and ruby necklace was revealed.

'I think we'd better call the police' said Yvonne, as she closed the box and placed it back in the box.

'Don't you know who these boxes belong to?' asked Maisie.

'One of the dealers perhaps?' suggested Alison. 'I'd feel a bit daft reporting boxes of jewellery found in an antiques shop.'

'No, I don't know, and I don't like it. Nobody should be coming down to the cellar without my permission, and if someone has changed this tunnel door and added their own lock that makes me even more suspicious.'

The four of them looked at the boxes, trying to come up with an honest and logical explanation.

'It's a bit creepy if someone has gone to all this effort' said Alison.

Maisie gave an involuntary shiver and glanced up the steps to the room above.

'Where does the tunnel go?' asked Tabitha, trying to see past Yvonne. 'Do you think we should have a little look?'

Everything in Yvonne's body was screaming NO, but it was Maisie who verbalised it. 'No! Not on your nelly!'

'Why on earth would we go into a tunnel we already suspect is being used by people to store their ill-gotten gains?' exclaimed Alison.

'Because it is exciting' grinned Tabitha. 'This could all be perfectly innocent.'

'I don't see how' retorted Yvonne. 'Somebody has done all of this without my knowledge, and I don't like it.'

'Although' said Maisie slowly 'that somebody isn't here now.'

'True' agreed Tabitha. 'Now would be as good as time as any to explore.'

Yvonne had to admit she was tempted. This was her building after all, and if anything was going on, she would like to know about it. Quickly making up her mind she said 'Come on, let's have a look. Once we've told the police we'll probably be prevented from looking down here for months.'

'You have a point' agreed Tabitha. 'I'm still not able to use my field, even though the police said I could. There is still quite a lot of police tape in there, and I need to find the time to clear it up before I let the sheep back in.'

'One of us should probably stay here' said Alison.

'Why?' asked Tabitha. 'No one is going to shut us in because no one can get into Yvonne's shop. It is all locked up.'

'Yes, but some of the dealers do have keys' said Alison.

'No they don't have their own keys, but they can get access to one set I keep in the lock box outside' explained Yvonne, 'but they are hardly going to be letting themselves in at this time of night. Don't forget Zebedee is a great guard dog and would make a huge amount of noise if anyone was in the practice of unlocking the front or back doors in the dead of night. But don't come if you're worried. None of us know what else is in here, or how far we can get.'

'I think a lot of these tunnels are blocked off' said Maisie who had changed her mind about exploring. 'I'm keen to see how far we can get. Stay here Alison.'

'No, I'm coming!' said Alison. 'I'd rather be with you three than left to face any intruders on my own!'

Yvonne picked up the box she had opened off the stack, and they used it to prop open the door. Tabitha left her sandals off, retrieved her jacket and bag from Alison, and because the tunnel was cold and damp all four women slipped their jackets or scarves over their shoulders, and with Yvonne re-united with her own phone, and Tabitha with hers, the four of them began to explore.

'It's like something out of Scooby-Doo' giggled Tabitha.

'Bagsy me be Daphne' said Alison.

'I'm Scraggy' laughed Yvonne.

'I'm Velma!' said Maisie.

'Isn't it Shaggy?' asked Tabitha.

'Oh yes, Shaggy, not Scraggy!' said Yvonne. 'Are you Fred or Scooby-Doo, Tabitha?'

'If it means I get scooby snacks then I'm Scooby-Doo. All this adventure is making me hungry.'

'Where do you think we are?' asked Alison. 'We've been going slightly uphill, so I wonder if we're under the Italian restaurant?'

'Look, here's a doorway!' Yvonne indicated the rotten wooden door on her right.

The four women shone their torches at the door and peered through the gaps to see what was on the other side.

'I can't make it out. Is it a wall?' asked Alison.

'I think it is. It must be bricked up from the other side' said Maisie. 'I think you're right; I think this must be somewhere in the Italian restaurant. We'll have to go in tomorrow and see if we can work out where it is.'

'Come on, let's keep moving a bit further' said Yvonne, as she led the way forwards.

After less than a minute, Tabitha called 'Look up!'

Four lights shone on a hatch in the ceiling. Reaching up, Tabitha attempted to open it, but was thwarted. It was well and truly jammed shut.

'I wonder if we are at Muston's?' asked Maisie.

'Could be, or we have been going slightly downhill now, so I think we could be below the old pub, The Crown' said Tabitha.

'We have reached a crossroads' said Yvonne, shining her torchlight at the three tunnels in front of her.

'I think I'd like to go back now' said Alison. 'I'm getting really cold, and quite scared.'

'Yes, me too' agreed Maisie. 'I think we should head back and phone the police. What if the people who stacked those boxes come back and find us? I have been thinking about when they could have been doing it, and surely they must have been doing it when no one else was around?'

'That would be easy during the day when the shop is open' explained Yvonne. 'If the person or people behind this are legitimate antiques dealers in my shop then they could arrange to be working in there on the same days, no one would question them bringing in boxes of stock because it is what we all do all of the time, and there are plenty of times when no customers come in. It wouldn't take long to move the bookcase and open the doors so they could carry a few boxes down there.'

Yvonne didn't want to believe anyone was letting themselves into her shop while she was asleep in her bed above, but she did want to keep exploring. She didn't think anyone else would be in these tunnels, and thought it was likely whoever was responsible for storing the boxes had been using her shop to gain access to them. It made her angry that someone was using her home in this way, and she wanted to find out as much as she could about the layout before access was denied to her. She was about to object when she saw Alison's face and realised how scared she was. Immediately she felt guilty and gestured to the others to turn back.

'Of course, come on, let's head back to my kitchen. There's a delicious curry waiting for us.'

It didn't take them as long to get back to Yvonne's cellar as it had to reach the crossroads, and they replaced the box on top of its friends and closed the door. Tabitha retrieved her sandals but decided her feet were too dirty to put them on, and they climbed back up the stone steps. Yvonne locked the door at the top behind them and led her friends through the shop's rooms and into her kitchen. Silently, everyone set to turning on lights, laying the table, turning on the oven to heat up the food, and putting the rice onto cook on the hob. Wine was opened and poured into glasses, Indian snacks were put into bowls and onto plates, Tabitha ran lightly up the spiral stairs to wash her feet in Yvonne's bathroom, and Zebedee tucked into her own dinner.

Everyone jumped when the buzzer was pressed, and then fell about laughing at their own and each other's tension.

Yvonne went to answer, and saw Tom Archibald standing at the gates. What did he want at this time of night? She was starting to get annoyed at his and Tim's almost constant presence, and snapped 'Tom, what do you want?'

Understandably, Tom looked a little surprised at the tone of her voice. Yvonne was always friendly and welcoming, and this was unexpected.

'Sorry to disturb you. I've been trying to get hold of you but was getting worried because you didn't reply to my texts. Are you OK?'

'I'm fine, I'm with friends and haven't been looking at my phone' Yvonne tried to rein in her frustration and thought by the look on Tom's face she had succeeded, at least in moderating her voice.

Holding his hands up in an apology, Tom said 'Good, good, that's good. I'm sorry to disturb you. We've had definite confirmation of the identity of the body, and I thought you'd like to know, but it can wait until tomorrow. Sorry again.'

'Tom wait!' called Yvonne, hoping he could hear her as he walked away. She could see him turn back, and she pressed the button to open the gates, and ran to the back door. 'Come on in' she called. 'We have something you probably need to see.'

The four friends, the dog, and the policeman walked through the shop to the end room. Yvonne had left the bookcase out of place and was able to walk around the back of it to unlock the door again, and led everyone down the stone steps to the ill-fitting door at the entrance to the tunnel. Tabitha moved forwards and pulled it open. While she stood holding it, Yvonne gestured for Tom to go inside the tunnel, where he hesitated when he saw the boxes.

'What is all this?' he asked.

Yvonne shrugged. 'I did not know these were here until we found them this evening, but we've just had a quick look inside that one on the top, and there is a load of jewellery in there.'

Tom looked around 'Are you telling me this is not part of your stock?'

'I am telling you that no one has my permission to store anything here, and therefore I suspect this is stolen goods.'

'I haven't got any forensic gloves on me' said Tom, searching the pockets of his jeans and denim jacket.

'Wait a moment' said Yvonne and disappeared back up into the shop. Less than a minute later she reappeared with a box of disposable gloves left over from the days when the dealers all wore them when handling their stock after the first pandemic lockdowns. 'Will these do?'

'They will' nodded Tom, as he expertly pulled on the blue gloves, and had a quick poke around in the box Yvonne had opened. 'What's in here?' he asked, pointing down the tunnel.

Before anyone could speak, Yvonne jumped in 'No idea. We didn't know this cupboard existed. What can you see?'

'Not a lot! I'd better call it in. Can you go back and be ready to let my colleagues in please? They will probably take a while to get here, so I am sorry to keep you from your bed.'

'We're not ready for bed, and we haven't had our dinner yet' said Tabitha.

'Oh no, I forgot about that!' exclaimed Maisie. 'It will probably be cooked to a crisp by now!'

As she disappeared up the steps, Yvonne said to Tom 'Have you eaten? There's plenty of curry and rice if you'd like some.'

'I have, thank you. You go ahead. I'll be fine here, although if there is a cup of coffee going I'd love one.'

'I'll bring one back to you' said Tabitha.

'Why don't we all eat down here' suggested Yvonne. 'We can bring a table and some chairs, and then Tom won't have to wait on his own. Tell your colleagues to come to the front door, and then we'll hear them when they knock.'

Fortunately the dishes in the oven were perfectly re-heated, and the rice on the hob actually needed another few minutes, and so by the time a small table, five chairs, a table cloth and place mats to protect the table which would still be for sale when they finished eating, and cutlery had been brought down to the basement, Maisie, Alison and Tabitha were able to carry the food down too. Maisie had included a plate and cutlery for Tom, and he didn't need much persuasion to put a spoonful of everything onto his plate.

'Cheers' said Tabitha, raising a glass of red wine. 'To the best hen night any of us will ever have!'

'Cheers' said Tom. 'To the one and only hen night I will ever attend.'

'Cheers!' said everyone.

Chapter 19

It took Tim less than fifteen minutes to turn up at the front door to Angel Lane Antiques, but another hour and fifty minutes after that before the rest of the team arrived. The impromptu dinner party had been cleared away, and the women had moved to Yvonne's kitchen, and carried on chatting over late night glasses of damson gin and sharing handmade chocolates from the delicatessen. By midnight it was all over. The boxes were briefly checked and carried out from the tunnel and taken away in an unmarked police van. The tunnels were explored by three police, who were back in Yvonne's cellar after twenty minutes, reporting that there was no access through to anywhere else. They finished their investigation for the night by fixing police crime tape across the tunnel doorway and the door at the top of the cellar steps. They then informed Yvonne she would not be able to open the antiques shop until further notice.

'But surely by closing the shop you will tip off whoever is doing this before they find out for themselves?' she argued. 'Wouldn't it be better to have surveillance? Remove the tape from the door behind the bookcase, and then catch whoever is doing this when they go to open it.'

'She's right!' exclaimed Tabitha. 'These two local policemen are always in here, so nobody would be surprised to see them. Tim and Tom could keep watch and provide protection for Yvonne at the same time!'

Alison looked worried 'Do you think Yvonne needs protection?'

Maisie said 'I think she does need protecting from whoever has been storing those boxes containing stolen jewellery.'

Yvonne argued 'We don't know yet that those boxes contain stolen jewellery. For all we know someone has fallen out with their business partner, or is going through a messy divorce, and is hiding stock so they don't have to declare it.'

Tim said 'I think Yvonne has a point about keeping the shop open. By letting the antiques dealers and members of the public in we won't be contaminating the crime scene. If there has been a crime, and I think there has been Yvonne, whatever scenario you can think up there cannot be an innocent explanation for what has been going on here. The cellar and tunnels are the areas of interest, and that is where we need to observe and protect. Although it wouldn't be either me or Tom doing the surveillance as we are needed elsewhere.'

The police team went into a huddle for so long the women got bored of waiting and made preparations to leave.

'You can come home with me' Maisie said to Yvonne. 'Zebedee too.'

Yvonne had to admit she was feeling a little unsettled by the unknown origin of the boxes and who brought them into her shop. Although she was pretty sure no one was sneaking in when the shop was closed, the thought did worry her.

'Thank you Maisie, I may take you up on that kind offer.'

'What's that?' asked Tim, who had emerged from the meeting with his colleagues.

211

'Maisie offered me and Zebedee a bed for the night, if we need it' Yvonne told him.

'If it makes you feel safer then go ahead, but we're going to set up a team to stake out the cellar door, starting from tomorrow morning, although there will be a police presence outside the shop tonight.'

Yvonne paused for a moment and curbed her instinctive response to argue about having one or more people in her shop at night. It made sense and would mean she and Zebedee could stay in their home. It also meant the police believed someone could be coming and going out of hours.

With a shiver, she said 'It's all got quite serious hasn't it?'

'It was very serious when you found that murdered woman in my field!' Tabitha pointed out. 'Who was she, by the way?'

'She has now been formally identified as Jane Poundsmith' confirmed Tom, who had also joined them. 'Yvonne, you don't need to know who they are, but a couple of the team will be setting up in the cellar in the morning, and the teams will change over every few hours, depending on how long this takes. The front and back doors to the building will also be always under surveillance. I know it won't be easy, but please do not acknowledge, or even look for, the people who are working.'

'It will be odd if I don't acknowledge the ones in here when the shop is open' observed Yvonne. 'But I know what you mean. Thank you for the offer Maisie, but we'll stay here tonight, and see how it goes.'

Maisie, Alison and Tabitha all hugged Yvonne good night, and prepared to walk home.

'I declare that was the most unique hen party ever in the history of hen parties!' said Tabitha, breaking the tension and raising the mood a little.

Tim and Tom also said goodbye to Yvonne and said they would be in to see her in the morning, with more information about Jane Poundsmith. They offered to walk everyone else home.

'Thank you' said Maisie. 'I must admit I am a little spooked by finding those boxes of jewellery and the tunnels I had no idea existed. For all I know there is one which goes right underneath my house!'

'Are you sure you want to walk us home?' asked Alison. 'You know we live down on the farm and it's at least a half an hour walk from here. It will take you just as long to walk back again. We're always walking down there in the dark and are used to it.'

'Please let us go with you. We'd be happier if we knew you were safely home after this evening's adventures' said Tom. 'I'm sure there is nothing to worry about, but we need to tick all the boxes.'

'We'll pick my car up on the way' said Tim. 'We can all walk Maisie back to her house, and it's only another few minutes on to mine.'

Alison and Tabitha accepted the officers' offer of a lift, all the time stressing they weren't worried, while Maisie was happier to have so many people to accompany her home. Once everyone had gone, Yvonne sat at her kitchen table, while Zebedee snoozed on the sofa. The police officer in charge, who she thought she recognised from the morning when she and George found the body in Tabitha's field, had repeated what Tim and Tom had told her about the surveillance, and stressed that no one was to use the door down to the cellar, and Yvonne was to contact him if she noticed anyone moving the bookcase to reach it before the officers took up their posts the next day. As she hadn't been aware of anyone carrying all those boxes to the tunnel, she thought it unlikely she would know if someone tried to access it, but she nodded and said she would phone him immediately.

Taking advantage of the delay in surveillance, Yvonne decided to make the most of having the place to herself. Changing into a pair of plimsols, pulling on a fleece jacket with pony nuts and dog treats in the pockets and retrieving the head torch she had used for the night ride on Toby, she whistled to Zebedee and together they headed for the cellar door.

It was easy to slide around the side of the bookcase which hadn't been placed the way she had originally found it, and by-pass the tape which had not yet been removed. She assumed the surveillance team would do that when they arrived in the morning. Yvonne unlocked the small door, reached in to turn on the lights, and with Zebedee's claws tap tap tapping down the stone steps behind her Yvonne headed for the tunnel. The police tape wasn't so easy to negotiate on the tunnel doorway because it was holding the ill-fitting door into place, but Yvonne reasoned that no one would remember the exact way it had been fixed, and she used the tape to hold the door open against the wall behind it.

Zebedee raced off ahead, and Yvonne was glad she had thought to put one of the many collars with inbuilt lights on her dog. This one was orange, and the coloured glow was comforting, until it disappeared. Those collars were not designed to light the way, only to be seen on the roads or in the fields. Yvonne wondered if she had made a mistake in bringing her dog down here. She would never forgive herself if something happened to Zebedee. Too late to do anything about it now, and afraid that if she went

214

back to her cosy safe kitchen she may not want to leave it again, Yvonne followed Zebedee. She decided not to use the dog whistle just yet, but checked it was in her pocket. When she passed the doorway on the right which they had guessed led into the Italian restaurant she took a photo with her phone, and another photograph of the hatch which could have opened into the former Crown public house. When she reached the crossroads she found Zebedee waiting. The dog looked back at her before trotting off along the one on the right. Yvonne saw no reason to call her back, and followed, keeping a close eye out for any more doorways or hatches. Along the route she discovered and photographed five more doors but no more hatches. Zebedee had stopped and was investigating a pile of rubble which blocked any further access along the tunnel. After a quick sweep with the light from her head torch, Yvonne decided that attempting to dig her way through was going to be messy and dangerous, and turned back. Taking the middle tunnel, she and Zebedee came across a similar blockage, and recorded three more doorways and another hatch along the way. The left-hand tunnel was different to the other two. This had no doorways or hatches but ended up with a wall at the end. Yvonne wondered why it had been built because it didn't appear to lead to anywhere. She took a photograph of the wall, which was made of the same greenstone as the rest of the tunnels and looked as though it had been there for as long as the tunnels had existed. Turning back, she began to retrace her steps, when a loud noise made her freeze. She hadn't been aware of listening out for anyone else in the tunnel, but now every fibre of her body was trying to work out where the noise was coming from, and what it was. She turned off the torch, so as not to give away her presence, and sunk down to the ground with her hand on Zebedee's collar, fumbling for the switch to turn that off too.

Without the light from the head torch or the dog's collar the pair of them were in complete darkness. There were no chinks of light anywhere, no moonlight or streetlights to cast shadows. It made Yvonne realise she was never completely in the dark. Until now.

There was also no noise, except for the sounds of her and Zebedee breathing, and the occasional clicks of Zebedee's claws on the ground as she shifted, keen to get moving.

'Shh, just stand still' Yvonne tried to breathe the words to her dog and wondered if she could have screamed if she wanted to. Her lungs seemed to have stopped working.

Complete silence. Total blackout.

Zebedee didn't appear to be concerned by their environment, nor was she letting Yvonne know they had company. Yvonne was sure her dog would have given some indication if they were not alone in the tunnel, and after a while, Yvonne had no idea how long, she switched Zebedee's collar back on and let go, watching while her dog weaved her way back up the tunnel. Satisfied there was no one lurking, Yvonne stood up and switched her head torch back on. She had not been able to hear anything since that loud noise and wondered if the sound had come from a building above the tunnel, or perhaps they were underneath a road and it had been a vehicle. Her confidence had deserted her, so she decided not to hang around any longer, and with her dog leading the way, this time choosing to stay just ahead of Yvonne rather than disappearing to explore in the darkness, Yvonne walked back to where she had propped open the tunnel door. The tunnel was beginning to look familiar to her now, and she was enjoying exploring although her heart was still beating rather fast after that scare.

Carefully putting everything back the way she remembered it, Yvonne closed the tunnel door and the cellar door, and headed back to her kitchen. While she was wandering through the tunnels she had been giving some thought to who could have been responsible for storing the jewellery down there, and as she walked back through the antiques shop she knew she was right.

Marion Close.

It was Marion's bookcase which was positioned in front of the cellar doorway. Dealers and customers alike had often commented on the high price Marion had written on the label she attached to the bookcase, and now Yvonne guessed why Marion had done that. She did not want to have to find another piece of stock big enough to hide the door from enquiring eyes, and easy enough to move to enable access to the doorway. Yvonne wondered if Marion had always known about the cellar and tunnels, or if it had been a happy discovery after she had begun to rent space in Angel Lane Antiques.

Yvonne double checked the doors were locked, and the alarms were set. Marion was one of six dealers who were entrusted with the code for the lock box to access the key to the front door of Angel Lane Antiques, and with the alarm code for the shop. Nobody had keys or alarm codes to her home, or even to the security gates outside the back of the shop, not even Rob Kemp, but it was still disturbing to think that someone could have been using her shop while she was asleep in her bed.

The fact that Marion hadn't been seen for a while suggested to Yvonne that she might be Jane Poundsmith. But this was something Yvonne couldn't believe. Marion was a lovely, gentle lady, who volunteered at her local cat rescue centre and spent the quiet times at antiques fairs crocheting post box toppers. Surely the woman who

217

headed up a national, maybe international, crime business wouldn't have time for abandoned animals and crafting skills? As Yvonne showered and prepared to go to bed her mind was buzzing with the events of the evening, and she wondered if she would be able to go to sleep.

Before she got into bed, she ran back downstairs, negotiated the alarms and locks to go through to the shop, opened the front door and removed the front door key from the lock box. She would have to make sure she was up in time to let in the two dealers who were working the next day. Although as it was now three o'clock in the morning she was tempted to make a pot of tea and settle down to some admin in her office. As a compromise she made a cup of tea and took a couple of chocolate digestives upstairs to her bedroom, put on a book on Audible with the timer set to the end of the twenty-five-minute-long chapter, and settled down with Zebedee lying comfortingly across her feet at the end of the bed.

Chapter 20

Yvonne awoke naturally at six o'clock, an hour before she had set her alarm to go off. The morning was sunny, and despite her late night she felt wide awake and full of energy. She pulled on her riding clothes, brushed her teeth because chocolate digestives in bed are not conducive to a healthy mouth, and went downstairs to make herself a travel mug of coffee. While she was waiting for the kettle to boil she went outside and put the front door key back in the lock box. Good luck to anyone who wanted to access the cellar this morning, and to be honest Yvonne didn't fancy being there when they discovered what had happened during the night.

The lanes were quiet as she and Zebedee drove to Hannam Livery, but the yard was already full of fellow early morning riders. It was the time of year when horse flies made their appearance by nine o'clock in the morning, and although they weren't too bad in this area, it made for a more pleasant experience if you could beat them to it. While Toby ate his breakfast, Yvonne drank her coffee, and sat quietly watching as horses were brought in from the fields, brushed and tacked up, and set off either down the driveway or in the opposite direction across the fields. Deciding a short walk around the fields would be a good idea, Yvonne gave Toby a brief once over with the orange rubber curry comb, didn't bother to brush out his mane and tail, and tacked him up with an orange rope hackamore, and his saddle. Checking her pockets for horse treats and dog treats, she led him over to the mounting block where she could easily climb into the saddle, and whistling for Zebedee she set off with her horse and dog around the outside of three fields. The farm was a mixture of arable and animals, as well as the fields set aside for the livery yard. Although the horses' fields were specifically designed for them, the way the farm worked meant that at certain times of the year sheep would graze those fields, and the horses would be let loose on the huge grassy fields used by the sheep and the cows. By mixing up the grazing in this way problems such as parasitic worms, over-grazing, and poaching of the ground could be minimised. The fields the horse riders had permission to ride over for a few weeks had been cut for straw which was used for bedding down the cows, sheep and goats in the depths of winter, and once they had ridden in there a few times Yvonne would be happy to let Toby have a good gallop, but today was their first time in this part of the farm since last summer, and she didn't want him to always think they galloped around. The day was warming up quickly, and she knew that if she and Toby set off at a trot or canter then Zebedee would try to keep up, and it was already too hot for dogs to be doing more than a sedate sniff and a wee. The three of them walked around the informal track which was created by the horse riders every year. It was on the edge of the harvested area, ensuring they did not disturb the wide wildflower margins where nesting birds, insects and tiny mammals thrived. Yvonne enjoyed the gentle forwards and backwards and side-to-side motion of her horse, the sunshine, the sounds of the birds, and watched as Zebedee made lazy tracks following scents in the stubble. For a couple of minutes she tipped her face to the sun and closed her eyes, allowing her horse to rock her body as they walked. The events of a few hours ago felt as though they had been experienced by someone else.

All too soon they had returned to the yard. Toby went back to his field mates, and Zebedee and Yvonne enjoyed a social chat with some of the other horse and dog owners, sitting on bales of the recently harvested straw in the relative cool of the barn. Everyone was excited about Tabitha and Alison's wedding the following weekend, and Lindy's party the weekend after that. Although Tabitha and Alison had only invited close friends, it seemed that everyone at the yard had some connection with one or both of them, whether it was as a client of Alison's at the hairdressing salon, or as a fellow local sheep farmer like Tabitha, or both. Yvonne sat back and relaxed as the chatter washed around her. This was real. This was what her life was all about. Not some awful crime being committed on her premises or a murder being carried out on one of her regular hacking routes. This. Women discussing timings for doing the horses and having a shower in time for the wedding; whether it was worth getting their nails done, or would the varnish have chipped by the time the wedding day arrived; how long would it take to style and dry hair on the day; what outfit to wear; could they get away with wearing the same outfit to both. Yvonne hadn't thought about dressing up for Lindy's party and made the decision to buy something new for the day. These days she rarely went to the type of event where dressing up was required, and decided to make the most of it.

Driving back in through the gates, she smiled to see that Rob was already hard at work at the back of the antiques shop, with one customer who had driven their Morgan classic car in for Rob to see.

'Good morning!' she called as she let herself and Zebedee out of her modern large dark blue Volkswagen SUV, bought for practical use rather than love, although she had bought it brand new eight years ago and did love it now.

She gathered from over-hearing their conversation as she and Zebedee walked up the wooden stairs to the door to her flat, that the man was looking for a new steering wheel for his car. It was as though none of the previous night's events had taken place. She showered and changed, choosing khaki green capri trousers and a bright pink sleeveless blouse. It was too hot to do battle with the hairdryer, so a naturally curly hairstyle was the order of the day, and minimal make-up but including Tropic Skin Shade, black mascara and clear lip gloss. White flip-flops and diamond stud earrings completed her look, and she and Zebedee went down the spiral stairs to the kitchen for breakfast. Just as she put Zebedee's food bowl down on the floor her phone pinged, and there was a message from George.

'Come and have breakfast and check-out the courtyard?'

She didn't need to think twice. Deciding that Zebedee was best left in the cool of her home, she replied to George with a thumb's up emoji, and walked up through the carpark making a conscious effort not to look out for members of the surveillance team, and along Bell Street to the black gates. As she opened the right-hand one, George appeared inside and helped her to close it behind her.

'I can't wait for you to see' he said, taking her hand and leading her past the five pale pink rose bushes in planters which lined the wall on the right. The water fountain had been completed and looked and sounded idyllic. The rest of the courtyard and furniture were more or less as she had last seen them, but George kept hold of her hand and led her into the building on the left.

'Oh my goodness!' she said. 'I can't believe how much work has been done in here!'

To the right was a large high-ceilinged room which had been transformed from a building site into an atmospheric dining room. A huge long dark wooden table ran down the centre of the room with a pink and silver striped runner decorating its length. On either side of the table were simple wooden chairs dressed with comfortable-looking pink and silver striped loose cushions to the seat and back, and above were three chandeliers with wine glasses instead of diamond droplets.

'Obviously this table can't accommodate everyone who will be coming to Tabitha and Alison's wedding' said George 'but you can see how this could be used for other events. These panels fold back, allowing everyone to be a part of the party.' He pulled open the wooden panels and revealed the courtyard beyond. Immediately the room looked as though it was as one with the courtyard.

'Yes, this is fantastic!'

'It is all down to Lesley. She is the one with the vision for this sort of thing. Come on, come and see the kitchen.'

The room behind had been filled with appliances, and Yvonne wouldn't have recognised it as the same space where George had been pacing out and indicating where various fixtures would be going. There were three people working in there, so Yvonne stayed in the doorway so she wouldn't get in their way.

'It is all plumbed in and working. Our buildings' team have shown their value in pulling all this together.'

'You must be so pleased' agreed Yvonne.

'There's more' grinned George and gestured for her to walk through the door marked 'TOILETS'.

Laughing, Yvonne opened the door, and then inspected what was behind each of the doors which led off the corridor beyond it. Three basic but functional unisex units, each big enough for a wheelchair, and special touches of vases of real flowers and locally produced luxury soaps and hand moisturisers were in each one.

'Keep going' nodded George, as she looked at the door at the end of the corridor.

Opening it, Yvonne said 'I am glad you didn't just bring me in here to show me the toilets. This is an amazing change!'

The café beyond had been remodelled, so that the floor space had been extended, and the cramped kitchen area had been replaced by a large counter area covered with lots of cake plates under domes, and a cool cabinet for cold drinks, sandwiches, cheeses and quiches stood against the wall, and a hot drinks machine for the staff to operate completed the area. The café was closed, but two members of staff were preparing to open up and catch the early Sunday morning breakfast crowd.

'Now that all their food is being prepared in the Courtyard or the TAA kitchens they can have more room for customers and a better space to display products. Choose what you would like, and we'll take it through and sit in the courtyard.'

As he spoke the door at the back of the counter area opened and one of the kitchen staff appeared, carrying a tray of warm hazelnut chocolate croissants.

'That was good timing!' said Yvonne. 'I'll have one of them and a mug of tea please.'

'I will have the same' said George.

George carried their food and drink on a tray, and he and Yvonne walked back past the toilets, the kitchen and the new dining room, to one of the sofas on the end wall of the courtyard.

'Is there anything you need me to do before Saturday's wedding?' Yvonne asked, as she gazed around at the flowers and chairs and tables.

'I'm not involved with the planning of the day,' explained George 'but Lesley has been in contact with Alison and Tabitha, and I think they are all sorted.'

'After all the recent stress I do hope so' said Yvonne. 'They thought they had everything planned up at Kenyon Hall. We couldn't believe it when they had to start again from scratch. They deserve a lovely wedding day.'

'We will do our best to make sure that happens' George assured her.

Yvonne stifled a yawn. 'Am I keeping you up?' teased George. 'How did the rest of the hen party go last night?'

'Sorry! I was up early for a ride with Toby before it got too hot, and very late to bed, although not because we were being wild and drinking a lot. Do you know if The Abbess Aethelgifu has a tunnel running underneath?'

'Yes, there is one. We found the doorway to it down in the cellar when we renovated the building. It is in a poor state of repair and is blocked by a pile of rubble where the roof has collapsed a few metres in. Why, does your building have one too?'

'Yes,' Yvonne wondered how much she should tell George. She was pretty sure he was trustworthy, but didn't want to jeopardise the work Tim, Tom and their colleagues were doing. 'Like you I saw the entrance when I bought Angel Lane Antiques, but haven't thought any more about it. I wonder what they were built for?'

'Smuggling rum' said George, in a peculiar voice. Seeing Yvonne's faint look of alarm, he explained 'That was my best pirate impression.'

225

'Oh dear, was it?' laughed Yvonne. Her phone pinged, and checking it she saw that Tim had sent her a message. 'I am sorry, I must go back to the shop. Thank you very much for breakfast, and for letting me see how amazing all of this looks. I am very excited for Alison and Tabitha's wedding. Thank you so much; I do believe you have saved the day for them.'

George's phone pinged, and he said 'Tim wants to talk to me; has he spoken to you?'

Yvonne waved her phone 'That was Tim. Do you want to come with me? He's going to be at the shop in five minutes' time.'

They carried their used mugs and plates to the new kitchen, thanked the staff, and walked along Bell Street and through the carpark to the back gates of Yvonne's shop where Rob was discussing a classic car with the owner.

'A 1939 MG VA!' exclaimed George, who was immediately welcomed into the conversation.

Yvonne left them to it, and climbed the stairs to her flat, where she found, as expected, Zebedee fast asleep in the middle of Yvonne's bed. Satisfied her dog was happy, Yvonne walked down the spiral stairs to her kitchen, and found her big glass jug, some ice cubes in the freezer, and homemade lemonade in the fridge from the Deli on the High Street. She poured the lemonade into the jug, added the ice cubes, set down the jug in the middle of the table, retrieved three glasses which matched it, and sat down to wait for Tim and George to find her. Checking her phone she noticed there was some activity on the group's wedding chat messages, and saw that Alison and Tabitha had received a partial refund from Kenyon Hall, with the promise of more to come.

'Knock knock' called Tim, as he pushed open the door.

'Come on in' said Yvonne.

'How are you?' Tim asked, closing the door firmly behind him and sitting down on the other side of the table. 'That was a lot to cope with last night.'

'I'm fine, if a little tired' said Yvonne. 'Don't worry about me. Is everything in place?'

'You mean the people in the cellar? Yes, the team is set up and ready for working in shifts. They will aim to come and go as unobtrusively as possible, and even though you know they are there you won't see anything of them. If no one turns up to retrieve the boxes or add more to the pile during the day, then the night team will already be in place before you lock up at closing time. If they are undisturbed during the night, they will swap with the next team after you open the shop the following morning. Just do everything you would normally.'

A thought occurred to Yvonne. 'Won't they need to use the staff toilet next door?'

Tim shook his head. 'Nope, they are fully self-sufficient. Nobody except you, Tabitha, Maisie and Alison know anything about this. For the sake of the investigation and the safety of the officers involved, please keep it that way.'

At that moment the door opened and George walked in. 'Hi Tim. You wanted to see me?'

Tim stood up and said 'Yes, hello George. I thought it would be easier to talk to you face-to-face and update you about what has been happening. The body the two of you found has now been identified as Jane Poundsmith, and the case is being investigated by a specialist part of the police force. The same goes for the jewellery you found. The whole thing has been taken out of our hands, and we are no longer involved. I thought you should know, because I am not going to be able to give you any more updates in the same way, although obviously if you think of anything

227

which could help those who are investigating then let me or Tom know, and we'll send you in the right direction to pass it on. I am sorry, but that is how these things work.'

'No problem' said George. 'I am glad the poor woman's relatives can now stop worrying about what has happened to her, although it must be devastating to know the truth. I do not know how I would cope if someone who I was close to died in those circumstances. So that is it for you then? Back on normal duties dealing with road accidents and local burglaries?'

'That's it!' shrugged Tim. 'I must admit I am not sorry to be stepping back from all that stress. I'll leave you two to it; it looks as though you're expecting someone' he said, nodding to the lemonade jug and glasses in the middle of the table, and he walked out.

'Sorry,' said George. 'Are you expecting someone else?'

'No, I set this out for the three of us, but Tim obviously has places to be and people to see' laughed Yvonne, worried now that she had said the wrong thing by mentioning the existence of the tunnels to George. Tim had not said a word about them, and clearly George was not to be included in the small group who needed to know. 'Would you like a glass?'

'Thank you, but no thank you. I'd best get to work. Nice of him to take the time to formally tell us the state of play wasn't it?'

Yvonne simply nodded in reply. This was going to be harder than she thought. She was used to keeping secrets, but not when the secret was happening all around her. She wondered if anyone had noticed the first surveillance team coming into the shop and going down to the cellar. How could they not see them? She realised George was still in her kitchen and was talking to her.

'Yvonne?'

'Sorry! I was thinking about that poor woman's family' lied Yvonne.

'Are you going to be OK?'

'Yes, yes of course. You go, get to work. I have to start working too. Thank you, George.'

With a small wave he was gone.

Yvonne put the jug of lemonade into the fridge and hurried out to the shop. Seeing William Drake behind the counter she slowed down. 'Hello William. How are you?'

'I'm fine thank you Yvonne. I have brought a salmon and asparagus quiche in today if you would like some.'

'You are very kind William!' Salmon and asparagus was her favourite. Glancing around in what she hoped was a casual manner, she asked 'Has anyone been in yet?'

'Yes, we had a spate of ones and twos coming through the door soon after I opened, but they have all left now. Sold that table over there' he indicated a large old pine table 'and Rob will deliver it later today.'

'I hope I will be able to deliver it!' said Rob as he walked through from his room at the back of the shop. 'The directions sounded a bit complicated, even for the Donheads.'

Chapter 21

The days leading up to the wedding passed as though nothing else was going on. Yvonne felt as though it was the only topic of conversation in the antiques shop, when she saw any of her friends, including George, and at the livery yard. It seemed as though the whole town was involved either by supplying food or clothes, or as guests, or both. Tabitha and Alison were involved in many of the town's activities, whether it was school fund-raising or the Thursday Market, hair and beauty treatments or helping to water the plants for Shaftesbury In Bloom. Both Tabitha and Alison had been born in the town, and gone to the local schools, and so even though the marriage ceremony in the town hall was going to be a private affair, many people wanted to be outside to welcome the couple afterwards, and there was a lot of discussion about where they were going to park, since the county council's carparks were notoriously tricky to navigate, and whether it was best to wait outside the town hall, where there was limited space on the pavement, or on Park Walk which was long and wide and perfect for scenic photographs overlooking the Blackmore Vale. Yvonne remembered her own wedding, which had been an enormous affair with hundreds of guests, regimented by the lady who arranged her flowers, the driver of the enormous white Rolls Royce, the vicar of the picturesque country church, the photographer before, during and after the service, and the master of ceremonies at the expensive country club where their reception was held. Tabitha and Alison's wedding day was going to be very different from her own, and hopefully this marriage would last.

True to his word, Tim's assurance that neither Yvonne nor her team of antiques dealers would notice the police team moving in and out of the cellar proved correct. To her frustration Yvonne discovered that the camera in the back room did not cover the doorway into the room, nor the area around the bookcase, instead concentrating on the three cabinets containing small and valuable items, such as jewellery and silver pieces. It was so long ago that the security system was installed, and Yvonne was so used to glancing at the views on the six screens on the counter, one for each camera in the shop, that she had forgotten what they were trained to focus on. She tried to view the playback facility to see if she could spot who was coming into the shop and not leaving, but there were too many people coming and going both on the camera and in real life in the shop for her to concentrate without drawing attention to what she was doing. It did make her think about what the purpose of the security system was, and she made a note to review it at a later date.

Yvonne's Matron of Honour dress was hanging in her dressing room, and she had worn the matching strappy sandals every day for a couple of hours while she was working in the shop, so that they were comfortable to wear all day on the Saturday. Maisie came over and showed her how to style her hair and do her make-up, and she had opted to have a manicure and a pedicure with Maisie at the salon on the afternoon before the big day. Yvonne was amazed that after almost forty years of doing her own hair and wearing make-up there was still more to learn. All four women agreed that they didn't want fancy hairdo's or lashings of colour on their faces, and only Tabitha was having a significant change to her own hair but that was because she was the only one who didn't have a public-facing job and chose to spend all day with it shoved under a cap.

The day of the wedding dawned with a peaceful sunrise. The weather forecast was for a hot sunny day, with the threat of a thunderstorm mid-afternoon. Yvonne was awake early, and together with Zebedee drove to see Toby before she needed to begin her matron of honour duties. She was at the yard before half-past five, and no one else was about. One of the other livery owners, Lindy Speake, was going to be taking care of the horses for the weekend, and so Yvonne left Toby's feed bucket behind, and she and Zebedee strolled down to the field where her horse was grazing with his friends. She wandered between the horses, saying 'Hello' to each one, and was rewarded with an inquisitive nose on the back of her proffered hand. The herd were calm, their only thoughts were on which blade of grass they were going to eat next. Yvonne sat down on the grass, Zebedee lay next to her, and one by one the horses migrated towards her, some eating as they moved, others taking the opportunity to stand and snooze. Toby was the only one who came close, and he stood behind her with his muzzle resting on her head. She felt his hot breath, and the sensation was soothing. The last few days had been exciting, frightening, disturbing and unsettling, and so to sit here in the noisy peace and quiet of a field of horses, with the birds singing loudly and numerous buzzing insects flying around, with her dog and her horse, was the relaxation Yvonne needed.

The sound of a car coming up the drive alongside the field broke her reverie. Toby lifted his head to see who it was, and some of the other horses began to walk towards the field shelters. How did they know this was the human who was going to be feeding them, and not Yvonne when she had turned up?

'Come on Zebedee, let's go and help serve breakfast to this lot' she said, as she pushed herself up from the ground.

By the time she had walked up to the feed room all eight buckets were ready to be transported down the track, loaded into the handcart which could easily be pulled by one person. Lindy admired Yvonne's pale pink nails with sparkly diamante decorations and refused to allow her anywhere near the cart or the buckets but welcomed her company. Lindy, supervised by Zebedee, distributed the right feed to the horses while Yvonne stood around feeling guilty for not helping. They all had the same basic feed of unmollassed sugar beet and a mix of minerals to support their forage, but some had more than others, and one had a tablet every day to help to slow down the effects of a degenerative disease.

While they waited for the horses to clean their buckets, Lindy allowed Yvonne to push the wheelbarrow while she poo-picked the day paddock. This was a soothing job on a day when nerves could set in. The people who had fed the horses and let them out into their night field the previous evening had cleared up the dung before leaving, but inevitably more had appeared over night because the horses had the choice of moving between the two fields. There were security cameras dotted around the farm, and some of them were fixed to the horses' field shelters. The livery owners had access to the videos and live viewing on these cameras on their mobile phones, and Yvonne knew that all eight horses had a tendency to come up to the shelters and rest between midnight and three in the morning, before returning to their night field.

'It is going to be a wonderful day' said Lindy as she scraped and tipped the droppings from the dry earth into the wheelbarrow.

'It is. I am so pleased everything has worked out for them' said Yvonne. 'Are you excited for your party next weekend?'

'Oh yes!' said Lindy 'Although it won't be anything like the scale of the wedding party today, we have had our own share of dramas.'

Yvonne's ears pricked up 'Really? What has happened?'

Lindy rolled her eyes. 'It's all a bit awkward, but my dad's cousin is an antiques dealer, and my mum gave her a load of jewellery to value for an insurance policy they were taking out. Something to do with raising the money for yet another major renovation the old house needs. I don't know the whole story, but it turns out that Dad didn't know what Mum had done, and he's furious because apparently this cousin of his is dodgy and not to be trusted. You probably know all sorts of people like that in your business.'

'I know a few.'

'Anyway, Mum is cross with Dad because he has never told her about his cousin's reputation, but he is always going on about her brother who was banned for drink-driving forty years ago.'

'He must have been well over the limit to be banned. I thought everyone drank and drove in those days!'

'Well, quite, that was always Dad's point. Anyway, every time they have an argument about anything, Dad manages to bring Mum's brother's crime into it, when all the time he was hiding the secret of his cousin's criminal existence! I think that's all of it.' Lindy said as she scanned the paddock around them.

'I can't see any more. What had she done?' asked Yvonne, steering the wheelbarrow over to one of the three trailers the farmer left in the fields for storing and moving the horse muck so he could spread it over the other fields as fertiliser for the crops.

'It turns out that when they were children, teenagers I think, Dad's cousin set up a business of stealing cars and selling them on to unsuspecting buyers. She would recruit boys to do the actual breaking in and driving away, get them to take the vehicles to several different garages with whom she had an agreement, fake the documents, and pocket the cash.'

'That sounds as though she had good organisational skills!' laughed Yvonne.

'It does, doesn't it? Can you imagine doing all of that when you were about fifteen years' old?' Lindy collected the empty feed buckets and stacked them into the cart, before pulling it by the handle as they walked up the track.

'How did she get caught?' asked Yvonne.

'She didn't. She has never been arrested, but the lads who worked for her were always getting criminal records. For all Dad knows she's been part of these industrial scale thefts of farm machinery where the tractors get whisked off to Romania or Poland or somewhere before the farmer even realises it is missing from his farmyard. He suspects she will have been involved in dealing drugs, although he is sure she has never taken them, and he also seems to know that she is in the business of buying and selling houses, the top-end-of-the-market mansions rather than two-up-two-down terraced houses, and luxury yachts to people who need to clean their cash.'

'What is she like?'

'I have no idea; I have never met her. My family are always meeting up for weddings, funerals and big birthdays. There are so many of us there is usually some event worth celebrating at least once a month, but Aunty Marion has never been invited to anything. I think that is why my dad is so upset with Mum. It is because she and Aunty Marion have been secretly meeting up at some posh hotel for spa sessions and afternoon tea for years, and he had no idea what they were up to. According to Mum, Aunty Marion is a lovely woman, gentle, kind and always pays her share of the bill. According to Dad so she bloody well should because his cousin can afford to buy the bloody hotel a million times over. Or words to that effect. Mum says Dad is over-reacting, and Dad keeps asking Mum where's the jewellery then?'

'And where is it?' asked Yvonne, pretty sure she knew. 'Here, I'll do that.'

'No you won't, you need to protect those nails, at least until this evening. I can rinse these buckets out. But you ask a good question' said Lindy. 'Mum has not heard from Aunty Marion since she handed over approximately two million pounds worth of earrings, rings, tiaras, cufflinks, necklaces, you name it. Mum gave it to someone who, according to Dad, is one of the biggest, if not the biggest criminal in England!'

Chapter 22

Yvonne decided to go straight from her flat to her car, and not let anyone see her in her wedding finery. It had only taken her about half an hour to shower, dry and style her hair, put her make-up on, and slip into her dress. She said goodbye to Zebedee, who was of course stretched out in the middle of Yvonne's bed, and let herself out of the door and down the steps outside. About four steps down she saw the man who had been watching her a few weeks ago. She hadn't forgotten about him in the intervening time, but had become less alert to his presence, and was trying to convince herself that he was an innocent person, probably several different men, who just happened to be around. All her convictions disappeared as he tried to dive back into the shadows of the trees at the far-left corner of the carpark. Unfortunately for him a family were coming down the path and they prevented his escape. Yvonne made no secret of the fact she had seen him, and stood with her hands on her hips openly trying to catch sight of his face, but he was too good and managed to keep it hidden beneath his baseball cap.

'Yvonne, you look gorgeous!' George called out as he crossed the carpark, carrying a large box.

Yvonne blushed, and hoped he was far enough away not to be able to see her burning cheeks. 'Thank you! What do you have there?'

'It is the bottom tier of the wedding cake. I decided it was safer to transport it like this, rather than risk braking sharply in my car. I will go back for the other two tiers once this one is safely in its place.'

'Walk carefully!' warned Yvonne. 'I think I might have gone for the all-in-one-go option in the car.'

'Believe me, I have been dithering over which is the best way to do it,' laughed George. 'At least this way if anything happens to this one, the other two tiers will be safe.'

'True! I'll see you later.'

'I look forward to it' George grinned.

Yvonne continued down the stairs, unlocked her car and pressed the key fob to open the gates. As though he had been waiting outside, Rob walked through. He made her jump because she hadn't seen him out there while she was talking with George.

'You scrub up well!' he said admiringly, as she manoeuvred herself carefully into the driver's seat, trying not to rumple her dress or shut it in the door as she closed it. 'Not that you don't look good the rest of the time. I think I'll shut up now.'

Yvonne was giggling at the expression on his face 'Thank you, Rob, I know what you mean, and I appreciate it. Have a good day in the shop.'

As she started the car she reflected that it was funny how Rob's compliment didn't make her face burn as George's had.

She drove through the town and along the lanes to the farmhouse, where she parked next to Maisie's car. She opened the boot and pulled out a large bag which had been stored overnight. For once she wasn't greeted by dogs or children as she let herself in through the open back door. Alison, Tabitha and Maisie were sitting around the kitchen table in their wedding clothes, with an unopened bottle of champagne and plates of fruit salad and small pastries in the middle.

'Where is everyone?' Yvonne asked.

'Scott took the girls and the dogs to his house last night, and he's going to bring the dogs back here later on, after dropping the girls at the town hall' replied Alison. 'The girls really want him to come to the wedding, and I think he is going to give in and come with them. I hope he does.'

Maisie said 'He has all the instructions on how to dress them and how to do their hair, and I'm going to put in the finishing touches when they arrive. We thought the chances of the flowers staying in their hair for any longer than the actual service are too low to risk putting them in any earlier.'

'Good idea' agreed Yvonne. 'Let's get that champagne open then shall we!'

The friends enjoyed twenty minutes of toasting each other while they sipped from their glasses, carefully eating slices of banana and green grapes, and tiny cinnamon buns.

'I could do with a cup of tea' admitted Tabitha.

'No!' chorused the other three.

'We agreed' said Alison. 'Nothing which can stain our clothes.'

'It is lucky I brought these' said Maisie, as she produced four gowns from the hairdressing salon. 'I thought this might happen.'

Laughing, the friends put them on, and Tabitha made a pot of tea.

After they had drunk their tea and polished off the pastries, each of them made a last trip to the toilet, Maisie and Alison touched up everyone's hair and added the flowers, and then Yvonne unzipped the bag she had brought in from her car.

'Alison and Tabitha, in here I have a few special things for both of you. During the past week various members of your family have popped into the shop and given me these items for safe keeping, to be given to you this morning. Something blue for you Alison, from your Uncle Brian.'

Yvonne handed Alison a small blue gift bag decorated in silver stars. Alison took it from her with an expression of surprise mixed with suspicion. 'Uncle Brian has refused to have anything to do with me since I came out as gay. He hasn't put a dog turd in here has he?'

Everyone present knew how difficult Alison's family had made her life in recent years, but her sense of humour about the occasion prompted them to laugh with her. Hamming it up a little, she carefully peered into the bag, and pulled out some of the silver tissue paper inside, revealing a blue velvet-covered box. Her expression was replaced with one of astonishment as she carefully opened it. 'Wow these are stunning! Look at these!' she handed the box to Tabitha, who then passed it along to Maisie.

'They are gorgeous; where did he get them from?' said Maisie, as she stroked the sapphires and diamonds which made up the delicate drop earrings inside the box.

Alison peered into the bag and pulled out more of the tissue paper. 'There is a little card inside too' she said as she opened the envelope and withdrew it, before reading it out to her friends.

'Dearest Alison, please accept these earrings from me with all my love. They belonged to Deidre's mother Joan, who was a true free spirit and chose to defy conventions of the time by flying airplanes for the RAF during WW2. I am sorry that Deidre and I did not give you the love and support you deserved when you made the decision to live your life in the way which best suits you, but I hope this gift goes some way to mending broken bridges. I hope you

have a lovely wedding day with Tabitha, All my love, Uncle Brian.'

The four friends sat in silence. After a while Tabitha said 'How do you feel?'

'Like I need a tissue!' said Alison. 'Wow. I don't know what to feel.'

'I remember how upset he and Deirdre made you' said Maisie.

'To the extent I wasn't sure if I would be welcome at her funeral a couple of years ago' agreed Tabitha.

'I wasn't sure if I would be welcome!' said Alison. 'Wow. I think it took a lot for him to do this for me.'

Yvonne had stayed quiet until now. Gently she said 'He made an appointment to come and see me last month on the pretext of having some antiques he wanted me to value. He spent two hours crying in my kitchen. I think the death of his wife, and being a widower for the past couple of years have made him realise how badly they treated you.'

'Not just them' commented Tabitha.

'Funny you should say that' said Yvonne, as she rummaged in the bag and produced another present for Alison. 'This is also for you.'

Alison took the tiny cream-coloured bag and looked questioningly at Yvonne. 'Silk? she asked.

Yvonne nodded and watched as Alison untied the drawstrings and pulled out a neatly folded piece of paper. As she unfolded it a small coin dropped out onto the kitchen table. Alison picked it up and peered at it, turning it so she could see one side or the other. 'It's a sixpence! What does this note say. Oh!' Tears sprang to her eyes as she saw who it was from. 'It's from Mum and Dad.'

This time she didn't read the contents aloud but absorbed the words before handing the paper to Tabitha. Tabitha read *'Our darling Alison, we wish you all the luck for your*

*wedding day. Here is a family tradition which was first
started with your great great grandmother, and today it is
your turn to continue that tradition, if you wish to do so.
Slip the bag containing the sixpence into your shoe for the
day. All our love to you and to Tabitha, Mum and Dad.'*

'Did you know about this?' Alison asked Tabitha.

'Yes' she nodded. 'Scott almost fell out with them at
Christmas over their behaviour when your daughters were
telling them about our wedding plans. The girls were so
excited, and your parents kept trying to shut them down.
Then your parents started on him, and he said it was as
though they were blaming him for turning you gay and
embarrassing them in front of their friends.'

Maisie took up the story 'According to Scott he spelt out
that they should be proud of their daughter for having the
courage to make a loving home for herself and her
daughters with someone as good for her as you are
Tabitha. He pointed out that the girls love you both, and
are happy and healthy and thriving in this environment, so
what was their problem with their daughter's life-
decisions? If he didn't have a problem with it, why should
they, after all he was the one who had been left for a
woman.'

'Oh my goodness, did he really say all that? Well done
Scott!' Alison clapped her hands and laughed. 'I can
imagine their faces. He used to hate the way they treated
me when we were together, and I had to caution him from
saying too much once Mum started picking on me about
my clothes and Dad started criticising my lack of work-
ethic as he saw it.'

'Says the woman who runs her own successful business
and works hard, while managing to balance that with
always being there for her girls when they have a school

242

play or gymnastics competition' said Tabitha, rolling her eyes. 'You have Scott to thank for this miracle.'

Alison said 'I think I do, yes. I wonder why they didn't give this to me when I married Scott?'

Yvonne judged the time was right to produce another gift from the bag. 'Tabitha, your turn!' she said as she handed over a small flat parcel wrapped in white paper with a pink ribbon.

'Well this can't be a massive family turnaround, because they've known for years about my sexual preferences. I can't remember a time when they weren't accepting and supportive of me' she shrugged. 'Oh! What is this!'

As she untied the ribbon and the paper fell away, the silver photo frame was revealed, holding a picture of a couple on their wedding day. A small card explained *'Great Granny and Great Grandad Leighton, June 17th, 1935'*

'I have never seen this before, they look so young,' she said, tracing their outlines with her finger. 'You know what this means Ali?'

Alison was still composing herself after the emotional revelations which went with the presents, and shook her head. 'No, what does it mean?'

'It means that Great Granny and Great Grandad Leighton were married on the same date as us, eighty-seven years' ago.'

'What a wonderful coincidence!' at last Alison was smiling. 'Look at her dress and hat, they would both look fine if she wore them today. Isn't it funny how some things change, and some things seem to last for ever.'

'One more' said Yvonne, as she produced two small packages from the bag, and handed one to each of the brides. 'But before you open them, here's the card which goes with it.'

'It's from my Nana' said Tabitha. 'Here is what she has written *"A bit of fun for the two of you to wear if you wish. One was mine, and one was my mother's, your Great Grandma Truckell".* Trust Nana!' she laughed, as she and Alison tore open the gold wrapping to each reveal a blue garter.

Alison was reading the label attached to hers 'This says Carol Shoopman Truckell, so that was your great great grandma?'

'That's right. Mine says Mary Symons Court, my nana. I know we said we weren't doing any of these stupid tacky things, but I think you need to slip that sixpence down the side of your shoe, and we both need to wear these garters.'

'I agree. As TV's Miranda's mum would say "Such Fun". Thank you for organising all these Yvonne.'

'All I did was store them for the people who wished you to have them. Scott put in a lot of work with your parents, Alison, and your parents, Tabitha, wanted to give you these presents themselves but once they heard about the efforts Alison's family were making they wanted to join in with this morning's occasion. You'll be seeing them all in an hour and can thank them for yourselves.'

'Do you mean my parents and Uncle Brian are coming to the wedding?' asked Alison.

'Only if you want them there' said Tabitha. 'I have told them they are welcome to come and stand outside the town hall to wish us well, if they want to, but I haven't said anything else.'

Alison looked at her friends while she thought about this. 'Do you know what, life is too short to chase after people who don't want you in their lives, and too short to turn away genuine offers of apology, so if they want to come to the party afterwards at TAA they are welcome, but I do think we should stick to only having those we have already invited to be with us in the room for our marriage ceremony because they are the people who have always been there for us.'

'I think you are right!' said Tabitha and gave her bride-to-be a big kiss.

'Enough of that!' said Maisie, as she gathered up the wrapping paper and gift bags. 'Come on, or we'll be too late for the wedding to take place.'

Chapter 23

The four of them travelled up into Shaftesbury in two separate cars: Alison with Maisie, and Tabitha with Yvonne. Maisie parked her car at her home in Victoria Street, and she and Alison walked along Bell Street to the top of the High Street, and approached the Town Hall from The Commons, while Yvonne left her car at her shop on Angel Lane, and she and Tabitha walked down to the High Street, and up towards the Town Hall. They ended up walking in the road because the narrow uneven pavements were filled with well-wishers, as friends, local shopkeepers standing in their doorways, and people who were visiting the town and became caught up in the occasion cheered and clapped as Tabitha and Yvonne smiled and waved back. Inevitably the road was also filled with cars, buses and delivery vehicles, but even these had stopped and waited while the couple walked by, some beeping their horns and calling congratulations out of their windows.

'I think they think we are the ones who have just got married!' laughed Yvonne.

'You should be so lucky' teased Tabitha.

Up ahead they could see Alison and Maisie were receiving the same treatment, and for a few minutes the centre of Shaftesbury was filled with the spontaneous noise of celebration as friends and strangers alike united. As soon as the two couples came together it was clear who were the brides and who were the matrons of honour.

Tabitha and Alison were wearing beautiful long dresses of gold lace with minute rose-red detail, over champagne-coloured silk. Alison's bodice was fitted, with a round neck and three-quarter length sleeves, the fitted waist flowing into a loose skirt which swished as her long legs moved revealing gold-coloured court shoes into which she had slipped the small silk bag containing her family's silver sixpence. The rose-red detail on her dress was of tiny hairdresser's scissors, round brushes, and combs. Tabitha's skirt was fitted down to her ankles, with a long split up the side to her left knee, and she was wearing gold-coloured sandals revealing her newly pedicured feet with their glittering gold-varnished toenails. Her arms and legs were naturally tanned because she lived in shorts and polo shirts from May until October, but Maisie had given both her and Yvonne a treatment which included fake tan to even out the sock lines and unexplained bruises which go hand-in-hand with a life outdoors. Tabitha's bodice was strapless, revealing her tanned and toned shoulders and arms and a surprising amount of cleavage. Although Tabitha did wear dresses and skirts when she wasn't working, several people did not recognise her because she was usually covered up. Her decision to wear something more revealing for her wedding day had been a surprise, but she was keen to enjoy the glamour of the day and thought that she may wear less buttoned-up tops in future. The rose-red detail on her wedding dress was of tiny sheep, three different designs, and tractors. From a distance their wedding dresses looked as though they were gold with tiny red roses stitched into the fabric.

The four women had spent a lot of time searching for the appropriate underwear for the day, and whereas Alison and Maisie were slim and small-chested and could wear almost anything, Tabitha and Yvonne both had bosoms they usually kept contained in sports bras or minimiser bras. Since they had been measured and probed in ways neither of them ever expected to be by someone with whom they were not in an intimate relationship, Yvonne had taken delight in spending a fortune on pretty bras which fitted and supported her, in different styles and colours, and wearing them at every opportunity, which was all of the times in between horse riding and walking for miles with Zebedee. For practical reasons Tabitha had remained wedded to her sports bras, albeit in a bigger cup size and smaller back size than she had previously believed she fitted, but for the past week she had been wearing one of five strapless bras she had invested in, which came with attachable straps, so that on her wedding day the familiar grooves over her shoulders caused by the straps which for years had been supporting her breasts would be almost invisible. Although she had had a few occasions in recent days when one or both boobs had escaped from their cups, always when she was grappling with a lively lamb, she had been amazed at how they had stayed put for the rest of her farm jobs.

The crowd parted to allow the brides to enter the Town Hall, and then the invited guests streamed in after them and the High Street returned to a normal Saturday morning within minutes, as though the pre-wedding celebrations had never taken place.

Maisie and Yvonne were both wearing mint green dresses with a sweet-heart neckline, fitted bodice, full dipped hem skirts which came to just below the knee so that Maisie's prosthetic leg was visible, and gold lace bolero shrugs. Footwear had been surprisingly easy, because Maisie could only walk in a flat heel and certain styles to fit her prosthetic foot and they had thought it would be difficult to find anything suitable. A chance meeting with a fellow prosthetic leg-wearer whilst sitting outside King Alfred's Kitchen in Shaftesbury had led to a great website which catered for people who wanted to wear pretty and practical footwear. In the same way Yvonne had splurged on new bras, Maisie ended up buying several pairs of boots, shoes, trainers and sandals, after years of wearing one brand of shoe in navy blue or black. For their wedding outfits they wore strappy gold sandals, Maisie in flat heels and Yvonne in two-inch heels which brought her up to Maisie's height.

Inside the Town Hall's Council Chamber Alison's daughters and her ex-husband were waiting for them. Maisie and Alison deftly completed the girls' hairstyles with rosebuds, and complimented Scott on his hairdressing skills. Scott, Alison was relieved to see, looked genuinely happy to be there, and was sporting a mint-green tie. The ceremony was fun, serious, emotional and inclusive, so that everyone felt they had a part to play in Alison and Tabitha's relationship. Afterwards there were a few minutes for hugs and kisses, photographs and congratulations, before they were ushered out of the building and back on the street. Alison made a point of looking for her uncle and parents but couldn't see them amongst the waiting throng. It was Scott who brought them to her, and daughter and niece spent a few quiet minutes with her formally estranged family, before her daughters grabbed everyone's hands and pulled them down the steps to Gold Hill. The tourists were willing to sacrifice a few minutes of their visit to allow people to take photographs of the happy couple as Tabitha and Alison posed and smiled, before calling time and leading their happy cortege between the buildings to Park Walk, where more smiling and posing for photographs could take place in a wider space. Alison and Tabitha had booked a local wedding photographer, Louisa Jane, and she had been taking photographs of them since they started walking towards the Town Hall. They knew she would be capturing their day without the need for formal poses, but they also allowed her, with the help of Maisie and Yvonne, to make sure she captured one or both of them with everyone who was invited. Camera phones were also much in evidence, and the pair posed and smiled for everyone who called to them, and with everyone who asked. When they had started on this adventure they wanted to enjoy the day, and they wanted their friends to enjoy it with them, and with the sun shining and everyone smiling it was exactly how they wished it to be.

Eventually it was time to head to the venue for the party, and Tabitha and Alison hung back while Maisie and Yvonne ushered their guests away from Park Walk and up the High Street, where Lesley Martin and her team were welcoming and directing people along Bell Street and through the open black gates. When the arrangements at Kenyon Hall had fallen through, Maisie had taken on the task of re-inviting all the guests who had accepted the original invitation. At Lesley Martin's suggestion, bearing in mind the new location of the wedding reception, Maisie had included a gold-coloured token, and as they walked down the path between the high walls towards the courtyard there were staff holding trays of fizzy wine from a local vineyard, fruit juice from a local farm shop, and glasses of iced water. The guests exchanged their token for a drink, and those who were trying to sneak in without a token were ushered straight through to the back of the TAA restaurant and found themselves outside on the High Street. George counted seventeen people who exited the courtyard in this way, although this didn't include Alison's parents or uncle because Yvonne had already prepared George to receive them personally.

Alison and Tabitha did not want any formal speeches, or a top table, or anything like that, but chose to make their personal vows to each other in the centre of the courtyard with their friends and family surrounding them, and then it was straight into the party. Local musician Conor Smith began singing and playing his blue guitar in the corner by the fountain, food was brought out at regular intervals by smiling staff, plenty of drink whether alcoholic or not was available, Louisa Jane was taking photographs as people shared confidences, laughed and congratulated the newlyweds. Eventually Louisa Jane put down her camera, and she and her team were able to enjoy the party, Conor also put down his guitar and joined in, and The Songsmiths left their families and came together from various parts of the courtyard to begin singing and playing their music. A rumble of thunder went almost unnoticed, as did the subsequent flash of lightening. The skies darkened, guests began to wonder if they were imagining a raindrop until they were smacked in the face by another, the sky above was suddenly lit up, an incredibly loud clap of thunder made everyone jump, and Lesley and George set the roof in motion to close over the courtyard. The lead singer Pete made a dry comment, and started playing his guitar and singing again, the rest of the band nodded to each other and joined in, and before long the thunder and lightening overhead was forgotten, the sound of the rain on the roof became background noise, and the wedding party continued.

There was a pause while The Songsmiths re-joined the party, and Lesley opened the doors to the room with the long table. Ooohs and aahs greeted the sight, as the wedding cake was revealed. Louisa Jane popped up again with her cameras, Tabitha and Alison thanked everyone who had helped them rescue their party after almost all of

251

their arrangements fell through, and thanked their guests for making their wedding day special, before cutting into the bottom tier and stepping away to let Lesley cut the slices. By the time Joni and Sarah of the Belle Street Duo had started singing, the cake was being eaten, and guests were joining in and dancing.

Gradually the guests began to leave, the remainder of the cake was packed away, and a skeleton staff remained. Tabitha and Alison were sitting with Maisie and Yvonne on two sofas at one end of the courtyard, all feeling remarkably sober. The thunderstorm was long past, the roof had been re-opened, the sky was dark because it was eleven o'clock at night, Lesley had lit a couple of firepits, and instead of fizz and juice, teas and hot chocolates were being passed around.

'What a fantastic day' smiled Alison. 'I can't believe my family were here, and I loved it.'

'I am so happy for you' said Tabitha. 'Their behaviour was the one dark spot on our life together, even though it didn't really affect us.'

'True,' Alison agreed. 'I also think that Charles Diamond did us a favour by cocking up our wedding plans for Kenyon Hall. This has been so much better, and far less hassle, than traipsing everyone up there.'

'I could have done without the stress of trying to arrange everything in a fortnight' said Tabitha. 'But yes, you are right, this has been brilliant. A real Shaftesbury wedding.'

'What on earth are we going to do with our time now?' laughed Maisie. 'This wedding has consumed every spare minute for weeks!'

'You know who I didn't see here today? I didn't see either Tom Archibald or Tim Smith,' said Alison.

'That's true. We did invite both of them and their families, didn't we?' asked Tabitha. 'Although I don't

252

think Tom has a partner, Tim has a wife and kids, but I didn't see any of them.'

'Curious' said Yvonne. 'Everyone else who replied to say they were coming were here, and both Tom and Tim said they were coming. Perhaps they have been caught up in some police emergency.'

Maisie yawned, before clamping her hand over her mouth. 'Gosh I am sorry! I didn't mean to do that.'

Alison yawned 'You've set me off now.'

Both Tabitha and Yvonne started to yawn, and then Maisie did it again which made everyone laugh.

'I think we ought to call it a day' said Tabitha as she looked around the courtyard where there were still a few people sitting at tables or chatting on the sofas. 'Do you think they'll mind if we leave our own party before they do?'

'Not at all!' said Maisie. 'The bride and groom are usually the first to leave their own party.'

'We left ours before the evening entertainment' said Yvonne, causing everyone to look at her. 'What?' she asked.

'You never talk about your wedding' said Tabitha. 'Or your husband.'

'I'm not going to start now. Are you two ready to leave, because I'll get hold of Andy the taxi driver to drive you home if you are.'

Alison and Tabitha looked at each other. 'I fancy walking home, how about you?' Tabitha asked.

'I'd like that' said Alison. 'Even with this coin in my shoe I'd rather walk home than get a taxi. I am still wired from today, even though I am tired. I think walking back through the lanes will be a lovely way to end the day.'

'Come on then, let's say goodbye and thank you to George and Lesley and the team' Tabitha stood up, and held out her hand to Alison.

'They make a lovely couple' commented Maisie as she watched them walk towards the kitchen where the last of the clearing up was taking place.

'They do, and I am really glad today has been as good as it has been' said Yvonne.

'We have George to thank for that. I mean, this place is perfect for weddings, and birthday parties. In fact, any celebration.'

'When you consider today is their first day, it has been amazing' said Yvonne. 'I don't think I noticed anything go wrong.'

'Nor me, although it must have done, it always does' said Maisie. 'Are you going straight home, or do you think we should walk back with them?'

'I am ready for my bed now, but I also think they want to be alone.'

'Thank goodness, I am so tired! I was being serious though; what are we going to spend our time doing now this is over?'

Chapter 24

Yvonne slept late into the next morning, and only awoke because Zebedee told her she needed to go out. Checking the mobile phone on her bedside table she saw it was almost half-past eight in the morning.

'Sorry Zeb, your legs must be crossed!' Yvonne rolled out of bed and opened the door to the wooden steps outside. As it was a Sunday morning the carpark was almost empty, and no one else was around. Leaving the door open, Yvonne went back inside, down the spiral stairs, and made herself a coffee, before returning to the top of the outdoor steps where she had created an area she liked to call her tree house. It was on the wooden balcony which ran around the back facing west and to the side facing south of her building. On the southern side she had a greenhouse built along the wall with a sloping roof following the line of her flat's roof, and accessible from her bedroom through a large sash window. Yvonne rarely climbed into her greenhouse, preferring to walk out of the door from her bedroom onto the balcony, and then through the door into the greenhouse, and instead chose to use the wide seat inside the sash window to cosy up with Zebedee during the winter and watch the rain pour down the glass of the greenhouse. In summer it was the perfect place to lean out to pluck peaches or grapes when they were in season and ripe. On the west-facing side of the balcony was the tree house, which was semi-enclosed by a metal trellis made by a local blacksmith. Yvonne had bought a huge teak swing seat the size of a bed, and the blacksmith designed the arch over the top of it. Yvonne placed big metal troughs on the outside of the arch and along the balcony's railing, into which she had built wooden planters, and all year round she enjoyed seasonal flowers, berries and fruits as she sat or lay in the swing seat. The planters along the railing gave her a degree of privacy from anyone using the carpark below, and the ones to the sides of the arch provided shade or shelter from the wind as well as wonderful scents and fresh salad, fruit and vegetables. Marion Close had sourced some large outdoor wine-coloured cushions which covered the base and back of the seat, and Yvonne had added smaller navy-blue bolster cushions and even smaller gold cushions which she stored in a box around the corner next to the greenhouse. The box was sturdy and had a flat lid, so it could also double up as a table or another place to sit.

Yvonne sat in the swing seat cradling the mug, while she leaned back and enjoyed the sunshine on her bare legs. She was wearing a blue and white t-shirt and shorts pyjama set and reasoned that if anyone saw her they would think she was dressed for the day. She wiggled her gold-painted toes and smiled as she thought back to the wonderful day before. Zebedee tap tap tapped back up the stairs and lay down on the wooden planks with a sigh, stretching out and looking as though she had been there for hours. Yvonne had barely seen George during Tabitha and Alison's wedding day, even though he was an invited guest. She knew he would have been busy working, but she had been expecting to have a quiet moment or two with him, maybe a little slow dance? She wondered if she was reading too much into their friendship, after all the staff at the TAA managed perfectly well when he wasn't there, and the courtyard catering business was designed to work in the same way. She kept checking the carpark to see if he was walking through it, but he did not appear.

Her tummy rumbled and reminded her she had usually eaten something in the morning by now. At the party there had been delicious little pork sausages baked in a honey dressing, and she had eaten quite a few of them but obviously not too many because that was what she fancied to eat now. She decided to have a quick shower and dress and have a wander up the High Street to see what was available for breakfast. Leaving Zebedee to sunbathe, Yvonne closed the dog gate at the top of the steps so that Zebedee wouldn't disturb Rob when he arrived, discarded her coffee mug on her bedside table, showered and washed her hair, and slipped into a sleeveless red and yellow striped maxi-dress. It was too hot for drying her hair or make-up so a big pair of sunglasses hid most of her face, she retrieved her dog from the balcony, and together they walked down the steps to the gates. The maxi-dress had pockets, and Yvonne double checked she had her phone and her keys as well as doggy treats and poo bags before opening the gates.

They crossed the carpark to walk through the old churchyard to Mustons Lane, turned left and joined the High Street. It was funny to think that less than twenty-four hours earlier she had been walking up here with her friend in their finery, as people called out to them and applauded. Now there were a handful of dog walkers, a couple of runners, and a pack of cyclists, none of whom acknowledged her.

King Alfred's Kitchen was open, so Yvonne ordered bacon and maple syrup pancakes, and she and Zebedee settled down at one of their outside tables on the edge of the High Street. Yvonne enjoyed watching the world go by from behind her sunglasses, as her curly hair dried in the sunshine. A few more people began to appear, either on foot or driving their cars, and she smiled and waved to someone she knew every few minutes. After breakfast she and Zebedee strolled back down the High Street and home, where she greeted the two antiques dealers, Rob Kemp and William Drake, who were manning the shop for the day, and then went back up to her bed for a rest.

It occurred to her that for the first time in weeks she had not seen either George, Tim, Tom, or the sneaky man who hid in the shadows. She couldn't remember the last time she had been out in Shaftesbury and hadn't seen one or more of them. She toyed with her phone, tempted to message George, but unsure what she would say. Instead she lay on her bed and switched on the audio book she had been listening to for a few days. There were only five more chapters to go, so she nestled down with Zebedee as the sun streamed through the bedroom window, and fell asleep before more than a minute had passed.

When she woke up it was gone midday. She checked her phone for messages, stretched and yawned, and got up. She wandered downstairs to the shop and saw everything was calm in there. Rob and William were sitting behind the counter having a cup of tea and invited her to join them. While Zebedee lay at their feet, the three of them chatted about an upcoming auction in which there were some beautiful pieces of diamond jewellery for sale. Yvonne's eyes kept flicking to the CCTV screen showing the room where the cellar door was hidden, but the scene did not change.

Rob noticed her watching the screen, and said 'Are you looking at Marion's stand? She still hasn't been in, or contacted any of us.'

'I haven't heard anything from Juliette either' said William. 'She usually rings me to have a moan about something, but she hasn't rung me for weeks.'

'Really?' Yvonne sat up a little straighter. 'When did you last hear from Juliette?'

William shook his head 'I can't remember.'

'You can check your call log?' suggested Rob.

'Good idea.' William pulled his phone from the pocket on the side of his shorts, and scrolled through the list. 'Here we are, she last rang me three weeks ago today. Look, you can see she was ringing at least once if not twice a week before that. Something must have happened to her.'

'I thought she was on holiday?' said Rob.

'Which one?' asked Yvonne.

'Marion went on holiday, not Juliette' said William, frowning at his phone. 'But surely Marion should be back by now?'

'Yes, she should' agreed Yvonne. 'I wonder if we should tell the police?'

'Might be a good idea' nodded Rob. 'Although Tim and Tom seem to have gone AWOL this last week too. I haven't seen either of those two cake-eaters all week!'

'No, now you come to mention it, I haven't seen them either' said William. 'Where is everyone going?'

'I'll pop over to the police station in the morning and see if I can speak to either Tom or Tim' said Yvonne. 'I would rather get some advice from one of them about what to do about Marion and Juliette's apparent absences in case we're making the same mistake the family of the so-called missing granny, Mrs Gooch, made when they reported her missing.'

'That's a good idea. I'm sure if something had happened to either of them someone in their family would have been in touch by now, or we would have heard about it through the antiques dealers' grapevine. I am sure there is nothing to worry about. How was the wedding yesterday?' asked Rob.

'It was wonderful' Yvonne smiled at him. 'Truly wonderful. Everything went to plan, the weather was gorgeous, the brides looked amazing, the wedding ceremony was beautiful, and the party afterwards was brilliant. It is incredible to see what George and his team have created in the space between the restaurant and the café.'

'That is interesting to hear' said William. 'My wife and I will be celebrating our fiftieth wedding anniversary next year, and we would like to splash out and have a party. We didn't do anything when we were married because I was in the army, and we weren't given more than a few days leave. We also did not have enough money to throw around at the time, but now we are in a much better position financially and have children and grandchildren. We would like to have a big family gathering to celebrate with them. Do you think it would be suitable?'

'Absolutely!' said Yvonne. 'Shall I ask George if you can go and see it now? I can cover here in the shop for you.'

'Yes, why not? Thank you' said William. 'My wife will have to see it too, obviously, but at least if I go and have a look I will know if it is not right for us.'

Yvonne was pleased to have a reason to contact George. She sent him a short text asking if she could send William round to the gate on Bell Street and waited for his reply. Several minutes went by without a response, so she checked if the message had been received. Frustratingly it showed it had not been read. She thought about ringing his number but held back. It wasn't as though it was urgent that William visited the courtyard today, and there will have been a lot of clearing up to do after the wedding party. As it was Sunday the restaurant would be busy with Sunday lunches and the café filled with visitors to Shaftesbury. To keep her mind occupied while she was waiting, Yvonne decided to follow up on some research she had been doing into Lindy Speake's family history. It took her a few minutes to settle down in front of her computer in her office, but when William knocked on the door she realised she had been sitting at her desk for almost ninety minutes.

'Hi William, I am sorry, he hasn't got back to me' she said as she waved her phone at him.

'Not to worry! It would probably be better if my wife is with me anyway' said William, graciously. 'I'll phone the restaurant and arrange a time for next week. Thank you for trying for us.'

'Sorry it didn't come to anything.' Yvonne wondered why George still hadn't replied. The text now showed it had been received and read.

'We're both off now' said William. 'We had a sudden rush of customers at half-past three and made three sales, so it was a worthwhile afternoon. See you next week!'

'Thank you William, and sorry again.' After William had closed the door, Yvonne turned back to the screen. She had been exploring Lindy's family tree and discovered that both names Marion and Juliette regularly appeared through her father's line. A thought began to take shape in her mind.

Chapter 25

Monday morning saw Yvonne rising early as usual and driving with Zebedee to the livery yard for an early hack with Toby. They managed to beat the heat of the day and the flies, and enjoyed an hour of walking, trotting and cantering around the fields before returning to the yard. Sally had brought in some homemade lemonade, and Yvonne joined Charlotte, Lindy and Sally in the hay barn, which had become their meeting place since the new hay bales had been brought in for storage.

'It is all very relaxed' Lindy was saying. 'Just turn up any time after five o'clock in the afternoon and leave whenever you have had enough.'

'Would you like a lift to Lindy's party?' Charlotte asked Yvonne. 'My mum has offered to drive us, and there's room for you too.'

'Thank you, that would be lovely. What sort of time are you thinking of going?'

Sally answered 'We thought we'd probably get there a little later than five o'clock, so that Charlotte could help her mum close the shop. Would leaving from yours at five o'clock be alright?'

'Yes, of course, that would suit me too' said Yvonne, calculating it would probably take them roughly half an hour to get to the party venue, Kenyon House. 'You did a fantastic job on Tabitha and Alison's wedding cake, Charlotte.'

'Thank you! I am glad you thought so. They popped round yesterday with a lovely bunch of flowers as a thank you, which I really appreciated. They didn't have to, after all they had paid for the cake, but it was a lovely gesture.'

'It was an amazing wedding' said Sally. 'Who knew that party courtyard existed behind all those buildings in Shaftesbury! We were having such a good time we missed out on the excitement going on in Park Walk.'

'What do you mean?' asked Yvonne. 'What excitement?'

'Haven't you heard?' asked Charlotte. 'There was a massive police operation on Park Walk, police vans everywhere, and loads of people were carted off in them.'

'What? What happened? Was there a fight or something?'

Sally said 'There definitely wasn't a fight because one of my friends lives there, and she said they were sitting out in their garden enjoying the peace and quiet at the end of the day, watching the bats swoop overhead, when all of a sudden they could see several vehicles with blue flashing lights tearing down the A350 from Cann towards Shaftesbury, and the next minute there were vehicles coming from all directions onto Park Walk, lots of shouting and the sounds of people trying to run away, doors slamming, and then the vehicles drove off and they could see them all going back the other way up the A350 with sirens on and lights flashing! She reckons there were about a dozen of them, and her son, who was upstairs in his bedroom, said there were ten more unmarked cars and vans which headed down the B3091 in the direction of Sturminster Newton.'

'How does he know they were unmarked cars?' asked Charlotte.

'Because they were also on Park Walk with their blue lights flashing through the grills at the front, and they left after the marked ones but without their blue lights on,' said Sally.

'What kind of operation involves that many vehicles?' asked Lindy.

'Probably drugs' shrugged Sally. 'My friend said it was all over in fifteen minutes, from start to finish.'

'How many people must they have arrested if they needed over twenty cars and vans?' asked Yvonne.

'Who knows?' said Sally. 'My friend could only hear, she and her husband couldn't see anything, and their son didn't notice the blue flashing lights outside his bedroom window until it was almost over.'

'I can't believe this is the first I am hearing of it!' said Yvonne, as she wondered why no one had mentioned it while she was eating her breakfast on the High Street, or why none of the customers in the shop the day before had said anything about it.

'It is all over social media and was reported on Alfred radio' said Charlotte. 'That's how I knew something had happened.'

'I'll have a look when I get back home' said Yvonne. 'Speaking of which, I had better get a move on. I need to open the shop today because we seem to be missing a couple of staff.'

'I have checked the weather forecast, and we could do another night ride tomorrow evening if you would like to join us?' said Sally.

'Yes please!' all thoughts of drug raids flew from her mind as Yvonne remembered the fun she had on their last one.

'That's good, it will be the four of us again. Meet here at half-past eight?'

'I'll be ready!'

Yvonne drove home, making sure she had the car radio tuned in to Alfred, but instead of news of Saturday night's police activity she was treated to a short story by Sarah English which was far more enjoyable, and arrived at her gates just as the conclusion was reached. Great timing, she thought as she drove in and parked, pleased to see she had beaten Rob and hers was the only car in the driveway. He was lovely but tended to keep her talking when she had things on her mind. She unlocked the back door and let herself and Zebedee in, and quickly walked through the shop to the other side, where the cellar door was hidden behind the bookcase. She peeped around the corner but couldn't see anyone or anything. She carefully moved the bookcase so that there was room for her to walk behind it to the door. She hesitated, unsure whether to knock, but in the end decided to open it without announcing her presence. She needn't have worried, because the cellar was empty, no trace of the police team who had been on the stakeout. The tunnel door was closed, so Yvonne went over and tested it. It had been securely locked but had not been replaced and so she could peer through the wide gap between the door and the door frame. Using the torch on her mobile phone she could see that the tunnel was empty. She studied the lock and wondered what was happening. Surely the police would need to give her the key to it?

Zebedee, who had been giving the cellar a thorough sniffing, suddenly shot through the door into the shop, and within seconds Yvonne could hear the sounds of Rob being greeted by her dog. Hurriedly she too left the cellar, closing the door shut, and pushing the bookcase back into position. She hadn't turned on the screens at the desk when she arrived and knew he couldn't watch her on the CCTV. Casually she peered into one of the cabinets as if there was an item that interested her, before sauntering through the shop to where Rob was still being forced to make a fuss of Zebedee.

He looked up as she appeared and said 'I know she only loves me for the doggie biscuits in my pocket' he grinned.

The first customers were waiting outside the shop in Angel Lane, and from the moment Yvonne opened the front door until midday there was a constant stream of people coming in, either customers or dealers. Yvonne reflected on what a good bunch of people she had in her shop, as she looked around and saw one dealer after another answering questions, opening cabinets to show interested buyers the contents, or offering to carry the heavier items out to the customer's car. Her eyes kept straying over to Juliette's and Marion's stands, and she resolved to seek out either Tim Smith or Tom Archibald and make them tell her exactly what was going on.

'It must be lunchtime' observed Rob. 'The place is empty!'

All the customers had disappeared, and the only people who remained were antiques dealers trying to rearrange their stands to lessen the ravaging effects of the public. Just at that moment the bell rang, and Tim walked in. Yvonne looked behind him but could see no sign of Tom.

'That's my cue to go and put the kettle on!' said Rob with an air of proprietary which made Yvonne smile.

Skipping formalities, Yvonne asked 'Where's Tom?'

Tim grimaced. 'Poor Tom is in hospital, after a fall last night during a police operation.'

'Not this business on Park Walk?'

Tim nodded. 'Yes. He was dealing with some suspects and was injured.'

Yvonne was surprised to find how concerned she was for a man she barely knew, and who most of the time she

266

regarded as a bit of a nuisance. 'Is he alright? What about his dog?'

Tim gave her a peculiar look. 'His dog wasn't with him. Stan isn't a police dog, you know.'

Feeling foolish Yvonne said 'I know that. I meant, is anyone looking after his dog?'

'Oh, sorry, I see what you mean. I have no idea.' He stood for a moment, obviously working something out. 'I had better check on him, just in case.'

'I'll come with you' said Yvonne. 'I'll put Zebedee away.'

She made sure Rob was happy to run the shop on his own while she popped out for an hour, and left the shop with Tim.

'He lives on his own, does he?' she asked.

Tim nodded 'Yes.'

Yvonne waited a few moments, but he didn't seem to be any more forthcoming. 'Where does he live?'

'In Bimport.'

'Do you have a key?'

'What? No.' Tim glanced sideways at her, and said 'I'm sure the dog's fine, but we'll go and have a look, just to make sure. If I need to I'll break in.'

'Or we could give Tom a ring and ask if he has a spare key secreted anywhere around the place.'

Tim shook his head. 'Tom is not in any state to answer.'

He was walking quite fast, and Yvonne was struggling to keep up, let alone speak, but she persisted with her questions 'What's happened to him?'

'I told you; he fell.'

They had already passed the black gates to George's courtyard venue and were heading into Bimport. As they marched on, Yvonne noticed the amount of police vehicles and tape around the Trinity Centre. An awful thought struck her. 'He didn't fall from there, did he?'

Tim looked at her, and she pointed at the tower. 'No, he didn't fall from there, but he did fall inside there. Come on, this is Tom's house.'

They had arrived at a large house set back from the road and surrounded by tall iron railings. The gates were locked, but Tim held a small machine up to the electronic pad, and they swung open. Wondering if his machine worked on her gates, Yvonne could feel the concern she had about him a few days ago rushing back. She looked around but could see nobody else in their vicinity. Tim was already heading around the back of the house, and Yvonne decided she had no choice but to follow him. She caught up as he approached the back door, but before he could try the handle the sound of barking nearby stopped them both in their tracks. They looked around, but no dog appeared although the barking continued. They were standing on a gravel path which bordered a small lawn surrounded by mature shrubs and trees. The barking appeared to be coming from the other side of the house, and so Tim and Yvonne walked along the path towards a building on the back of the house an estate agent would describe as a garden room. As they approached Yvonne could see there was a sturdy trellis roughly six feet high forming a tunnel which filled one side of the garden. It was covered in a variety of climbing plants, including roses and jasmine, and both looked and smelled attractive. Suddenly Stan appeared inside the tunnel. To Yvonne's relief she realised it was actually a dog run, and fully enclosed with wire mesh. The dog run started at the end of the garden room, where a dog flap enabled Stan to come and go as he pleased.

'Hello Stan!' Tim greeted him, and at the sound of his voice Stan immediately came rushing over wagging his tail. Tim looked up and down the inside of the run. Satisfied he said 'He's alright for water and getting out into the garden when he needs to, but I don't suppose Tom left him with a tin opener.'

They explored the exterior of the run, and although there were a couple of gates into it, both were securely locked. Standing back, they scrutinised the rear of the house for any windows which were open, but as expected for a policeman's home there were no easy points of entry.

'I suppose we could push food through the holes' said Yvonne, looking at the sturdy wire mesh. 'If Tom went out to work yesterday evening, Stan hasn't been fed for at least fourteen hours.'

Tim shook his head 'I think it would have to be liquidised. Those gaps aren't very big.'

'Probably designed to prevent birds and small mammals from getting trapped inside. What do you think? We could cut a hole in the mesh, or break a window or break down one of the doors?'

Tim sighed. 'Tom went on duty at ten o'clock yesterday morning, which means his dog hasn't been fed for over twenty-four hours. If we had more time I wouldn't do this, but I think for the animal's sake I need to do something I am going to have to pay for with large amounts of cake' and he pulled his mobile from his uniform.

Although Yvonne could only hear his side of the conversation, she could tell the person on the other end of the phone was enjoying the request for a favour. Within less than seven minutes Tim had let another man into Tom's garden.

'This is Adam.'

Adam gave Yvonne a big grin 'The police always have to call the firefighters to get them out of trouble.'

Tim started to try to defend himself 'I could do it, but I don't have any equipment on me.'

Ignoring him, Adam started to work on the back door lock, and in no time the door was open. Stan, who had been watching the humans, worked out what was happening and went flying through the dog flap into the house. The back door opened into a huge kitchen, low ceilings and dark in a typical cottage-style, with an AGA on one wall and a large butler-style sink opposite it under a window overlooking the garden. Tim's six-foot two-inch frame had to stoop, and he made his way carefully across the kitchen negotiating the large pine scrubbed rectangular-shaped table in the middle and making sure to duck under the low beams which ran across the ceiling lowering the height even further. Yvonne could see a door at the end behind which they could hear Stan gently whining. The door was painted a strong yellow and matched the AGA

'I assume he's friendly?' Adam asked.

Tim shrugged 'We're about to find out.'

'Sorry mate, I must go so I won't be finding out. I'll leave you to it. Good luck!'

'Thanks for doing this. No doubt I'll be paying for it for years to come' Tim grinned.

'You can bet on it' said Adam, as he sketched a wave and disappeared through the back door, closing it behind him.

Tim opened the door, and Stan launched himself through it, greeting everyone with enthusiasm. Tim walked into the large utility room, which Yvonne guessed must have been a larder originally, and started to search through the cupboards for a bag of dog food. Yvonne went straight to the tall free-standing fridge, and inside were five

Tupperware boxes containing a mixture of meat and vegetables. When Tim's search proved fruitless, Yvonne took one of the boxes and emptied the contents into a dog bowl which had been lying on the draining board.

'I feed Zebedee like this, so it is possible Tom does too.'

'You don't think you have just given Tom's dinner to the dog?'

'Possibly! But then from what you've said Tom won't be home to eat it any time soon.'

On the kitchen noticeboard was a card for the doggy day-care in Hannam where Tom took Stan when he was going to be working consecutive long shifts. Tim rang the number and spoke to a lady called Sue, explained the situation, and Sue agreed to have Stan for the foreseeable future. After Tim finished the call he said 'She knows Stan, and says he gets on with her dogs so she'll keep him in her home until Tom can look after him again. She's coming up for him now.'

'Are you going to tell me exactly what is wrong with him?'

Tim sighed and rubbed his face. Yvonne realised he must have been part of the team on Park Walk the night before last, and wondered how much, if any, sleep he had managed since then. 'Did you see any milk in that fridge?'

Yvonne opened the door again, and Stan looked up, hopefully. 'I suppose he's missed a meal, if Tom went to work yesterday morning' she said, and took out another Tupperware box, and the bottle of local cow's milk. 'By the way, one of my antiques dealers has been missing for a while, well two of them have. One called Marion Close who we knew was going on holiday, but she hasn't returned to work and isn't answering emails or phone calls, and the other called Juliette Monk who seems to have vanished.'

'Message their details to me and I'll see what I can do' said Tim. 'I'll put the kettle on to boil.'

While Tim made the tea, he told her a few more details about the previous evening. 'I don't suppose it matters now, since you have been involved, but things are still operational and haven't been confirmed yet. What I am saying is, please don't discuss this with anyone else. Except for George, because he was involved too.'

'George was involved! Is he under arrest?'

'No, not like that. Let me explain. The tunnel which ended at your shop starts at the abbey ruins, and runs under the town from west to east, with branches off at various points. The gang headed up by Jane Poundsmith have been moving mostly stolen jewellery from all over the United Kingdom down to Shaftesbury, and depositing it in the tunnel entrance at the Abbey or through the one in the bakery on the High Street.'

'Surely someone would notice if people were going into the Abbey with bags and leaving without them?'

Tim shook his head 'Jewellery isn't a big bulky item like, for example, the farm machinery this gang also steal, or the kilos of heroin they buy and sell. You can have several thousand pounds worth of rings in a normal size shoulder bag, and no one would know. The couriers were able to walk into the grounds and drop the bags containing the jewellery down a small shaft hidden behind a low wall, eat an ice cream or have a coffee, and walk out again. There are several different ways of accessing Park Walk, and so the same person could come and go without raising suspicion for years. The bakery would pretend to be having a delivery of ingredients, and those bags would be stored in the opening to their part of the tunnel. Jane would walk along the tunnel from your shop and collect the bags of stolen goods, and walk back again, storing the items in those boxes you found.'

'How does George fit in to this?' Yvonne was desperate to hear that he was on the side of the police, and not Jane Poundsmith and her gang.

Tim studied his tea before lifting the mug and draining it. 'It is complicated, but a large part of Jane Poundsmith's business was laundering the money she made from the drugs and stolen property by obtaining high end food and drink and selling it through up-market establishments.'

'Like Kenyon Hall?'

Tim nodded 'Like Kenyon Hall. George is an astute businessman, who travels around the country checking in with the businesses in the Jimmy Mack chain, and for several years he has been curious about how some of the competition are able to obtain certain products. When Tabitha and Alison began to have problems with their wedding plans he asked his contacts about other places similar to Kenyon Hall, and a pattern began to emerge of failures to provide the food and drink which had been promised. He came to us with the information, most of which we were aware of, but some was not on our radar, and it helped to fill in a few gaps in the intelligence. The tunnel from your shop runs underneath The Abbess Aethelgifu too, and George has allowed us to access the tunnel from his restaurant.'

'So where does Tom falling down inside the Trinity Tower come into it, if all the action was going on underground and on the ground?' Yvonne asked.

'I don't suppose it matters if I tell you. No doubt the Shaftesbury grapevine will make up something even more implausible' said Tim. 'Have you ever been up there?'

Yvonne shook her head. 'No, I haven't even been inside the building, let alone up the tower.'

'It is a fantastic viewpoint. We have access to it for surveillance purposes.'

Yvonne looked at him disbelievingly. 'You're kidding. Surely these days everything is done with cameras and listening devices.'

'You can't beat eyes on the ground. Or in this case up in the air.' A message came through on Tim's phone. 'Sue is here. That was quick. I'll go and let her in.'

While he was gone, Yvonne looked around for anything Stan might need to take with him for his mini break. When Tim reappeared with a friendly blond-haired lady she had gathered up a lead, a dog bed, and a clean food bowl.

'Hello Stan!' Sue greeted the dog affectionately, and his levels of excitement went up three notches from the greeting he had given his rescuers half an hour earlier. Seeing the small pile Yvonne had collected on the table Sue said 'Oh we won't worry about any of that. Stan sleeps in any of the dog beds in my kitchen or on the sofa, and I have plenty of dog bowls. I will pop his harness on' she said as she unhooked a fluorescent yellow dog harness from the back of the door.

Stan happily trotted after her, and Tim, having found a spare key in one of the kitchen drawers, waited while Yvonne washed their tea mugs up before locking Tom's house. Together they walked through the electronic gates, and he repeated his magic trick with the small gadget, before turning to her and asking 'Would you like to see the view from the top of the tower?'

No fan of heights, Yvonne took a moment to think about it before saying 'yes please!'

They walked in silence to the base of the tower, where Tim unlocked the arched door painted gunship grey, and she followed him up the steep narrow spiral stairs. There was no handrail or even rope, and Yvonne found she

274

needed to put both hands onto the cool stone on either side of the winding staircase as she climbed. She ran up and down her own iron spiral staircase all the time, but she realised that hers spiralled anti-clockwise, and the treads were much wider than this one. Approximately halfway up was a small stone landing with a wooden door.

'What's behind there? She asked, trying not to breathe too heavily. She really must take up another form of exercise.

'It's where we have a special operations room, lots of technology and dead birds.'

'Dead birds!'

'Yes, it's the former bell tower, and pigeons always get in somehow. If no one goes in there for a week there is always at least one dead bird on the floor. Beats me why they can't go back out the same way they came in. Anyway, I can't show you in there for obvious reasons, but Tom was working in there and someone came up here and attacked him.'

'You mean he fell down the steps we have just climbed?'

Tim nodded. 'Come on, we have more to climb before we get to the top.'

They emerged into bright sunlight, through another wooden door, and stepped out onto wooden floorboards. 'Wow!' All thoughts of Tom and his terrible fall were temporarily forgotten as Yvonne slowly turned three hundred and sixty degrees as she gazed at the stunning landscape. She noticed that she didn't feel any fear considering they were over one hundred feet from the ground, and the town of Shaftesbury is over seven hundred feet above sea level. The wide chest-high wall surrounding them enabled her to enjoy the view without breaking out into a sweat. She ventured closer to the wall and looked over at the Abbey gardens below. Her eyes followed the paths and roads so familiar to her when she was walking, riding or driving along them, but the change in perspective gave her a new vision of her town.

'I can see why you would use this as an observation post. Although it is limited because of the height. You can't tell who those people are down there, let alone what they are doing. And the trees and bushes obscure much of the view if you were tracking somebody.'

Tim made no comment.

Yvonne continued to study the countryside around them, spotting routes that she and Toby regularly rode, and wondering if it was possible to reach others on horseback.

'We do live in a beautiful area' she said, eventually.

She followed Tim back down the stone steps, imagining how terrifying it would be to slip and tumble down, hoping that Tim would break her fall without falling himself. She had been too busy concentrating on keeping her legs moving and breathing properly on the way up to notice the blood stains on the walls, although someone had attempted to remove them. She shivered and resolved to find out when she could visit Tom as soon as possible.

Back on the ground, Tim relocked the door, and Yvonne said 'If there is anything I can do for Tom, will you let me know?'

He nodded. 'Someone will be coming to see you later today, to talk to you about the tunnel from your cellar. It won't be me. I'm heading for my bed.'

'Thank you for showing me that amazing view. Go and get some rest.'

One of the clocks chimed the hour, and glancing at her watch Yvonne realised she had been gone from the shop for two hours. She hurried back along Bell Street to Angel Lane and walked in through her shop's front door to find a huddle of antiques dealers around the counter.

'What's happened?' she asked, as she looked from one upset face to another.

'It's Juliette' said William. 'She's dead.'

Chapter 26

There were no customers in the shop, and so Yvonne turned the sign to CLOSED and locked the door. In a departure from her usual etiquette, she invited everyone into her kitchen, and made them tea or coffee as they sat around her kitchen table. Although Juliette had not been a popular member of the team, in fact she had been the only unpopular dealer, it was clear that the news of her death had shocked those present. Yvonne did a quick calculation and thought that there were five members of the team who were missing. Then she remembered that if she was right she wasn't expecting to see Marion again, and Juliette definitely wasn't coming back, and revised the number to three absent dealers. She placed mugs in front of people, but no one picked them up.

Yvonne took her place at the table and asked 'How do you know she has died?'

All eyes turned to William. He said 'My wife and I use the same paper shop as Juliette for our newspaper to be delivered. I went in to pay our monthly bill, and the woman behind the counter told me.'

'How come the newsagent told you?' Rob asked. 'Did she know you knew Juliette?'

'No, I asked her how she was, and she started to tell me about it. She was worried because Juliette used to have a copy of every newspaper delivered to her home every day, and the bill was almost three months outstanding. It's only a little village shop, and they don't have the margins to cover that sum of money and they had been putting a lot of effort into trying to get in touch with her. They had been to her house on several occasions, and eventually contacted the police because they were worried about her. Apparently she always paid on time, and with two missed payments and a third rapidly approaching it was so out of character the police took it seriously and did some investigating. None of her neighbours had seen her for weeks, just as we hadn't either. Her car was in the garage to the side of her house, her plants in the garden and on the windowsills were unwatered and either dead or dying, and she had a weekly food delivery from the local farm shop which had sat uncollected on the doorstep for the first week until they came to deliver the second week, and sensibly took the first away as well as the undelivered second box. People in the area had begun to talk and ask questions, so when the local police turned up there were several neighbours who wanted to help.'

Firstly, it was news to Yvonne that anyone read newspapers anymore, let alone had them delivered. Secondly, although she could imagine William settled down with a copy of The Guardian, she couldn't imagine Juliette sitting down and reading anything. Juliette was a busy person, always late, always running out of time to do the jobs expected of her in the antiques shop. The thought of her spending time quietly reading newspaper articles was unimaginable.

William took a sip of his coffee, and sighed, looking down at the mug he cradled in his hands. 'Her body was found in an armchair in the conservatory. She had been tortured. That's all the police told the newsagent. But it's enough. My imagination has been working overtime. Especially with the state of that body you found, Yvonne.'

Quietly, Yvonne said 'I believe that body was Marion.'

A collective intake of breath went around the table.

Nobody spoke, until Rob asked 'How do you know?' Does that mean the two murders are related?'

He was looking at Yvonne, as though she had all the answers, which she supposed was fair enough although she didn't know everything. She had suspected that Juliette and Marion were connected in some way, but to hear that they had both died brutal deaths was difficult to comprehend. Were they both mixed up in this gang? Was it Juliette who was Jane Poundsmith, and not Marion as she thought? She shook her head. All she had was suspicions from which she had drawn her own conclusions. It would be wrong to share her thoughts with these people, particularly as the only fact she had been given by the police was that the dead body in the field was that of Jane Poundsmith. The antiques dealers had not been told about the jewellery found inside the tunnel, or the police operation in the cellar. She was desperate to talk to somebody, but didn't know who to trust.

'I am sorry Rob, I don't know for sure. This is a lot to take in. There has been a lot going on since George and I found that body, and there are things I can't reveal until they are made official by the police. Whatever the truth, at least one of our team has died, and I am shocked and saddened.'

There was a general murmur of agreement.

Yvonne continued 'I think we should close up for the rest of the day, perhaps even the week. What do you all think?'

'I think it would be a good idea to close until the weekend,' said Rob. 'Give us all a little time to get our heads around what has happened to Juliette, and perhaps allow some time to find out about Marion.'

'I agree,' said William. 'I think we should close as a mark of respect for Juliette, and while there is some uncertainty about the whereabouts and health of Marion I'm not sure I can put on a happy welcoming face to customers as they walk through the door.'

'Alright then, we'll reopen on Saturday' said Yvonne. 'We will need to sort out a few practical issues like redoing the rotas, but leave that to me and I'll be in touch via email if that's OK with everyone?'

The subdued team nodded in unison, and one-by-one took their mugs to the sink, rinsed them, and put them on the draining board. They left via the back door, leaving Yvonne alone with Zebedee in her kitchen. She picked up her phone and texted George.

'Are you "At Home"?' she asked.

Immediately the reply came back 'No. I'm over the road from you. Can I come over when I'm finished here?'

Deducing he must be at the police station, Yvonne replied 'Yes.'

Not knowing if he was going to be five minutes or five hours Yvonne decided to keep busy. She went into the shop and armed with a large roll of bubble wrap and a stack of boxes began packing up the stock belonging to Marion and to Juliette, deciding that if she was wrong about Marion she would have a substantial amount of apologising to do. Focusing on wrapping and packing different sizes and shapes into some of the many banana boxes the shop accrued was just what she needed while her mind reviewed the events of the past few weeks. She made use of the bigger items of furniture such as Marion's bookcase, and a large table on Juliette's stand, to create a closed-off section, behind which she could stack the boxes out of the public's reach. Obviously if someone was desperate to steal something it wouldn't take too much effort, but Yvonne thought the presence of manned CCTV cameras and the location of the stock in the end room of the shop might put a stop to that. She wondered why the police had not been in touch with her about the deceased women's belongings.

Her phone pinged just as she had finished and was surveying her work to see if she could arrange the barricades any better. She was surprised that almost two hours had passed, and that she was hungry. She walked through to the kitchen and pressed the button to let George in through the gates, before washing her hands at the sink. Glancing down she could see that her t-shirt was filthy from close proximity with all those antiques, and she was sweaty from the exertion. Nice.

'I don't know if you are hungry, but I popped up to your friend Charlotte's bakery and bought these strawberry and cream tarts.'

Realising she hadn't had any lunch, Yvonne said 'Wow those look delicious! I am just going to quickly make myself some toast first, before I eat all that sweetness. Would you like any toast?'

'Yes, please. A lot has happened since we were last together. How are you?'

'I am not sure. I found out today that there are now two of my Angel Lane Antiques dealers who have been murdered. It is all a bit scary.'

'Two?'

Yvonne told George what she knew about Juliette's death, which was very little, while they passed butter and marmite to each other, and ate their toast. She gestured to her t-shirt. 'That is why I look like this. I have been packing up their stands. Although I have no idea what I am going to do with it all. What have you been up to?'

George told her about the supply contacts and the rumours in the trade, and they compared notes about their tunnel. It turned out that George knew all about the police presence in the tower, and apparently it was common knowledge in the town.

'Not that common!' exclaimed Yvonne. 'What is going to happen to the tunnels now, do you know?'

George shook his head 'I have no idea. I have secured the entry into it from the restaurant, and I assume you have done the same here?'

'Not really, although the police put a new lock on the door.'

'I think it would be a good idea for you to make it secure, especially considering the value of the items you have in your shop.'

'Of course it would, I don't know why I haven't got onto it before.'

All conversation stopped while they tucked into the tarts, laughing at each other as they got cream down their chins and up their noses.

'Would you like to come to a party with me on Saturday?' asked Yvonne before her brain could stop her mouth from running away. 'It's nothing exciting, just someone from the livery yard. It's her fiftieth birthday, and she's having a little celebration.'

'I'd love to,' said George. 'I am sorry I didn't see you at Tabitha and Alison's wedding, but I got caught up with the police shortly after their ceremony, and I couldn't leave the station until late on Saturday night by which time you had all gone home. I gather it all went well? Lesley said they had a few hiccups, but otherwise everything went to plan.'

'Oh my goodness your team were fantastic,' gushed Yvonne. 'Lesley is a marvel, isn't she? Tabitha and Alison were so pleased, and if there were a few hiccups we didn't notice them.'

'That's good' said George. 'Always better to appear to be the swan gliding along the water, than reveal those feet madly paddling underneath.' He yawned. 'I am sorry. It was a late night last night, and then I have been at the police station for several hours today. Hopefully they have finished with me now, because there was very little I could tell them after the initial information.'

'I am feeling a bit tired now too, and I haven't had any of the stress you have had. I think I need a bit of time to take in everything that has happened recently.'

'Perhaps I will see you tomorrow?' asked George.

'Definitely. We have decided to keep the shop closed for the rest of the week, which will free up my time. Anything you would like to do?'

There was a brief pause before George answered, where Yvonne felt a frisson of excitement. Really, with all the death and injury going on around her she shouldn't be thinking about sex.

'Would you and Zebedee like to come with me for a sail on my friend's boat? He has recently bought it and wants to take it for a trip over to the Isle of Wight and back.'

'I would love to! I need to be back here in time to go out for an evening hack with the girls, but that won't be a problem, will it?'

'No, we should be back in Shaftesbury by five o'clock tomorrow afternoon.'

'Are you sure it will be alright for Zebedee to come?'

'Absolutely. He has two dogs who always go out on the boat with him, and he has doggy buoyancy aids and clips the dogs onto a line so they can't jump or fall overboard. I must confess I have already asked if the two of you can join us.'

After George had left, Yvonne went upstairs to her tree house and sat with a glass of rosé wine, curled up in one corner of the bench swing, and allowed her mind to relax. So much had happened in the previous few weeks she was struggling to process it all. Once the glass was empty, she went down to her office for some paper and a pen, returned to her place on the swing bench and wrote it all down in the notebook she had found in one of the drawers of her desk. Discovering the jewellery, the murdered body, George, the problems with Charles Diamond and Kenyon Hall, the breakfast ride to the airfield, the night ride, the mystery man always lurking whenever George was around, the policemen's unusual behaviour with telephone messages and hanging around outside her home, the relief of the wedding venue, catering, cake, musicians, discovering the stolen jewellery on her premises, discovering the tunnel, discovering the body was that of someone she had known, walking up the High Street with Tabitha on her wedding day, the joy and celebration of that day, learning about Tom's injuries, finding out that Juliette had been murdered.

When she had finished she closed the notebook, she looked across the carpark to the roofs which stretched out in front of her. The scene always brought to mind the chimney sweeps singing and dancing along the roof tops in Mary Poppins, but now her mind was on people scurrying along the tunnels underneath the town.

Chapter 27

Yvonne slept deeply that night and awoke refreshed the following morning. George came to pick her and Zebedee up in his Jaguar, and Zebedee sat proudly in the back in her car seat harness, enjoying the sensation of the wind on her face as he drove them with the car's roof down. George's friend and his wife were welcoming to both Yvonne and Zebedee, and Yvonne realised with shame she hadn't brought anything for them. It hadn't even crossed her mind, and so once they landed at the marina on the Island, she insisted on buying everyone's food in the beachside pub. A substantial ploughman's lunch filled their bellies ready for the return journey, and it felt as though time had passed in a flash when they moored back at the boat's home. Zebedee and the couple's German Shepherd dogs had become firm friends on the boat, and the couple invited Yvonne to join them and George on their next trip over to the Island the following week, which she enthusiastically accepted, resolving to make sure she brought a marine-appropriate gift with her next time.

George drove into the carpark before the town's various clocks chimed five o'clock and came in for a quick cup of tea before he had to rush back to the restaurant ready for evening service. Yvonne took Zebedee for a half hour walk around the town, making sure she passed Tom's house so she could have another look at it. It really was a magnificent place for one person to live in, and she wondered what his story was. Not expecting an answer, she sent him a text wishing him well, and continued on her way home. She fed Zebedee, retrieved her equipment for the night ride from the downstairs loo and checked it was all still in working order before loading it into her car. A quick change into riding clothes, and she drove down to the livery yard, leaving Zebedee at home for once flaked out on one of the sofas in the kitchen rather than the middle of Yvonne's bed.

After the sea air and socialising for several hours, Yvonne was feeling tired, but didn't want to miss out on the adventure with her friends. She left the other three to chatter about Tabitha and Alison's wedding, and Lindy's upcoming party, and enjoyed being out with her horse in the warm summer's evening. As before the women took care to make sure all four horses were calm and confident in the company and position within the ride, and Charlotte's horse Sparkle surprised everyone by settling in straight away and even allowing Charlotte to open and close one of the gates without any drama. Sally had worked out a different route this time, and they ventured through tracks and fields Yvonne had not ridden in before, and again she was taken aback by the stunning views and countryside they had on their doorstep.

As they turned towards home the sun was setting behind Duncliffe Woods, and for a few minutes they rode alongside each other in a line watching as the colours of the sky changed from blue to a yellow haze, pinks, reds, oranges, until finally dark blue. Their way home was along quiet country lanes and so everyone had turned on their lights on their riding hats and hi-vis waistcoats, but before they needed to switch on the lights on the horses' tails they were able to leave the roads and join the fields belonging to their home farm. They turned their lights off and revelled in the freedom of riding their horses in the light of the darkness, the horses having no difficulty in seeing their way.

A pot of mushroom soup had been left for them by the farmer, and although Yvonne had planned not to stay for supper but go straight home to bed, the enticing smell of the soup and her stomach reminding her that she hadn't eaten since lunchtime, meant it was gone midnight before she eventually showered and changed into sleeping vest and shorts, and climbed into bed.

Just as she was dropping off to sleep she realised it was the first time since she had discovered the tunnel that she hadn't checked for signs of use before locking up and going to bed for the night. Convincing herself that there hadn't been any evidence that anyone other than the police had been near it for the past few weeks, and as the police operation was now over there wouldn't be anyone left to carry on using it, she decided not to get out of bed to check.

The following morning she and Zebedee went to the livery yard to check and feed the horses, because it was her turn on the rota. It was a beautiful, calm sunny summer's day, and Yvonne enjoyed being the only human at the yard, although she could see the farmer's tractor in one of the distant fields and knew he had been out of bed long before she had. She gave Toby a quick brush with a rubber curry comb, just to get the last of the dried sweat patches off from behind his ears and under his girth. They had all washed the horses with wet sponges the evening before, but Toby had enjoyed a good roll in the dirt by the shelters, and the soil had clung onto the wet patches.

Satisfied he was looking much cleaner, Yvonne left her horse to spend the day sheltering from the forecast sun, and drove home. As soon as she opened the back door to the shop her phone rang. It was Tim Smith.

'I just thought I would let you know that Tom is coming home today. I am going to collect him some time after two o'clock.'

'Thank you Tim, that is good news. Is there going to be anyone to help him once he is home?'

'No, although a few of us will be dropping in to make sure he is alright and fetch any shopping he needs. He is going to be capable of doing most things for himself, although he has arranged with Sue to keep Stan until the weekend.'

'That sounds positive! Can I drop in once he is home and settled in?'

'He would like that' said Tim. 'I'll get him to text you once he's home. I am sure he would appreciate some company.'

Yvonne had been walking slowly through the shop while they chatted, and as they said their goodbyes she stopped in her tracks. The pile of boxes that she had neatly stacked belonging to Marion and Juliette had disappeared, leaving empty tables, chairs and the bookcase.

She realised Tim was still talking on the phone. 'What's happened? Yvonne! Are you alright? What's going on?'

'Sorry, I have just discovered that Marion and Juliette's stock has been stolen!'

'Where from?'

'My shop!'

'I'm coming over. I am ten minutes away. Don't touch anything.'

True to his word, in less than nine minutes Tim arrived at the front door, with four other policemen and women. One of the women started to question Yvonne about what had been stolen, who had access to it, and when she had last seen the items, while the others listened. Yvonne explained that she had decided not to open her shop for a few days, and no one except her had access. She had got into the habit of removing the key from the lock box outside the front door at night and replacing it in the morning, and after all her antiques dealers had left following William's revelations about Juliette, she had removed the key and put it in her office. She was kicking herself for not checking the tunnel door before she went to bed the previous evening. She had checked it before George came to collect her and Zebedee at nine o'clock in the morning, which gave the police almost twenty-four hours in which the items could have been stolen.

The policewoman obviously wasn't satisfied with Yvonne's answers and asked her to walk over the road to the police station for a formal interview. Yvonne was in a daze and agreed. She didn't want to stay in the building. The policewoman said Zebedee could come too, and Yvonne left her home and shop in the safe hands of the remaining police.

The formal interview wasn't any different to the informal one, as far as Yvonne could tell, other than they were in the stark interview room in the police station and being recorded, rather than her cosy little shop. She could only give the same answers to the same questions the policewoman had posed on the other side of the road, but her mind was whirring. Had George deliberately got her out of the way with that trip to the Isle of Wight so that others could sneak in through the tunnel from his restaurant to her home? It had to be someone who knew she would be away that day, and that the shop was closed. As her shop was usually open seven days a week it was too much of a coincidence that the first time it was closed in eight years was the day she was burgled.

Tentatively she began to ask her own questions. 'Do you have any suspects?'

'I'm afraid I can't tell you that.'

'Is the death of Juliette Monk related to the disappearance of Marion Close? I reported her missing recently.'

'Are you a relative of either of these people?'

'No.'

'Then I cannot give you any information.'

'Can you at least tell me if you have finished with using my premises as a convenient place for you to catch criminals?' Yvonne was getting a little tetchy with this one-way sharing of information and decided to remind the police that she had been cooperative throughout their investigations. It didn't work.

'I can't. But we are discussing whether it is safe for you to go back home. It may be a good idea to start to think about where you could stay for a little while.'

Yvonne had been shaken by the sight of the empty spaces in her shop and had already been thinking about packing Zebedee and a few belongings into her car and taking that trip to Ireland she had always promised herself. Until the policewoman added 'Somewhere local, where we can reach you at short notice should we wish to speak to you again.'

'I'm not a suspect am I? I called you! Why would I do that if I had stolen their stuff?'

Hurriedly the policewoman assured her 'No, no, you are not a suspect in this case, but we may need your help in identifying anything we find as a result of this recent theft. Is that something you would be able to do?'

Yvonne backed down, feeling a little foolish at her outburst. After spending weeks checking the contents of the two ladies' stands to see if anything new had been added, and then packing it all away into boxes, she was familiar with every item. There were a couple of local hotels she could stay in, but she wondered if they accepted dogs. She would rather not beg a favour from any of her friends, because everyone had their own families and busy lives and she was used to being on her own, although she was sure that any of them would gladly welcome her into a spare room or at a push a sofa. Until a couple of hours ago her first thought would have been to ask George, with the possibility of progressing their budding romance, but there was no way she was going to do that now.

The police obviously felt they couldn't get any more information from her, and accompanied her back across the road to fetch a few belongings. Packing a bag of clothes and toiletries for herself, and a bed, a couple of bowls and some food for Zebedee was easy. She dithered over taking riding clothes and horse tack, after all if she couldn't work in the shop or even enjoy the comforts of her home, she would have plenty of time for riding. While she was trying to work out how much she could fit in her car, and whether it would be safe to leave in her car if she stayed in one of the two hotels or whether she should risk leaving it at the livery yard for a few nights, her phone rang, and she saw it was Tom calling.

'Tom! Oh my goodness, how are you? Are you home?'

'Hello Yvonne, not yet but Tim is here, he has just picked me up from the hospital and we are driving back now. But he says he thinks you have to move out for a few weeks, and I wondered if you and Zebedee would like to move in with me and Stan? There is plenty of room in my house, and to be honest I could do with an able-bodied person to keep Stan exercised. It would mean the world to me if he could come back home today.'

Yvonne recognised emotional blackmail when she heard it, but also understood that Tom was genuine in his offer and in his wish to have his dog with him. Now that she had seen his house she knew that it would be easy to store Toby's tack there without it getting in Tom's way, and Zebedee and Stan had appeared to get on well on the couple of occasions they had met.

'Of course I will accept your offer Tom, thank you very much. How long before you'll be there?'

She could hear Tim and Tom conferring, before Tom said to her 'About twenty minutes.'

'I'll see you there. Thank you!'

It was only after they had hung up she realised he had said she would have to move out for a few "weeks".

Chapter 28

In the end the police were only too happy to help her move out, after confirming her absence from her home would be more like weeks rather than days, and they loaded Toby's tack, a couple of boxes of papers and her computer from her office, all the perishables and a few staples from her kitchen, and a lot more clothes than she had originally packed into one of their police vans. By the time they arrived at Tom's gates he was already installed in the kitchen, with Tim, and Yvonne's belongings were unpacked from the van and carried into the house in less than five minutes.

Yvonne was shocked by Tom's appearance, even though having seen the stone steps in the tower and the large areas where blood had been partially cleaned from the steps and walls she was prepared for him to be in a bit of a state. One leg was in a removable brace, and the opposite wrist was in a permanent cast. His face was a mass of bruises and stitches, and Yvonne could see that there were a couple of wounds in his scalp too. She dreaded to think what the state of his body was like under the clothes he was wearing.

'It's OK, I'm not going to be asking you to help me to the toilet or bathroom' Tom grinned, although the facial movement was obviously painful. 'But I am very grateful to you for agreeing to stay here, not just for your company, but I was going to have a team of this lot coming in three times a day to feed me.'

His colleagues laughed. They had helped themselves to tea and coffee and raided the box from Yvonne's kitchen containing one of Rob's uneaten cakes from a couple of days ago. One of them handed a mug of tea to Tom, and a slice of cake on a piece of kitchen roll, and another passed tea and cake to Yvonne. As she pulled out a pine kitchen chair and sat down at the table she tried to adjust to the weirdness of going from the tense atmosphere of the police interview room to the cosy laughter-filled environment of Tom's kitchen with the same people.

By the time they left Yvonne had another two phone numbers to call in case there was more information she could provide or if she was concerned about anything. She remembered a time when she had a page in her slim paper telephone and address book full of police telephone numbers. She wondered where that book was now. It had replaced her bulky Filofax when she had to change direction in life and had gone everywhere with her.

'Let me show you around' said Tom as he eased his way up from the carver dining chair.

'Can you walk on that?' asked Yvonne, gesturing to his booted leg.

'Yes, no problem with this thing on. Come on, this way. Along there is my room. Fortunately I live on the ground floor anyway, and everything I need is down here. You can choose any of the rooms upstairs except Mum's, because she'll need somewhere to stay when she comes over for a visit. I haven't been up here for ages, so you may need to open a window and give the bathroom a wipe down, but there is clean bedlinen and plenty of towels.'

Yvonne followed behind him as Tom climbed the narrow wooden stairs, using a crutch on the side of the damaged leg but obviously not able to use his plastered wrist on the other side. At the top were a series of closed doors running off a long corridor to either side of them. The ceiling height was higher, and as they opened one door after another and looked inside she could see the windows were bigger, and the rooms were lighter than downstairs.

'This was my sister's room, this was my room, here is the family bathroom, this is Mum's room, these two were guest bedrooms, with a Jack and Jill bathroom. You might want to choose one of these rooms because this is the best bath and the best shower in the house, but it's up to you. Bedding and towels are all in that cupboard at the end of the hall.' One by one Tom showed Yvonne into the clean and recently decorated rooms, the colour schemes were cream and pale green in the bedrooms and white and blue in the bathrooms, and didn't look as though anyone had been in since the new carpets, fresh paint and curtains had been installed.

'Don't worry about bedding and towels. I managed to bring my own but thank you. This is very kind of you.'

'I am sorry I can't help you bring your belongings upstairs.'

Yvonne laughed 'Of course you can't! I must go and see Toby for an hour or so, and then I'll come back and cook something for our dinner. Shall I collect Stan on my way home?'

'I was hoping you would say that' grinned Tom. 'Thank you. I'll give you the code for the gates so you can come and go as you please. You won't need a key for the house because I won't be going anywhere except for the occasional hospital visit, and then I'll leave my keys for you. If you could put things in the AGA and pull them back out again then dinner is going to be easy. There is a pheasant curry I made a few months ago in the freezer, and if you put it in the bottom oven before you leave, it will have defrosted and you can put it in the main oven when you get back.'

'Sounds delicious!'

Yvonne decided to collect Stan on her way to see Toby, so that he and Zebedee could have an on-lead walk with her together, just to check they were going to be happy to live with each other for a while. She needn't have worried, as the two of them settled into the car together without any issues, and after checking on Toby she took them for a walk around one of the fields for half an hour. She didn't know Stan well enough to trust him off the lead, but neither he nor Zebedee were desperate to run around in the heat of the late afternoon.

When she got back to Tom's house she let the dogs out of the car but kept Stan on a lead. With Tom's wrist in a plaster cast she didn't want the dog to bang into him if she could help it. As expected as soon as he saw Tom he tried to leap across the room, so Yvonne kept hold of him and let Stan drag her at a more sedate pace.

'Hello boy. I am so glad to see you.' Man and dog revelled in their greeting while Yvonne kept Stan from getting too close to Tom's injured body, until Tom eventually said 'That's enough, settle down. You are going to have to be gentle with me.'

Stan looked as though he understood and licked Tom's outstretched hand. Yvonne decided it was safe to unclip his lead but was ready to grab him if he started jumping up at his owner. Instead he shook himself, and trotted off into the garden, where Zebedee had been exploring during the homecoming.

Yvonne turned down Tom's offer of a drink 'I'm going to get my room organised first, because after the day I've had

I think I might just go straight to bed once I've had my dinner. Is there anything I can get for you first?'

'No, I'm fine thank you. You go ahead.'

As Tom had suggested, Yvonne chose one of the guest bedrooms, made the bed and hung her towels in the bathroom, dug out pyjamas and toiletries, and decided a quick shower before dinner was called for. Washed and dressed in shorts and a t-shirt she came back downstairs, transferred the pot of curry into the cooking section of the oven, and opened a couple of cold bottles of lager for them both. Tom had moved out into the garden, onto one of four teak garden chairs, and the dogs were happily mooching around him. Although Yvonne had what seemed like a million questions for him, she was too tired to chat, and he didn't appear to be in the mood either, so they sat in comfortable silence enjoying the evening sun and the distant sound of the town.

Over dinner, which was delicious, they discussed and shared their experiences of the last few days, tongues and minds loosened by the red wine from Tom's impressive wine cellar below the kitchen. Tom was curious to know everything that Yvonne knew about the tunnels, the jewellery, and the deaths of the two women who had been major contributors to her business. She resisted sharing her suspicions about George, although she wasn't sure why. Tentatively she asked him about how he got his injuries, and the way he talked she felt it was cathartic for him. He was one of four officers who were in the Trinity Tower, either in the surveillance room keeping watch on the cameras and reporting to the officers on the ground what they could see, or up on the tower roof observing the operation as it went down. He had been in the surveillance room when there was a kerfuffle on the steps outside, and he ran out to assist his fellow officers. One of the criminals had tried to hide in the tower, not realising it was full of police. The door on the ground floor should have been locked, but it was overlooked when the team arrived to set up allowing the man easy access. The door into the surveillance room was shut, so the man had no idea there were two officers inside, but had run past intending to get to the roof and let his mates know how to escape the police presence on the ground. Of course, the moment he squeezed through the door at the top of the stone steps he realised his mistake, and tried to turn and run back down, but the nature of the spiral stairs meant he slipped and fell onto his backside, and slid. Tom had heard the shouts from above, opened the door and stepped out to see what was going on, and was unfortunate to get knocked over by the man's body, the momentum taking the pair of them a distance down, bouncing off the walls as they went. Tom had several gashes to his head and face, but was lucky not to have broken his neck, although he did end up with a broken wrist and wrenched elbow, and twisted knee and ankle.

'It was the knocks to the head which have caused more problems than the twists and breaks' he said. 'There was quite a bit of swelling on my brain, and they had to keep me sedated until that all went down.'

'You must have been in so much pain'

'Not really. I was on a lot of medication. I still am. Probably shouldn't be drinking this' he said, the thought just occurring to him that lager, red wine, and pain and anti-inflammatory medications are not a good combination.

'No, you shouldn't. Sorry, that's my fault, I didn't think!'

For the first time that day, Yvonne began to giggle. Tom joined in, and the pair of them ended up laughing. Eventually Yvonne said 'Come on then, I'll make us a hot drink and then I'm going to bed. Are you sure you don't need me to help you with anything before I go? I'll have my phone with me just in case.'

Tom waved his cast in the air 'No thank you, I'm fine. Fortunately I am left-handed and this is my right, so I can manage to clean my teeth and all that. But thank you. I'm going to sit outside for a bit longer. I feel as though I have been stuck in that hospital bed for too long.'

Yvonne had left her phone upstairs, and before she climbed into bed she checked it for messages. She had been keeping Tabitha, Alison and Maisie informed about the events concerning the shop, and had messaged the antiques dealers' WhatsApp group about the possible need to keep the shop closed for longer than they had planned. She hadn't worked out what she was going to do if the police did want her to cease trading for more than a few days, but knew she had insurance which should cover it. She made it clear that any dealer who wanted to leave without giving the usual one month's notice was welcome to do so without penalty, after all it is probably what she would have done.

She hadn't contacted George but saw he had left a message asking if she was alright, because customers had told him about the police being at her shop that afternoon. She wasn't sure what she wanted him to know at that point, and decided to reply with 'I'm fine. Will tell you all about it when I can' hoping that would satisfy his curiosity if he was innocent, without telling him anything useful if he wasn't.

Chapter 29

Yvonne and Zebedee slept well in their new surroundings, and Yvonne woke early feeling refreshed and ready for the day ahead. When they entered the kitchen they were greeted by Stan, who always slept there, and Yvonne took both dogs out for a walk, turning left out of Tom's gates and heading down the footpath to Castle Hill. It was too early for most dog walkers, but there were a couple of runners, and a local nature expert called Joe, with his two Jack Russells. Yvonne decided to risk letting Stan off the lead, knowing that Joe's two dogs were friendly and that she had good recall with Zebedee. Neither Jack Russell was particularly interested in playing, so after exchanging pleasantries with Joe, Yvonne continued walking down Castle Hill while Stan and Zebedee played Chase Me games the whole way. Before they reached Breach Lane she popped them both on a lead, although there was no traffic, and then kept them on their leads as they walked along a section of Breach Common. She enjoyed this peaceful place, where a small group of locals worked hard all year round to keep the dreaded Himalayan Balsam weed at bay, and restoring former ponds and other vital areas for the plants, amphibians, insects and mammals who thrive in the environment. She was sad to see the damage local vandals had done to the living willow chairs but enjoyed the bird song all around. Leaving the common and walking up a short section of

Foyle's Hill her mind turned to what she could do about her business, if anything, and what the future might hold. Would anyone want to stay trading from somewhere connected to so many deaths? She didn't need to earn a living, and could apply for permission to turn the building into a residential home and sell it, and then move to … where? She was happy in Shaftesbury, she loved her little antiques business, she had enjoyed working with her fellow antiques dealers, she had friends in the town, and couldn't imagine finding somewhere as idyllic to keep Toby as the Hannam Livery Yard.

She suddenly realised she was walking up Stoney Path heading towards Park Walk, following one of her normal routes home, but of course she wasn't going home, she was going back to Tom's house. Turning left onto Park Walk instead of right, she wiggled her way along the tiny lanes back to Bimport and let herself in through the gates. The dogs took it in turns to try to drink their shared water bowl dry, so after they had finished she refilled it, gave them their breakfast, and put the kettle on. Tom had two kettles, one an electric jug kettle, and another she assumed was suitable for the AGA. She used the electric kettle to make her morning cup of coffee, and the electric toaster for toast, sure that there was probably a way of making toast on the AGA but deciding she preferred to be sitting out in the garden with her breakfast sooner rather than later.

She spent the next hour sitting in Tom's garden listening to the sounds of the town waking up, a couple of times an ambulance from their base across the road went out on an emergency, but mostly it was the sounds of people calling their dogs, dogs barking, someone's chickens clucking and occasionally squawking to each other, and general traffic noise. She decided that if she had to close her business she would stay in Shaftesbury, probably in her present home. She loved the Tree House, and the convenience of having everything she needed to buy so close, especially now that Charlotte's bakery had opened around the corner from the butchers, not that the local Reeves bakery was very far away. Her phone pinged, and she saw it was an invitation from Tabitha to join her and Alison at TAA for dinner that evening. She delayed replying. George was bound to be there, and she didn't know what to think about him, whether he could be trusted.

Tom appeared at the kitchen doorway and asked if she wanted another cup of tea. 'Please could you collect the eggs for me? I don't think I can manage that just yet' he said, holding out a woven willow egg basket.

Yvonne looked around the garden 'Where are the chickens?'

Tom used his arm in the cast to point to the end of the garden 'Down there, can you see the gate in the fence? Don't let the dogs in, or Stan will eat all the eggs.'

Yvonne had no doubt Zebedee would too, and she also wasn't sure how chicken-proof her dog was. She had seen enough dead bodies for one lifetime.

Behind the gate was chicken heaven, with a fully enclosed run similar to Stan's dog run but it was a huge square-shape filling the bottom of the garden, with three large hutches inside all with easy-access nesting boxes, and plenty of space for the chickens to scratch around and fly up onto the roofs of the hutches. Yvonne opened each box and picked up the eggs inside, ignoring the chickens who were sitting firmly in their sections obviously laying more eggs. She wondered if she could create something similar in her small garden area. It would be nice to have her own fresh eggs in the morning, and she wouldn't want this number of hens, perhaps two or three at the most.

Back in the kitchen she helped Tom to make scrambled eggs by breaking the eggs for him, because that was something he couldn't manage one-handed, although he had been willing to give it a go. She also had to slice the bread, because she always bought whole loaves but decided it would be kinder to get them sliced before leaving the shop at least for the next week or so until the plaster cast was removed. They ate breakfast, making idle conversation, planning their day. Afterwards they washed up together, although Tom had a dishwasher in his kitchen they both agreed they only used them when they'd had a lot of guests for dinner, and then went their separate ways: Tom out into the garden for a nap and Yvonne upstairs to set up the second guest bedroom as her office. Tom suggested that if she was going to be homeless for a while it would be a good idea to have a base for her business as well as somewhere to live, and if she needed to meet anyone then it could double up as an office or her sitting room. She pushed the twin beds against two walls and positioned the pillows and added bedspreads from the cupboard so they turned into a corner sofa. One wall of the room was fitted out with wardrobes, chests of drawers and a dressing table, which Yvonne was able to utilise as her office cupboards and desk, although she needed to bring her chair from her home office as neither the dainty bedroom stool nor the low plush bedroom chairs were suitable for hours spent at her computer or doing paperwork. She messaged Tim to see if she could go home and collect a few more belongings, and he said he would meet her there in a couple of hours' time. She used those two hours to sort through everything she had on Marion and Juliette as antiques dealers in her shop, from original email conversations to records she kept in the big A4 size shop diaries, paper contracts and private diary entries in the smaller A5 desk diaries she kept in her home office. She set up a spreadsheet on the computer with two columns, one for Marion and one for Juliette, and logged everything chronologically, from their first contact with her to the last time they were in the shop. Because her record-keeping was so thorough, and because the two women appeared to have a fortnightly routine of communicating online and appearing in person, it was easier than she had been expecting. Next she turned her attention to their sales. All of this was recorded on a bespoke program on her computer and was collated and on the screen in seconds.

Checking with Tom that it was alright to leave Zebedee with him, she drove home, and found Tim already there with the gates open, waiting for her.

'I wondered if you used the magic gate opening thingy on my gates' she said archly.

He held his hands up 'I promise yesterday was the first time.'

Not sure if she believed him, Yvonne ran up the wooden stairs to her flat, noticing that someone had watered the plants on the balcony. She picked a few ripe tomatoes, new potatoes, lettuces, broad beans and peas and put them in a cloth bag from the greenhouse, before letting herself in through the door and locking it behind her. In her bedroom she picked up another few personal items which she put inside a shoulder bag, and then walked down the metal spiral stairs to her office and collected her chair. She was tempted to go through into the shop, but decided she'd rather not see it again until the police were ready to release it back to her. She carried the chair and bags out through the shop, surprised but pleased to find the connecting door from her home was locked, weaving her way through

Rob's automobilia and a complete Austin 7 to the shop's back door, which Tim had opened for her.

'Someone has been watering my plants up there. Can you thank them for me please?'

'I will. None of us want you to be inconvenienced any longer than necessary, and the least we can do is look after the place until you're back.'

'Any idea when that will be?'

Tim shook his head 'No, I am sorry. You're happy to stay at Tom's aren't you?'

His query sounded genuine, and Yvonne replied 'Yes, it suits us both, and of course the dogs love it too.'

'That's a relief. We were wondering how we were going to look after him. He's had a rough time, and none of us want him to go back there. Have you thought of anything else which could help us with our enquiries?'

'Yes I have, but I think it only fair if you share what you know with me too' said Yvonne.

'I am telling you what I can' said Tim. 'Do you want to tell me now?'

'I think it best if we do this over at the station. I don't know if any of this can help, but I have spent the morning working out some interesting patterns of behaviour between Marion Close and Juliette Monk.'

To save time later Yvonne drove her car across the road to the police station carpark, and then joined Tim and a couple of his colleagues in one of the interview rooms. She had deliberately left her computer and diaries at Tom's house but had brought a printout of the two spreadsheets she had created containing the dates of the various communications she had with Marion and Juliette, and a list of their respective sales since they had joined her shop five years' earlier. She hadn't made the connection before, but her memory had been jogged by the realisation that the two women joined within a few weeks of each other, and that the two previous dealers who had rented those spaces had both suddenly packed and left before giving notice. She remembered now that Marion had come into the shop expressing a desire to rent the space by the cellar door before the dealer who was settled in there left, and that when the space next to it became available none of the people on the waiting list wanted to move in. At the time she had thought it curious, but now she thought it suspicious. She shared her belief that Marion Close was Jane Poundsmith.

The police thanked her, but didn't seem surprised, nodding when she said she thought Marion was Jane, but didn't share anything further. Even Tim clammed up, and she wondered if she should have told him what she had found out in the relatively relaxed environment of her kitchen instead of the formal police station. Everyone at the police station she met expressed their gratitude for her decision to stay with Tom while her home was out-of-bounds, and she couldn't help wondering if they had engineered the need to take over her property. She wasn't going to bring it up, because she was unnerved about staying in her home until she knew what was going on, and Tom's house seemed ideal until then.

As she had the car with her she went and did some food shopping, leaving her car in the police station carpark and coming back to it to drop off meat and bread, before heading up the High Street to the delicatessen for cheese. While she was there she bought a couple of fresh hot caramelised sausage rolls for their lunch, wondering as she did so if Tom would prefer a plain sausage roll. Just in case she also bought two of those, reasoning they could cool down and keep in the fridge until the next day. The shopping expedition took longer than it should because people kept stopping her and asking what was going on with her shop. She appreciated those who were genuinely concerned, and didn't mind those who were gossiping, because when she could reopen she had a feeling it would be the place to be in Shaftesbury for the day. The one person she didn't see was George, and for that she was relieved.

When she got back to the car she texted Tabitha and thanked her for the offer of a night out, but declined. She decided that a hack around the fields with Toby and Zebedee was more appealing than eating in a busy restaurant run by someone of whom she was a little bit afraid.

The next couple of days passed quietly, with Yvonne rising early and walking the dogs around the town before heading back to Tom's for breakfast in the garden. She could see him beginning to move more easily, and the bruises on his face were fading. Tim turned up to take him for a hospital appointment in Salisbury, and when he came back a few hours later the plaster cast on his wrist had been replaced by a removable Velcro brace, similar to the one on his leg.

She caught him in the kitchen having a serious word with Stan and Zebedee. 'You see this?' he said, holding up his healing wrist, 'this is at a critical time in its life. One knock from an overenthusiastic dog and I'm in trouble. Do you understand?'

Both dogs licked their lips.

'I'm not sure the dog whispering classes are working' laughed Yvonne as she came into the room.

'They look as though they want to eat it!' he complained. 'Tim's coming back later. Are you going to be around?'

'I'm going over to the yard to ride Toby at some point this evening. What time is he coming?'

'I think he was hoping to have some supper with us because his wife has taken the kids away for a week and he's feeling lonely. I said we were having lamb chops with new potatoes, peas and beans. You'd rather eat after your ride wouldn't you, so shall I say nine o'clock? It doesn't matter if you're not back; it's easy enough to keep it all warm until you want it.'

Yvonne loved riding later in the evening, to avoid the heat of the day and the flies, and regularly ate her evening meal after half-past eight at this time of year, as opposed to the dark winter months when she was ready for dinner by six o'clock in the evening. She also felt she could get used to having someone else cooking for her at a time that suited her. Before she could reply her phone pinged, and there was a message from George.

'That sounds perfect, thank you Tom. I'll aim to be back in time, but you don't have to cook for me if I'm not. I can do it. Sorry, I had better deal with this.'

She walked out to the garden and made herself comfortable on one of the chairs, before picking up her phone and reading George's message.

'Are we still on for tomorrow night? What time shall I pick you up?'

Damn, she had completely forgotten that she had invited him to Lindy's party with her. And that she had accepted Charlotte's invitation for a lift to the party. She needed to let one of them down. Before she replied, she decided she needed some answers for herself. She went back into the kitchen.

'Tom, this is important. Is George mixed up in this criminal investigation in any way?'

Tom looked surprised. 'George? No way. He's one of the good guys. You know he used to be in the special forces?'

'No, I did not.'

'Why did you think he was involved?' Tom was curious, rather than concerned.

'Because he is always there whenever something happens. Because he has access to my shop through that bloody tunnel. Because someone is keeping an eye on him.'

Instantly Tom sat up straighter and winced. 'Ow, I can't do that. What do you mean someone is keeping an eye on him?'

Yvonne told him about the man who kept spying on either her or George, but she thought it was more likely George who was under surveillance. 'Although I haven't seen him for a while.'

'When was the last time you saw him?'

Yvonne shook her head. 'I can't remember.'

'Think, Yvonne, this could be important.'

Yvonne tried to recall the last image of the shadowy man but couldn't remember seeing him for several days.

'Have you seen him since Tabitha and Alison's wedding?'

'No, no I haven't. The last time was before the wedding, I am sure.'

'I'm going to tell Tim what you have told me' said Tom as he picked up his phone.

Chapter 30

Yvonne packed her car with Toby's saddle and bridle, and with Zebedee, and drove down to the yard. Lindy was about to take Astrid into the school, but when she saw Yvonne drive in she stopped to ask if she was going for a hack.

'Yes I am, just around the fields so that Zebedee can come too. Do you want to join us?'

'Yes please, it's far too hot to be schooling. I'm not in the mood, but a lovely ride around our countryside is just what we need.'

It didn't take Yvonne long to bring Toby in from the paddock and tack him up, and the two women and their horses, and one dog, walked across one stubble field leading to another, and then another, all with the gates wide open.

'Isn't this heaven! The birds singing, the sun shining, a decent breeze to keep the worst of the flies away' Lindy was smiling as she spoke. 'The perfect way to spend my birthday.'

'It's your birthday today? Happy Birthday Lindy!'

'Thank you! I always try to go for a ride on my birthday, and at Christmas.'

'So do I, especially at Christmas. I've had some super hacks on Christmas Day.'

They spent the next few minutes comparing horse rides, and then moved onto Lindy's planned birthday party the next day.

'Honestly, I am dreading it. My dad's side of the family are upset about the problems at Kenyon Hall and are trying to get the business back up and running, but public confidence has been knocked, and they are having major problems trying to buy supplies. Mum and Dad are barely speaking. The atmosphere between them is awful. Thank goodness I don't live with them.'

'Is this about your mum handing over the jewellery to your dad's cousin?'

'Yes! They still haven't heard from her, which is unusual because she is normally in touch with Mum once a week or so, although that was before Dad knew about their contact.'

Yvonne decided she needed to say something. 'Lindy, have you heard anything about the problems I have been having at my antiques shop?'

'Oh no! What has happened? I haven't heard anything.'

Yvonne was surprised that there was anyone in Shaftesbury who hadn't heard something, even if it wasn't true, but Lindy looked genuinely surprised. 'Lindy, what did you say your cousin's name is?'

'My dad's cousin you mean? She is called Marion Close.'

'Oh Lindy, I am afraid I may have some terrible news for you. I think that your aunt could be the body I found on Tabitha's farm.'

'No, that can't be right. I thought you had found some gangster mastermind? Oh!' Yvonne could see that suddenly Lindy was realising that the rumours her father had always spoken about her mystery aunt could be true. 'But I never really believed him. Mum and I always thought he was jealous because Aunty Marion didn't have the constraints in her life that he did because of who he was. I mean, we believed that she was probably involved in illegal activity, but that woman you found was evil, wasn't she?'

'So I understand' said Yvonne. 'But it would explain why your mother hasn't heard from her, wouldn't it? The police have said that the name Jane Poundsmith was a pseudonym which Marion Close was hiding behind.'

They rode in silence for a while. Yvonne kept glancing at Lindy, but her face never changed from one of horrified confusion until eventually she said 'But surely the police would have got in touch with us? If the body really was that of Aunty Marion.'

'They would have done if you were her nearest relatives. Presumably she has other family?'

'Not that I know of. I mean, obviously she has other relatives, because we are a big family, but as far as I'm aware she doesn't have a husband or children or anything, and there weren't any brothers or sisters; she was an only child.'

'It might be worth contacting the police and asking them,' suggested Yvonne.

'If it was her, then where is the family jewellery?' asked Lindy.

'Have you reported it missing?'

'No, because we didn't know it was. Although to be fair, Dad has kept going on about Marion stealing it.'

Yvonne noted that 'Aunty Marion' had become just 'Marion'.

She said 'Perhaps it is time to report it now.'

They rode into the yard and untacked and took their horses back to their fields in silence, Yvonne piecing a few things together, and Lindy trying to comprehend what was happening.

'It's no good, I'm going to phone them now. But I can't call 999 can I?'

'I have a number you could try' said Yvonne. 'I can phone it first if you like, and explain for you, and then you can talk to them?'

'Thank you, you know more about this than I do' said Lindy. 'Can you phone them now please?'

Yvonne phoned Tim and explained that she believed Lindy's cousin was the Marion Close who the police believed to be Jane Poundsmith. 'The thing is Tim, shouldn't her relatives have been informed if it was her?'

'Ah, there has been a bit of confusion there. Can you ask Lindy to come in to see us?'

'At the police station in Shaftesbury?'

'Yes.'

'Now? We're about fifteen minutes away.'

'We'll see you both in fifteen minutes. I'd like to talk to you about the mystery spy you have been seeing.'

Lindy had heard Yvonne's side of the conversation and said 'I'll follow you in the car. You will come in with me, won't you? I don't think I have ever been inside a police station before!'

For the second time that day Yvonne drove into the carpark at the police station opposite her home. Lindy needed to show her driving licence to the policewoman at the desk to prove who she was, and then Tim appeared and ushered them into one of the interview rooms that Yvonne was becoming familiar with.

'Would you like a tea or a coffee, or perhaps some water?' he asked them.

This was the first time Yvonne had been offered anything to drink, but she thought it probably wasn't going to be very good tea and declined, as did Lindy. Yvonne hoped they weren't going to be very long, and her stomach rumbled at the thought of the lamb chops Tom was going to cook for them all. She looked at Tim, and guessed he was thinking the same thing.

They had been joined by a woman in plain clothes, who wore a name badge on a lanyard which stated that she was a Detective Chief Superintendent. To Yvonne's knowledge this was the highest rank she had spoken with since she found the body in the field. Things must be serious now, she thought.

The policewoman spent some time asking Lindy questions about herself and her family but ignored Yvonne. Eventually she must have been satisfied with Lindy's answers and included Yvonne in the conversation.

She said to Lindy 'Officers are speaking with your parents now. I am sorry to inform you that the body Yvonne found three weeks ago was that of your relative, Marion Close. Two hours ago we arrested the people we believe are responsible for her murder. These people included the remainder of a nationwide gang we have wanted to catch for too many years, and some of the intelligence we used came from you, thank you' she said to Yvonne.

Yvonne was so surprised she tuned out for the next few things the DCS said, before composing herself and listening again. She realised that the DCS had been recapping the events of recent weeks for Lindy's benefit and wasn't telling her anything she didn't already know. Although shocked, Lindy was calm and listened to everything the policewoman was saying.

Then, as far as Yvonne was concerned, came the interesting bit.

'We had always believed that Jane Poundsmith was a real person, but in recent months we came to realise that the name was a character used by more than one person. In effect there were two women called 'Jane Poundsmith', neither of whose real names were Jane Poundsmith. Whether this had always been the case, or whether it was a recent change in the way the gang worked, we are unsure at the present time, although we do believe that your aunt, Marion Close, has always been in the position of power attributed to that character. In recent years we believe she was joined by a second woman, whom you knew as Juliette Monk' she said to Yvonne.

Yvonne had worked this out already, but simply nodded to encourage the DCS to continue.

The DCS asked Lindy 'Did you know that your aunt had a cousin called Juliette Monk?'

Lindy shook her head.

The DCS continued 'There is no doubt that your aunt and Juliette Monk were powerful women in the gang, but it wasn't until recently that we discovered there was a third person, who was even more powerful, and who was the one who ran the whole operation. That person was a man.' She looked at Yvonne, who stared back blankly. This was news to her. Then she broke out into a cold sweat. Surely not. Not George. Not after Tom had reassured her he was someone she could trust.

'Please could I have some water?' she asked Tim, who immediately got to his feet and left the room.

'Are you alright?' Lindy asked her. 'You've gone very pale.'

'I don't feel very well. I think I know who that man is' Yvonne said, and then shut her mouth in case she was going to be sick. All that time George was there with her, in the field, he had known all along what they were going to find because he had done it! And she had been alone with him on several occasions, in her home, in his bedroom, fantasising about him. She was glad she hadn't

316

been home for her dinner, because she was sure she would have thrown it up by now.

Tim reappeared with a tray carrying a litre bottle of mineral water and four glasses. He poured a glass for Yvonne and slid it along the table. She didn't trust herself to pick it up in case she spilled it, her hands were shaking so much, so instead she mumbled a 'thank you' and kept looking into the glass.

'We arrested him this morning. His name is William Drake. Did you have any idea before this evening?' the DCS asked Yvonne.

'What?' Yvonne looked up, startled. 'William? No, you've got that wrong' but as she was defending him she realised it made sense. George wouldn't have been able to bump his mates up the waiting list, let alone create room for them in the shop. George wouldn't have been able to have easy access to her end of the tunnel from her cellar. And George wasn't old enough to have recruited Lindy's aunt when she was a teenager. She took a big gulp of water, and immediately felt better. Even though she had known William for a long time, enjoyed his company, and his quiche, she was relieved it was him and not George who had been deceiving her. It wasn't a good feeling, but it was a relief.

Lindy was looking confused. 'Who is William Drake?'

Yvonne let the DCS explain. She thought she knew a little about him, but as the DCS spoke Yvonne realised she knew nothing about him.

'He was born William Henry Cole in 1936, in Brighton. We don't know much about his early years, but by 1959 he was calling himself William Drake, probably in memory of someone he had been at school with and who had died, an early example of identity theft. He was running a café on Southsea seafront in Hampshire. Over the years there were brushes with the law, but nothing serious, and nothing he could be charged with. He then seems to have taken on a few more seaside cafés along the south coast, before moving inland. At the time no one noticed, or if they did they weren't saying anything, but now we can see that every café was physically linked to a car repair shop or a beauty salon or a pawn shop. We cannot find any evidence of criminal behaviour, but it is beyond belief to think that he was not involved in organised crime given the locations of his businesses. Every café earned enough to cover its costs, and more. He earned a good living from those businesses, and never lived beyond his means. There was no reason to suspect him of being anything other than an astute business owner in the hospitality sector.'

'What changed?' asked Yvonne, intrigued now she had got over her panic that George was the villain.

'Nothing' Tim took over. 'He continued to keep up the façade of being a good citizen, regularly gave money and time to local charities, was on the board of governors for his children's schools, he and his wife regularly attended church on a Sunday, and the family took holidays in their caravan before they upgraded to a motor home. When he retired he handed the running of the legitimate family business over to his three children, all of whom had worked in the cafés since they were old enough to do so, and those cafés are still trading today.'

'Where does Aunty Marion fit into all of this?' asked Lindy, who had poured herself a glass of water, and was offering one to Tim and the DCS sitting opposite her.

'We understand she got hold of some of your father's jewellery?' asked the DCS, who clearly knew the answer.

Lindy nodded. 'My mum gave it to her, without my father's knowledge. He's furious about it.'

318

'I'm not surprised. Your aunt has been on our radar for over fifty years, but we have never been able to hold her for anything. Then this mysterious Jane Poundsmith started being mentioned. The woman was everywhere, but no one could give a good description of her. We were arresting drug dealers and they'd tell us she was their boss; car thieves said the same; sophisticated prostitution rings named her as the person behind them. We'd get a description, or a location, or a phone number, even once an address, but information was conflicting and misleading. Of course now we realise she was two people: Marion Close and Juliette Monk were both 'Jane Poundsmith', but the real Jane Poundsmith was William Drake. As a man he was a non-descript average height, average build, nothing to stand out in a line-up, but together with two real women William Drake could don his own disguises and be anyone he wanted to be. The three of them had wigs and outfits for every occasion, so if one of them was meeting up with some gangster one week, another would go in their place wearing the same wig and outfit. Where Marion slipped up was meeting your mother and receiving her jewellery dressed as herself, for obvious reasons. Quite why she involved her family we will never know.'

'Perhaps she got tired of living like that and was trying to find a way out?' said Lindy hopefully.

Neither Tim nor the DCS looked as though they believed that theory, but both nodded for her benefit. The DCS said 'It looks as though she was trying to set up on her own, without William but possibly with Juliette. We think they were trying to close down William's operation and have him put out of action, permanently, but he got there first. William had been increasing the human trafficking side of their business, and we have been given numerous tip-offs in recent years enabling us to shut off the routes. We are

319

working on the theory that Marion and Juliette were behind the tip-offs, and William discovered what they were doing. It was extremely risky for them to betray him.'

'So was it William who killed Marion?' asked Yvonne.

'No, at least not with his own hands. He was employing a particularly nasty group of thugs to get rid of rival drug dealers on what he considered to be his patch in Mold in Flintshire, Wales, and he set them loose on her. But he did murder Juliette. We think he tried to use the manner of Marion's death as a warning to Juliette not to stray from the rules they had successfully worked within for years, and she wasn't having any of it. She was a strong woman by all accounts and had a temper.'

Yvonne nodded. She had witnessed a few of Juliette's outbursts, and had given her a warning that one more and she'd have to leave the shop. Now she was wondering what would have happened if she had carried out her threat. Never had she believed her life would be in danger for terminating a contract with an antiques dealer in her business, but now she realised it could have been a possibility.

'How did you catch him?' she asked.

'It is thanks to you' the DCS smiled at Yvonne.

'Me?'

'William had remained undetected, or even suspected, for so long we think he thought he was invincible. He didn't recognise how much Marion and Juliette had enabled his business to run successfully, and that without them he wouldn't have achieved the level of crime that he had, and so after he had Marion killed he carried on in the way he had for years. Unfortunately, he no longer had Marion to clean up after him or clear the way before him. He only had Juliette, but she went on the run and managed to evade capture for a short time. Unfortunately for Juliette she put her trust in someone who betrayed her, and William caught up with her when she made a brief visit to her home. When he killed Juliette, possibly in self-defence, there was no one left to cover-up his actions. He willingly gave his fingerprints when you invited us into your shop because at the time he knew we didn't have his fingerprints in the system, after all it was never him who got his hands dirty. But then we found matching fingerprints on Juliette's neck. Once we had a positive connection, the rest was possible to link up.'

'So where does the man I have been seeing lurking over in the corner of the carpark and elsewhere fit into this?' asked Yvonne.

Tim answered 'That was Juliette. After you told me what you had seen we went back through the CCTV footage from around the town, and found her. It wasn't you or George she was watching, it was William, that is why you kept seeing her; she wasn't trying to keep hidden from you. She was trying to keep tabs on him and who he was meeting. The gang preferred to work old-style, in-person, and kept their digital communications to the minimum, thus reducing the risk of being monitored by us. We don't have the budget for full-time surveillance on everyone involved.

But of course, every time she realised you had spotted her, she had to hide. Like William, she wasn't used to doing things on her own. She had always had Marion or William to work with. The three of them needed each other to succeed.'

'But what was it all for?' asked Lindy. 'If William was living within his legitimate publicly known means, and he was the boss, then who was benefitting?'

The DCS spread her hands in front of her on the desk. 'They all had a good standard of living, drove nice cars, lived in nice houses, took nice holidays, but no one had the enormous villa in Majorca or the private plane to fly them there. None of them had a drug habit, or even a drink problem. They just seem to have thrived on the organising of serious crime.'

'Until it killed two of them' observed Lindy.

Chapter 31

Yvonne phoned Tom and asked if Lindy could come home for supper with them. It was odd asking someone else if she could have a friend over, but also a nice feeling to think someone else was going to be getting the meal ready. Tim turned up a few minutes later, and the four of them sat down to a delicious meal cooked entirely by Tom with one hand, although Yvonne had to lift the dish containing the lamb chops out of the oven, and she drained the potatoes despite him insisting he could do it.

'There is no point straining the other hand' she pointed out.

By an unspoken agreement no one talked about the revelations of the past few hours until after they had eaten, and even then none of them felt there was much they could say.

'How are you feeling about moving back to your flat?' Lindy asked Yvonne.

'Fine' she said. 'After all, none of the murders took place in my building. What I am less comfortable about is reopening the shop, when it turns out that a quarter of the team were criminals.'

Tom said 'I think the odds are stacked against that situation ever occurring again. Although ...' he stopped, clearly remembering Yvonne's past.

She grinned at him, letting him off the hook. 'It's OK.' She turned to Lindy. 'This isn't the first time I have encountered deceit and death in my life. But let's not talk about that now. I am grateful that we are all safe, and although this probably wasn't the fiftieth birthday Lindy wanted, it is certainly one she will never forget. Happy Birthday Lindy!'

Everyone raised their glasses in the slightly bizarre toast, and Lindy laughed along with them.

'Thank you, Yvonne. I am genuinely grateful you were with me this evening, or all of this could have come out tomorrow and ruined my party. You are right, I am never going to forget my fiftieth birthday. Nor am I going to take my father's warnings about people lightly, ever again!'

After Tim and Lindy had left, Yvonne checked her phone and realised she hadn't made arrangements for the next day with her friends. It was almost midnight, too late to start texting now, but as she was still wide awake she took the dogs out for a last stroll around the town. She found herself walking down the High Street, on the opposite side of the road to George's restaurant. George just happened to be locking the doors after the last of his staff had left. Yvonne waved and crossed the road to join him.

'George! I'm so glad I've caught you.'

'Only just,' he said, yawning. 'It's been a long day. What are you doing out at this time of night, and who's this? A new dog?'

He bent down to make a fuss of Zebedee and say hello to Stan.

'I couldn't go to bed yet, so much has happened. I needed to have some time on my own, and the dogs were happy to come with me. This is Tom's dog.'

George took a step back 'Tom Archibald? Why have you got his dog at this time of night?'

'We're staying with him for a few days while the police have taken over my building.'

'So that's why you haven't replied to my text about tomorrow? You're going to the party with Tom. It would have been nice if you had told me earlier.'

Before he could turn away and lock himself inside the restaurant, Yvonne caught his arm 'It's not like that. I am sorry I didn't reply. But really George, an awful lot has happened, and I am trying to take it all in. Please accept my apologies, and come with me to Lindy's party tomorrow, assuming it is still on.'

'Why wouldn't it be?'

Yvonne glanced up and down the street. George said 'Come inside. I was going to make myself a drink before bed anyway. I'm sure you can tell me what has been going on over a glass of something.'

'I could do with a brandy.'

George locked the doors behind them, and led the trio upstairs, where Yvonne let both dogs off the lead. She texted Tom to let him know not to wait up for them, and after he replied with a winking emoji she realised both dogs had disappeared.

'Don't worry, they've gone to bed' laughed George, as the sound of two dogs moving around upstairs could be heard. 'Leave them to it and start at the beginning.'

Yvonne accepted the glass he gave her, and they sat at the little table in the window, overlooking the town at night. Yvonne told him about the murders and William's involvement, and then about her plans for the future. It felt good to be talking about something other than stolen jewellery and dead bodies for the first time in days. Suddenly she was overcome with tiredness and could see he was stifling one yawn after another.

'Thank you for the drink, and the opportunity to off load. I am sorry to keep you up so late. I'll go and retrieve those dogs and head home.'

They walked up the stairs to George's bedroom, where Zebedee was stretched out on one side of the bed, and Stan was curled up by George's pillow. Yvonne pointed at him 'That one sleeps on his own dog bed in the kitchen!'

She made the dogs get up, and everyone trooped back down the stairs, where George let them out through the front of the restaurant and insisted on accompanying them back to Tom's house. When Yvonne objected at the lateness of the hour, George said 'It's not far, and I'll sleep better knowing you are safely back.'

The walk through the town was uneventful, and when Yvonne entered her temporary bedroom she realised she was still wearing her riding clothes. She wondered if having a shower would wake up Tom but decided he wouldn't hear a few minutes of running water. Feeling clean and refreshed, she climbed into bed, shoving Zebedee over from the middle which she had claimed as her own, and was asleep as soon as her head snuggled down onto the pillow.

Chapter 32

In the morning Yvonne was the last one out of bed and volunteered to walk to Charlotte's bakery and buy croissants for breakfast. Accompanied by the two dogs she walked along the roads with a swing in her step, tired from the events of the day before but relieved that William Drake was in custody. Tim had already been in to see Tom before she got up and told him that the police were expecting to be handing her shop back to her some time the following week, and she would be free to reopen immediately. She knew she wouldn't be reopening any time soon and felt an immense sense of release at making that decision. Of course, she would need to make arrangements with the remaining dealers, but the freedom of not having a business open seven days a week for the first time in eight years made her feel light and happy.

Charlotte was serving customers, even though it wasn't yet eight o'clock, and Yvonne thanked her for the offer of a lift to Lindy's party but explained she was now going with George.

'Aha' Charlotte winked. 'You have had a better offer! He is seriously gorgeous.'

'Talking about me?' a voice from the doorway made them both jump, and George walked in. Giving Yvonne a light kiss on the cheek, he said to Charlotte 'I have come to collect the order for the restaurant.'

Blushing furiously, Charlotte rushed off as Yvonne said 'Hey, you're jumping the queue!'

Charlotte's mum handed her a brown paper bag and said 'Here you are Yvonne, on the house,' and waved Yvonne's protests away.

'What's that, breakfast for you and Tom?' asked George with a slight edge to his voice.

'It certainly is' smiled Yvonne. 'Shall I walk down to the restaurant for half-past five?'

'No, I'll come and collect you. It is just us isn't it? Your mate Tom isn't coming too?'

Yvonne laughed 'Yes, it is just us. My mate Tom will be sitting in his armchair, home alone like Cinderella.'

'Stop it, or I'll start to feel sorry for the fella.'

On the way back she walked up Angel Lane past the front of her shop and continued to Bell Street and back to Tom's house, happy with her decision for the future of her shop. She would reopen it, but not in the same form, and it was going to take some time to organise. As she and the dogs walked along, occasionally stepping into the road after checking there were no vehicles coming when the pavements were too narrow to pass people coming in the opposite direction, it seemed as though she knew everyone they met. It was a lovely way to start the day, to smile and say 'Morning!' every few steps, and very different to her days of driving up and down motorways and main roads for work.

Tom popped the croissants in the AGA and made the coffee, while Yvonne sat at the kitchen table and told him about the numerous goodwill wishes people had sent him when they saw her. Word had obviously got out that she was staying with him. Neither of them were surprised.

'Have you left here other than for hospital and doctors' appointments?'

'No, I haven't, why? Do you think it's time I met my public?'

They decided to go into town for lunch, Tom walking with a stick as a walking aid but also to ensure other people gave him space and didn't expect him to jump out of their way. Yvonne and the dogs ambled slowly in front of him, clearing the way on Shaftesbury's pavements which are narrow and uneven. They had lunch outside King Alfred's Kitchen, sitting on chairs set up by the roadside, and as Yvonne expected, allowing passers-by to question both of them about recent events. It was a pleasant way to spend a couple of hours, but in the end they made their slow way back to his house.

While Tom had a nap, Yvonne popped down to see Toby, taking the dogs with her. Stan had fitted easily into the dog pack at the farm, and was an accepted part of the family, playing with the lively ones before flopping out in the shade of the haybarn where Sally said she'd keep an eye on him while Yvonne and Zebedee went to check on Toby. Toby didn't move from his spot inside one of the shelters where he was dozing with two of the other horses. Yvonne stood with him, listening to his breathing and feeling an overwhelming sense of calm.

Ninety minutes later she walked into the kitchen, having retrieved Stan from his slumber with three of the other dogs and driven back to Tom's place, showered and changed, and spent some time on make-up and hair.

'Wow look at you!' exclaimed Tom.

Yvonne twirled around, showing off the floaty skirt of the turquoise dress she was wearing. 'George will be here in a minute. Is there anything you need me to do before I head off?'

'No, nothing thank you. Go and have fun!'

'Don't wait up!'

Yvonne decided to wait for George out on the pavement, but by the time she walked through the gates he was pulling up to the kerb. As she slid into the passenger seat he leaned over and gave her a kiss on the cheek 'You look amazing' he said. 'Roof up or down?'

'I have come prepared for the roof to be down' she said and lifted the white silk organza scarf she had draped across her shoulders over her hair.

'I will leave it down,' he said and smoothly turned the car around, and drove them out of Shaftesbury to Sherborne.

The entrance to Kenyon House was grand, with a large stone archway through which they drove following the 'Lindy's Birthday Party' signs in gold-coloured paint on pale-blue painted wood. The drive to the house was winding, in and out of trees allowing them glimpses of the house before it was shielded from view again.

'I'm glad I opted for shirt and trousers, and not the shorts and t-shirt I almost wore' said George. 'This place looks even more grand than Kenyon Hall!'

They were directed to the field for parking by two young boys dressed in top hat and tails, and Yvonne felt pleased she had chosen to wear sandals rather than high heels. She had guessed the party would be held mainly on grass and didn't want to be tottering around trying not to get spiky heels stuck in the earth, or worse scratching and marking expensively polished wooden flooring if the party was indoors. She could see several mucky 4x4 vehicles she guessed belonged to Lindy's equestrian friends, alongside smart sports cars, ancient Volvos, and several flashy clean 4x4s. A group of girls dressed in fairy costumes were directing guests around the side of the house onto a huge sandstone veranda overlooking a gently sloping expanse of lawn leading to a sparkling blue lake. Looking around at the guests Yvonne recognised plenty of people, even though they looked completely different from their usual equestrian appearance. Over to the right was a five-piece band playing gentle music, and all around were waiters carrying trays of food and drink. Yvonne and George accepted glasses of wine and tasted everything which was offered to them in the space of five minutes.

'I am going to have to stop' admitted Yvonne. 'It's all delicious, but we really must find Lindy and wish her a happy birthday. Where is she do you think?'

They had been moving with the flow of people towards the lake, when they saw that to the left behind some impressive pine trees was a fairground complete with a Big Wheel, and Lindy was waving from one of the gondolas near the top. They both waved back, unsure if she was waving to them. Lindy called out to Yvonne to wait for her to reach the ground, and George and Yvonne watched the slow progress of the Ferris Wheel as it turned on its axis until Lindy could make her exit.

'Happy Birthday, Lindy! This is an amazing party!' said Yvonne, and she hugged her friend.

'Happy Birthday, and thank you for inviting me' said George, as he gave Lindy a kiss on the cheek. Strictly speaking she hadn't invited him, it was Yvonne who had done that, but Lindy didn't correct him and accepted their birthday wishes with a smile and a hug back.

'Come over here, I have something to tell you' Lindy said, as she took Yvonne's arm and led her onto a wooden jetty which had been roped off. 'You too!' she called to George.

Once the three of them were some distance from the partying guests, Lindy said 'My poor dad is putting on a brave face. I did offer to cancel all of this, but he insisted we went ahead. He said he wasn't going to let his criminal family stop the celebrations of his only daughter's fiftieth birthday.'

'Poor man, even if he didn't approve of his cousin's life choices she was still his relative' said Yvonne. 'And your mum must be upset too if she and Marion had become friends recently?'

'Mum's furious that Marion deceived her! She isn't grieving. I think Dad is embarrassed more than sad, but Marion wasn't the only bad apple in the family since she was working with her cousin, a woman called Juliette Monk, who you also knew.'

Yvonne nodded 'When I was researching your family tree I wondered if they were related. There were a number of women named Marion or Juliette in your father's family.'

'Were there? I have never investigated it. Fortunately, this Juliette isn't a close relative of Dad's because Marion was Dad's mother's brother's daughter, and Juliette is the daughter of his wife's sister.'

George looked confused. 'Not that it matters, but Marion was the daughter of your dad's uncle, and Juliette's mum was Marion's aunt.'

'You've got it! Anyway, the good news is that all the jewellery will be returned, once the police have completed their investigations. It doesn't look as though the gang had time to move more than a few items on, because Marion and Juliette were attempting to set up on their own. Dad keeps meticulous records of everything belonging to the Speake family. I think it was his great great grandfather who started the record-keeping, and subsequent members of the family have maintained and updated them.'

'What does this mean for Kenyon Hall?' asked George.

'It is damaging' admitted Lindy. 'The good news for the business is that neither Marion nor Juliette were close relatives of Dad's family who run the business, and to our knowledge they never visited let alone worked there. But Dad's brothers are having to make some major changes to the management of the place, and of course Charles Diamond's part in the criminal gang is being investigated. I know my uncles and cousins believe he is a victim. I am going to be working with them, and we wondered if you would be willing to come in with us as a consultant, George? Obviously we'll do it properly with all the paperwork next week, but I wanted to see if you were open to the idea first?'

'I would be happy to' said George.

'Great news, thank you. Now, would you like some more fizz? It's not champagne, but it is delicious, from the local vineyard. We had better get back to the party!'

The trio negotiated the rope barrier, and immediately Lindy was ushered away by some other friends for photographs. Neither George nor Yvonne wanted any more to drink, and instead joined the queue for the Ghost Train, placing their empty champagne glasses on the tray of one of the waiters before climbing into a carriage. For the next few hours they rode the merry-go-round horses, drove the dodgems, screamed on the Wurlitzer and on the Ghost Train, and laughed at their shapes in the hall of mirrors. Yvonne won a huge pink teddy bear on the shooting range, and George won an equally big green crocodile in the egg and spoon race. Sally beat Yvonne in the sack race, and Yvonne beat Charlotte on the coconut shy. Everyone had their faces painted with glitter, even George, and by the time the sun began to set Yvonne and George were sitting in a gondola on the Big Wheel, with a giant pink teddy and huge green crocodile, enjoying the stunning views across the lake and grounds of Kenyon House, and over the surrounding Somerset countryside.

The temperature had dropped, and the party was moving indoors. Sally and Charlotte and Charlotte's mum were sitting on one of the sofas in a sitting room, where Yvonne and George joined them. Lindy appeared, and the six of them giggled and laughed at the fun they had at Lindy's birthday fun fair.

'It's not bad you know, this being fifty lark' said Lindy.

'My turn next year,' said Charlotte's mum.

'Mine too' said Yvonne. 'I wonder what adventures we'll have between now and then?'

'No more adventures please' groaned Lindy. 'I had enough yesterday to last me a lifetime!'

'Yes, more adventures!' said Sally. 'Horse riding adventures! More night rides and breakfast rides.'

'You know, that lake looks inviting' said Charlotte. 'We could bring the horses over and try swimming with them in there.'

'I have never thought of that!' exclaimed Lindy. 'I stand corrected. More adventures, please.'

Eventually everyone began to drift away, and by two o'clock in the morning Yvonne and George were able to find his car easily in the moonlit field because it was one of only half a dozen. They talked all the way home about the fairground, the music, the food and drink, and the people they had met. George dropped Yvonne at the gates to Tom's house, and they arranged to meet up for Sunday lunch at one of the local pubs later that day.

Yvonne let herself into Tom's kitchen, was greeted by the dogs, and made herself a cup of tea to take to bed. Tomorrow, or rather today, she would enjoy some peace and quiet now that the mystery of the murder and the jewellery she had found with George was solved. On Monday she would begin to put the plans for her future into action.

THE END

Printed in Great Britain
by Amazon

27912445R10192